PORT MOODY PUBLIC LIBRARY

D0088968

CRYOBURN

BOOKS by LOIS McMASTER BUJOLD

The Vorkosigan Saga:

Shards of Honor • Barrayar
The Warrior's Apprentice • The Vor Game
Cetaganda • Borders of Infinity
Brothers in Arms • Mirror Dance
Memory • Komarr
A Civil Campaign • Diplomatic Immunity
Cryoburn

Falling Free • Ethan of Athos

Omnibus Editions:

Cordelia's Honor • Young Miles
Miles, Mystery & Mayhem • Miles Errant
Miles, Mutants & Microbes • Miles in Love

The Chalion Series:

The Curse of Chalion • Paladin of Souls
The Hallowed Hunt

The Sharing Knife Tetrology:

Volume 1: Beguilement • Volume 2: Legacy
Volume 3: Passage • Volume 4: Horizon

The Spirit Ring

ALSO AVAILABLE FROM BAEN BOOKS

The Vorkosigan Companion, edited by
Lillian Stewart Carl and John Helfers

CRYOBURN

LOIS McMASTER BUJOLD

CRYOBURN

This is a work of fiction. All the characters and events portrayed in this book are fictional, and any resemblance to real people or incidents is purely coincidental.

Copyright © 2010 by Lois McMaster Bujold

All rights reserved, including the right to reproduce this book or portions thereof in any form.

A Baen Books Original

Baen Publishing Enterprises
P.O. Box 1403
Riverdale, NY 10471
www.baen.com

ISBN: 978-1-4391-3394-1

Cover art by David Seeley

First printing, November 2010

Distributed by Simon & Schuster
1230 Avenue of the Americas
New York, NY 10020

Library of Congress Cataloging-in-Publication Data

Bujold, Lois McMaster.
  Cryoburn / Lois McMaster Bujold.
      p. cm.
  ISBN 978-1-4391-3394-1 (hc)
  1. Life on other planets—Fiction. 2. Immortalism—Fiction. 3. Cryonics—Fiction.
I. Title.
  PS3552.U397C79 2010
  813'.54—dc22

                                    2010029989

10 9 8 7 6 5 4 3 2 1

Pages by Joy Freeman (www.pagesbyjoy.com)
Printed in the United States of America

CRYOBURN

Chapter One

Angels were falling all over the place.

Miles blinked, trying to resolve the golden streaks sleeting through his vision into mere retinal flashes, but they stubbornly persisted as tiny, distinct figures, faces dismayed, mouths round. He heard their wavering cries like the whistle of fireworks from far off, the echoes buffeted by hillsides.

Ah, terrific. Auditory hallucinations, too.

Granted the visions seemed more dangerous, in his current addled state. If he could see things that were not there, it was also quite possible for him to not see things that *were* there, like stairwells, or broken gaps in this corridor floor. Or balcony railings, but wouldn't he feel those, pressing against his chest? Not that he could see anything in this pitch darkness—not even his hands, reaching uncertainly before him. His heart was beating too fast, rushing in his ears like muffled surf, his dry mouth gasping. He had to slow down. He scowled at the tumbling angels, peeved. If they were going to glow like that,

1

they might at least illuminate his surroundings for him, like little celestial grav-lights, but no. Nothing so helpful.

He stumbled, and his hand banged against something hollow-sounding—had that bit of wall *shifted*? He snatched his arms in, wrapping them around himself, trembling. *I'm just cold, yeah, that's it.* Which had to be from the power of suggestion, since he was sweating.

Hesitantly, he stretched out again and felt along the corridor wall. He began to move forward more slowly, fingers lightly passing over the faint lines and ripples of drawer edges and handle-locks, rank after rank of them, stacked high beyond his reach. Behind each drawer-face, a frozen corpse: stiff, silent, waiting in mad hope. A hundred corpses to every thirty steps or so, thousands more around each corner, hundreds of thousands in this lost labyrinth. *No—millions.*

That part, unfortunately, was not a hallucination.

The Cryocombs, they called this place, rumored to wind for kilometers beneath the city. The tidy blocks of new mausoleums on the city's western fringe, zoned as the Cryopolis, did not account for all the older facilities scattered around and underneath the town going back as much as a hundred and fifty or two hundred years, some still operational, some cleared and abandoned. Some abandoned without being cleared? Miles's ears strained, trying to detect a reassuring hum of refrigeration machinery beyond the blood-surf and the angels' cries. Now, there was a nightmare for him—all those banks of drawers bumping under his fingertips concealing not frozen hope, but warm rotting death.

It would be stupid to run.

The angels kept sleeting. Miles refused to let what was left of his mind be diverted in an attempt to count them, even by a statistically valid sampling-and-multiplication method. Miles had done such a back-of-the-napkin rough calculation when he'd first arrived here on Kibou-daini, what, just five days ago? *Seems longer.* If the cryo-corpses were stacked up along the corridors at a density, on average, of a hundred per ten meters, that made for ten thousand along each kilometer of corridor. One hundred kilometers of corridors for every million frozen dead. Therefore, something between a hundred and fifty and two hundred kilometers of cryo-corridors tucked around this town somewhere.

I am so lost.

His hands were scraped and throbbing, his trouser knees torn and damp. With blood? There had been crawlspaces and ducts, hadn't there? Yes, what had seemed like kilometers of them, too. And more ordinary utility tunnels, lit by ceiling tubes and not lined with centuries of mortality. His weary legs stumbled, and he froze—um, *stopped*—once more, to be sure of his balance. He wished fiercely for his cane, gone astray in the scuffle earlier—how many hours ago, now?—he could be using it like a blind man on Old Earth or Barrayar's own Time of Isolation, tapping in front of his feet for those so-vividly-imagined gaps in the floor.

His would-be kidnappers hadn't roughed him up too badly in the botched snatch, relying instead on a hypospray of sedative to keep their captive under control. Too bad it had been in the same class of sedatives to which Miles was violently allergic—or even, judging by his present symptoms, the identical drug. Expecting a drowsy deadweight, they'd instead found themselves struggling with a maniacal little screaming man. This suggested his snatchers hadn't known everything about him, a somewhat reassuring thought.

Or even anything about him. *You bastards are on the top of Imperial Lord Auditor Miles Vorkosigan's very own shit list now, you bet.* But under what name? *Only five days on this benighted world, and already total strangers are trying to kill me.* Sadly, it wasn't even a record. He wished he knew who they'd been. He wished he were back home in the Barrayaran Empire, where the dread title of Imperial Auditor actually *meant* something to people. *I wish those wretched angels would stop shrieking at me.*

"Flights of angels," he muttered in experimental incantation, "sing me to my rest."

The angels declined to form up into a ball like a will-o'-the-wisp and lead him onward out of this place. So much for his dim hope that his subconscious had been keeping track of his direction while the rest of his mind was out, and would now produce some neat inspiration in dramatic form. Onward. One foot in front of the other, wasn't that the grownup way of solving problems? Surely he ought to be a grownup at his age.

He wondered if he was going in circles.

His trailing hand wavered through black air across a narrow cross-corridor, made for access to the banks' supporting machinery, which he ignored. Later, another. He'd been suckered into exploring down too many of those already, which was part of how he'd got so hideously turned around. Go straight or, if his corridor dead-ended, right, as much as possible, that was his new rule.

But then his bumping fingers crossed something that was not a bank of cryo-drawers, and he stopped abruptly. He felt around without turning, because turning, he'd discovered, destroyed what little orientation he still possessed. Yes, a door! If only it wasn't another utility closet. If only it was unlocked, for a change.

Unlocked, yes! Miles hissed through his teeth and pulled. Hinges creaked with corrosion. It seemed to weigh a ton, but the bloody thing moved! He stuck an experimental foot through the gap and felt around. A floor, not a drop—if his senses weren't lying, again. He had nothing with which to prop open the door; he hoped he might find it again if this proved another dead end. Carefully, he knelt on all fours and eased through, feeling in front of him.

Not another closet. Stairs, emergency stairs! He seemed to be on a landing in front of the door. To his right, steps went up, cool and gritty under his sore hand. To his left, down. Which way? He had to run out of up sooner, surely. It was probably a delusion, if a powerful one, that he might go down forever. This maze could not descend to the planet's magma, after all. The heat would thaw the dead.

There was a railing, not too wobbly, but he started up on all fours anyway, patting each riser to be sure the step was all there before trusting his weight to it. A reversal of direction, more painful climbing. Another turning at another landing—he tried its door, which was also unlocked, but did not enter it. Not unless or until he ran out of stairs would he let himself be forced back in there with those endless ranks of corpses. He tried to keep count of the flights, but lost track after a few turnings. He heard himself whimpering under his breath in time with the angel ululations, and forced himself to silence. Oh God, was that a faint gray glow overhead? Real light, or just another mirage?

He knew it for real light when he saw the pale glimmer of his hands, the white ghosts of his shirtsleeves. He hadn't become disembodied in the dark after all, huh.

On the next landing he found a door with a real window, a dirty square pane as wide as his two stretched hands. He craned his neck and peered out, blinking against the grayness that seemed bright as fire, making his dark-staring eyes water. *Oh gods and little fishes let it not be locked . . .*

He shoved, then gasped relief as the door moved. It didn't creak as loudly as the one below. *Could be a roof. Be careful.* He crawled again, out into free air at last.

Not a roof; a broad alley at ground level. One hand upon the rough stucco wall behind him, Miles clambered to his feet and squinted up at slate gray clouds, a spitting mist, and lowering dusk. All luminous beyond joy.

The structure from which he'd just emerged rose only one more storey, but opposite it another building rose higher. It seemed to have no doors on this side, nor lower windows, but above, dark panes gleamed silver in the diffuse light. None were broken, yet the windows had an empty, haunted look, like the eyes of an abandoned woman. It seemed a vaguely industrial block, no shops or houses in sight. No lights, security or otherwise. Warehouses, or a deserted factory? A chill wind blew a plastic flimsy skittering along the cracked pavement, a bit of bright trash more solid than all the wailing angels in the world. Or in his head. *Whichever.*

He was still, he judged, in the Territorial Prefecture capital of Northbridge, or Kitahashi, as every place on this planet seemed to boast two interchangeable names, to ensure the confusion of tourists no doubt. Because to have arrived at any other urban area this size, he would have had to walk over a hundred kilometers underground in a straight line, and while he would buy the hundred kilometers, considering how his feet felt right now, the straight line part was right out. He might even be ironically close to his downtown starting point, but on the whole, he thought not.

With one hand trailing over the scabrous stucco, partly to hold himself upright and partly from what was by now grim superstitious habit, Miles turned—right—and stumbled up the alley to its first cross-corri—corner. The pavement was cold. His captors had taken away his shoes early on; his socks were in tatters, and possibly also his skin, but his feet were too numb to register pain.

His hand crossed a faded graffiti, sprayed in some red paint and then imperfectly rubbed out, *Burn The Dead.* It wasn't the first time he'd seen that slogan since he'd come downside: once on an underpass wall on the way from the shuttleport, where a cleaning crew was already at work effacing it; more frequently down in the utility tunnels, where no tourists were expected to venture. On Barrayar, people burned offerings *for* the dead, but Miles suspected that wasn't the meaning here. The mysterious phrase had been high on his list of items to investigate further, before it had all gone sideways...yesterday? This morning?

Turning the corner into another unlit street or access road, which was bounded on the opposite side by a dilapidated chain-link fence, Miles hesitated. Looming out of the gathering gloom and angel-rain were two figures walking side-by-side. Miles blinked rapidly, trying to resolve them, then wished he hadn't.

The one on the right was a Tau Cetan beaded lizard, as tall, or short, as himself. Its skin rippled with variegated colored scales, maroon, yellow, black, ivory-white in the collar around its throat and down its belly, but rather than progressing in toadlike hops, it walked upright, which was a clue. A real Tau Cetan beaded lizard, squatting, might come up nearly to Miles's waist, so it wasn't *exceptionally* large for its species. But it also carried sacks swinging from its hands, definitely not real beaded lizard behavior.

Its taller companion . . . well. A six-foot-tall butterbug was definitely a creature out of his own nightmares, and not anyone else's. Looking rather like a giant cockroach, with a pale pulsing abdomen, folded brown wing carapaces, and bobbing head, it nonetheless strode along on two sticklike hind legs and also swung cloth sacks from its front claws. Its middle legs wavered in and out of existence uncertainly, as if Miles's brain could not decide exactly how to scale up the repulsive thing.

As the pair approached him and slowed, staring, Miles took a firmer grip on the nearest supporting wall, and essayed cautiously, "Hello?"

The butterbug turned its insectile head and studied him in turn. "Stay back, Jin," it advised its shorter companion. "He looks like some sort of druggie, stumbled in here. Lookkit his eyes." Its mandibles and questing palps wiggled as it spoke, its male voice sounding aged and querulous.

Miles wanted to explain that while he was certainly drugged, he was no addict, but getting the distinction across seemed too much of a challenge. He tried a big, reassuring smile, instead. His hallucinations recoiled.

"Hey," said Miles, annoyed. "I can't look nearly as bad to you as you look to me. Deal with it." Perhaps he had wandered into some talking animal story like the ones he'd read, over and over, in the nursery to Sasha and little Hellion. Except the creatures encountered in such tales were normally furrier, he thought. Why couldn't his chemically-enchanted neurons have spat out giant kittens?

He put on his most austere diplomat's tones, and said, "I beg your pardon, but I seem to have lost my way." *Also my wallet, my wristcom, half my clothes, my bodyguard, and my mind.* And—his hand felt around his neck—his Auditor's seal-ring on its chain. Not that any of its overrides or other tricks would work on this world's com-net, but Armsman Roic might at least have tracked him by its ping. If Roic was still alive. He'd been upright when Miles had last seen him, when they'd been separated by the panicking mob.

A fragment of broken stone pressed into his foot, and he shifted. If his eye could pick out the difference between pebbles and glass and plastic on the pavement, why couldn't it tell the difference between people and huge insects? "It was giant cicadas the last time I had a reaction this bad," he told the butterbug. "A giant butterbug is actually sort of reassuring. No one else's brain on this planet would generate butterbugs, except maybe Roic's, so I know exactly where you're coming from. Judging from the decor around here, the locals'd probably go for some jackal-headed fellow, or maybe a hawk-man. In a white lab coat." Miles realized he'd spoken aloud when the pair backed up another step. What, were his eyes flashing celestial light? Or glowing feral red?

"Just leave, Jin," the butterbug told its lizard companion, tugging on its arm. "Don't talk to him. Walk away slowly."

"Shouldn't we try to help him?" A much younger voice; Miles couldn't judge if it was a boy's or a girl's.

"Yes, you should!" said Miles. "With all these angels in my eyes I can't even tell where I'm stepping. And I lost my shoes. The bad guys took them away from me."

"Come on, Jin!" said the butterbug. "We got to get these

bags of findings back to the secretaries before dark, or they'll be mad at us."

Miles tried to decide if that last remark would have made any more sense to his normal brain. Perhaps not.

"Where are you trying to get to?" asked the lizard with the young voice, resisting its companion's pull.

"I ..." *don't know*, Miles realized. *Back* was not an option till the drug had cleared his system and he'd garnered some notion of who his enemies were—if he returned to the cryonics conference, assuming it was still going on after all the disruptions, he might just be rushing back into their arms. *Home* was definitely on the list, and up till yesterday at the top, but then things had grown...interesting. Still, if his enemies had just wanted him dead, they'd had plenty of chances. Some hope there... "I don't know yet," he confessed.

The elderly butterbug said in disgust, "Then we can't very well send you there, can we? Come *on*, Jin!"

Miles licked dry lips, or tried to. *No, don't leave me!* In a smaller voice, he said, "I'm very thirsty. Can you at least tell me where I might find the nearest drinking water?" How long had he been lost underground? The water-clock of his bladder was not reliable—he might well have pissed in a corner to relieve himself somewhere along his random route. His thirst suggested he'd been wandering something between ten hours and twenty, though. He almost hoped for the latter, as it meant the drug should start clearing soon.

The lizard, Jin, said slowly, "I could bring you some."

"No, Jin!"

The lizard jerked its arm back. "You can't tell me what to do, Yani! You're not my parents!" Its voice went jagged on that last.

"Come *along*. The custodian is waiting to close up!"

Reluctantly, with a backward glance over its brightly-patterned shoulder, the lizard allowed itself to be dragged away up the darkening street.

Miles sank down, spine against the building wall, and sighed

in exhaustion and despair. He opened his mouth to the thick-
ening mist, but it did not relieve his thirst. The chill of the
pavement and the wall bit through his thin clothing—just his
shirt and gray trousers, pockets emptied, his belt also taken.
It was going to get colder as night fell. This access road was
unlighted. But at least the urban sky would hold a steady
apricot glow, better than the endless dark below ground. Miles
wondered how cold he would have to grow before he crawled
back inside the shelter of that last door. *A hell of a lot colder
than this*. And he *hated* cold.

He sat there a long time, shivering, listening to the distant
city sounds and the faint cries in his head. Was his plague of
angels starting to melt back into formless streaks? He could
hope. *I shouldn't have sat down*. His leg muscles were tightening and cramping, and he wasn't at all sure he could stand
up again.

He'd thought himself too uncomfortable to doze, but he
woke with a start, some unknown time later, to a shy touch
on his shoulder. Jin was kneeling at his side, looking a bit less
reptilian than before.

"If you want, mister," Jin whispered, "you can come along
to my hide-out. I got some water bottles there. Yani won't see
you, he's gone to bed."

"That's," Miles gasped, "that sounds great." He struggled to
his feet; a firm young grip caught his stumble.

In a whining nimbus of whirling lights, Miles followed the
friendly lizard.

Jin checked back over his shoulder to make sure the funny-
looking little man, no taller than himself, was still following
all right. Even in the dusk it was clear that the druggie was a
grownup, and not another kid as Jin had hoped at first glance.
He had a grownup voice, his words precise and complicated
despite their tired slur and his strange accent, low and rumbly.
He moved almost as stiff and slow as old Yani. But when his

fleeting smiles lifted the strain from his face it looked oddly kind, in an accustomed way, as if smiles were at home there. Grouchy Yani never smiled.

Jin wondered if the little man had been beaten up, and why. Blood stained his torn trouser knees, and his white shirt bore browning smears. For a plain shirt, it looked pretty fancy, as if—before being rolled around in—it had been crisp and fine, but Jin couldn't figure out quite how that effect was done. Never mind. He had this novel creature all to himself, for now.

When they came to the metal ladder running up the outside of the exchanger building, Jin looked at the bloodstains and stiffness and thought to ask, "Can you climb?"

The little man stared upward. "It's not my favorite activity. How far up does this castle keep really go?"

"Just to the top."

"That would be, um, two stories?" He added in a low mutter, "Or twenty?"

Jin said, "Just three. My hideout's on the roof."

"The hideout part sounds good." The man licked at his cracked lips with a dry-looking tongue. He really did need water, Jin guessed. "Maybe you'd better go first. In case I slip."

"I have to go last to raise the ladder."

"Oh. All right." A small, square hand reached out to grip a rung. "Up. Up is good, right?" He paused, drew a breath, then lurched skyward.

Jin followed as lightly as a lizard. Three meters up, he stopped to crank the ratchet that raised the ladder out of reach of the unauthorized and latch it. Up another three meters, he came to the place where the rungs were replaced by broad steel staples, bolted to the building's side. The little man had managed them, but now seemed stuck on the ledge.

"Where am I now?" he called back to Jin in tense tones. "I can feel a drop, but I can't be sure how far down it really goes."

What, it wasn't *that* dark. "Just roll over and fall, if you can't lift yourself. The edge-wall's only about half a meter high."

"Ah." The sock feet swung out and disappeared. Jin heard a thump and a grunt. He popped over the parapet to find the little man sitting up on the flat rooftop, fingers scraping at the grit as if seeking a handhold on the surface.

"Oh, are you afraid of heights?" Jin asked, feeling dumb for not asking sooner.

"Not normally. Dizzy. Sorry."

Jin helped him up. The man did not shrug off his hand, so Jin led him on around the twin exchanger towers, set atop the roof like big blocks. Hearing Jin's familiar step, Galli, Twig, and Mrs. Speck, and Mrs. Speck's six surviving children, ran around the blocks to greet him, clucking and chuckling.

"Oh, God. Now I see chickens," said the man in a constricted voice, stopping short. "I suppose they could be related to the angels. Wings, after all."

"Quit that, Twig," said Jin sternly to the brown hen, who seemed inclined to peck at his guest's trouser leg. Jin shoved her aside with his foot. "I didn't bring you any food yet. Later."

"You see chickens, too?" the man inquired cautiously.

"Yah, they're mine. The white one is Galli, the brown one is Twig, and the black-and-white speckled one is Mrs. Speck. Those are all her babies, though I guess they're not really babies anymore." Half-grown and molting, the brood didn't look too appetizing, a fact Jin almost apologized for as the man continued to peer down into the shadows at their greeting party. "I named her Galli because the scientific name of the chicken is *Gallus gallus*, you know." A cheerful name, sounding like *gallop-gallop*, which always made Jin smile.

"Makes...sense," the man said, and let Jin tug him onward.

As they rounded the corner Jin automatically checked to be sure the roof of discarded tarps and drop cloths that he'd rigged on poles between the two exchanger towers was still holding firm, sheltering his animal family. The tent made a cozy space, bigger than his bedroom back before...he shied from that memory. He let go of the stranger long enough to jump up on the chair and switch on the hand light, hanging by a scrap of wire from the ridge-pole, which cast a bright circle of illumination over his secret kingdom as good as any ceiling fixture's. The man flung his arm up over his reddened eyes, and Jin dimmed the light to something softer.

As Jin stepped back down, Lucky rose from the bedroll atop the mattress of shredded flimsies, stretched, and hopped toward him, meowing, then rose on her hind legs to place her one front paw imploringly on Jin's knee, kneading her claws. Jin bent and scratched her fuzzy gray ears. "No dinner yet, Lucky."

"That cat does have three legs, right?" asked the man. He sounded nervous. Jin hoped he wasn't allergic to cats.

"Yah, she caught one in a door when she was a kitten. I didn't name her. She was my mom's cat." Jin clenched his teeth. He didn't need to have added that last. "She's just a *Felis domesticus.*"

Gyre-the-Falcon gave one ear-splitting shriek from his perch, and the black-and-white rats rustled in their cages. Jin called greetings to them all. When food was not immediately forthcoming, they all settled back in a disgruntled way. "Do you like rats?" Jin eagerly asked his guest. "I'll let you hold Jinni, if you want. She's the friendliest."

"Maybe later," said the man faintly, seemed to take in Jin's disappointed look, and after a squinting glance at the shelf of cages, added, "I like rats fine. I'm just afraid I'd drop her. I'm still a bit shaky. I was lost in the Cryocombs for rather a long time, today." After another moment, he offered, "I used to know a spacer who kept hamsters."

This was encouraging; Jin brightened. "Oh, your water!"

"Yes, please," said the man. "This is a chair, right?" He was gripping the back of Jin's late stepstool, leaning on it. The scratched, round table beside it, discarded from some cafe and the prize of an alley scavenge, had been a bit wobbly, but Custodian Tenbury had showed Jin how to fix it with a few shims and tacks.

"Yah, sit! I'm sorry there's only one, but usually I'm the only person who comes up here. You get it 'cause you're the guest." As the man dropped into the old plastic cafeteria chair, Jin rummaged on his shelves for his liter water bottle, uncapped it, and handed it over. "I'm sorry I don't have a cup. You don't mind drinking where my mouth was?"

"Not at all," said the man, raised the bottle, and gulped thirstily. He stopped suddenly when it was about three-fourths empty to ask, "Wait, is this all your water?"

"No, no. There's a tap on the outsides of each of these old heat exchanger towers. One's broken, but the custodian hooked up the other for me when I moved all my pets up here. He helped me rig my tent, too. The secretaries wouldn't let me keep my animals inside anymore, because the smell and noise bothered some folks. I like it better up here anyway. Drink all you want. I can just fill it up again."

The little man drained the bottle and, taking Jin at his word, handed it back. "More, please?"

Jin dashed out to the tap and refilled the bottle, taking a moment to rinse and top up the chickens' water pan at the same time. His guest drank another half-liter without stopping, then rested, his eyes sagging shut.

Jin tried to figure out how old the man was. His face was pale and furrowed, with sprays of fine lines at the corners of his eyes, and his chin was shadowed with a day's beard stubble, but that could be from being lost Below, which would unsettle anybody. His dark hair was neatly cut, a few gleams of gray showing in the light. His body seemed more scaled-down than distorted, sturdy enough, though his head, set on a short neck, was a bit big for it. Jin decided to work around to his curiosity more sideways, to be polite. "What's your name, mister?"

The man's eyes flew open; they were clear gray in color, and would probably be bright if they weren't so bloodshot. If the fellow had been bigger, his seedy looks might have alarmed

Jin more. "Miles. Miles Vo—well, the rest is a mouthful no one here seems able to pronounce. You can just call me Miles. And what's your name, young...person?"

"Jin Sato," said Jin.

"Do you live on this roof?"

Jin shrugged. "Pretty much. Nobody climbs up to bother me. The lift tubes inside don't work." He led on, "I'm almost twelve," and then, deciding he'd been polite enough, added, "How old are you?"

"I'm almost thirty-eight. From the other direction."

"Oh." Jin digested this. A disappointingly old person, therefore likely to be stodgy, if not so old as Yani, but then, it was hard to know how to count Yani's age. "You have a funny accent. Are you from around here?"

"By no means. I'm from Barrayar."

Jin's brow wrinkled. "Where's that? Is it a city?" It wasn't a Territorial Prefecture; Jin could name all twelve of those. "I never heard of it."

"Not a city. A planet. A triplanetary empire, technically."

"An off-worlder!" Jin's eyes widened with delight. "I never met an off-worlder before!" Tonight's scavenge suddenly seemed more fruitful. Though if the man was a tourist, he would likely leave as soon as he could call his hotel or his friends, which was a disheartening thought. "Did you get beaten up by robbers or something?" Robbers picked on druggies, drunks, and tourists, Jin had heard. He supposed they made easy targets.

"Something like that." Miles squinted at Jin. "You hear much news in the past day?"

Jin shook his head. "Only Suze the Secretary has a working comconsole, in here."

"In here?"

"This place. It was a cryofacility, but it was cleared out and abandoned, oh, way before I was born. A bunch of folks moved in who didn't have anywhere else to go. I suppose we're all sort of hiding out. Well, people living around here know there's people in here, but Suze-san says if we're all real careful not to bother anyone, they'll leave us be."

"That, um, person you were with earlier, Yani. Who is he? A relative of yours?"

Jin shook his head emphatically. "He just came here one day, the way most folks do. He's a revive." Jin gave the word its meaningful pronunciation, *re*-vive.

"He was cryo-revived, you mean?"

"Yah. He doesn't much like it, though. His contract with his corp was just for one hundred years—I guess he paid a lot for it, a long time ago. But he forgot to say he wasn't to be thawed out till folks had found a cure for being old. Since that's what his contract said, they brought him up, though I suppose his corp was sorry to lose his vote. This future wasn't what he was expecting, I guess—but he's too old and confused to work at anything and make enough money to get frozen again. He complains about it a lot."

"I . . . see. I think." The little man squeezed his eyes shut, and open again, and rubbed his brow, as if it ached. "God, I wish my head would clear."

"You could lie down in my bedroll, if you wanted," Jin suggested diffidently. "If you don't feel so good."

"Indeed, young Jin, I don't feel so good. Well put." Miles tilted up the water bottle and drained it. "The more I can drink the better—wash this damned poison out of my system. What do you do for a loo?" At Jin's blank look he added, "Latrine, bathroom, lavatory, pissoir? Is there one inside the building?"

"Oh! Not close, sorry. Usually when I'm up here for very long I sneak over and use the gutter in the corner, and slosh it down the drainpipe with a bucket of water. I don't tell the women, though. They'd complain, even though the chickens go all over the roof and nobody thinks anything of it. But it makes the grass down there really green."

"Aha," said Miles. "Congratulations—you have reinvented the garderobe, my lizard-squire. Appropriate, for a castle."

Jin didn't know what kind of clothes a *guarding-robe* might be, but half the things this druggie said made no sense anyway, so he decided not to worry about it.

"And after your lie-down, I can come back with some food," Jin offered.

"After a lie-down, my stomach might well be settled enough to take you up on that, yes."

Jin smiled and jumped up. "Want any more water?"

"Please."

When Jin returned from the tap, he found the little man easing himself down in the bedroll, laid along the side wall of an exchanger tower. Lucky was helping him; he reached out and absently scritched her ears, then let his fingers massage expertly down either side of her spine, which arched under his hand. The cat deigned to emit a short purr, an unusual sign of approval. Miles grunted and lay back, accepting the water bottle and setting it beside his head. "Ah. God. That's so good." Lucky jumped up on his chest and sniffed his stubbly chin; he eyed her tolerantly.

A new concern crossed Jin's mind. "If heights make you dizzy, the gutter could be a problem." An awful picture arose of his guest falling headfirst over the parapet while trying to pee in the dark. His *off-worlder* guest. "See, chickens don't fly as well as you'd think, and baby chicks can't fly at all. I lost two of Mrs. Speck's children over the parapet, when they got big enough to clamber up to the ledge but not big enough to flutter down safely if they fell over. So for the in-between time, I tied a long string to each one's leg, to keep them from going too far. Maybe I could, like... tie a line around your ankle or something?"

Miles stared up at him in a tilted fascination, and Jin was horribly afraid for a moment that he'd mortally offended the little man. But in a rusty voice, Miles finally said, "You know—under the circumstances—that might not be a bad idea, kid."

Jin grinned relief, and hurried to find a bit of rope in his cache of supplies. He hitched one end firmly to the metal rail beside the tower door, made sure it paid out all the way to the corner gutter, and returned to affix the other end to his guest's ankle. The little man was already asleep, the water bottle tucked under one arm and the gray cat under the other. Jin looped the rope around twice and made a good knot. After, he climbed back onto the chair and dimmed the hand light to a soft night-light glow, trying not to think about his mother.

Sleep tight, don't let the bedbugs bite.

If I ever find bedbugs, I'll catch them and put them in my jars. What do bedbugs look like, anyway?

I have no idea. It's just a silly rhyme for bedtimes. Go to sleep, Jin!

The words had used to make him feel warm, but now they made him feel cold. He hated cold.

Satisfied that he'd made all safe, and that the intriguing off-worlder could not now abandon him, Jin returned to the parapet, swung over, and started down the rungs. If he hurried, he would still get to the back door of Ayako's Cafe before all the good scraps were thrown out at closing time.

Chapter Two

When Armsman Roic woke for the second time—or maybe
it was the third—the opaque drug-mush in his head had
cleared to a thin, throbbing haze. He felt for his wristcom and
found it, unsurprisingly, gone. Groaning, he turned on his musty
mattress thrown on the floor of this...place, and opened his
eyes to plain daylight and his first clear view of his prison.

It was bare of furnishings. Some kind of old hotel room,
he decided after a minute from the shape, stains, outlets,
corroded-looking sprinkler overhead, and cheap light above
the only door. His mattress lay in what might once have been
a clothes niche, opposite a small working bathroom with the
door removed. A chain bolted around his ankle led in turn
to a bolt on the wall. The links were long enough to let him
use the facilities, he remembered that from the blurry night,
but not to reach the outer door.

He visited them again, and, hoping to wash out more of the
mush, drank thirstily from a flimsy plastic cup apparently left

for his use. A long, narrow window stretched above a stained bathtub. He stared out onto a featureless rise crowded with tall, arrow-shaped conifers, dark and tangled. He rapped on the glass; it gave back that dull tone that said *unbreakable,* at least by anyone not armed with a power drill or perhaps a plasma arc.

He tested the length of his chain. It didn't go even halfway to the door, but by standing upright, he found he could see out the front picture window, unobscured by curtains or a polarizing filter. *They must not expect visitors.* This room seemed to open onto a second-storey gallery. The view beyond the railing ran downhill to a broad patch of flat scrub that curved out of sight, framed by more tangled taiga. Not another building to be seen.

He wasn't in the city anymore, that was certain. Had there been any urban glow on the horizon last night? He could only remember the night-light in the loo. He could be ten kilometers from Northbridge or ten thousand, for all he knew. Which could make a difference, later.

He folded his considerable length back onto the mattress, and began working at the bolt in the wall, the only item even remotely resembling a weak point. It didn't budge, and his big fingers could scarcely get a purchase on the annoying little thing. If only he could get it started wriggling...

How t' devil did I end up in this mess? He imagined Armsman-commander Pym critiquing his actions of yesterday, and cringed. This was a thousand times worse than the infamous bug butter debacle. Yet it had all started so benignly, four weeks ago.

If abruptly, but there was nothing new to that—Lord Auditor Vorkosigan's galactic assignments from Emperor Gregor usually arrived abruptly. After a dozen off-world trips in m'lord's wake, Roic was getting practiced at the scramble to arrange m'lord's luggage, in his role of sometime-batman, m'lord's and his own travel documents, in his role as personal assistant—the job title Roic traveled under, as explaining the ancient and honorable rank of *Armsman* to galactics was always a losing game—and m'lord's security. And—though m'lord almost never discussed this aloud—private medtech for m'lord's lingering health issues.

The competent Vorkosigan House staff, under the even more competent supervision of Lady Ekaterin Vorkosigan, had actually relieved him of the first of these tasks. Canceling his own affairs had cost more of a pang, as he'd just worked up the courage to invite Miss Pym down to Hassadar to meet his parents for the first time. But as an armsman's child, Aurie had understood perfectly. Courting his commander's daughter had been an oblique process this past year, rather like those Earth insects Lady Vorkosigan had described, where the male approached with painful caution lest he be mistaken for a meal by his intended. But it was Armsman-commander Pym who would tear off Roic's head and eat it if he made a mis-step.

Still, in less than a day they'd boarded the shuttle for orbital transfer to the jumpship, and begun three boring, if comfortable, weeks of travel to New Hope II, or Kibou-daini as it was called by the locals to distinguish it from two other planets and a transfer station of the same name in the wormhole nexus. Kibou for short, thankfully. M'lord, accustomed from his old days in Imperial Security not to waste travel time, had handed Roic quantities of homework about their destination, and himself plunged into even larger and more classified reports.

Roic himself couldn't figure this gig out. Granted, Lord Vorkosigan was the only person Roic knew who had actually died and been cryo-revived, making him the hands-on expert in the subject among Gregor's Auditors, the Emperor's personal stable of troubleshooters. And he knew his galactics, no question there. And he had just successfully concluded, in his other hat as the-Count-his-father's voting proxy to the Council of Counts, several years on committees devoted to upgrading Barrayaran law on reproductive technologies to galactic standards. Cryonics, Roic supposed, was the other end of these life-tech issues, and so a logical extension. But the Northbridge Invitational Conference on Cryonics, hosted by a consortium of Kibou-daini cryorevival corporations, had proved as harmless a hotel-full of misty-eyed science boffins and well-fed lawyers as Roic had ever seen.

"Don't underestimate the viciousness of academics when funding is at stake," m'lord had said, when Roic had pointed this out. "Nor attorneys' command of ambush tactics."

"Yeah, but they don't generally use stunners or needlers," Roic had returned. "It's all words. My skills seem wasted. When they start firing off those paragraph grenades, I'd rather hunker down behind you."

He'd spoken too soon, it seemed.

He'd sat in on every program m'lord had attended, in the back of the room where he could watch all the exits, and been hard-put to stay awake, though m'lord recorded everything indiscriminately. He followed m'lord to meals with other attend-ees and to lavish evening parties provided by the conference's sponsors, at varying distances from looming over m'lord's short shoulder to leaning against the far wall, as m'lord signaled. He learned far more about cryonics and the people who dealt with it than he had ever wanted to know.

And he had just about come to the conclusion that the entire jaunt was a put-up job between Lady Vorkosigan and Empress Laisa, to give Ekaterin a much-needed holiday from a spouse who diagnosed all complaints as a sign of boredom, to be alleviated with an exciting new task. Since Lady Vorkosigan already ran an enormous household, rode herd on four children under the age of six and a teenage son from a prior marriage, played political hostess for her husband in his roles both as an Imperial Auditor and as the Count's heir, had undertaken supervisory responsibilities for agriculture and terraforming in the Vorkosigan's District, and tried desperately, in her spare seconds, to maintain a garden design business, bets were on below-stairs as to when she would break and respond to m'lord's idea of husbandly help by defenestrating the little man from the fourth floor of Vorkosigan House. This trip seemed a reasonable substitute to Roic.

But even the most loyal armsman had to go to the loo sometimes, which was why, economy be hanged, Roic argued constantly for a back-up man, or better, two, on these excursions. He'd returned . . . night before last?—or had he lost more than one day in this dazed captivity?—to the main room of the reception to discover m'lord gone, though a quick ping found him up a floor, past some winding stairs, in an even more private section of the party. Their wristcoms ran a scrambled security channel; no *come-here-I-want-you* code called, so Roic jittered impatiently and controlled his nerves. When m'lord at last trod back down the winding stairs, spotted Roic, and joined him, tugging down his cuffs in a self-satisfied way, his appearance was anything but reassuring. To anyone who knew him well, that is. It was the manic glitter in his eyes, and the fleeting smile, and the general air of elation. The *damndest* things could elate him.

"What?" Roic had murmured in alarm, and "Later," m'lord had replied. "The walls have ears."

Roic had to grind his teeth till midnight found them back in their shared room, where m'lord unpacked the anti-bug silencer for the first time, and his message encoder as well. He sat at the room's sole desk and began typing.

"And so?" asked Roic. "Why do you look so happy all of a sudden?"

"I've had my very first break in this case, after days of dead time. Someone just tried to bribe me."

Roic stiffened. An attempt to bribe an Imperial Auditor could warrant the death penalty, on Barrayar. *But we're not on Barrayar, more's the pity.* "Er . . . and this is a good thing?"

"Where there's smoke, there's fire, they say." M'lord continued cheerfully keying in whatever he was composing for Imperial Eyes Only. "Or maybe mirrors. Mind you, it was a subtle and elegant bribe. I'm almost glad I'm not dealing with idiots, here. Oh, Laisa, you were right, you were right. However did your cute Komarran nose know?"

"What did you say?" asked Roic anxiously.

"That's right, you were never in a galactic mercenary outfit. Or covert ops. They both have tested policies for bribes. Back in my old fleet, the rule was accept everything, register it with Command, and go do exactly what you were going to do anyway. Covert ops was similar—accept and follow up as far as the string leads. Because strings run two ways, you know. Play it out, pull it in...see what's on the other end...Hah!" He finished his entries with a flourish.

"What kind of bribe?" Roic pressed. "Or—should I not know?" *Please, don't make me work in t' damned dark!*

"Some very interesting stock options in the Shiragiku-sha— the White Chrysanthemum Cryonics Corporation, in full. WhiteChrys is the company in process of establishing a franchise on Komarr, you know. I could get in on the ground floor at a very favorable rate, it seems. In fact, they would lend me the money at no interest, to be paid back after my value doubles. Because what could be better for them than to boast a local stockholder with my insanely high connections? Though I am not, curiously enough, offered *voting* stock. The votes are reserved for their sub-zero patrons."

Of all the brain-bending twists of democracy Roic had encountered, even worse than the secondary market in Komarran planetary voting shares, it was Kibou-daini's custom of votes by the dead that most made his head hurt. Proxies, naturally—left in the hands of the cryocorps that shepherded their frozen charges into an unknown and curiously receding future. Because if you were going to trust a company with your death and next life, your vote was a small thing in comparison.

"It had doubtless," m'lord had remarked crisply, upon first learning this fact, "seemed a good idea at the time." Two, three hundred years ago, when New Hope's strange burial customs,

as Roic could not help thinking of them, were just beginning
to gain popularity.

"Heh," muttered m'lord, and sent his message on its coded
and circuitous way.

Roic knew that *Heh*. It gave him cold chills.

And so to bed, to rise and face the last day of the conference, which had gone, as near as Roic could tell, as *no one*
had expected, not even m'twisty lord.

And now, oh God, he'd gone and *lost* the little maniac...

Or had he? Belatedly, he wondered if m'lord had been captured in the melee in the lobby as well.

He could be *here*. Roic abandoned the bolt and shuffled over
to rap three times three on his room's side wall. Again. *Nothing*.
He tried the other side of the room, though he had to stretch
to reach. Silence. The adjoining rooms could be empty, or his
fellow captives still too drugged to hear, or answer. Or maybe
it was his captors over there, and he'd just alerted them of his
return to consciousness. *Damn*. Try again later?

He went back to working on his bolt, which was produc-
ing blisters on his fingers but no discernable loosening, and
brooded. He'd only taken his eyes off m'lord for a *moment,* and
then his old street guard reflexes had cut in, as he'd hustled at
least half-a-dozen potential kidnap victims into a lift tube and
escape, because they were unarmed civilians but that *wasn't
his job* even though no one else was doing it. He'd sure won
a whole lot of angry attention from their attackers by that,
at least till the stunner beam had caught him. *Maybe m'lord
escaped, and will rescue me.* An embarrassment, Roic decided,
that he could happily live with.

At the sudden clack of the door being unbolted, he started
and dropped his hands hastily to his lap. The door opened,
and a skinny young man with lank dark hair, and a slitted eye
set in a swollen magenta-and-purple contusion, eased through
and stared for a suspicious moment at Roic, seated on his
mattress. He limped forward to just beyond the arc of Roic's

chain, set some sort of commercial Reddi-Meal tray on the
floor, and pushed it toward Roic with what appeared to be a
broom handle. The tray was still sealed. So, Roic was not to
be starved—or poisoned? *Don't make premature assumptions,*
he could almost hear m'lord's voice intone. Roic realized he
was terrifically hungry, but he made no move toward the tray.

"I've seen you before," Roic said suddenly. "In the hotel lobby."
Up close. Things had been happening too fast at the time for
Roic to tell if the snatch had been an amateur or a pro job,
but thinking back, he guessed a mix. The marksman who'd
clocked him with the stunner had been cool enough, yet the
mob of men assigned to control and cart away captives, well,
they sure hadn't been up to Roic's idea of a standard—military,
paramilitary, or youth scout troop. It had been a *mass* snatch,
however, therefore not targeted especially upon Barrayarans—
m'lord's ego would be wounded at that—but Roic wasn't sure
if it made things more or less of a puzzle.

The skinny man touched his swollen eye and stepped back
a pace, scowling. It seemed he remembered Roic, too.

"Who *are* you people, anyway?" asked Roic. "Why t'devil
did you kidnap me—us?"

Skinny's head jerked up; his good eye lit. "We're the New
Hope Legacy Liberators. Because this generation"—he thumped
his fist on his chest—"is finally doing what it takes to stand up
to the power-grubbing corps. They've grown so fat and corrupt,
there's no choice left but to burn the whole rotten structure to
the ground and start over. We're standing up to bite the dead
hand of the past that grinds us into the dust!"

Roic squinted in dismay as Skinny, impassioned if garbled,
elaborated on this theme. The N.H.L.L. appeared to be some
sort of local political action group, who, grown frustrated at
their inability to win verbal arguments—if this was a sample,
Roic could see why—were trying to up the ante with physical
demonstrations. Bits and pieces from more considered critiques
of local affairs that Roic had overheard at the conference bobbed

by in the torrent of complaint, but the gist of harangue seemed to be that Skinny and his fellows were busted and down on their luck, and they figured that if only dead people didn't persist in owning everything in sight, there would be more left for the living. The corps and the corpses seemed muddled together in Skinny's head. Roic refrained from pointing out that actually, the wealth of Kibou-daini was being managed by live people in the name of the dead ones, and even if those were replaced by different live people, it seemed improbable that anyone would choose the N.H.L.L. for the task.

"Burn the dead!" Skinny finished, in much the tone that one might say *Amen* at the end of a rote prayer.

Burn, bury, freeze, Roic didn't see much to choose, except for the loss of some recycled organics. "But what's that got t'do with us?" said Roic plaintively. "We don't vote here. We're leaving next week. Are you after ransom?"

Skinny made a gesture of proud denial. "No! But we're determined that the Nexus will know of the injustice and suffering and *theft* on Kibou! No one—not you galactics, not the complacent old salary-folk, fat sheep dreaming only of their own meat lockers, not our own oppressed generation planet-wide—will remain in ignorance after this, no matter how they shut their eyes and ears!"

"Ah," said Roic. "Publicity stunt, huh?" Roic would have preferred ransom, actually. M'lord could have arranged it in a heartbeat, as soon as he was allowed to contact the Barrayaran consul here, and doubtless some sneaky way of recovering the money afterward, too. And yet, Roic had never heard of a political fringe group that wasn't strapped for cash. "It could be ransom," he essayed cautiously. "Or even reward, depending..."

Skinny looked scornful, but maybe give the idea time to work? Roic had more pressing concerns. "Lord Vorkosigan— t' fellow I work for, you can't mistake him, top of his head would be about level with your shoulder, carries a cane, talks a blue streak—is he here?"

Was that blank look feigned? Roic wasn't sure. He went on more urgently, "Because if he is, you've got to put us in a room together. I'm his private medtech, and he needs me. He gets these terrible seizures. He's a very important Vor lord, back on Barrayar. They'd pay a lot to get him back *unharmed*. But if he *dies* on you, well, you've no idea how ugly it could get." Roic wasn't sure how far to push this theme. M'lord had presumably been keeping a low profile here for a reason, and Roic didn't want to run the ransom price up inadvertently.

Lord Vorkosigan's post-cryorevival seizures actually consisted of him sinking down, shivering with his eyes rolled back for a couple of minutes in an unattractive manner, and then waking up very, very cranky. The fits were unlikely to be fatal, at least since Lady Vorkosigan had extracted his promise never, ever to attempt to drive himself in any powered vehicle—ground car, aircar, lightflyer, shuttle, or mode unnamed. Horses and bicycles had been a compromise, and though m'lord hated the helmets, he did comply.

Skinny didn't need to know this, however, so Roic embroidered the medical facts to the limit of his invention till Skinny, doubt growing in his eyes, weakened and said, "All right! I'll ask." He added—as no professional would have—"I didn't see anyone who looked like that guy here, though."

Skinny withdrew, leaving Roic thinking, *Uh-huh. Minion, not master.* Skinny seemed a type Roic had met often in his early days as a street guard in the Vorkosigan District capital of Hassadar. While not reliable enough to be put in charge of anything more complicated than a dishwasher, they were very easy to convince that all their troubles were someone else's fault. Roic knew this because they used to tell him so, at great and often incoherent length, while he was hauling them somewhere safe to sleep off their current binge of drink or drugs or arguments. That didn't mean they couldn't be truly dangerous, especially when they found themselves in over their heads, and it didn't take a very deep pool of troubles to manage that, either.

His own pool seemed an abyss, right now. Did the Legacy Liberators' plans for their captives include killing them one by one till their demands were met? *Our fringe loonies on Barrayar sure would,* Roic thought semi-proudly. Yet the affair had been oddly bloodless, so far—stunners and sleepy-drugs, not needlers and nerve gas. But maybe, maybe—dare he hope?—m'lord *wasn't* in their queue.

Because if m'lord died on Roic's watch, there would be nothing for it but to file the testimony by secured comlink and slit his own throat right here. Death would be better than making that report to certain persons in person. He pictured the faces of Count and Countess Vorkosigan, of Lady Ekaterin, hearing the news. Of Commander Pym, of Aurie. He imagined Sasha and little Helen, five years old—he'd have to kneel to look them in the eye—*Where's Papa, Roic?*

He lacked a suitable blade. He'd heard of prisoners choking themselves by swallowing their own tongues—he curled his experimentally—but he doubted it would work for him. There was the wall. Strong enough to hold that damned bolt, certainly. Could he run against that wall hard enough to break his own sturdy neck?

It seemed premature, but it was something to keep in mind. M'lord, now, he was very big on getting a good meal on board before making life-or-death decisions, and so was m'lady, come to think. Roic sighed, crawled over, and collected his Reddi-Meal.

Miles woke in a blink to broad daylight, a canvas roof, and a curious feline face staring into his from a cat's breath away. Glad to discover the weight on his chest was not some alarming new medical condition, he lifted the three-legged beast off and gingerly sat up. Post-drug headache, check. Fatigue, check. No screaming angels, double-check and an exclamation point or two. His vision seemed clear of all unrealities, and his surroundings, though odd, were not out of any nightmare he owned.

He pushed his blanket aside and looked around the rooftop refuge. All of the castlelike details had faded, to be replaced by a utilitarian flat quadrangle with a couple of exchanger towers supporting the canvas room. Or barn. Or zoo. In addition to the bird-of-prey on its perch, elegant and haughty and clearly the Vor lord of all it surveyed, some battered metal shelving displayed the cages harboring the black-and-white rat collection, along with several glass-walled terrariums. Though most of their occupants were out of sight behind artfully-arranged vegetation, he was fairly sure he saw a turtle. Along the wall opposite his bedroll, three boxes lined with shredded flimsies made nests for the chicken population; Twig, the brown hen, still dozed in hers. Miles eyed the clothesline still tied around his ankle. *Have I been collected?* He'd known worse fates.

And here was his zookeeper. Jin, sitting at the little round table, turned around and smiled at him. "Oh good, you're awake!"

Freed of an upwhacked brain chemistry's re-imaging, Jin proved a skinny kid just shy of puberty, with a shock of straight black hair in need of a cut and bright brown eyes, his features typical of the multi-racial blends of the local founder populations. He was dressed in a shirt too large for him, the sleeves rolled up and the shirttail trailing down over a pair of baggy shorts. Worn sport shoes without socks slopped on his feet. "Would you like breakfast?" Jin asked. "I have fresh eggs this morning—three of 'em!"

A proud young farmer; Miles could see that eggs loomed in his near future. "In a bit. I'd like to wash up first."

"Wash?" said Jin, as if this were a novel notion.

"Do you have any soap?" Miles went on. "I don't expect you have any depilatory."

Jin shook his head at this last, but jumped up to rummage on his crowded shelves and came up with a bar of rather dry soap, a plastic basin, and a grayish towel. Miles had to ask for Jin's help un-knotting the safety line, then accepted the soap and supplies with thanks and shuffled around the exchanger tower to the working water tap, where he stripped off his clothes, what was left of them, knelt, and managed a wash and rinse not only of his face, but head and whole body, including a good soaping of his sore feet and knees. The latter were contused and scabbed this morning, but showed no sign of infection, good. Jin tagged along to watch, frowning curiously at the pale scars lacing his torso. Miles slid back into his ragged and somewhat smelly garb, combed his hair with his fingers, and shuffled back to sink gratefully into the lone chair, toward which his young host gestured him.

Jin set a metal pot of water to boil on an ordinary, if battered, rechargeable camp heater. The boy's rooftop realm was clearly furnished out of back-alley scavenges, but some fruitful ones. The water heated quickly, and Jin slipped his three eggs, precious treasures, gently in. "Twig laid the brown one," Jin informed Miles, "and Galli the other two. They're fresh last night. And I have salt!"

Jin bustled about and produced a couple of plastic plates, the bottle of water refilled and ready for sharing between them, and half a loaf of what proved to be surprisingly excellent bread, if a trifle dry. With an air of confession, Jin lowered his voice. "Eggs come out of chickens' butts, you know."

"Yes, I knew that," Miles returned gravely. "We have Earth chickens, and other birds, where I come from, too."

Jin relaxed. "Oh, good. Some people get upset when they first find that out."

"Some people think Barrayar is a primitive world," Miles offered.

Jin brightened. "Does it have many animals?"

"Yes, the usual Earth imports, atop its own native ecosystem. The native animals are mostly small, like bugs, though. There are larger creatures in the seas."

"Do people fish?"

"Not in the seas. In stocked lakes, yes. The Barrayaran plants and animals are mostly toxic to humans."

Jin nodded wisely. "Around here, the native stuff they first found on the equator was mostly microorganisms. They figure that's where the oxygen came from, before the last big freeze. They set up a lot of Earth plants to follow the melting glaciers, north and south. But not many animals."

"Kibou-daini is a lot like Komarr—that's the second planet of my Empire," Miles said. "A cold world, being slowly terra-formed. Sergyar—that's the third world—you'd probably like it. It has a fully-developed native ecosystem, and lots of amazing animals, or so my mother tells me. It's only been colonized in the last generation, so scientists are still finding out new things about the biota."

Jin looked at Miles more warmly. It seemed he had just risen in the boy's estimation—were adults who could make sensible conversation rare in Jin's world, perhaps? For a certain value of sensible equating to *zoological,* apparently.

"I don't suppose you have any coffee. Or tea," Miles said, without much hope.

Jin shook his head. "I have a couple of cola bulbs, though." He darted back to his shelves to return with a pair of bright plastic drink bulbs. "Except they're warm."

Miles took one up and squinted at the ingredients label, a vile concoction of cheap sugars and chemicals, and decided he couldn't manage this before breakfast even if one of the chemicals might be caffeine. *So, when did you grow so nice, my Lord Auditor?* Or was it *grow so old?* The eggs, bread and water would be challenge enough for his queasy stomach. He shook his head no-thanks and set the bulb down.

The eggs were still simmering. Miles looked around and said, "Interesting place, this. Not at all like anything I've been shown on Kibou so far." Not with the cryocorps stage-managing the tours, certainly. "How many other people live here?"

Jin shrugged. "A hundred—two hundred? I'm not sure. Suze-san would know."

Miles's eyebrows rose. "That many!" They stayed out of sight well. He supposed a community of illegal squatters would have to be discreet in order to last. "How did you come here?"

Another shrug. "I just found it. Or it found me. A couple of folks out collecting tripped over me sleeping in a park, and sort of collected me, too."

A tradition, it seemed. "Do you have other family here?"

"No."

An atypically short response, from the chatty—lonely?—child. "Family anywhere?"

"My dad's dead." A hesitation. "My mom's frozen."

A distinction with a difference, on this planet. "Siblings?"

"I have a little sister. Somewhere. With *relatives*."

That last word had almost been spit out. Miles controlled his brows, maintaining an empty, inviting silence.

"She was too little to take with me," Jin went on, a bit defensively, "and she didn't understand anything that was going on anyway."

"And what was, er, going on?"

The shrug again. Jin jumped up. "Oh, the eggs are done!"

So was Jin an orphan? A runaway? Both? Miles dimly thought Kibou-daini maintained the sort of children's social services usual to technologically advanced planets, if perhaps not up to the relentless standards of, say, Beta Colony. Jin was a mystery, but not, alas, the most pressing one on his hands this morning.

Jin rolled hot eggs onto their plates, making sure Miles got the special brown one, and Miles kept the wits not to argue about his guestly double-portion. Jin handed over a restaurant packet of salt from someplace called Ayako's Cafe, and they divided the bread and shared the water. "Excellent," said Miles around a mouthful. "Couldn't be fresher." Jin smiled.

Miles swallowed a bite of bread, and said, "So, you said someone around here had a comconsole? Would they let me use it?"

"Suze-san." Jin nodded. "She might. If you get to her early in the day, when she's not so grouchy." He added more reluctantly, "I could take you."

Was he regretting untying that ankle-rope? "I'd like that very much, thanks. It's rather important to me."

The *I'm-pretending-I-don't-care* shrug again. As if the only way Jin could imagine keeping any living thing was by tying it up and feeding it, lest it run away and never be seen again.

Jin bustled about after breakfast to feed meat shreds to the falcon, bread bits to the chickens, and other carefully sorted scraps to the rats and the residents of the glass boxes. He cleaned cages and swished out and refilled water pans with fresh drinks all round. Miles was quietly impressed with his thoroughness, though the boy might have also been dragging his feet, reluctant to end this visit. In due course, and feeling much stronger and less dizzy, Miles followed his guide cautiously down the ladder once more.

Chapter Three

Miles trailed Jin through another unlocked metal door, down some stairs into a disturbingly darkened corridor, through a utility tunnel, and into yet another building. Subliminal sounds and smells, as well as better lighting, suggested this one was occupied, and indeed, around another turn they came to what had obviously once been an employee kitchen and cafeteria. About a dozen people lingered there, some cooking, some eating. All watched in wary silence as the pair passed, except for a young woman working at an industrial-sized mixer who spotted Jin, waved a large spoon in the air, and called him to breakfast.

Jin faltered, sniffing at the aroma of baked goods wafting from her vicinity, but then smiled and shook his head. "Later, Ako! I got a guest!" Miles stared back over his shoulder as Jin drew him onward.

Along a corridor two flights up, they passed a row of doors to what formerly, Miles thought, might have been offices, but now seemed to be living quarters. Through the open ones he saw filtered daylight, and piles of personal junk variously tidy or messy, the sort of shabby, battered goods that only folks who feared they couldn't get more would ever use, or save. The people he glimpsed seemed to be mostly dozing in bedrolls on the floor, or puttering quietly. A few residents squinted back at Miles as they passed. While they seemed a mix of ages, a disproportionate number were elderly. Maybe the able-bodied young ones, like Ako-the-cook, were out doing things?

This place was drawing power and water enough to maintain decency, if not such luxuries as lift tubes. No signs of buckets used as chamber pots, stairwells doubling as urinals, or cook-fires set in wastebaskets or bathtubs. So where was the power coming from, and the sewage going to? Was someone here paying for utilities, or were they being secretly siphoned from the municipal systems? The answers, Miles thought, might be revealing, if only he had time to pursue them.

Up another floor lay a corridor with fewer doors. Jin stopped at one on the end and knocked briskly. He waited a minute, leaning his shoulders on the wall and swinging one foot, then rapped again, louder.

"Yah, yah," a gruff voice sounded from within. "I hear you. Don't get your undies in a knot."

The door opened a hand-span. Miles dropped his gaze to not much higher than his own eye level, and found a seamed face scowling back at him. "What's this?" the grumbling voice demanded sharply. "Oh, it's you, Jin. What are you doing, bringing a stranger up here?"

"Yani and I found him last night," said Jin. "He was lost."

The red-rimmed eyes narrowed. "What, is that Yani's druggie?"

Miles cleared his throat, conscious of his piratical beard stubble. "Drugged, ma'am, but not a druggie. I had an unfortunate allergic reaction to some medication, in the course of which I was robbed and stumbled into the Cryocombs. It took me quite a while to find my way out again."

"You're not from around here."

"No, ma'am."

Jin jumped in: "He wants to use your comconsole, Suze-san."

The scowl deepened. "You can't call out on it. It only inloads."

This seemed unlikely to Miles, but for starters, he would take whatever he could get. It was plain this Suze really didn't like him here. An un-trusted outsider who Saw Too Much could come to a bad end, in a secretive community. Granted, he hadn't spotted any bully boys, but murder didn't take muscle; slyness would do as well. "I just want to check the news, ma'am. Till I get my wallet and IDs back, I have to beg kindness from strangers."

Suze snorted. "You find many kindly strangers where you come from?"

"I've always found enough." A dozen times over, Miles's life had been handed back to him by people he barely knew. "I figure it gives me an obligation to take my turn being one."

"Huh," said Suze.

"Jinni and Lucky both like him," Jin testified in anxious aid.

Thin lips quirked. "Oh, well, if the rat and the cat both agree, who am I to argue...?" After another moment, the door swung open, and Jin shooed him in.

Suze might have been any age from a hard-worn eighty to a well-preserved century. She had certainly, Miles thought, been a head taller a couple of decades back; now she would need sturdy shoes to top five feet, but instead wore flat plastic sandals that snapped her dry-skinned heels as she stepped. That head was covered with frizzed and unruly gray curls. She might have seemed younger if she'd smiled, but the frown-grooves were deeply set around her pursed mouth. Her loose trousers, shirt, and over-shirt were not a set, but being black, black, and black, they could not mis-match.

Her quarters consisted of two rooms. An antechamber filled with much the same sort of junk storage Miles had glimpsed below-stairs might once have been the domain of some recep-tionist. The room beyond, a generous corner office with windows on two sides, had surely been executive territory. A rumpled bedroll lay along one inner wall; he spied the comconsole, with desk and chair, along the other. A battered table held a ewer and washbasin, damp towels, and a faint scent of soap competing with the close, old-woman air of the place. The tall storage cupboard, doors shut, might have held anything. A couple of spare swivel chairs, a couch leaking stuffing, and two armchairs, all used office furniture, suggested that Suze might not be as reclusive as she looked.

Suze gestured him to the comconsole. "It's open."

"Thank you, ma'am," Miles said, sliding into the station chair. Suze and Jin watched over his shoulder. Finding the local news feeds took only moments. He selected Nexus standard English from a menu of some dozen supported local language options, half of which he could not identify. Although Barrayaran Russian was most certainly not among them, which might come in handy should he need private speech with his bodyguard—if Roic was still alive. . . .

As he'd suspected, yesterday morning's uproar at the cryo-conference was well covered. The vid commentary, as usual, was cursory and not too informative, but the detail-supplements proved more useful; they included a complete list of the kidnapped, with pictures, and pleas from the local authorities for anyone with information to step forward. Roic and Miles were both on the list, as was Dr. Durona, unfortunately. Two different extremist organizations, neither of which Miles had previously heard of—so much for his ImpSec reports on Kibou-daini—were claiming credit, or blame, for the kidnappings.

"That's you!" said Jin in excitement, pointing to Miles's face on the holovid. Miles didn't think it a flattering shot, but apparently it was recognizable. He wasn't sure if that was a good thing or not, just now. Jin went on, "Miles Vor—vor—vorka*seegain.*"

"Vor-*ko*-suh-g'n," Miles corrected automatically.

"So, you were caught up in that stupid mess," said Suze. "Galactic, are you?"

She was not as unaware of the news as Jin. Interesting. "The kidnappers seemed to be targeting off-worlders. A group of us had been assembled in the lobby for a guided tour. It was listed on the public schedule, so the snatch wasn't necessarily an inside job."

"You just said you were robbed."

"So I was, right down to my shoes. But the sedative they jabbed me with as they were dragging me off was an unfortunate choice. Instead of knocking me out, it made me manic. I broke away."

"Why didn't you go back to the hotel?"

"Well, and then there were the hallucinations. About ten hours of them, I think."

Suze regarded him in deep suspicion. Miles hoped it sounded too screwy a tale to have been made up.

Nine delegates taken—no, eight, subtracting Miles, although the kidnappers hadn't confessed to losing him. The Barrayaran consulate here, tiny as it was, would surely already have reported this, though the message could not yet have arrived home. *Damn.* Admiral Miles Naismith, free mercenary, had never owned a home address, nor hostages to fortune. Lord Auditor Miles Vorkosigan did. He couldn't *not* report in. And yet, what an *interesting* chance to become temporarily invisible had been handed to him....

His old covert ops instincts were kicking in, and he wasn't at all sure he wanted them. He could walk out of here and into any store or restaurant, and sooner or later find someone who would let him call and get help and a pick-up. The call would, of course, be unsecured and wide-open to anyone else looking for him, not limited to the authorities. Yet if the authorities, or at any rate, the powerful people who he suspected ran them, hadn't drawn his negative attention night before last, he'd not hesitate to do just that. But he was hesitating now.

Suze pulled up a swivel chair and plumped down on it,

watching more closely as he read on. Jin shifted from foot to foot, growing bored as Miles, frowning, sped through holo-screens of mostly non-useful data. "Hey Suze-san, you want me to bring you some cinnamon rolls? Ako was just getting them out of the oven."

"Do they have coffee down there?" Miles asked, diverted. "Can you bring me coffee? Black?"

Jin wrinkled his nose. "I don't know how anybody can stand to drink that stuff."

"It's a taste you acquire when you're older. Rather like an interest in girls."

Suze made a noise in her throat that might have been either a laugh, or phlegm.

Jin's nose wrinkled further, but he bobbed a sort of nod with his whole body, and trotted off.

"Two coffees!" Suze called after him. He waved an acknowl-edging hand as he thumped out the door.

Miles turned in his chair and looked after him—the boy was out of earshot already. "Nice kid, that."

"Yah."

"Good of you to take him in. What do you know about him?" *Prime the pump, my Lord Auditor.* "He told me his father was dead and his mother was frozen, making him an orphan of sorts, I suppose. I'd think his mother would have been too young for long-term cryo-sequestration. Usually at that age it's only used as a last-ditch emergency procedure to hold people till they can be treated." As Miles had once been. He couldn't even add, *To my cost,* because despite the imperfections of his revival, his life and everything in it for the past decade had been its grant. *And a gift of the kindness of strangers, don't forget them.* The Durona Group being about as strange as they came.

Suze's snort this time had a decidedly editorial tone. She looked him over and evidently came to some decision in his favor, for she went on: "Jin's father was killed in a construction accident. He didn't have a cryo-contract or cryo-insurance, so he was denied treatment till it was too late, though I expect things were happening brutally fast at the time."

Miles nodded. Emergency cryo-treatment was either fast or useless, giving a new meaning to the phrase, *the quick or the dead*. There was little point in reviving a body when the mind was irretrievable; you might as well just clone the victim and start over.

"Jin's mother went a little crazy after that. Launched a campaign for freezing as a universal public right, and went after the corps' grave-robbery as well. She became quite the spokeswoman, a few years back. Lawsuits, protests. Then one of her rallies went violent—they never did figure out who was to blame, though I have my own suspicions—and she was arrested. They rammed though an allegation of mental illness—not quite a charge of criminally insane, because that would have had to meet stricter standards—and some kindly friend of the court offered to fund her freezing till her cure could be discovered."

Miles's teeth tightened. "That chilled the opposition, did it?"

"You could say."

"Didn't her relatives protest? Or anybody?"

"Her campaign group was broken up by the expenses of it all. Her relatives were embarrassed by her—put at risk of losing their own jobs, don't you know. I expect they were secretly glad when she was shut up." Suze eyed him. "You don't seem especially shocked."

Miles shrugged. "I've seen a fair number of worlds, met a lot of people. Encountered a variety of systems. I've seen worse. Granted, Jackson's Whole, which is run by what are in effect high-tech warlords and their thugs, has a certain refreshing straightforwardness about its corruption. They don't have to pretend their evil is good in order to sell it to voters."

"Let me tell you, young man—the dirty little secret of democracy is that just because you get a vote, doesn't mean you get your choice." She sighed. "Though up till twenty, thirty years ago, it wasn't so bad, here. There were hundreds and hundreds of cryocorps, all run by different people with different ideas, so their vote-bags offset each other. Then some of them grew big enough to start gobbling up the others. Not because it was good for Kibou, or for their cryo-patrons, or for anyone but their top men in the grip of their greed, but just because they *could*. Nowadays it's down to half a dozen big corps that control most everything, plus a few scattered holdouts too small to matter."

"Jin called you Suze the Secretary," said Miles slowly. "What are you secretary *of*?"

Her lined face, briefly animated by her anger, grew more closed. "This place, once. It was a closely-held family corp, and I was executive secretary to our chief. Then we were bought out—swallowed up and stripped. Not because the buyer wanted us, but because they wanted to eliminate us."

"Who bought it out? WhiteChrys, by chance?"

Suze shook her head. "No, Shinkawa Perpetual. WhiteChrys got *them* later, though." A twisted smile suggested she thought this justice was cosmic, if a little too late.

"But how did you end up living in this shell?"

"A lot of us lost our jobs then, you know. No golden tram rides to retirement for mere employees. We had to go somewhere." She hesitated. "Other folks drifted in later."

"Executive secretary, huh? I guess you would know where all the bodies were buried."

She cast him a sharp look—what, frightened? This tough, haggish creature? But before Miles could pursue this line further, Jin banged back in, bearing a laden tray. It held—besides the promised rolls, redolent of cinnamon, a carton of milk, and two mismatched cups—an entire insulated *carafe* of coffee. Miles, proud of his restraint, did not fall on it rabidly, but waited for his hostess to serve him.

She dismayed him with delay by shuffling to her tall cupboard and returning with an unlabeled square glass bottle. She poured a... shot, Miles fancied, into her own cup, and, after a pause, raised her brows at Miles. "Want any freshener?"

"Er, no thanks. Just coffee." It sluiced down his throat, tonic enough all on its own. Jin sat back on the other swivel chair, contentedly munching rolls and swiveling with a steady *squeak-squeak-squeak* that made Suze wince and take a long swallow of her doctored drink.

Her scowl returned, contemplating Miles. He wasn't sure what he'd said to wind her up, just when he'd thought he was winning her favor. Clearly, she wasn't merely someone lucky enough to have salvaged a working comconsole, but a leader of sorts in this odd secret community.

"Jin can take you to Ayako's Cafe," she said suddenly. "You can call your friends to come get you from there."

Jin sat up and protested, "But I haven't shown him how Gyre flies, yet!"

"He can't stay here, Jin."

Jin wilted.

It was plain Suze liked Miles even less as a kidnapped conference delegate than as a mere lost tourist with a weakness for recreational hallucinogens. He decided to try another lure. "I came to that conference to learn about Kibou-daini's cryo-law and science, but actually ended up being hand-fed some very slick pitches for various cryocorps franchises. After four days of it, a lot of the delegates were ready to sign contracts on the spot. In a way, the extremists' attack was a fortunate misfortune. I was sent here by my employer to make a complete report on your cryonics system, but it seems I was missing some rather large pieces."

"Then you'd best be on your way to hunt for them, hadn't you?"

And what kind of piece are you? To be sure, *Puzzle.* "Actually, now the conference is over, my time is my own. But I could use another day of rest from yesterday's ordeal, if Jin is willing. Although I do need to report in to one fellow. Jin, if I gave you directions, do you think you could hand-carry a letter across town for me, and give it to a man?"

Jin perked up. "Sure! Uh...maybe. What part of town?"

"East side."

"Um...yah, I could do that."

Miles decided to ignore the faint tinge of doubt in his voice. "Where are we now, by the way?"

"South side," said Jin.

"Go yourself," said Suze. "I'll give you the tube-tram fare. Just don't come back."

"And when the police ask me where I've been, what shall I tell them?"

Her face grew grimmer. "Tell them you were lost."

"I could—if it were worth my while."

The snort this time was savage. "If we had money for bribes, would we be *here*?"

"You mistake my meaning, ma'am. My coin is information. Although, you know, you're the second person on Kibou who's tried to bribe me. Is this some sort of local custom?"

Her mouth worked. "Who was the first?"

"WhiteChrys."

"Impressive."

"It impressed me, although not in the way they intended. Small gifts are for selling things. Large gifts are for hiding things. It made me very, very curious."

"So did you take your large gift, Vorkosigan-san?"

He did not bother correcting it to *Vorkosigan-sama*, or possibly *-dono*; at least she had the pronunciation right. "At that level, a scornful *no* is not only shortsighted, but potentially dangerous. I think a day or two of rest here might be good for my health."

"And how do I know that letter to your friend won't bring more trouble down on *us*?"

"It won't if I say not. I outrank him."

Her lips twisted. "Yah, you have that swagger, don't you?"

And Suze had undoubtedly seen a lot of upper management swagger in her time. Miles wondered if her bosses had realized how closely they were observed.

Jin had been following this exchange with anxious squeakings of his chair. "I could take his letter, Suze! I don't mind a bit."

Miles opened a hand to Suze, half persuasion, half plea. "Think it through. You lose no secrecy you haven't lost already"—he cut the *unless you propose to have me murdered*—no point in planting suggestions—"and you gain my gratitude."

"And what's that worth?"

On Barrayar, quite a lot. But they were not, as Roic had several times pointed out, on Barrayar. "I'll think of something."

Her eyebrows signaled severe skepticism. But she spoke instead to Jin: "Didn't Yani tell you to leave him out there? See what trouble comes of good deeds, Jin!" Miles wasn't sure if this counted for a yea or a nay, but she heaved a sigh and went on, "Take Vorkosigan-san down to the storerooms and find him something to write with. And on."

Jin shot eagerly to his feet. Miles made his thanks and followed him out before Suze could change her mind.

Jin watched, shifting from foot to foot, as Miles-san, as he'd decided to think of him, because that last name was a jawbreaker, sorted through the few half-empty boxes of notepaper on the shelf in the storeroom. It was mostly the kind that old ladies used for writing formal thank-you notes, decorated with flowers and such, though Jin eyed one that bore puppies with a certain covetousness. With a quirk of his eyebrows, the little man made his selection, then turned to testing pens from the box of assorted discards. He found two that worked, stuck them in his pocket, and looked around.

"This place looks like a junk shop. Or the attic of Vorkosigan House..."

"Whenever anybody has findings that they don't want, they bring them down here for anybody to use," Jin explained. "Or else when...um." *When they go downstairs to Tenbury for the last time,* but he couldn't say that. He wasn't sure he was even supposed to *know* that.

Miles-san's gaze caught. "Ah! Shoes!" He limped over to the pile. Jin tagged along, and helpfully also began sorting. The galactic's feet were a little smaller than his own, but then, Jin had had to find replacement shoes here just a month ago, when his toes had pushed through his last pair like spring shoots through soil. The ladies' fancy shoes were all useless even to most of the ladies here, and tended to accumulate, but Miles found a pair of sport shoes that fit at last. They were a girly flowered print, but he didn't seem to notice as he shoved them on and fastened the straps. "That's better. Now I can move." He turned, scanning the stores more closely. "Huh. Canes!"

He went to the collection leaning in a corner and picked though it, passing up some sturdy medical ones with multiple rubber feet, and others that were too long. He made his final choice by sweeping them around like swords and thwacking them against the wall, so that Jin wasn't sure if he was looking for a prop or a weapon. But just in case it was the former, Jin led him back to his rooftop home by the inside route, up the emergency stairs and out the exchanger tower door.

Miles-san took over the table and chair, set out his paper, and frowned, face intent. The he bent and began scratching with the pen, with occasional long, thoughtful pauses. Jin had cleaned out the chickens' boxes, counted the chicks just in case any had found the parapet again, and brushed Lucky before the man finished writing, sealed the note, and looked up, squinting around.

"Do you have a clean, sharp knife? Or pin, or needle?"

"I'll look." Jin eventually found a little scalpel in the half-a-medicine-kit he'd once collected, and handed it over. Miles-san eyed it, shrugged, and to Jin's alarm poked his thumb with the sharp end. After squeezing out a drop of blood, he bent and pressed it over the flap, leaving a clear thumbprint across the line, which he then circled and initialed.

"Yah, wow," said Jin. "Why'd you do that?"

"DNA. Thumbprint's as good a mark as my grandfather's

seal-dagger. Better. They didn't do DNA scans in his day. After all, one couldn't expect the attaché to bestir himself for just any anonymous note off the street."

He then proceeded to give Jin a rather complicated set of directions for after he'd reached the east side, which he made Jin recite back; the result made him sigh, and bend again to write the man's name and address on the outside of the envelope after all. "I expect you'll get there one way or another. Don't give this into the hand of anyone but Lieutenant Johannes or Consul Vorlynkin, mind. It's very private."

Jin promised this, and went to find his box of coins, fishing out enough for the tube-tram fare, both ways. It didn't leave much.

"Is that your whole bank?" Miles-san asked, peering over his shoulder. Jin nodded. "Well, if you make my delivery, you'll get it back."

Jin wasn't sure how much store to set by this, but he nodded anyway. In turn he gave Miles-san a set of instructions should any animal emergencies arise while he was gone, which made the man blink a little. But *he* recited them back flawlessly. Jin tucked the letter inside his shirt, cast one last doubtful look over his shoulder, and descended the ladder.

Jin was nervous on the tube-tram, afraid people were looking at him, but no one seized him by the arm and dragged him to Security. He almost lost himself in the big transfer station downtown, the east side routes being unfamiliar to him, but he kept his eyes rigidly on the wall maps and made an effort to not look panicked. Helpful people could be as dangerous to him as suspicious ones. He found the right tube and the right stop at last.

A six-block walk, without too many turns, brought him to his destination. The neighborhood was full not of tidy apartment buildings of the sort he'd grown up in, but of forbiddingly fine houses in walled gardens. Several bore shiny brass plaques beside their gates labeling them as planetary embassies—Escobar's was an especially large and impressive mansion. The Barrayaran Consulate, thankfully also clearly labeled, was not so intimidating by contrast—quite a small house, really, set close to the street so Jin didn't have time to get scared going up the walk. No uniformed guards, and the decorative iron gate was so low Jin might have hopped over it, if it hadn't been left invitingly open. Jin gulped and pressed the buzzer.

The door was opened by a blond man in shirtsleeves, his slim green trousers held up by braces. He looked rumpled and tired and in need of a depilatory. He stared at Jin with lowered brows. "No solicitors or beggars," he said unencouragingly.

He had the same rumbly accent as Miles-san, and Jin realized to his dismay that not all Barrayarans were short. This man was very tall. "Please, sir, I'm a messenger. I have a letter for Lieutenant Johannes or Consul Vor, um, Vorlynkin." From Miles-san's brief description of the lieutenant, Jin thought this might be him, but did lieutenants answer doors? Further, Jin thought with some outrage, Miles-san had called him *a nice kid,* not *a scary grownup.* Though he supposed lieutenants had to be grownups.

"I'm Johannes."

Jin reached inside his shirt; the man tensed, but eased again when Jin drew out the letter. "From Miles-san—from Mr. Vorkosigan." Jin was careful with the pronunciation.

"*Shit!*"

Jin flinched. Lieutenant Johannes then terrified him further by grabbing his arm, dragging him into the front hall, and slamming the door shut. He snatched the letter, held it up to the light, then tore it open, pausing only to shout up the stairway, "*Stefin!*"

He began running his eyes down the neat, tightly-written lines. "Alive, oh thank God! We're saved!"

A second grownup, somewhat older and even taller than the first, clattered down the stairs. He was dressed like any Northbridge businessman right down to the hakama-like trousers, except that his wide-sleeved haori coat hung open, and he looked as squinty-eyed and tired as the lieutenant. "What, Trev?"

"Look at this! A letter from Lord Vorkosigan—he's free!"

The second man looked over his shoulder, and echoed, "Thank God! But why didn't he call in?" Then, after a moment more, "What? *What?*"

The lieutenant turned the letter over and they both read on. "Is he *insane?*"

The older man cast Jin a very narrow look, stirring up all Jin's worst fears. Policemen loomed in his imagination.

"Is this real?" the older man demanded.

Jin bent, picked up the fallen envelope, and held it out mutely. He swallowed and managed, "He said you'd like the thumbprint. He said it would be just like his grandfather's seal."

"Is that *blood?*"

"Um, yah...?"

The older man handed the envelope to the lieutenant. "Take that downstairs and check it."

"Yes, sir." Trev-san disappeared through the doorway at the back of the hall. After a moment, Jin heard a door slam, and feet thumping down some other stairs.

"Excuse me, sir, are you the consul?" Jin had gained the vague notion that a consul was something like an ambassador, but smaller. Rather like his house, really. "Because Miles-san said, only give his letter to the lieutenant or Consul Vorlynkin." He managed to get that last name out without stumbling over his tongue, this time. Jin would have expected an ambassador proper to be stouter and older, but this man was lean and not as old as Miles-san, or at least, he didn't have any gray in his brown hair.

"I'm Vorlynkin." His stare at Jin intensified. His eyes were very blue, like a hot summer sky. "Where did you see Lord Auditor Vorkosigan?"

"I, um, met him last night. He'd been lost in the Cryocombs. He said."

"Is he all right?"

The answer seemed more complicated than the question, but Jin decided to skip all that and just reassure him: "He's much better this morning. I gave him eggs."

Vorlynkin blinked, and looked at the letter some more. "If this wasn't a letter in his own hand—if this *isn't* a letter in his own hand—I'd have you under fast-penta so . . . eh. *Where* did you see him?"

"Um, where I live."

"And where's that?"

He was in trouble now, between Suze and this alarming stranger. He was never supposed to talk to strangers, or tell anyone about the facility, he'd been told that often enough. He wondered if he could bolt back out the door and down the walk before the consul could grab him. "Um, my place . . . ?"

"What . . ." To his surprise, Vorlynkin did not pursue this, but turned the letter over again. "What did he seem to be about?"

"Um . . . he asked a lot of questions." Jin thought a moment, and offered, "He's not kidnapped anymore, you know."

"But why send a *child* as a courier . . . ?" Vorlynkin muttered. Jin wasn't sure if the question was addressed to him, so did not attempt to volunteer an answer. It didn't seem the time to explain about *almost twelve*, either. He was beginning to think that the less he said, the safer he would be.

The other fellow—Lieutenant Johannes, Trev-san, whatever—stumped back into to the entry hall, waving the envelope at his boss. "This part's real. Now what, sir?"

"We still have to find his armsman just the same—he seems to think Roic was taken. No change there with respect to the locals. I suppose we have to do exactly what this says. But send a holo of the letter to ImpSec Galactic Affairs on Komarr, priority, scrambled."

The lieutenant looked hopeful. "Maybe they'll have an order. Some other order. One that makes more sense."

"Not for some days. And think who they'd have to go to for an override." The two men looked at each other in mysterious perturbation. "We're still on our own, here."

Jin diffidently cleared his throat. "Miles-san said I was to bring back a reply."

"Yes," said the consul. "Wait there." He pointed to a spindly chair against the wall, one of a pair flanking a little bureau with silk flowers atop it, and a mirror above. Both men thumped downstairs again.

Jin sat. Only the firmness and brevity of that *Yes* gave him the courage not to run away while he had this chance. However doubtful they were of Jin, they seemed to take Miles-san's letter seriously, which was a relief.

He was left alone for a long time. He got up once, to peer into the rooms flanking the entry hall. One was a sort of living room, very fancy; the other was more severe and officelike. No sign of pets, not even a bird in a cage or a cat. He was glad he hadn't gone poking around searching for any when another man emerged from the back hall, looked at him in surprise, and said, "May I help you?"

This fellow spoke in a normal Kibou accent, at least. Jin shook his head vigorously. "Lieutenant Johannes is seeing to, um, it. Me."

The ease with which Jin spun off the lieutenant's name seemed to reassure the man. "Oh," he said, and wandered into the office, to sit at the comconsole and begin some sort of work there. Jin stayed in his seat after that.

After a great deal more time, Vorlynkin came back. He held another sealed envelope in his hand, plain and businesslike, much bulkier than the one Jin had delivered.

"Do you think you can give this back into the hand of Lord Vorkosigan—only?"

Jin stood up. "I got this far."

"So you did." With visible reluctance, the consul handed the envelope over. Jin stuffed it into his shirt once more, and lost no time in escaping.

I didn't understand any of that. Jin looked back apprehensively as he passed out the iron gate once more. But he was glad Miles-san seemed to have some friends. Of a sort.

Chapter Four

As soon as he'd seen Jin safely over the parapet, Miles retraced his steps to the basement cafeteria, careful to make no wrong turns. He was apparently early for lunch, as only a few heads turned in suspicion to follow him. It occurred to him that he was less conspicuous here in his tattered garb than if he'd been wearing his full-on Imperial Auditor grays, a suit so severe as to signal *Serious Person Here* anywhere in the Nexus regardless of the vagaries of local fashion. *Street Refugee Here* was a much better choice for his current needs.

The scattering of tables was divided from the cooking area by a long serving counter, with metal cupboards above. He made his way around it to find a sort of large electric samovar promising tea. Next to the dispenser was a mismatched collection of mugs, with a hand-lettered sign over it, *Wash your cup!* He couldn't quite tell if these were personally owned or up for grabs, which gave him a perfect opening for conversation with the woman, evidently Ako's replacement, who was stirring a ten-liter pot of soup.

He addressed her, "May I use one of these?"

She shrugged. "Go ahead. Wash it after, though." She tapped her spoon on the pot rim and laid it aside. "You new here?"

"Very new."

"Rules are, cook what you want, clean up after yourself, replace what you use, contribute money to the pantry when you can. Sign up on the cleaning duty roster on the front of the fridge."

"Thanks. Just tea for now..." Miles took a sip. It was stewed, cheap, bitter, and served his purposes as a prop in both senses. "You been here long yourself?"

"I came with my grandmother. It won't be much longer."

As he was figuring out how to lead her on to parse that, a familiar, querulous voice sounded from beyond the counter: "That soup ready yet?" A tall, bent old man stooped to peer through the serving hatch. Impressive white mustachios drooped down, framing his frown, and wriggled as he spoke. Like an insect's palps, ah.

"Another half hour," the woman called back. "Just go sit."

"I believe I've met him," Miles murmured to her. "Name of Yani?"

"Yah, that's him."

Yani shuffled in to collect a mug of tea from the dispenser. He scowled at Miles.

Miles returned a cheery smile. "Good morning, Yani."

"So, you've sobered up. Good. Go home." Yani clutched his mug in two hands, to average out the shakes perhaps, and shuffled back to one of the tables. Miles, undaunted, followed and slid in across from him.

"Why haven't you gone away?" asked Yani.

"Still waiting for my ride. So to speak."

"Aren't we all."

"Jin says you're a revive. Did you really have yourself frozen a century ago?" That would have been just about at the end of Barrayar's Time of Isolation, on the verge of a torrent of new history all of which Yani had more-or-less slept through.

"I would think the oral chroniclers around here would be all over you."

Yani vented a bitter laugh. "Not likely. The people here are glutted with revive interviews. I thought the journals might pay me, but there are too many of us up walking around. Nobody wants us here. Everything costs too much. The city's too big. Settlement was supposed to be more spread out. Hell, I thought the terraforming would be halfway to the poles by now. The politics have gone all wrong, and nobody has any manners...."

Miles made encouraging noises. If there was one skill Miles had honed in his youth, it was how to please an old man by listening to his complaints. Yani needed no more than a nod to launch into a comprehensive denunciation of modern Kibou, a world with no need nor place for him. Some of his phrases were so practiced they came out in paragraphs, as if he'd told them over to anyone who would stop to listen. Which, by this point, was no one—the few other residents who drifted in gave Yani's table a wide berth. His rheumy eye brightened at this new audience who didn't show visible signs of wanting to chew through his own leg to get away, and Miles's suspect druggie status was temporarily forgotten.

As Yani maundered on, Miles was thrown back in memory to his own grandfather. General Count Piotr Vorkosigan, planetary liberator, un-maker and re-maker of emperors, and cause of a lot of that history that Yani had missed, had sired his heir late in life, as had Miles's father, so that it was more nearly three generations between grandfather and grandson than two. Still, they had loved each other after their own peculiar fashion. How would Miles's life have altered if Piotr had been frozen when Miles was seventeen, instead of buried for real in the ground? His impending return always a promise, or a threat?

Like a great tree the old general had been, but a tree did not only give shelter from the storm. How would Barrayar be different if that towering figure had not fallen, permitting sunlight to penetrate to the forest floor and new growth to flourish? What if the only way to effect change on Barrayar had been to violently destroy what had gone before, instead of waiting for the cycle of generations to gracefully remove it?

For the first time, the notion occurred to Miles that it might not be vote-grubbing alone, nor even the lack of medical progress in reversing geriatric decay, that caused the cryocorps to freeze more patrons than they revived.

Yani had now segued into a long screed about how his cryocorp had cheated him, evidently by not delivering him into this new world physically youthful, rich, and famous, which was roughly where Miles had come in on this rant. Yani seemed a time-traveler who had found out the hard way that he did not like his destination any better than his point of departure, failed to notice the one common factor was himself, and now could not go back. So just how many like him were haunting the streets of Kibou? Miles made the emptiness of their mugs an excuse to grab both and take them for refills.

As he was washing his mug and topping up Yani's, Miles murmured to the cook, "Is it true Yani was rejected for being a revive?"

She snorted. "I daresay nobody wanted him around a hundred years ago, either. I don't know why he thought that would have changed."

Miles muffled a smile. "I daresay."

The half-smile caught her eye, and she looked at him more closely. "You're not very old. Are you sick?"

Miles blinked. "Do I look that hung-over?"

"I thought that might be why you were here."

"Well, I have a chronic medical condition, but I don't much care to discuss it." How had she guessed? A seizure disorder hardly showed on the outside like, say, skin lesions. Miles suspected a conversation at cross-purposes, again, and that he'd just been handed a clue. So what was it?

But before he could follow this up, she turned away and said, "Oh! Tenbury-san!"

A lot of heads swiveled at the entry of a man in threadbare coveralls, a shirt with the sleeves rolled up, and an enormous quantity of hair, but the looks were mostly followed up with brief nods or friendly waves. The greetings were returned as silently. The man came into the kitchen area. He shoved his hand into his thatch of brown-gray beard to scratch his chin, greeted the cook with another nod, and held out a familiar carafe, which she took to rinse and refill with coffee. "Your lunch is all ready, Tenbury-san," she called over her shoulder. "Sack's in the fridge."

The man grunted thanks and went to poke inside the industrial refrigerator. He was not, Miles, realized, actually of a bearlike build under all the mad hair, but lanky and pale. He pulled out a cloth sack, turned, and eyed Miles. "You're new."

"I'm a friend of Jin's," Miles answered, not quite directly. *Or at least, he collected me.*

"Really? Where is the boy?"

"I sent him to run an errand for me."

"Eh. Good. Time he did some work."

"There's a faucet leaking in two-ten," the cook informed him.

"Right, right. I'll bring my tools after dinner," said the man. He took the carafe and ambled out.

"Who was that?" Miles asked, as the cook picked up her spoon again.

"Tenbury. He's the custodian here."

Miles dimly remembered that term going by a few times earlier, and wondered if its meaning was as far outside the usual as Suze the Secretary's. But if he really wanted to know where the power came from and the sewage went to, now was his chance. Should he wait for Jin to broker an introduction? Miles didn't have infinite time to explore, here...his feet were already in motion, deciding for him.

He waved his own thanks to the cook, dropped the refilled mug by Yani, rapped a friendly farewell on the tabletop, and made it to the door just in time to tail Tenbury's receding footsteps. The worn rubber soles on Miles's scavenged shoes were as silent as he'd hoped. Hinges squeaked; Miles nipped around the corner to discover a door closing again on another stairwell. He drew a breath and followed.

The steps descended into stygian blackness. His breath quickened. To his intense relief, a sudden glow reflected off the walls ahead—Tenbury had unshipped a hand light. So, the man didn't see in the dark like a werewolf, good. At the fourth landing, the scrape of a heavy door being shoved open was followed by loss of the reflected light. Miles sped his steps, put out his hands, and found the handle. He opened this door more cautiously, turning sideways to slide through the gap and easing it closed with the minimum sound.

The bobbing light receded to his right; he turned after it, thinking of will-o'-the-wisps luring unwary travelers to their doom. As he followed, he became aware of tiny twinkles dancing in the corners of his vision like floating fireflies, adding to the night-swamp effect. He blinked, and they resolved into scattered indicator lights, green for all's-well, tacking randomly up the corridor walls on either side.

Reluctantly, Miles reached out and let his hand trace across the now-familiar bumps of closely-set banks of cryo-drawers. Except these were not abandoned and cleared, but working, or a portion of them were. Well insulated, the drawer faces were at room temperature—there was no danger of his skin freezing to the surface and trapping him in a growing cocoon of icicle-glass, really. He drew in his hands anyway, making his way down the center of the corridor by witch-light.

He stopped short as, at the end of the corridor, another door opened. Ordinary office-lab-living-quarters glare temporarily blasted his eyes, making a nimbus around a hairy head that fortunately did not turn around. The door shut, and Miles was plunged into blackness once more. As his night vision came slowly back the dense dark was relieved, if that was the word, by the scattered green specks. He could just make out his corpse-light sleeves.

So, he hadn't found the pumping station or the electrical transformers. He'd found the deeper secret of this place—working cryochambers. A number of mysteries fell neatly into place.

Suze and companions were running a secret cryocorp. No—a cryo-*cooperative*. And, unless he missed his guess, unlicensed, untaxed, and uninspected. Clandestine, off the books in every way.

Kibou-daini—a whole planet so obsessed with cheating death that even the *street people* managed to scavenge hope.

Which beat living, and dying, in a cardboard box all to flinders, Miles had to admit. He opened his mouth in what might have been a silent laugh. *And I thought I'd pulled some audacious stunts in my time...* How the hell Suze and whatever helpers she'd suborned had managed to palm an entire facility, back when this place was being decommissioned and stripped, its patrons shifted to the elegant new Cryopolis on the west end, gaudy with its floodlit pyramids, was a tale Miles was suddenly dying to hear.

Bad choice of phrase, my Lord Auditor.

Less than a third of the cryo-drawers in this corridor sported those glow-worm lights, and how many other corridors might there be? Plenty of room for more customers. And, because his mind worked that way, he considered how easy murder by cryo-drawer would be. The ultimate shell game, one live body hidden among hundreds of dead ones. Asphyxiation would come quickly in the sealed black box, even without the freezing, and no one would know where to look till much too late....

It's nothing I haven't undergone before.

It was curious how much that reflection *didn't help*.

He stepped forward to the end door, raised his hand to touch the cool metal surface, and just stood there for a minute. Then, curling his fingers into a fist, he knocked.

The creak of a chair. The door opened partway, and a hairy face thrust through. "Yah?"

"Tenbury-san?"

"Just Tenbury. What did you want?"

"To ask a few questions, if I may."

Beneath shaggy brows, dark brown eyes narrowed. "Did you talk to Suze?"

"Jin took me to see her this morning, yes."

Tenbury's lips pursed amid their thatch. "Oh. All right." The door swung wide.

Miles did not correct the misperception that Suze had therefore gated him into this covert community, but slipped inside at once.

The room was part office, part control chamber for the banks of cryo-drawers, and part living space, or so the unmade bedroll by one wall and the piles of personal junk suggested. Beyond, another door stood open on what might be some sort of repairs facility. Miles glimpsed workbenches and racks of tools in its shadows. There was only one station chair, by which Miles guessed this Tenbury was less sociable than Suze, but the custodian politely gestured his guest into it and leaned against a control console. Miles would have preferred it the other way around, so as not to risk a crick in his neck, nor the embarrassment of swinging his short legs above the floor. But he dared not impede the useful exchange he'd started, so he sat and half-smiled upward.

Tenbury cocked his head, and echoed the cook's observation. "You look too young for us. You sick or something?"

Miles repeated the reply that had seemed to work before: "I have an incurable seizure disorder."

Tenbury winced in sympathy, but said, "You'd do better to go back to the docs. Off-planet, maybe."

"I have. It was costly." Miles turned out his empty pockets as if to demonstrate.

"That why you ended up here? Broke, are you?"

"In a sense." It wasn't as if Miles was trying to beat a fast-penta interrogation through excessive literalism, yet he found himself oddly reluctant to lie outright to this man. "It's more complicated than that."

"Yah, it always is."

"Can you show me what I might be getting into? If I stayed here, that is?"

The hairy eyebrows jerked up. "You've nothing to worry about with *my* work. Come on, and you'll see."

Tenbury led through his shop, which seemed half-engineering-half-medical. Dismantled freezer parts lay strewn across a workbench. "I keep a portion of the chambers usable by cannibalizing the others," Tenbury explained.

Miles encouraged the tech to expand upon the arcana of his craft with much the same noises he'd used on Yani, to better effect. When Miles had absorbed as much about how cryo-chambers were built as he could stand, he asked, "But won't you run out of parts?"

"Not for a while yet. This facility was originally set up to serve twenty thousand patrons. In twenty years, we've only accumulated about a ten-percent occupancy. I admit we started much smaller, back when. We can go for decades yet. Till I'm gone, for sure."

"And what then? Who are you relying on for your revivals?"

"We don't need anyone to do the revivals, yet. Anyway, they're much trickier."

Indeed. "Who does the cryoprep, then?"

"Plant nurse. You'll meet her sooner or later. She's real good, and she has an apprentice, Ako, too. I need to get myself a couple of youngsters like that, I guess."

Miles didn't marvel at this. Emergency cryoprep was a common enough medical procedure that even he had learned it, at least theoretically, as part of military field-aid. Under non-emergency conditions there were doubtless more refinements, resulting in less cryo-amnesia and other unwanted side-effects, after. Less trauma to start with left less trauma to recover from, but to choose to go down to that darkness in cold blood, so to speak, while still breathing... "It's still frightening to think about," he said honestly.

"For most folks, it's a last choice, not a first one. We all come to it in time, though. No one wants to go of a coronary in the night and not-wake-up warm and rotting. Safer not to wait too long." Tenbury's lips twisted. "Although some of the corps are trying to increase market share these days by encouraging folks to freeze early. I'm not sure if the math works out."

"It does seem an inelastic demand, yes," agreed Miles in fascination. "More customers now can only mean fewer later. A short-term strategy for such a long-term enterprise."

"Yah, except maybe for those who'd miss their chance."

It was Miles's turn to tilt his head in consideration. "I suppose they're not up to one-hundred-percent market saturation, even now. What about the religious types?"

"Oh, yah, there are still a few refusers."

"Refusers?"

"You're not from around here, are you? Figured from your accent, but I'd have thought you must have been on Kibou longer. In order to end up here, I mean."

"It was something of an accident. I'm glad I stumbled on you, though."

Refusers, like *revives,* were another item the careful corps tours had neglected to mention, but they hardly needed even Tenbury's brief explanation, which he obligingly supplied, for Miles to figure out. Tenbury's judgment was that those who chose burial over freezing for superstitious reasons were a self-limiting phenomenon. Miles thought of those fringe utopian communities that had practiced strict celibacy and thus died out within the first couple of generations, or non-generations, and nodded provisional agreement.

Tenbury then kindly took Miles through the far door, out of the workshop and into another corridor—thankfully lit, though even with illumination the general effect was of an unsettling cross between a space station corridor and a morgue. There he opened an empty cryo-drawer, recently reconditioned, and pointed out its features, rather like a very restrained used-vehicle salesman.

"It seems . . . small," said Miles.

"Not much head room," Tenbury agreed. "But you're past sitting up suddenly by the time you arrive in it. I've often wondered if folks would retain any memory of their time in these, but the revives I've met all say not." He slid the drawer closed and gave it a fond thump to seat the latch.

"You just go to sleep, and then wake up in a future somebody else picked for you. No dreams," Miles agreed. "Blink out, blink back in. Like anesthesia, but longer." An intimate preview of death, and doubtless a lot less traumatic when the *blink out* part wasn't accomplished by a needle-grenade blowing out one's chest, Miles had to allow. He spread his palm on the drawer-front. "What happens to all the poor frozen people"—or *frozen poor people*—"if this place is discovered by the authorities?"

A brief, humorless grin ruffled the beard-thatch. "Well, they can't just let us thaw and rot, then bury us. That's illegal."

"Murder?"

"Of a sort. One of the grades of murder, anyway."

So this place was not as futile an effort as Miles had first guessed. Somebody *was* thinking ahead. How far? Who might find the future legal responsibility for these frozen souls on their hands? The municipality of Northbridge? Some unwitting entrepreneur, buying the rediscovered property for back taxes without inspecting it first? *Cheating death,* indeed. "Illegal at the moment, then. What happens if the law changes?"

Tenbury shrugged. "Then several thousand people will have died calmly and without pain, in hope and not despair. And won't know the difference." He added after a thoughtful pause, "That would be an ugly sort of world to wake up in anyway."

"Mm, I don't suppose the authorities would go to the trouble and expense of reviving folks just to let them die again immediately. Blink out, and . . . stay blinked." There were worse ways to arrive at an identical fate. Miles had seen many of them.

"Well, I need to get back to work," Tenbury hinted away his uninvited visitor. "I hope this helped you."

"Yes, yes it did. Thank you." Miles let Tenbury shepherd him back through the shop to the first corridor. "I suppose I'd better go feed Jin's pets. I did promise the boy I would."

"Odd kid, that. I had hopes for a bit he might apprentice to me, but he's more interested in animals than machinery." Tenbury sighed, whether in regret or bafflement Miles was not quite sure.

"Um..." said Miles, staring up the darkened corridor.

"First door on your left," said Tenbury, and thoughtfully held his office door wide to light the way till Miles had found it in the gloom. The stair rail and a careful count of the turns guided Miles after that. He emerged again in the basement near the cafeteria, and from there found his way back up to Jin's roof via the interior stairs.

Emerging into the daylight and greeted by milling chickens, he thought, *Damn, but I hope the boy makes it back here soon.*

The big downtown tube-tram transfer station was just as confusing going back as forward, Jin found when he'd taken his second wrong turn. The crowd made him nervous, and it was only going to get worse as the time edged toward rush hour. He needed to get out of here. Scowling, he turned around a couple of times, reoriented himself, and made his way upstream through an entry corridor, bumping a lot of folks going the other way.

What was in that big thick envelope Counsel Vorlynkin had handed to him? It crackled against his skin. Entering the second-level rotunda, he dodged out of the way of a woman with a pram, then leaned his shoulders against a pillar and fished out the letter. To his disappointment, it wasn't sealed with a bloody thumbprint, but it was certainly sealed. No peeking. He sighed and thrust it back inside his shirt.

He finally found the right escalator, and rode it up two flights to the top-level gallery. He was worried about his animals. Would Miles-san take proper care of them? You never could tell, with adults. They pretended to take you seriously, but then laughed behind your back at the things that were important to you. Or said that because you were just a kid, you would forget it all soon. But Miles-san had seemed to genuinely like Jin's rats, letting Jinni sit on his shoulder and nibble at his hair without flinching. Jin could tell when grownups didn't really appreciate how sleek and funny and friendly rats could be, and they didn't bite hard at all unless they were accidentally squeezed, and who could blame them for that?

The squeeze on Jin's shoulder made him jump and yelp. If he'd been equipped for it, he might have bitten the hand as well, but all he could do was twist and stare upward. Straight into the face of his worst nightmare.

Brown hair, a pleasant smile, the blue uniform of municipal security. Not just a tube-tram safety officer; their uniforms were green. A real policewoman, the sort who'd come for his mother.

"What's your name, child?" The voice was friendly, but the undertone steely.

Jin opened his mouth: "Jin..." Oh, no, that wouldn't do. Lying to grownups made him scared inside, but he managed, "Jin, um, Vorkson."

She blinked. "What kind of name is that?"

"My Dad was a galactic. But he's dead now," Jin added with hasty prudence. And half truth, for that matter. He tried not to think about the funeral.

"Does your mother let you come downtown alone? It's school hours, you know."

"Um, yes. She sent me on an errand for her."

"Let's call her, then."

Jin held out his skinny wrists. His stomach felt cold and quivery. "I don't have a wristcom, ma'am."

"That's all right. You can come along to the security booth, and we can call her from there."

"No!" In a panic now, Jin tried to wrench away. Somehow, he found his arm cranked up behind his back, hurting. His shirt tail came loose, and the envelope dropped to the pavement with a loud slap. "No, wait!" He tried to dive for it. Without releasing his arm, the woman scooped it up first, staring at it with a deepening frown.

She murmured to her own wristcom, "Code Six, Dan. Level One."

In moments, another policeman loomed. "What ho, Michiko? Catch us a little shoplifter?"

"I'm not sure. Truant, maybe. This young fellow needs to come to the booth and call his mother. And get ID'd, I think."

"Right."

Jin's other arm was taken in an even stronger fist. Helplessly, he let himself be marched along. He was wild for a chance to break away, but neither grip slackened.

The security booth had big glass windows overlooking the rotunda. It was cool inside, and when the door shut a wonderful silence fell, which usually would be a relief to Jin, but not now. A lot of screens were running, and Jin realized that some of them were from vidcams that looked right into people's faces as they went up or down on the escalators. He hadn't noticed them among the noise and confusion and hurry of the place. The woman plunked him down in a swivel chair. His feet didn't quite reach the floor.

The wide man, Dan, held up a light pen. "Let me see your eyes, child."

Retina scan? A red flash. Jin squeezed his eyes shut as tightly as he could, and clapped his palms over his face for good measure. But it was already too late. He heard the man moving away to his comconsole.

"He's scared, Dan," said the woman. Jin peeked through his fingers to see her holding up the envelope, squeezing and rattling it like a birthday present. "Think the reason might be in here?"

A ping from the console. "Aha. I believe we have a match. That was quick." Officer Dan looked up and asked, "Is your name Jin Sato?"

"No!"

"It says here he's been missing for over a *year*."

Without letting go of Jin's arm, the woman edged around to look at the holoscreen. "Good heavens! I'll bet his family will be relieved to get him back!"

"No, they won't! Let me go!"

"Where have you been hiding for a whole year, son?" Officer Dan asked, not unkindly.

"And what is this?" Michiko asked, hefting the envelope and frowning.

"You can't have that! Give it back!"

"So what's in it?"

"It's just a letter. A, a very personal letter. I'm supposed to deliver it. For, for some men."

Both officers went rigid. "What sort of men?" asked Michiko.

"Just...men."

"Friends? Relatives?"

Relatives were not a good thing, in Jin's world. "No. I just met them today."

"Where did you meet them?"

Jin's mouth clamped shut.

"Not addressed. Not postal-sealed. No legal reason we can't peek, is there?" said Dan.

The woman nodded and handed the envelope over. Dan popped a folding knife and slit it open from the bottom, holding it above the countertop. A thick wad of currency thumped out, followed by a fluttering note.

It was more money than Jin had seen in one place in his life. From their widening eyes, it was more money than the two security officers were used to seeing in one lump, too, certainly in the hands of a kid.

Dan riffled the wad and vented a long, amazed whistle.

Michiko said, "Drug ring, do you think? Feelie-dream smugglers?"

"It could be—gods, it could be anything. Congratulations,

Michiko. Shouldn't wonder if there's a promotion in this." Staring at the envelope with more respect, Dan belatedly pulled a pair of thin plastic gloves from his pocket and donned them before he picked up the note. It seemed to be printed on half a flimsy.

Dan read aloud, "We must trust that you know what you are doing. Please contact us *in person* as soon as possible." He turned the note in the light. "No address, no date, no names, no signature. Nothing. *Veery* suspicious."

Michiko bent to look Jin sternly in the eyes. "Where did you meet these bad men, child?"

"They *weren't* bad men. They were just...men. Friends of a friend."

"Where were you taking all this money?"

"I didn't know it was money!"

Michiko's eyebrows rose. "Do you believe that?" she asked her partner.

"Yah," said Dan, "or he might have taken off with it."

"Good point."

"I wouldn't have! Even if I had known!"

"No one can threaten you now, Jin," Michiko said more gently. "You're safe."

"No one *did* threaten me!" Jin had never felt less safe in his life. And if he blabbed, Suze and Ako and Tenbury and everyone who had befriended him wouldn't be safe, either. And Lucky and the ratties and the chickens, and big, beautiful Gyre... Lips tight as he could press them, Jin stared back at the officers.

"Call Youth Services to pick up the boy," said Michiko. "The rest of the evidence had better go to Vice, at a guess."

"Yah," said Dan, his gloved hands sliding Jin's precious envelope, the wad of cash, and the note into a transparent plastic bag.

"My *animals*," Jin whispered. Such a simple task Miles-san had entrusted him with, and he'd screwed it all up. He'd screwed *everything* up. Between his scrunched eyelids, tears began to leak.

With a grating noise and a puff of powder, the bolt popped out of the concrete.

"*Finally*," breathed Roic.

Chapter Five

Roic waited for dusk to deepen, and for the occasional echo of footsteps along the gallery to fall silent for a good long time, before venturing a cautious reconnoiter. The door lock yielded to force, or rather, the flimsy doorframe splintered and gave up the mechanism whole, more loudly than he would have liked, but no one called out or came to investigate. Crouching to slip beneath any view from the windows, bare feet silent on the boards but for an occasional tiny clink from the chain swathing his ankle, he discovered that the gallery wrapped the rectangular building on three sides, with stairs down on either end. About a dozen rooms like his lined this level. There was no third storey.

Another building, with faint yellow gleams leaking from its windows, lay down the slope to the right. Obscured in the trees behind it seemed to be a parking area, but a marked lack of security lighting made the details invisible—both to Roic and to anyone passing overhead in a lightflyer, he guessed. Right now he was grateful for the shadows. He slipped around to the far end. A third building, vaguely shedlike, sat low and black in the gloom down at the border of the level scrubland. Roic wondered if there'd been a fire, to so clear out the crowded conifers.

Roic's heart nearly failed him when a voice above his head hissed, "Roic! Up here!"

He jerked his head back to see a pale smudge of a face peering over the edge of the roof. A long black braid swung forward over the figure's shoulder, triggering recognition and relief. "Dr. Durona? Raven? So they got you, too!"

"Sh! Not so loud. We were in the same lift van. You were out cold. Come up, before someone comes back." A pair of lean arms extended downward; Raven was apparently lying prone. "Careful of my hands..."

With no more noise than a grunt and a scrape, Roic scrambled up to the flat rooftop. Their careful foot-slides making no thumps that could be heard through a ceiling below, they took shelter of sorts in the lee of a vent housing.

Raven Durona could have passed for a Kibou-daini native—a slim intellectual Eurasian in body and face, with a high-bridged nose and straight black hair to his waist—till he opened his mouth and that un-local accent came out. Delegate from the Durona Medical Group on Escobar, he'd been the only other person at the cryo-conference Roic had known, and moderately well at that, but m'lord, inexplicably, had signed them away from each other. Raven had accepted the signal with the merest nod and eyebrow twitch, and steered around Roic and m'lord thereafter. Leaving m'lord clear, Roic realized in retrospect, to trawl for his own targets.

Roic lowered himself to sit cross-legged, the Escobaran cryo-surgeon wrapped his arms around his knees, and they put their faces close together.

In a nearly voiceless murmur, Roic said, "Seen any guards?"

"No, but our captors are still awake," Dr. Durona returned

in a matching tone. "They're mostly still down in the dining hall, but some wander back up here at random. They sleep below us."

"How'd you get out of your room?"

"Surgery on my bathroom window-lock."

An exit doubtless aided by the fact that the man was lithe as a snake; Roic's shoulders would not have fit. "And the chains?"

"Chains? You had chains? Special, Roic!"

"Never mind. How far are we from Northbridge, did you see? And where t'hell are we?"

"About a hundred, hundred and fifty kilometers, I'd guess. The one glimpse I had was all forest as far as I could see. There don't seem to be any roads—everything must come in by lightflyer or lift van. This place used to be some kind of lake resort for Northbridge weekenders, before the dam blew out in a storm and the lake ran down the river. The rebuild got tied up in lawsuits, so the resort has been defunct for a couple of years. One of our kidnappers owns it, turns out. Which may have been how the Legacy Liberators came up with this crazed scheme in the first place."

"What t'hell are they doing—no, wait. First, have you seen Lord Vorkosigan?"

Raven shook his dark head. "I thought I saw them tackle him, back in the lobby when they grabbed me and you were throwing people into the lift tube and bellowing at them to keep climbing—I swear some of those poor delegates were more scared of you than of our attackers—but I haven't seen him since. There are only six other hostages here, plus me and you. All locked in for the night. It seems the N.H.L.L. was setting up to host three times that many. They're not best pleased with you for that."

"How many bad guys?"

"What a Barrayaran turn of phrase! About a dozen here, at a guess. I've not seen them all together. They take it in shifts to harass us."

"Huh?"

"Lecturing us, mostly. About the stern and glorious goals of the New Hope Legacy Liberators."

"Oh. I had a sample."

"Only a sample? The rest of us have endured *hours* of it. They marched us down to the dining hall and harangued us till they were hoarse."

"How come I wasn't invited?"

"*You* have a reputation as a bold Barrayaran barbarian—say that six times really fast—too dangerous to let loose. Chains, huh? You were fortunate to miss class. I think they might be trying to inculcate some sort of identify-with-one's-captors syndrome in us, but are doing it wrong. Old Baron Ryoval could have eaten them all for breakfast."

Roic had heard m'lord's clone-brother Lord Mark quote the late Baron Ryoval of Jackson's Whole only once—some mutter about, *And then we shall explore the interesting focusing effects of threatening your* remaining *eye*—and had not been moved to inquire further. He'd been moved to edge away, actually, despite overtopping Lord Mark by half a meter of height. Roic only knew that the entire Durona Group, thirty-five or so cloned siblings possessing extraordinary medical talents, felt they owed their escape from Jacksonian techno-slavery to a new, free life to Lord Mark and Lord Vorkosigan. The *reason* for Raven's peculiar mélange of an accent, and that of every other Durona, was that they were all refugees from Jackson's Whole who'd been living for over a decade on Escobar. The reason that the infamous Baron was *the late* was Lord Mark. The reason Roic and Raven found themselves sitting on this roof together... was still unclear.

Well, Raven had been invited to the conference to give an illustrated lecture on cryorevival techniques after death from extreme trauma, which m'lord and perforce Roic had sat in on three days ago, after Raven had hinted, during a chance encounter in a hotel lift-tube, that m'lord would find special interest in the very complicated case of Patient C, a messy death by needler-grenade to the chest. It was, Raven had informed his audience, one of his earliest and most memorable cases as a young assistant surgeon. M'lord had indeed been riveted. Roic had closed his eyes. But *besides* that.

"Yes, but *why* are these idiots lecturing you?"

"Pitching their cause, I think. Rather like the past several days at the cryo-conference, really, except in reverse. And with much worse food."

"Are they suppressed by the government, or censored by the local media?"

"Not at all, apparently. They even have a site on the planetary net that tells everyone all they would want to know about their views. No one wants to know much, it appears, so they've turned to more forcible ways of getting attention. Now, robbing at gunpoint actually works. *Selling* at gunpoint—not so good. We all started today scared to death. But by the end, it was just *dreary*." Raven rubbed his nose. "They seem to plan to keep it up for days. Hence my escape attempt, but it's not going too well."

"We both got this far..."

"Yes, but here we are in the middle of a hundred kilometers of woods—lots more if you take a wrong turn—and even if this forest isn't stocked with people-eating predators, it would be insane to plunge off into the darkness with no shoes or gear. And all the vehicles in the parking lot are neatly locked. I just checked."

"Huh. Pity."

Raven eyed Roic in speculation. "Now, by myself I don't think I could jump someone coming out to his lightflyer and grab it after it was opened, but if we worked an ambush together..."

Roic took this, resignedly, as, *If you jumped him and I cheered you on...*

Raven frowned. "Except this crew doesn't seem to come or go very often. All locked down tight, making no noise. Till you came along, I was starting to wonder if I should let myself back into my room and pretend this never happened, wait for some better chance."

"I don't think I could do that," said Roic, remembering his ruined doorframe. He craned his neck to stare over the roof edge at that third darkened structure. If that was an old shore-line down there... "What's that other building?"

"Don't know. I haven't seen anybody go in or out."

"I'm thinking it could be a boathouse. Or a tool shed—an isolated place like this would need one—but likely a boathouse."

Raven glanced wryly at the dried lake bed, and murmured, "I've never ridden in a boat. This doesn't seem the night to start. Tools, now... do you think you could pry open a light-flyer? But then you'd still need the code keys to power it up. Crowbar's no use there. Except maybe to hit the owner on the head?"

"M'lord keeps boats. He has a place on a lake down in the Vorkosigan's District, back on Barrayar, couple hours from the capital by lightflyer." A thought niggled in Roic's aching head. "I say, let's go see."

Raven gave him a dubious look, but shrugged agreement.

With painful caution, they lowered themselves from the roof and tiptoed down the far stairs. They made a straight line for the cover of the trees, then circled to come out on the shore side of the low building. The effect of the sticks, rocks, and debris on Roic's bare feet made him reluctantly agree with Raven's negative view of any longer walk in the woods.

The window glass was unbreakable, the entry facing the ex-lake padlocked, but it gave way to the same method Roic had used on his room door. Raven winced at the rending crunch; they both froze, listening hard, but no outcry came. They edged inside.

The outer door opened onto an office; the door beyond was, thanks be, unlocked. Roic swung it open upon a garagelike space. Also very dark, but—could one *smell* boats? The scent of wood and oil and old bilge and dried waterweed was quite unmistakable, and strangely happy, like preserved summer. As his eyes adjusted, Roic could just make out half a dozen kayak-or-canoe shapes slung from the ceiling, and a couple of wider hulls up on sturdy cradles. Workbench on the far side of the room, mostly cleared away. Raven started for it, hands held out before him in wariness of head-cracking pillars or other shadowy obstacles, but Roic whispered him back.

"Come over here. This big power boat—help me get the cover off."

"Roic, even if we could haul it out the doors, the lake is *dry.*"

"That's not it. Just help, all right?"

The hull was maybe five meters long and half that wide, and a stretched plastic cover protected a large open cockpit. The fastenings parted reluctantly, and Roic dragged the cover aside and climbed in. Raven followed in curiosity.

Roic felt his way to the controls, just behind a windshield, and opened what proved—yes!—to be a small vid plate cover. Now, if this comlink was independently powered, as it bloody well should be—Roic's fumbling fingers found the on-switch at last, and green and amber lights threw back the pools of darkness.

"Hey!" said Raven, in a hearteningly impressed tone—most Duronas daunted Roic. "Did you know that would be there?"

"I had a guess. If this place rented out boats to its customers, it would've had to keep something to go rescue them in. Comlink is a pretty standard built-in for pleasure boats this size, along with the depth-finder and nav links and so on."

The emergency channel was easy to find. Within minutes, Roic had talked his way back through the system to the Northbridge police. His years as a street guard gave him a good idea of just what to say to smoothly reach the folks with clout, and the boat's navigation aid provided a precise location. He reported, briefly, his experiences and Raven's to the startled but pleased Northbridge detective officer in charge of the—by now highly publicized, Roic sensed in his tone—kidnapping case. To Roic's intense worry, it seemed no one had found Lord Vorkosigan yet. As the Northbridge police scrambled, Roic closed the link and leaned back.

"Now what?" asked Raven.

"Now we wait."

"For rescue? Do you think we ought to do something for the others?"

"Lying low's better. No point in stirring up anything if our captors aren't going to miss us for a while yet. Let the Kibou fellows do their job, and hope they get here first." Roic recalled some of m'lord's cautionary lectures on *local liability,* a concern that m'lord himself seemed to take to heart only intermittently.

Speaking of locals... Roic leaned forward again and searched out the number of the Barrayaran consulate in Northbridge. Unfortunately, the public net only supplied the public number, not the secured emergency link coded on his wristcom, presumably discarded back in the city by his captors for well-founded fear of tracers. A polite recorded voice told him to call back during office hours, or leave a message. The muted background music was a popular Barrayaran military march that gave Roic a twinge of homesickness. He was halfway through recording a succinct report on his current situation when, to his relief, he was interrupted by a live human.

Roic recognized Lieutenant Johannes, the young driver who—along with Consul Vorlynkin himself, because m'lord was, after all, m'lord—had picked them up at the shuttleport nigh on a week ago and transported them to the conference hotel. Military attaché, ImpSec of sorts, and for all Roic knew, cook, gardener, and the consul's batman. He felt a dim sense of comradeship, contemplating Johannes.

"Armsman Roic!" Johannes's voice was curt and anxious. "Are you all right? Where are you?"

Roic began his summary once more; halfway through, the strained face of Consul Vorlynkin joined Johannes's image above the vid plate.

"If you follow up with the Northbridge police from your end, you'll likely know as soon and as much as we do," Roic finished.

Vorlynkin said, "Lord Auditor Vorkosigan is not with you—right?"

"We haven't spotted him here. Any sign back there?"

A too-long pause. "We aren't quite sure."

What t'hell did *that* mean?

"When you get free, report in to the consulate at once," Vorkynkin went on. "Should I send Johannes to coordinate with the police?"

Roic scratched his head. "If m'lord's not here, there's no point t' get in a panic about us. I'll get back with the others."

"What about me?" said Raven, either indignant or amused, it was hard to tell.

"Who is that?" said Vorlynkin sharply.

"Dr. Durona. An acquaintance from Escobar, one of the delegates," Roic replied.

Raven obligingly leaned forward into range of the vid pick-up and smiled benignly. Vorlynkin frowned back.

"M'lord would want to know he was"—*safe* seemed a premature claim—"with me," Roic explained.

Vorlynkin said distantly, "You know, if you people would be more forthcoming, we could do our job of supporting you much better."

The faint bitterness in the consul's voice was more reassuring to Roic than the man could possibly imagine. It sounded quite like Vorlynkin *had* undergone some recent dealing with m'lord, one that he was loath to transmit over an unsecured comlink.

"Yes, sir," said Roic, in a mollifying tone.

He cut the com.

"Now what?" said Raven. "Just sit here and wait for the sirens?"

"There had better not be sirens," said Roic. "Best they drop down and secure the hostages first before making any noise." That was what he'd suggested, at least.

After a longer pause, Raven said, "The Liberators didn't really act like they wanted to kill us. Just convert us."

"Panic does odd things to people."

Raven sighed. "You could stand to be more reassuring, Roic, you know?"

Huddling around the indicator lights as if at a very tiny campfire, they waited in the darkness.

Miles rattled the consulate's wrought-iron front gate, found it locked, and stared over it wearily. Beyond a dainty front garden sat a dinky house, overshadowed by its grander neighbors, although at least it looked well-kept. Maybe it had once been servants' quarters? Kibou-daini had never been considered strategically important enough to spend much Imperial money upon, its system being in a wormhole cul-de-sac on the far side of Escobar, well outside of Barrayar's web of influence. This consulate existed mainly to ease the occasional Barrayaran or more likely Komarran trading venture through planetary regulations, aid any members of the Imperium who found themselves in local trouble, and direct and quietly vet the even rarer Kibou traveler planning to visit the Imperium. Miles's arrival was likely the most excitement the place had endured in years. *Yeah, well, it's about to get more so.*

The pre-dawn chill was damp and penetrating, his legs were cramped, and his back ached. He sighed and clambered awkwardly over the gate, retrieved his cane, stumped up the short walk, and leaned on the door chime.

The porch and hall lights flicked on; a face peered through the glass, and the door opened a crack. A young man Miles didn't recognize spoke in a Kibou accent: "Sir, you'll have to come back during business hours. We open in about two more—"

Miles wedged his cane through the opening, levered it wider, put his head down, and barged in.

"Sir—!"

The minion was only saved from a shattering blast of Auditorial ire by Consul Vorklynkin strolling through an archway at the back of the hall, saying, "What is it, Yuuichi?...Oh my God, Lord Vorkosigan!"

Showing a swift sense of self-preservation, Yuuichi fell back from between them.

Vorlynkin, tall and lean, was half-dressed in trousers, shirt, and slippers, bleary-eyed, and clutching a mug that steamed with the gentle perfume of hot green tea. Miles was so distracted by the smell that he was almost thrown off his well-rehearsed opening, but he'd had a *lot* of hours this past night to rehearse.

"Vorlynkin, *what the hell have you done with my courier?*"

Vorlynkin's spine snapped straight, unconsciously revealing a military hitch sometime in his earlier life. A look of partial, but only partial, relief lit his blue eyes. "We can answer that! My lord."

"So Jin did make it here?"

"Um, yes, sir."

The problem had occurred on Jin's way back, then. Not good... Miles had waited in growing anxiety till midnight, then pressed Ako into substitute pet care and taken matters unto his own hands, or feet. The hours it had cost him to make it here unobserved had not improved his mood. Neither had the rain.

The consul's brows drew down as he took in Miles's appearance in turn, a very far cry from Miles's cultivated gray-eminence-look of their brief meeting last week. Although the ragged, stained clothing, two-day growth of face stubble, general reek, and peculiar shoes might not be the whole of why he flinched. But, showing a keen eye that was well-placed in the diplomatic corps, he caught Miles's gaze tracking his waving mug, and added smoothly, "Do you want to come to the kitchen and sit down, my Lord Auditor? We were just having breakfast."

"Tea, yes," said Miles, relieved from his impulse to wrench the mug out of the man's hand. *Gods, yes.*

Vorlynkin led through the back archway, saying, "How did you get here?"

"Walked. Thirty-odd kilometers since midnight, back ways, dodging twice because I didn't want to explain myself in my current condition to the local street guards. Needless to say, this was *not* my original plan."

The kitchen was a modest tidy room, with a round dining table squeezed into a sort of bay overlooking the walled back garden. The windows mostly reflected the room's bright interior, but beyond, the night's damp blackness was turning to bluer shadow. The blond kid, the attaché Johannes, turned from the microwave and almost dropped whatever pre-packaged bachelor fare he'd just heated. At his boss's head-jerk, he hastened to pull out a chair for the very important, if very unkempt, visitor. Miles fell into it, trying not to let his gratitude overcome his exasperation, because the latter was about all that was keeping him functional.

"Can I get you something, my lord?" asked the lieutenant solicitously.

"Tea. Also a shower, dry clothes, food, sleep, and a secured comconsole, though I'd settle for just the comconsole, but let's start with the tea." Or else he risked pillowing his head on his arms and going for the sleep first, right here. "Did you get my don't-panic message off to Barrayar, and my wife? Coded, I trust?"

Vorlynkin said, a little stiffly, "We notified ImpSec Galactic Affairs on Komarr that we'd heard from you, and that you were not in the hands of the kidnappers."

"Good enough. I'll send my own update in a bit." Miles trusted it would overtake any word anyone had been maladroit enough to hand on to Ekaterin, or he'd have some groveling to do when he got home. "Meanwhile, I've had no news since yesterday. Have you heard more on the hostages taken from the cryo-conference? Anything on Armsman Roic?"

Vorlynkin slid into his chair a quarter-wedge around the table from Miles. "Good news there, sir. Your Armsman managed to escape his captors long enough to reach a comlink of some sort and call the Northbridge authorities. The police rescue team reached them not long ago—we've been up all night following developments. It seems everyone was freed alive. I don't know how long it will take him to get back—he said he had to stay till he'd given his testimony."

"Ah, yes. Roic has a deal more sympathy for police procedure than I do." Miles took his first swallow of hot tea with profound relief. "And the boy—wait. And who might you be?" Miles eyed Yuuichi, who had taken refuge with Johannes on the far side of the kitchen.

"This is our consulate clerk, Yuuichi Matson," Vorkynkin put in. "Our most valuable employee. He's been here about five years." The clerk cast his boss a grateful look and slanted Miles a civil bow.

The consulate's only employee, actually. And since Vorlynkin had been here two years, and Johannes had only arrived last year, Matson was also the oldest, in time of service if not age. *Who do you trust, my Lord Auditor?* In a situation like this, no one but Roic, Miles supposed, but misplaced paranoia could be as great a mistake as misplaced faith. Careful, then, but not bloody paralyzed. "So what happened to Jin?"

"We dispatched him back to you exactly as you directed, my lord. We did take the precaution of placing a microscopic ping tracer in the envelope, however."

Not exactly the *don't follow him* that Miles had written, but it would be hypocritical to quibble over fine points now. Results, after all.

"By early evening, the envelope had come to rest in what we think is the evidence room of the Northbridge central police station—it's in that building, anyway. The boy Jin, after apparently passing through the hands of the police, ended up at the juvenile detention center, where he's been all night. With that much to go on, Lieutenant Johannes was able to access the public arrest records for yesterday, and identify him by process of elimination. It seems the boy's full name is Jin Sato, and he's a runaway who's been missing for over a year!"

"Yes?" said Miles. "I knew that."

Vorlynkin's diplomatic tones grew notably strained. "How the *devil*—sir!—did you come to involve a child like that in your affairs—whatever they are?"

"He's eleven," said Miles.

"Eleven! Worse and worse!"

"When my father was eleven," said Miles reasonably, "he became aide-de-camp to the general-my-grandfather in a full-scale civil war. By age thirteen he'd helped to bring down an emperor. I didn't figure an afternoon's jaunt across his home town and back—on a peaceful planet at that—to be beyond Jin's capacity." Yet apparently, he'd figured wrong. Miles winced inside. He hadn't thought through the implications of Jin's runaway status in a heavily monitored place like this, even while picking his own route to avoid notice as a matter of routine. The boy would be frantic for his animals by now, and that was the least of it. "My mistake to fix, then. I don't abandon my people if I can help it. We'll just have to retrieve him."

Vorlynkin's jaw dropped. "He's a *minor child.* How? We have no rights to him!"

"He was carrying all our petty cash, too," put in Johannes. "I'd have gone after that myself, but I had no way to prove it was ours." He frowned at Miles, the *exactly as you directed* complaint implied.

Well, there's always your ping tracer, but before Miles could voice the thought, Vorlynkin went on.

"If your underage courier talks, I expect the Northbridge police will be calling *us.* With some very hard-to-answer questions."

Miles paused, alert. "Have they?"

"No. Not yet."

And if they didn't call, it would imply Jin had kept his mouth shut, and under conditions that had to be quite frightening to him. "That's...interesting."

"Where *did* you pick up that boy, my lord?" said Vorlynkin.

"Actually, he found me. On the street, more or less." Miles

did some rapid internal editing. He had, after all, given Suze his tacit word not to reveal her lair in exchange for information, and he had certainly received information, even if he wasn't sure what he wanted to do with it yet. "You read my note to you, right?"

Vorlynkin nodded.

"Well, as I said, the drug the kidnappers tried to sedate me with triggered manic hallucinations instead, and I ended up lost in the Cryocombs." No need to say for how long; the situation was certainly elastic enough to cover the missing day he'd spent with Jin and company. "When I came to my senses and found my way out, I was still a bit paranoid about my kidnappers finding me again, and too exhausted to go on. Jin kindly helped me, and I owe him."

Vorlynkin stared at Miles very hard. "Are you saying you weren't in your right mind?"

"That might actually be a good explanation, should one be needed. Does this consulate keep a local lawyer?"

"On retainer, yes."

Standard practice. *Can you trust him or her to keep our secrets?* was a question Miles wasn't ready to ask out loud quite yet. "Good. As soon as possible, contact the lawyer and find out what we can do to get Jin back." He held out his mug for more tea; Yuuichi, the clerk, politely filled it. Miles's hand was shaking with fatigue, but he managed not to spill tea on the way to his lips. "Shower's as good as three hours of sleep. Shower first, and then the comconsole, if you please."

"Shouldn't you rest, my lord?" said Vorlynkin.

Miles choked back an impulse to scream, *Don't argue with me!* which was a pretty good indicator that, yes, he damn well should rest, but there were a few key things that he had to know, first. "Later," he said, then conceded, "Soon."

After a moment, he added reluctantly, "You'd better let the Northbridge police know I escaped, was lost in the Cryocombs, and came back to the consulate on my own—I don't want them to waste their resources hunting me. You can tell them I'm uninjured but extremely fatigued, and am resting here. They can send someone to take a statement from me tomorrow, if they need one. Don't mention Jin unless they ask. If anyone else inquires after me...check with me."

This won another hard stare from Vorlynkin, but he only nodded.

Johannes led Miles upstairs to the sleeping quarters—it appeared that the two Barrayaran bachelors saved on rent by living on the premises—and the consulate personnel scored about a million points with Miles by providing his very own clothes and gear, retrieved along with Roic's from their hotel room after the kidnappings. Johannes eyed the Auditor's own secured communications equipment—ImpSec's best—with due respect, when handing it over. The personal belongings the kidnappers had stripped from Miles were still in the hands of the police, found discarded in a downtown alley and retained as evidence, except for his Auditor's seal, which Vorlynkin had managed to pry back from them with, Miles gathered, some vigorous diplomatic persuasion.

Half an hour later—washed, shaved, and dressed in clean clothes—Miles had Johannes lead him down to the consulate's basement communications tight-room, such as it was, and settle him before a secured comconsole. Miles stretched his back and spread his fingers, then entered his first search term: *Lisa Sato.*

"Who's that?" asked Johannes, looming over his shoulder.

"Jin Sato's mother."

"Is she important?"

"Someone thought so, Lieutenant. Someone definitely thought so." As the vid plate flickered, Miles bent to the data stream.

Chapter Six

A brief conversation with m'lord over the comconsole at Northbridge police headquarters, once the rescued delegates arrived there, relieved Roic of his worst nightmare, that of losing the little gi—m'lord. New curiosities thronged to take its place. Why was m'lord insisting that Roic bring Dr. Durona along?

"Actually, I'd planned to return to the conference hotel and collect my luggage," Raven interpolated, leaning into the vid pick-up.

"See me first," m'lord replied.

"I'll miss my jumpship."

"There's one every day. In fact, don't reschedule your berth yet."

Raven's black brows flicked up. "My time is money."

"I'll keep that in mind."

Raven shrugged amiably at m'lord's very dry tone, and followed Roic, both scuffing along in the paper slippers their hosts had provided while waiting for their stolen shoes to surface.

It was midafternoon when the police at last dropped Roic and his bemused companion off at the consulate. The four-square house seemed unduly modest, in Roic's view, though he supposed that upholding the dignity of the Imperium at this distance was costly enough. It did look as though it might provide a shower and a place to nap, Roic's two biggest remaining wants since the police had provided the freed captives with a meal, or at least as many ration bars as anyone would want to eat. High in protein and vitamins, tasting like chocolate-coated putty with kitty litter—some horrors were universal, it seemed.

Roic stifled his wish for a wash-up and had Lieutenant Johannes guide them directly to m'lord, already ensconced like an invasive spider in the consulate's communications tight-room. In most planetary embassies that Roic had visited in m'lord's wake, the tight-room seemed the secret nerve center of the embassy's affairs, hushed and urgent. Here, it felt more like someone's leftover basement hobby room—for some very odd hobbies—retrofitted in high tech.

M'lord swiveled in his station chair and waved Roic and Raven to seats, dismissing Johannes with a "Thank you, Lieutenant." Johannes, looking as though he longed to stay and eavesdrop, nodded and dutifully withdrew, closing the door with that muffled thump that betokened a good sound seal. Roic ignored the faint serial-killer ambiance of the windowless chamber, and tried to appreciate that here at last one might enjoy a truly private conversation.

"Are you two all right?" A perfunctory inquiry; m'lord didn't even wait for Raven's nod and Roic's grunt before continuing, "Tell me everything that happened to you. And yes, I want all the details."

M'lord listened, brows tightening, as the full tale of the kidnapping and rescue unwound, rewarding the tellers at the end with a mere, "Huh." He added to Raven, "I'm glad you're all right. I shouldn't have liked to explain your loss to your clone-siblings, or mine. I'd actually thought the Durona Group would send your sister Rowan."

"No, she's much too busy these days for off-planet jaunts,"

said Raven. "She's our department head for Cryonics—we have over five hundred employees, between our clinical services, research, and administrative overhead. And she and that Escobaran medtech she married plan to pop their second kid from the uterine replicator any day now."

"Not cloned, eh?"

"No, it was all done the old-fashioned way, an egg and a sperm in a test tube. They didn't even go for any genetic mods, beyond the routine check for defects, of course."

"Of course," murmured m'lord, without comment. "So good old Lily Durona is a real grandmother, now—or aunt, depending on how you look at it. She continues in good health for her age, I trust?"

"Very much so."

"Interesting."

Raven tugged absently on his frazzled braid, laid over his shoulder, and continued, "As a department head, Rowan says she misses the hands-on surgical work. She hardly gets to do two revivals a week, these days. I do two to six a day, depending on complications. Nothing as complicated as you were—*you* took Rowan, me, and two shifts of medtechs eighteen hours straight, back in the day."

"You did good work."

"Thank you." Raven nodded in what seemed to Roic rather smug satisfaction.

"Give Rowan my best, when you see her."

"Oh, yeah, she said to say hi to you, too."

This won an oddly ironic look, and a return nod.

"I take it," put in Roic, "that Dr. Durona, here, wasn't at the conference by chance?"

"Indeed, not. I'd asked the Durona Group to supply me with an independent technical evaluation of the cryo-conference, and whatever turned up at it."

"The Group had actually received the conference's call for presentations well before you asked, Lord Vorkosigan. We were going to send one of our junior residents—this place is not without interest to us, actually."

"And have you observed anything of special note so far? Technically." M'lord leaned back in his station chair and steepled his fingers, giving Raven a judicious stare.

"Nothing new to us on the technical side. I did notice that they seemed more interested in freezing people than thawing them."

"Yes, the cryocorps are plainly playing numbers games with their customers'—patrons, they call 'em—proxy votes."

"It's a game they've won, from the sound of things."

M'lord nodded. "It was barely discussed at the conference, yet there seems to be plenty of debate on the subject outside. In the streets and elsewhere."

Raven put in, "The N.H.L.L. were sure complaining vigorously."

"Yeah, but not very effectively," said Roic. "Loons like that are their own worst advertisement."

"Does it strike you both as a pretty free debate, as such things go? Noisy?"

"Well, yes," said Raven. "Not as noisy as Escobaran politics."

"Noisier than Barrayar, though," Roic said.

"*Much* noisier than Jackson's Whole," Raven granted, with a twisted grin.

"That's not politics, that's predators versus prey," muttered m'lord. But he went on: "Well, thanks to the N.H.L.L., I had a very useful two days. Now that you're both back alive, I suppose I can afford to be grateful to them."

"New answers?" asked Roic, with a sapient eyebrow-lift.

"Better. A whole raft of new questions."

And m'lord promptly topped—of course—Roic's tale with a hair-curling story of the appalling extent of the Cryocombs beneath the city, and of how m'lord had stumbled on a bootleg freezing operation run by, apparently, Kibou street geezers. Raven seemed less impressed by the bootleg cryonics—he was Jacksonian, after all. As near as Roic could tell, *everything* on Jackson's Whole was done illegally. Or, more precisely, lawlessly.

"Fragile and doomed," was Raven's succinct opinion of Madame Suze's on-going operation. "I'm astonished she's gotten away with so much for so long."

"Mm, maybe not. It's clandestine, but it doesn't really rock the cryocorps' boat. Everyone here being in the same boat, after all." M'lord rubbed his chin and squinted red-rimmed eyes that glinted a trifle too brightly. "Then we come to this woman Lisa Sato, and her group."

"Your little zookeeper's frozen mama?" said Roic.

"Yep. The N.H.L.L. is allowed to run its length, Suze's operation is overlooked, but Sato's seemingly much more reasonable and legal group is broken up, at considerable trouble and expense. All that ambient noise, and yet only one voice is silenced." M'lord gestured to the secured comconsole, now dark. "I've spent the past several hours doing some digging—"

And as a former ImpSec galactic operative, this sort of digging was meat and drink to m'lord, Roic reflected.

"—and in just that time, I've turned up anomalies galore. Lisa Sato was not the only member of her group to come to a bad end. Two others were frozen after supposedly-unsuccessful treatments for medical conditions that should not have been fatal, another died in an accident, and yet another was ruled a suicide of the fell-or-jumped sort. Even at the time, brows were raised, and quite a few people were offended, but the aftershocks were drowned out in the news by a flood of trivial sex scandals. What does this suggest to you?"

"That Lisa Sato's group was getting ready to rock somebody's boat pretty hard," said Roic slowly.

Raven nodded concurrence. "How?"

"That, interestingly, does not turn up in the public record. Nor even in the less-public records. Somebody did a first-class job on the cleanup, there, even if they weren't able to make it completely invisible. That now heads my list of shiny new questions—just what got cleaned up, a year and a half ago?"

Roic frowned. "Very riveting, m'lord, but...what has this got t' do with Barrayar's interests?"

M'lord cleared his throat. "It is far too early to say," he said primly.

Roic, glumly, read that as, *I haven't made up a reason yet, but give me time.* Was m'lord going all quixotic on account of that orphan boy? Emperor Gregor himself had warned Roic about m'lord's tendency to expensive knight-errantry, in one of their rare private conversations. From the Imperial sigh that had accompanied this, it had been unclear if Gregor actually expected Roic to restrain m'lord, or not.

The door hissed open, and Consul Vorlynkin stuck his head through. "I've heard back from the lawyer, Lord Vorkosigan."

"Ah, good!" M'lord waved him in; he stood, seeming a bit wary. "What's the word on Jin?"

"As I thought, there is nothing we can legally do. If he were an orphan without kin, you could apply for custody of him, but it would take some months and almost certainly be rejected by the Northbridge courts, especially if there was any hint of taking him off-planet."

"I didn't ask to adopt him, Vorlynkin. Just rescue him from the police."

"In any case, my Lord Auditor, it's become moot—the police have already turned the boy over to his blood-kin, an aunt who is in fact his present legal guardian."

"Damn!" M'lord slumped. "Damn. I hope Ako proves a more faithful zookeeper than I did."

"Well, it's not as if we could kidnap him," said Vorlynkin, with a faint smile. M'lord eyed him. Perhaps thinking better of this mild venture into humor, Vorlynkin cleared his throat and went back to looking bland. Roic wondered if he should take Vorlynkin aside later and warn him not to *say* things like that around m'lord, and not because the Lord Auditor might take offense.

Roic rubbed sandy eyelids. "Perhaps you'd best sleep on it, m'lord," he suggested, not without self-interest. M'lord had plainly had the advantage of a shower and fresh clothes, but still looked as if he'd been up all night, as had they all. And the shiny glitter in his eyes was a tip-off. "Have you checked your neurotransmitter levels since you got back?" The elevation of same being early warning of an impending seizure, and signal it was time to use the medical seizure-stimulator to short-circuit the fit—in some safe and controlled place.

M'lord addressed an unrevealing mutter to his shoes.

"Right," said Roic, in a very firm tone.

M'lord sighed and rubbed the back of his neck. "Yeah, yeah."

"Can I go back to my hotel now?" asked Raven hopefully.

"Yes, but stay in touch. In fact—Vorlynkin, please issue Dr. Durona a secured wristcom before he goes, eh?"

Vorlynkin's brows rose, but he said only, "Yes, my lord."

"I *need* more *data*," m'lord growled, to no one in particular. He looked up appraisingly at the consul. "All right, Vorlynkin. If WhiteChrys or any of our other late hosts call to inquire after me, I want you to tell them that I am very upset by the disruption of the conference and the kidnapping of my armsman. In fact, I'm furious, and as soon as I recover from my ordeal I plan to stalk home and give a very bad report of the affair to anyone who will listen, starting with Emperor Gregor."

"Er . . . and are you?" asked Vorlynkin, sounding nonplussed.

M'lord returned only an unreassuring grin. "I want you to test how far they'll go to reopen their lines of communication. Indicate you'll do your diplomatic best to calm me down, but you're not sure it can be done. If they offer you incentives for the task, take them up."

"You . . . want me to accept a bribe, sir?" A little real offense tightened Vorlynkin's jaw, as well as understandable alarm.

"Well, at least pretend to consider it, eh? It will show us who wants what, and how badly. If they don't come through, I'll have to think of another move, but if you're a tolerably good fisherman, I think you can hook them for me."

"I'll, um ... try my best, sir." Vorlynkin didn't exactly stare at the Lord Auditor as if the little man had sprouted two heads, but Roic could almost see the consul scrambling to keep pace. *Yeah, welcome to my world.*

The debriefing broke up.

The consulate harbored two spare bedrooms upstairs fitted out for guests, not much used for the purpose and slowly filling with assorted storage. One had been hastily cleared for the Lord Auditor. Roic turned down the bed and rummaged in m'lord's luggage for the seizure stimulator. M'lord stripped to his underwear, sat on the bed, and eyed the medical device with loathing.

"Kludgy thing."

"Yes, m'lord. Tell me, am I to trust the consulate fellows here, or not?"

"I'm not sure yet. I've been caught out before with embassy staff or even ImpSec couriers being suborned."

"Because if you mean to use them for backup, which we very much need, you're going to have to start including them in your loop. I could see Lieutenant Johannes, f'r instance, didn't know what to make of you leaving him out just now."

"It's this Lord Auditor thing. I *used* to be able to get almost anyone to talk to me, damn it. In your spare minutes, try your hand at evaluating them, eh? I've no doubt they'll be more willing to be frank with you, simple honest face and all that."

"Yes, m'lord."

"I already know that *somebody* out there is buying people. Question is, has the consulate been bought already, or did there seem no need to secure it before I showed up? At least neither of the Barrayarans have families here, so I don't have to worry about negative incentives." M'lord scowled, lay back, and set the stimulator to the curve of his skull. Roic handed him the mouth guard, which he fitted around his teeth. He took a breath and squeezed his eyes shut like someone about to down a dose of some nasty-tasting medicine, and triggered the stimulator.

Roic timed the seizure—it was a long one, suggesting m'lord had been pushing the limit. Roic was used to the rolled-back eyes, the weird grimace, and the shivering, but he doubted he'd ever be quite reconciled to the strange absence of that driving personality animating the face. In due course, the neural storm passed, and m'lord lay slack, his eyes opening again on the universe as though his gaze recreated it.

"God, I hate this," he muttered. His standard mantra at this point.

"Yes, m'lord," Roic soothed. His standard response.

"I'll be useless for the rest of the night even if I do get slept out. And tomorrow as well."

"I'll bring you coffee."

"Thanks, Roic." M'lord rolled over and drew up the covers, surrendering at last to the demands of his depleted body. Muffled into the pillow, almost inaudibly, "F'r everythin'..."

Roic shook his head and tiptoed off to find his own bunk.

Jin blinked open sore eyes in the semi-darkness of his sister Minako's tiny bedroom, then bit his lip on a groan. He'd meant to stay awake, outwait and maybe outwit his captors, but the exhaustion of the past day had betrayed him. He sat up on his elbow. A nightlight low on the wall shed a dim pink glow, but the room lacked a clock. It was still full dark outside, and the muffled rumble of Uncle Hikaru's snores sounded through the thin walls of the next room, so everyone else was asleep, but it could be any hour from midnight to near-dawn.

He swung bare legs out from under the covers of the narrow futon. Aunt Lorna had put him to bed in his underwear, since his cousin Tetsu's pajamas had been too big, and his cousin Ken's too small. His own clothes she had hauled away to wash, or maybe burn, she'd said, since there was no telling where they'd been. Jin sure wasn't telling, anyway.

Hopelessly, he went to the window and tried the lock. It unlatched, but the window only slid aside about three centimeters. Uncle Hikaru had climbed up on a borrowed ladder, after the argument at dinner, and blocked the window groove with a rod. Jin could just curl his fingers around the frame, but couldn't get his hand through. He wasn't going to be able to repeat his escape of last year.

Jin pressed his forehead to the cool glass and looked down at the patch of patio, one floor below. In a way, Aunt Lorna had made it easy for him, back then, by exiling all his animals out there. After he'd climbed out the window and dropped down, he'd only had to load them all up on Minako's outgrown stroller, left in the lee of the fence earlier that day. He'd been terrified at the time that Gyre's squawk and Lucky's meowing would alert the household, or that the glass box holding the rats and the turtle would tip and clatter, but it had been a cold night, the windows closed, and nobody but him paid attention to his creatures anyway.

Well, Tetsu had got in the habit of teasing Gyre, till Gyre had, naturally, bit him. Then there'd been the trip to emergency care, and the surgical glue and antibiotics, and Aunt Lorna screeching more than Tetsu, though mostly about the bill. Tetsu had shown off his battle scar at school the next day pretty smugly, Jin thought.

Jin slipped over and tried the door, turning the latch as silently as he could. Still locked. There had been another big argument about whether people had to get up in the night to let Jin go to the bathroom, which Uncle Hikaru had settled, in a very practical way, by providing Jin with a bucket, which had scandalized Aunt Lorna and made Tetsu and Ken make fun of him, till Uncle had thumped them. That had been after the squabble over where Jin was to sleep, since his sister was now judged too big to share a bed with him, or maybe it was the other way around. Tetsu and Ken, already dividing a cramped room, complained about having yet a third boy shoved in atop their clutter, and had also objected to being made Jin's watchers. Jin had endured much in silence, last night and today, in anticipation of a timely escape. He hadn't expected to be *locked in*.

"Just till the boy settles down," Uncle Hikaru had said—as if Jin would abandon his creatures. As if he would ever stay *here*.

Was Miles-san taking care of his charges properly? What must he think, when Jin never came back with his money? Would he think Jin had stolen it? The *police* had stolen it, really, but would even that extraordinary off-worlder believe Jin over the grownups? He swallowed a lump in his throat, determined not to cry again, because maybe letting go like that was why he'd fallen asleep, earlier. Although what was the point in forcing himself to stay awake when he couldn't get out? He returned to the futon and sank down in despair.

Maybe tomorrow night he could hide a screwdriver or some other tools in the room, and try to take the window or the door lock apart from the inside. Tenbury would have known how, Jin was sure. He didn't think he could pretend to be all settled down so quickly and thus lull his captors into relaxing their guard, not when he was growing more and more frantic inside. Aunt Lorna had threatened she was going to sign him right up tomorrow for Tetsu and Ken's school, because she couldn't afford to lose any more work days over him. School, he recalled, had seemed even less easy to escape from than— Jin refused to think of this narrow rented row-house as *home*.

The door lock clicked. Aunt Lorna, checking up on him? He could still hear Uncle Hikaru's snores. He rolled over to face the wall, hitched his covers up over his shoulder, and scrunched his eyes shut.

"Jin?" a shy voice whispered. "Are you asleep?"

Jin rolled back, both relieved and annoyed. It was only Mina. "Yes," he growled.

A short silence. "No, you're not."

"What do *you* want?" Some forgotten doll or stuffed toy, he supposed, although she'd taken a basket of them with her to her temporary bed on the couch downstairs.

The door rumbled, sliding into its slot, and small feet padded to the side of his futon. He rolled over onto his elbow again and stared up at her, staring down at him. She shared Jin's brown eyes and tousled mop of black hair, but she was taller and less chubby than he remembered from fourteen months ago. Then, she hadn't even started school yet—now she was in her second year. She seemed less . . . bewildered-looking, somehow.

"If I let you out," she said, "will you take me with you?"

"Huh?" Startled, Jin sat up and hugged his knees. What, she wasn't just lost on the way to the bathroom? "No, of course not. Are you crazy?"

Her face fell. "Oh." She retreated to the door and started to pull it shut behind her.

"No, wait!" Jin hissed, lumbering up.

Next door, the snores stopped. They both froze. After a moment, there came a creaking and a sort of gurgling-drain noise, and the snores started up again.

"We can't talk here," Jin whispered. "Let's go downstairs."

She seemed to think this over, then nodded, waiting in the hallway while he wrapped a blanket around his shoulders and trailed after her. Jin shoved the door closed again very slowly and quietly. The stairs squeaked under their tiptoeing feet, but no one came after them.

"Don't turn the light on," Jin said, keeping his voice low. There was enough light leaking from what Uncle Hikaru called the one-butt kitchen, in a niche off the living-dining room, to keep from tripping on things.

Mina settled back in her twisted nest of covers on the couch. Jin sat on the edge of Uncle Hikaru's chair and stared around.

Mina asked, "Do you remember Daddy?"

"Sort of. Some."

"I don't. Just his picture in the family shrine Mommy set up."

"You were three." Jin had been seven when their father had died. Four years ago—it seemed half a lifetime. He remembered his mother's extravagant grief and anger rather better, and how seldom he'd seen her after that—as if one death had stolen both parents, even before the policewomen had come for her. "Doesn't Aunt Lorna keep the family shrine anymore?"

"She let me keep it in my room for a while, but then we ran out of space when I needed a desk for school, so she boxed it up and put it away. I wasn't sure if to set your picture in it or not."

Mina was putting on her shoes, a determined look on her face.

"You can't go with me," Jin repeated uneasily. "Not where I'm going."

"Where are you going?"

"A long walk. Too far for you. Why do you want to come anyway?" She'd been Aunt and Uncle's pet, he thought.

"Tetsu and Ken are horrid to me. Teasing and bedeviling. Uncle Hikaru yells at them, but he never gets up and does anything."

Jin didn't quite see the problem with this. Well, he had a dim sense that maybe it was his job to heckle his own sister, but if somebody else wanted to take up the slack, he had no objection. "They're probably just jealous because you get all the girl stuff. Plus if you weren't here, Ken would have your room," he added in a fair-minded fashion.

"Uncle and Aunt were talking about 'dopting me, before you came back. But I don't want Tetsu and Ken for my brothers. I want my *real* brother."

"How can they adopt you when Mom's still..." He trailed off. *Alive?* The word choked in his throat, a wad of uncertainty. He swallowed it and went on: "You can't stay where I'm going. I—they wouldn't want you. You'd just get in the way." While Suze-san and the people at her place might be willing to treat a stray boy as casually as a stray cat, he had a queasy sense that a stray girl, and younger at that, might be another story. And while the police, not to mention Uncle Hikaru and Aunt Lorna, might be less excited about him running away a second time, would that boredom extend to Mina? "You couldn't keep up."

"Yes, I could!"

"Sh! Keep your voice down!"

Her mouth went mulish. "If you don't take me along, I'll set up a screech, and they'll catch you and put you back in my room! And I won't let you out again, so there!"

He tried to decide if she was bluffing. No, probably not. Could he hit her on the head with something and knock her out while he made his getaway? He had a feeling that worked better in holovids than in real life. And if he hit her with one of Aunt Lorna's pots or pans, the only blunt instruments immediately available, it would make a hellish bong and wake everybody up anyway, defeating his purpose.

She interrupted his hostile mulling, in a practical tone that reminded him of Uncle Hikaru: "Besides, I have money and you don't."

"...How much?"

"Over five hundred nuyen," she answered proudly. "I saved it up from my birthday and chores."

Enough for a dozen tram fares, except that Jin had sworn off the tube system. He craned his neck for a look at the kitchen clock—maybe two hours till dawn, and everybody getting up and missing them. That wasn't very much of a headstart, compared to the last time. It was now or never. Jin surrendered to the inevitable. "All right, get ready. *Quietly.* Do you know where Aunt Lorna put my stuff?"

They found Jin's clothes in the plastic basket, along with his shoes, in the closet off the kitchen that harbored the launderizer. Mina knew which kitchen drawer hid the lunch bars, too, and stuck a dozen in a sack. Within minutes, they both edged out the sliding back door. Jin latched the patio gate as quietly as he could behind them, and led off up the alley.

The occasional streetlights made cold halos in the clammy

night mist. "I've never been outside this late before," said Mina, still whispering, though they were well away from the row house. "It's weird. Are you afraid of the dark?" She made to walk closer to Jin; he strode faster.

"The dark's all right. It's *people* you have to be afraid of."

"I guess so."

A longer silence, while their feet thumped softly on the pavement. Then Mina said, "That thing Aunt Lorna said to you, about recid—recidiv... I can't pronounce it. Kids who run away over and over. They don't *really* freeze them, do they?"

Jin pondered it uneasily. "I never heard of it before. And it would cost a lot of money, I think."

"So she was just trying to scare you into being good?"

"Yeah." The *scare* part had sure worked, Jin had to allow that.

"But anyway, they don't freeze you the *first* time." Mina seemed to take undue satisfaction from this thought.

An unwelcome memory rose in Jin's mind. It wasn't the clammy smell of the night that triggered it, because the policewomen had come for his mother in the daytime, but the clammy chill in his gut that day had felt much like this. Mom kneeling down, gripping his shoulders, saying, *Jin, help look after Mina, all right? Be a good big brother, and do what Aunt Lorna tells you.*

Jin had given up on that last when Aunt Lorna had insisted that he get rid of all of his pets, yes, *all*, a clean sweep, there was no room and they smelled and pooped too much and that bird was homicidal and to top everything, Ken was supposedly allergic to Lucky, who was too lazy to scratch anyone. Jin just figured his cousin was doing all that sniffling and blowing on *purpose,* to be annoying, in which he certainly succeeded. Jin had forgotten the first part of that maternal parting...blessing, curse, whatever it was, because, after all, nobody yelled at Mina they way they'd yelled at him and his pets.

He wished he hadn't remembered that.

They had a good long walk ahead of them just to get out of

this area, which they needed to do before they were missed. Maybe they'd better lie up and hide during school hours. Jin selected a direction he was almost sure was south, and kept trudging.

Chapter Seven

Two days after his dawn return to the consulate, Miles's party assembled on the front walk and watched the WhiteChrys groundcar pull up to collect them. It was long, sleek, gleaming, and settled to the pavement with a sigh like a satisfied lover.

Roic's eyebrows rose. "Better t'n that bus-thing they ferried us conference delegates around in, I'll give it that."

"Indeed," said Miles. "Good job, Vorlynkin. It looks like WhiteChrys means to grovel in style."

This won an uncertain head-duck from the consul, who had spent a good part of yesterday in repeated calls to and from their would-be host to set all this up, while Miles played hard-to-get. At least the delay had given him time to recover from the induced seizure.

But while it would do no harm to Miles's cause if Barrayar's own diplomat plainly found him alarming, he was not altogether sure if the man was under control. *Or sure whose control he's under?* He favored the consul with a brief smile. "By the by,

Vorlynkin, please refrain from commenting on anything you hear me say or see me do today. For the duration, you're the yes-man."

An unreadable pause. "Yes, my Lord Auditor."

Capable of irony, was he? Good. Probably.

"It'll be just like watching a play," Roic reassured him. Vorlynkin's brows quirked, albeit not in an especially reassured way. Dr. Durona, engaged in examining the variegated hostas lining the walk, straightened and turned his braided head with interest as the groundcar's rear compartment canopy rose and a woman exited.

She was as sleek as the groundcar, if considerably more delicate. Her long black hair was drawn back and bundled with enameled combs in an elegant construction that Miles was sure Raven must envy. Kibou natives wore a variety of fashions both local and galactic-inspired; Miles had been here just long enough to decode her garb as business-traditional, female version. A skin-skimming top, a fitted undercoat, and the loose cord-fastened outer coat might be worn by either men or women, but then, instead of the wide trousers tied in at the ankles adopted by men, she showed off trim calves with a short skirt and leggings. All in subtle autumnal shades that set off her deep brown eyes. The overall effect was simultaneously upper-class and sexy, like a very expensive courtesan—Miles had once had the geisha tradition explained to him on a visit to Earth itself, on its island of origin, a side-benefit of having a bride with a mania for gardens. The sense that this woman was a weapon aimed directly at him came mainly from her diminutive height, which nearly matched his own, and the fact that she wore flat sandals.

"Good morning, *ohayo gozaimasu*." She favored them all with a formal bow, but her smile zeroed in on Miles. "Lord Vorkosigan, Consul Vorlynkin, Durona-sensei, Roic-san. Wonderful, you're all here. I am Aida, Mr. Ron Wing's personal assistant for today. I will escort you to WhiteChrys's new facility, and answer any questions you may have along the way."

I'll bet not mine, thought Miles, but returned appropriate greetings and allowed the pretty young lady to shepherd them all into the spacious groundcar. Miles wondered how much her boss had scrambled to find a hostess of that height on such short, as it were, notice.

Ron Wing was the man Miles had been holding out for yesterday, while Vorlynkin fielded oblique messages and visibly refrained from tearing his hair. Wing's official title was Head of Development; he was one of WhiteChrys's chief operating officers, and the man in ultimate charge of the Komarr expansion effort. It was his underlings who had spent so much effort cultivating Miles, and vice versa, during the cryonics conference. *Now we'll see what's on the other end of their string.*

Roic, Aida, and Raven took the rear-facing seat; Miles and Vorlynkin settled opposite. No one even risked bumping heads with each other in the shuffle.

"Reminds me of my Da's old groundcar," Miles murmured to Roic.

"Nah," Roic whispered back, as the driver in the front compartment, who had not been introduced, set them smoothly in motion. "This isn't even half the mass. No armor plating."

Soft-voiced Aida offered a startling variety of drinks from the car's bar, which everyone politely refused after Miles did. Miles tilted his face to the polarized canopy to get a better look at the capital from an above-ground vantage for a change. No actual mountains cradled Northbridge, but it had been long enough since the glaciers had retreated here for streams to have carved the moraines into something other than scraped-flat. The native plant species, rudimentary at best, had pretty much been displaced by urban landscaping based on Earth imports. The city was city, grown up around an infrastructure of galactic-standard transport and technology. If Miles hadn't walked through it himself, he'd have no guess of what strangeness lay below.

The view grew more interesting when they reached the west end and approached the Cryopolis proper.

"The Cryopolis began to be developed some forty years ago," Aida informed them in good guide style, "when further extension of cryofacilities beneath the city grew too expensive. Now Northbridge has grown out to meet it, and it has become its own municipality, named Western Hope."

"And how many representatives does Western Hope field to the Territorial Prefecture's legislature?" Miles inquired.

"Fourteen," she replied brightly.

As many as the parent-city itself, though it occupied a fraction of the area. "Interesting."

Roic's head swiveled around. "What t' heck...?"

"Pyramids!" said Dr. Durona happily, craning too. "Dozens of 'em! Is there a river around here called Denial?"

Miles reminded himself to repress Raven, too, at the earliest private opportunity.

Aida's permanent smile grew briefly pained, but recovered at once. "Those are the facilities of our largest cryonics services competitor, NewEgypt."

About a kilometer of sandstone wall was pierced by a high gate, flanked by huge statues of somber seated figures sporting slim canine heads.

"I saw those before," said Roic, "back at the conference. There was a fellow wandering around in a skimpy costume with a big plastic dog head, handing out flyers. Seemed more like an advertisement for a Jackson's Whole bioengineering firm."

Miles could fill in that one. "The figures are of Anubis, the Egyptian god of the dead," he explained. "They had a number of other gods with animal heads—hawks, cats, cows—that had various figurative meanings. That's actually not a dog but a jackal, which was a carrion-eating scavenger in their ancient deserts. A natural association with death for a preindustrial folk, I suppose." He glanced at Aida and refrained from expanding the parallel, though he did wonder if anyone had bothered to check the translations on those hieroglyphs decorating the walls, or whether they really read something like *Ptah-hotep is a louse!* or *Unas owes Teti one hundred wheat sheaves and a firkin of figs.*

Aida glanced at the receding figures and sniffed. "As you can see, they've taken up that era from Old Earth as their corporate theme."

More of a theme park, Miles thought.

Aida added with reluctant admiration, "The pyramids are their cryo-storage facilities. NewEgypt has found that patrons will pay a premium for the more limited luxury space on the upper levels."

"Luxury space?" said Roic. "Isn't it all t' same, once you're frozen? I mean, technologically?"

He glanced at Raven, who murmured, "One certainly trusts so ..."

"Yes, but the cryo-contracts are selected and signed by the living people," Aida explained. "It has been a very appealing and successful program for NewEgypt. They've trademarked that entire historical period to block imitators." She added in a tone of some disappointment, "They were giving away live sphinxes at the conference this year, but our department head was too late to get us one."

With effort, Miles didn't blink, and so he had a good view of the next facility along their route, which featured glass towers and glittering spires wrapped with lines of colored light. The groundcar was well sound-insulated, but he could have sworn a faint bass beat penetrated the canopy. "Music?"

"Shinkawa Consolidated," their guide explained. Sure enough, they passed another gate, with the cryocorp's name displayed over it in shifting rainbow hues. "I believe they are trying to appeal to a younger crowd."

Miles tried to digest that. It wasn't going down. "Surely that would be the smallest market segment."

"Patrons are normally older when their contract is activated, yes," said Aida. "But personal affordability is improved the sooner you sign on and begin your payments. It's actually been a very effective strategy for Shinkawa. If I didn't have a cryo-contract through my own employer, as part of my benefits package, I'd consider them myself." She hid a giggle behind one well-manicured hand. "Though I probably shouldn't tell you that."

Another cryocorp campus appeared on the opposite side of the highway. It seemed to have a lot of trees, but neither walls nor gates—nor gate guards—though a low stone divider bore the name *Northern Spring*. What buildings Miles could spot through the vegetation looked blocky and utilitarian. Miles pointed. "How about those folks?"

"Ah, Northern Spring," said Aida. "They have the distinction of being one of the oldest cryocorps in the region, and one of the first to develop a facility out here, but they are not what we would call top tier."

Actually, according to Miles's not-always-inadequate preliminary reports on Kibou-daini, they were the sixth largest publicly-owned cryocorp presently doing business, which would certainly make them what *he* would call top tier. But the general look of their place was staid to the point of stodgy.

A lot of money was being spent to woo . . . not the dead, Miles supposed, but the living. Although for personal long-term cryo-sequestration, one might well *want* an immortal entity like a corporation left in charge. Their impressive fronts promised a number of things, but mostly continuity. If only one didn't know that at the secret heart of all such organizations, corporations and governments alike, it still came down to a finite number of fallible people talking to each other . . .

The big groundcar slowed and turned, passing under an enormous red torii gate—WhiteChrys lost no time in asserting its chosen corporate style. The security beeped them through electronically without a pause. They rounded a stand of pine trees and pulled up before the headquarters building. An efficient tower block rose behind, but the visitor first threaded an imitation-traditional garden, all water and walkways, moss clumps, raked pebbles, and delicate red maples. The theme continued inside the big glass lobby with gnarled miniature trees and severe flower arrangements. Amid all this tasteful splendor their hosts awaited, bowing, and Miles shook off the last of his lingering seizure fatigue and gathered his wits.

Ron Wing in person proved middle-aged and trim in formal business attire: undercoat, wide-sleeved outer coat with just a hint of winged shoulders, and baggy trousers in subtle muted blues, complete right down to the split-toe socks and sandals. Style, fabric and cut all signaled status, money, and mode as surely as a Barrayaran Vor male's quasi-military tunic, trousers, and half-boots. The calculated dress was backed up by shrewd eyes and a sober attention.

At Wing's elbow hovered the fellow who had delicately conveyed WhiteChrys's bribe to the Lord Auditor at the party the night before the terrorists/activists/idiotists had struck, so rudely interrupting their promising exchange. Hideyuki Storrs bore the title of executive vice president for development. He wore a slimmer version of his boss's garb, much like Vorlynkin's studiously local dress, tradition modified by utility; Miles had pegged him as a high-ranking minion, but not quite inner circle.

The development department plainly wanted to take up where they'd left off, and Miles was reminded not to let himself be unruffled too soon. No point in wasting a free edge. Half of Miles's maneuvering yesterday had been to climb the chain of command up to One Who Knows. As Aida passed the party on to Storrs, who made the formal introductions to Wing, Miles thought with satisfaction, *Target acquired. Locked on.* By Wing's smile, Miles wondered if his opposite was thinking something similar.

I am more important to you than I ought to be. Why?

"I'm so pleased," said Wing, "that you have allowed us to make up for some of the inconveniences you have lately suffered, Lord Vorkosigan."

Miles made an it's-not-your-fault wave of his free hand, undercut by a thin grimace, and returned, "We can only be grateful that no one was seriously injured or killed in the whole escapade."

"Truly," agreed Wing. "In exchange, this does allow us to give you a much more detailed look at our facility than the general tour would have."

"Some exchange does seem due, yes."

"Would you care for some refreshments? Tea? Or shall we follow galactic custom and begin right away?"

"I'd prefer to jump straight in, actually. My time here is not unlimited."

"Right this way, then..."

The whole party shuffled off after Wing at Miles's cane-pace, not altogether feigned. Between his underground ordeal and the usual after-effects of the damned seizures, his aches and pains were catching up with him. Aida stuck to his side, as if ready to catch him should he fall over. The prettiest public parts of the HQ building were quickly displayed, then they were wafted by float cart over to another building where actual intake of patrons occurred. Both the front lobby and the back loading docks seemed busy.

"Our patrons come from two sources," Wing explained, leading them down the medically-scented corridors. "Some, who've suffered sudden and unexpected metabolic shut-downs, are actually processed by the hospitals, and then transferred to us for long-term storage. Others, who choose a less chancy mode, come in to our clinics and have us do the processing on-site."

"Wait, they come in *alive*?" asked Roic.

"The healthier you are when frozen, the better your chances of a healthy revival," said Storrs.

"That's quite true," murmured Raven.

Roic's brows drew down, and he shot a glance at Miles, who could only say, "Alas, yes."

"Would you care for a closer look at the technical processes?" said Wing. "That section isn't normally on the public tours, of course. We have some twenty or so freezings scheduled for today. The transfers are of course usually unscheduled."

Miles, who had once endured the whole process far too intimately, if not consciously, waved aside the macabre treat; Roic looked relieved. Vorlynkin bore it all with a wooden expression. Raven, at Miles's thumbs-up behind his back, took the suggestion and went off with Storrs. Miles was glad to exit the processing building; the smell of the place, while not unpleasant, was doing odd jumpy things to his backbrain.

"And how many cryorevivals do you do here in a day?" Miles asked Wing, once they were safely back in the float cart and in motion. He and Wing shared the front seat with the best view, Aida sat facing rearward at their backs, and Vorlynkin and Roic shared the last bench, not quite out of earshot.

Wing hesitated only slightly. "I would have to look that figure up." He glanced back as the cart bowled along through the well-kept grounds. "How did you come to know Dr. Durona?" Included in this jaunt at Miles's—well, not request; Raven had simply been announced in the seat count for the groundcar.

"He and my assistant Roic were rather thrown together during the kidnappings. A bonding experience, I gather."

"Ah, that would explain it. Your Roic looks a fellow I'd want to duck behind in a crisis, too." It was plain Wing had no trouble translating *assistant* as *bodyguard*. No one, looking at Roic and Miles together, ever thought anything else. Miles was fairly sure Wing had not yet decoded the complexities of *Armsman*. Wing went on, "I was intrigued to learn you have a relative who is a major shareholder in the Durona Group. Unless the name Vorkosigan is common on Barrayar?"

"Mark?" *So, you've finally caught up with that.* Another clue, one of several, that Miles's Auditorial visit to Kibou had come as a surprise to the cryocorp, and they were still on the scramble to peg him. Miles had met deep-laid plots, years in fruition; Wing's maneuvers smelled of stop-gap, maybe only days old. "My younger brother, actually."

"Really!" Wing smiled. "Do you think our Komarr expansion project would be of interest to him, as well?"

Yes, but not in the way you think. "I'd prefer to keep Mark out of this. He's a very shrewd businessman. While I've labored my whole life in public service for very little reward, he's piled up profits to envy, passing me by. One of the things that most excites me about your project is the chance at last to beat him at his own game." Miles arranged his lips in a smile of vulpine sibling rivalry.

Wing got it at once, which said something about Wing. "I quite see." He added after a moment, "And does he have anything like your influence in public affairs, Lord Vorkosigan?"

"No, he pretty much keeps to the shop."

"Too bad."

"Not from my point of view."

"And the rest of your famous family? Are you on warmer terms with them?"

"Oh, yes. Though a chance to show them *all* up doesn't come along every day." Miles let his voice turn faintly whiny. "I've always had more to prove, on Barrayar." There, let Wing digest that. A nice balance between jealous greed and the promise of an influence worth peddling. *And* it would stand up to surface inquiry. *Thank you, Brother.*

Wing's brow furrowed in doubt. "Won't Dr. Durona report back to him?"

"Let's just say I'm working on that." Miles softened his voice so the hum of the cart kept it from carrying. "You know the old saying, *Keep your friends close and your enemies closer?*"

Wing nodded. "That's a good one." He hesitated. "We've prepared a presentation on the Komarr Project for you, next. Should we invite the good doctor to view another part of the facility during that?"

"It won't be necessary. Unless you have some technical innovation you prefer not to disclose to potential rivals?"

"No, the Komarr installation will be based on tried and

trusted technology. Our innovations are all to the business model."

"No problem, then. I gather Raven is one of those techie types—business goes right over his head." How provincial was this fellow Wing? Raven was from bloody *Jackson's Whole*, where the Deal was art, science, war, and survival-till-dawn. "Have you ever been off-world, Mr. Wing?"

"Yes, I had a trip to your Komarr last year, when we were setting up. All business, I'm afraid—I had very little time to tour. I never got outside of the Solstice Dome."

"Ah, that's a shame."

Back in the headquarters building, they were all trundled off to a top-floor conference room, elegantly appointed with more gnarly potted treelets and fine art glass. Aida at last persuaded them to consume assorted beverages—Miles and Vorlynkin stuck to green tea, Roic to coffee—after which they were subjected to a glossy holovid presentation all about the large WhiteChrys cryonics facility presently under construction in the Solstice Dome, Komarr's planetary capital. Try as he might, Miles could spot nothing about it that was not perfectly aboveboard. Neither, with access to far more detailed data, had ImpSec Komarr. And they'd looked it over closely, incidentally picking up, with WhiteChrys's full cooperation and applause, two overcharging contractors, an embezzling customs clerk, and a ring of warehouse thieves, although none of that was mentioned in Wing's snazzy vid.

Raven and Storrs joined them about halfway through. The vid wound up in a burst of optimistic-yet-tasteful music.

Miles leaned back in his incredibly comfortable conference chair, steepling his fingers. "So, why Komarr? If you wanted to expand off-world, wouldn't Escobar have been closer?"

Wing sat up, looking happy to answer. "We did look into it. But Escobar's own cryonics services are far more mature, and are further shielded from competition by what I can only call highly protectionist regulation. Our analysts concluded that

Komarr, despite the extra distance, offered far more scope for growth, which is, after all, where most profits lie. Profits in which we hope Barrayarans like yourself will share, of course. Indeed, Solstice Dome is sharing already—all the work after the design stage was contracted locally."

"I expect," said Miles judiciously, "once everyone on a planet has been sold a cryo-contract, there's no place left to go but outward." He didn't add, *Though there's one born every minute,* but it was a struggle.

"It's the hazard of a mature market, yes, I'm afraid. Although some interesting work has been done in the past year with commodifying contracts."

"Beg pardon?"

Wing's voice warmed with genuine enthusiasm. "Cryonics contracts have not been historically uniform, having been collected over many years by many institutions, often under different local laws. They yield on wildly varying bases, any of which might have grown or shrunk since the contract was activated. Companies themselves have split, combined, gone bankrupt or been bought out. Formerly, contracts and the responsibility for them have changed hands only along with the institutions holding them. But it was recently realized that a secondary market in individual contracts could provide considerable opportunity, either for profit-taking or to raise operating capital."

Miles felt his brow corrugating. "You're buying and selling the *dead*?"

"Swapping all those frozen bodies around?" Roic's horrified expression was much less controlled.

"No, no!" said Wing. Storrs seconded his boss with vigorous headshake, *No, no, no!*

"That would be absurdly wasteful," Wing went on. "The patrons mostly stay right where they are, unless a facility is being upgraded or decommissioned, of course. The patrons are held on a reciprocal accounting basis, company to company.

It's only their contracts that are traded." He added piously, "It's hoped that, over time, this will result in a more uniform and fairer contract structure industry-wide."

Miles translated this as, *When we've squeezed the sponge dry, we'll stop*. Judging by Raven's remarkably blank smile, quite as if he hadn't understood a single word, he was making the exact same construction.

"And, er, will you be applying that model to Komarr?" Miles asked.

"Unfortunately, no. There is no one there to trade with." Although he sighed, Wing did not seem to be especially distressed by this. Miles read that as, *We plan to be a monopoly*.

"This is all quite stunning," Miles said honestly. "And what do you think of it all, Vorlynkin?" He cast the consul a jovial wink. "Ready to sign up? I suppose it's all old hat to you, though."

"Not . . . really," said Vorlynkin. "Most of my work has dealt with the concerns of the living. I had to expedite returning the remains of one poor Barrayaran tourist who was killed glacier-diving last year—very dangerous sport—and sign off on the delivery of a couple of Kibou business people who'd died of natural causes in the Empire and been shipped home. One frozen, one as ashes. There were complaints about the latter from the kin, which I forwarded to those responsible." Vorlynkin added diplomatically—how else?—"I do appreciate this behind-the-scenes view, Wing-san. It's proving an eye-opener for me." The glance under his lashes was at Miles, though.

They were all gathered up again and conveyed to lunch, which was served in a low building overlooking more gardens and a koi pond. The space was all paper screens and tatami mats, plus more art glass and those flower arrangements consisting of a handful of pebbles, three sticks, two buds, and a blossom. They sat on silk cushions at a couple of low lacquer tables. Miles had Wing on one side and Aida on the other, all to himself; Storrs hosted Vorkynkin, Roic, and Raven at the second table. A pair of servers brought in a succession of

delicate dishes all looking like miniature sculptures, and Miles
finally allowed Aida to serve him an odd-tasting clear wine in a
flat ceramic cup. He wondered if the vessel's design was meant
to be self-limiting; anyone too drunk must spill the contents
down their front. He managed not to, barely.

Aida facilitated the conversation onto a series of pleasant, neutral topics, all the while inching nearer, her coat and
undercoat loosened to strategically reveal the swell of her breasts
beneath her low-cut top. Miles suspected pheromone perfumes,
but the message hardly needed the boost; this young lady
could be part of his bribe if he wished. Alas, Aida had shown
no sign of knowing enough dirt to cultivate, and anyway he
didn't need to look *every* kind of corruptible. There was such
a thing as artistic restraint. Miles pulled out his holovid cube
and showed off pictures of his magnificent wife and adorable
children, and she backed off, although he also vented a few
complaints about the high costs of raising a family, and Wing
inched nearer, encouraging him in this vein. Miles drank more
weird wine and grinned foolishly.

WhiteChrys would have kept refilling Miles's cup till he slid
under the table, he was sure. He only wound up the party by
repeated hints about Vorlynkin needing to get back to his duties.
Aida slipped across to entertain the other group, while Wing
took Miles on a turn around the pond, "to clear our heads."
Miles's head, at least, cleared quite quickly when Wing at last
got down to some very specific details about how Miles's new
shares were to be secretly transferred. He supposed he shouldn't
think of it as *Quick work, my Lord Auditor; from foreplay to
coitus in one afternoon.* But who was being screwed? And why,
why, *why* was he being bribed?

"I truly *believe* in the Komarr project," Wing told him, with
apparent sincerity. And a touch of euphoria, though Miles
couldn't tell if it was induced by the wine or the closing of the
negotiations; to Wing, he suspected, they were interchangeable.
The man harbored an almost Jacksonian passion for winning in

the Deal. "In fact, I've switched all my own stock and options from WhiteChrys to WhiteChrys Solstice. I've even placed my own cryo-contract with the new facility, that's how much I'm behind it. So you see I've put my money *and* my life where my mouth is." His dark eyes almost sparkled with this revelation.

And Miles, connections boiling up at last, thought, *Ye gods. I think you've just handed me your head.*

Chapter Eight

The wolf spider was perky and sharp in a black coat with white stripes and neat dots, like an aristocrat in a historical holovid dressed for a night on the town. Jin could clearly count all eight eyes in its fierce little face, two bright black buttons looking back at him, crowned by four more above, and another on each side of its head. Beneath its—no, beneath *her* abdomen clung a bundle of fine white fluff, like a tiny cotton ball—an egg case? Was she going to be a *mama* spider? Prone on the floor of the musty garden shed, Jin stiffened with excitement, then drew slowly backwards, careful not to startle her into scuttling into the cracks in the floor or walls before he could find something to capture her in. She was a good size for her breed, over three centimeters, quite as long and wide as the end joint of Jin's thumb, so she was certainly a grownup spider. She seemed to wait patiently for him.

Jin stared around the shed in some frustration. It was taking a lot longer to walk from his aunt and uncle's outlying northwest suburb to the near south side of the city than he had imagined. It was partly from Mina lagging and complaining as soon as she'd grown tired, just as Jin had expected, but mostly he was afraid he'd got turned around and lost during their long trudge last night. Streets curved unexpectedly, mixing him up, and the towers of the city center, glimpsed now and then from a hill or clear space, looked much the same from any direction.

This shelter had been a splendid find, early this morning. They'd stopped to buy half-liters of milk in a corner store of a neighborhoody area, then spent the next few blocks looking for a place to hide out during school hours. One house had a *For Sale* sign out front, and a peek through the windows revealed it cleared of furniture and empty of people, safe. It had been locked up tight, but the door to the shed around back proved unlatched. The garden was high-walled and full of sheltering bushes and trees, good to hide them from prying busybodies. Better yet, they'd found an outdoor spigot with the water still turned on. Mina's lunch bars were holding out, if getting boring, but finding water had been more of a problem, though during the long march yesterday they'd twice lucked out with city parks that offered not only drinking fountains, but bathrooms. Mina had proved very cranky about going behind a bush, even in the concealing dark.

The shelves of this shed had been cleared of likely containers, unfortunately, as well as of garden tools except for one bent and rusty trowel. Jin's eye fell on his sleeping sister, curled up with her jacket folded under her head, her zippered yellow backpack beside her, decorated with smiling but anatomically mis-drawn bees. He squatted down and began rooting through it. Ah, there!

"Hey!" mumbled Mina, sitting up and yawning. Her sleep-pale face was marked with creases from her makeshift pillow, and her hair hung every which way. What was it about sleeping in the daytime that made people so hot and rumpled? "Are you stealing my money?"

Jim popped open the clear plastic box she kept her coins in and dumped the contents back into the pack. "No! I just need the box."

"What for?" asked Mina, enduring this rummage, but at least not theft, of her possessions with no more than a frown.

"Spider house."

"Eew! I don't like spiders. Their webs stick in your mouth."

"She's a wolf spider. They don't spin webs."

"Oh." Mina blinked, considering this. She didn't look altogether convinced, but at least she didn't set up any stupid shrieking. She did keep her distance till Jin had snuck up on and captured his prey. But once the lady spider was safe behind the transparent barrier, Mina was at least willing to take a closer look, as Jin pointed out the manifold, if miniature, splendors of fur and eyes and mandibles, and the promising egg case.

"She really does have eight eyes!" said Mina, crossing her own as if trying to imagine the spider's view of her. Emboldened by her brother's example, she tapped on the plastic lid.

"Hey, don't. You'll scare her."

"Will she be able to breathe in there?" asked Mina.

Jin regarded the box in new doubt. It was certainly secure, but it did seem rather airtight. The wolf spider scratched futilely at the walls of her prison with fine claws. "For a while, anyway."

"What's her name?"

"I haven't named her yet."

"She needs a name."

Jin nodded full agreement. All right, *sometimes* Mina could be sensible. It was said there were thousands of wolf spider species back on Old Earth, but the Kibou terraformers, stingily, had only imported half a dozen or so for their new ecosystem. But with no comlink here, he couldn't look up his new pet's real scientific name. He hoped it would turn out to be something as sophisticated as the spider herself.

"You could call her Spinner. Except you said she doesn't spin. Wolfie?"

"Sounds like a boy's name," Jin objected. "It ought to be a lady's name, to fit her. Something from Old Earth."

Mina scowled in thought a moment, then brightened. "Lady Murasaki! That's the oldest lady's name I know of."

Jin, about to pooh-pooh her idea in brotherly reflex, paused. He eyed his spider. The name *did* fit. "All right."

Mina grinned in triumph. "What does she eat?"

"Littler bugs. I should catch her some in the garden before we leave. I'm not sure how much longer it will take us to get, um. Home."

Growing more interested after all this, Mina said, "Can I help feed her?"

"Sure."

Mina stretched, and, perhaps reminded of food, dug in her pillaged backpack for another lunch bar. "Maybe we better split this. To make them last."

"Good idea," Jin admitted. He set the spider box aside and went out to rinse and fill their milk bottles with water from the garden spigot.

When he slipped back inside the shed, closing the door with a creak, Mina asked, "What time is it out there?"

"I'm not sure. Afternoon, anyway."

"Do you think school's out yet? Can we go on the streets again?"

"Pretty soon."

They divided the lunch bar and the water.

"Maybe you should put Lady Murasaki in one of our water bottles, instead," said Mina, draining hers and holding it up to the light falling through the shed's one grimy window. "We could poke breath-holes through it."

"I was going to rinse those out and fill them up with water to take with us. You know how you were yammering you were so hot and thirsty yesterday afternoon."

"My feet were so sweaty inside my shoes," Mina said. "They felt nasty." She looked up at him, still a bit puffy-eyed from their uncomfortable day's sleep. "How much longer is it going to take to get to your place?"

"Hard to say." Jin shrugged uneasily. "I've been gone way longer than I'd planned. I sure hope Miles-san is taking care of all my creatures."

"That's your galactic friend, right?"

During their winding journey, the past day and a half, Jin had slowly unburdened himself of what he suspected were far too many of his secrets to Mina, partly to shut up her incessant questions, mostly because, well, he hadn't *had* any other kids to talk to for so long.

"Yah."

Jin's own abysmal failure as a courier troubled his mind. Would Miles-san believe Jin hadn't stolen his money? How was he getting along with Gyre? You had to be gentle but firm with the bird. The chickens were easier, except for the part about climbing down and carrying them back up the ladder or the stairs when they fluttered over the parapet. With that cane, could Miles-san manage both an indignant chicken and the stairs?

"Does Miles-san have any children?" Mina asked.

Jin frowned. "He didn't say. He's pretty old—thirty-something, he said. But he's kind of funny-looking. I don't know if he could get a girl." Once the drug effects had worn off Miles-san had been a nice enough fellow, with that face where smiles seemed at home. Plus, he had seemed to understand Jin's creatures, which made him quite smart, for a grownup. Jin wasn't sure whether to wish him a short, understanding bride, or not.

After a long, thoughtful pause, Mina said, "Do you think he'd like some?"

"What?"

"Children. Like, if he's lonely."

At Jin's baffled stare, Mina forged on: "We read this book for school this year, about two orphans adopted by a man from Earth. He took them there and they saw everything about where our ancestors came from." She added enticingly, "They got new pets..."

Jin vaguely remembered that one from his own second school year, otherwise made burdensome by the infliction of beginning kanji. There had been a lot of sickly stuff about the girl getting a fancy kimono, but there had also been a chapter about going to the seaside which had featured some Earth sea creatures—much too short an episode, but at least there'd been pictures—and a cat who'd capped her excellence by having kittens at the end. "Miles-san isn't from Earth. He's from Barrayar, he said."

"Where's that?"

"Somewhere beyond Escobar, I guess." Escobar, Jin knew, was Kibou's closest nexus trading partner, by a shortish multi-jump route. Farther worlds didn't much come up till galactic history in high school, except for Earth. Jin had studied a lot about Earth on his own, because of the zoology. Now, if only some benefactor would come along and offer to take Jin to *Earth*... Although come to think, Barrayar as Miles-san had described it might be almost as good, with its double biota.

A sudden picture bloomed in Jin's mind of the odd little fellow living all alone in a cottage in the country—no, better, a big rambling old house with a vast overgrown garden. Like the book with that old professor who had taken in two children from the city during wartime—Jin didn't know what war, except it was from a period before anybody got frozen. There'd been a horse that drew a cart, and wonderful adventures involving a cave with blind white fish. Jin had seen a horse in the Northbridge Zoo, once, on a class field trip. The braver children had all been allowed to pat its glossy neck, while one of the keepers held its lead; Jin remembered the huge beast blowing air out its soft, bellowslike nostrils in a warm whoosh across his cheek. Jin understood there were littler versions bred just for children, called *ponies*. Mina wouldn't be scared of one that size. The looming beast at the zoo had alarmed even Jin, but he'd been younger then, too. A great rambling house, and animals, and...

It was all rubbish. Miles-san wasn't a professor, or their uncle of any kind, great or regular, and for all Jin knew he lived in a cramped city apartment and wasn't lonely at all. Jin decided he didn't like that country daydream. It hurt too much when it stopped. He frowned at Mina. "Nobody's going to adopt us and take us away from here. That's a stupid idea."

Mina looked offended. She turned one shoulder to him and began pulling on her socks. They were blotched with pinkish-brown stains where her blisters had popped and bled, and Jin gulped faint guilt. They both donned their shoes, Lady Murasaki was safely lodged in Mina's backpack, where, Jin argued, she would endure less bouncing than in his pocket, and they sneaked out onto the street once more.

A winding kilometer farther on, during which Jin kept looking for, and not getting, a glimpse of the downtown towers for orientation, they came upon a busier street with a tube-tram station entry.

Mina's footsteps had grown short and gimpy already. She looked at the entrance in some longing. "If you want to go on the tram"—she swallowed a bit—"I'll pay our fares."

"No, the police have vidcams in the stations. That's how I got trapped day before yesterday. We can't go in there." But Jin's eye was caught by a big colorful display on the outside of the entry kiosk. A map! He peered up carefully for scanning vidcams on this side, didn't spot any, and ventured nearer, Mina trailing.

The lighted *You Are Here* arrow horrified Jin. They were nowhere near the south side of town, as he'd hoped from how far they'd trudged. They'd somehow ended up on the residential east side, instead, and still had maybe thirty kilometers left to hike before they reached the light industrial zone of the south, quite as far as they'd already come. Well, that explained why the houses were so nice around here. Jin stepped closer, squinting.

Just two stops farther on this line was the very station he'd exited to reach the Barrayaran consulate. It was about a three-kilometer walk above ground. Jin stared, thinking. He had dimly planned to offer Mina's money to Miles-san, when they arrived at their destination, but his sister was proving pretty tight-fisted, in Jin's view. She was sure to set up a screech, even though Jin was nearly certain Miles-san would replace it as soon as he could. But if he stopped at the consulate first and explained his loss, editing his situation a bit maybe, would they give him more money for the Barrayaran? Miles-san seemed fairly important to them. And they wouldn't turn Jin in, because they were protecting their own secrets, right?

Contemplating this confession made him feel a little sick, but not as sick as going all the way back to Miles-san empty-handed as well as three days late. He stared harder at the map, trying to memorize the streets and turns.

"I know where we're going now," he said to Mina, trying to sound confident and big-brotherly. "Come on."

After the WhiteChrys groundcar dropped them all off again at the consulate, Roic followed m'lord upstairs and watched him down two headache tabs and several glasses of water. Returning to the entry hall, m'lord stuck his head into the room Roic thought of as the parlor, where Raven Durona had been left to cool his heels, and said, "Debriefing downstairs again, I think."

Raven nodded and unfolded himself to tag along. There had been little conversation on the way home; Aida had still been escorting, m'lord had settled into himself heavy-eyed, Vorlynkin had stared out the canopy with a set jaw, Roic considered himself an observer, and Raven had been disinclined to buck the obvious trend. They arrived downstairs at the door to the tight-room to discover it closed and locked.

M'lord hit the intercom. "Vorlynkin? Are you in there? Open up."

"Just a moment, m'lord," Vorlynkin's voice came from the

speaker. The moment turned into several minutes, while m'lord tapped his foot and Raven sat on the nearby step and yawned.

"Reminds me of a house with only one bathroom when the relatives have come to visit," remarked Roic, as the wait stretched.

M'lord cast him a dry look. "I wouldn't know. I've never lived in a house with only one bathroom." Roic returned him an ironic head-tilt.

At length, the doorseal popped, the vaultlike door swung open, and the consul admitted them. His eyes seemed electric blue, and he was breathing fast, as though he had been running. "You're too late," he announced.

M'lord's brows rose. "Not a first. What for this time?"

A muscle jumped by Vorlynkin's scowling mouth. "I just sent a full report of what I witnessed by tight-beam to General Allegre at ImpSec HQ, Barrayar. I never thought I'd live to see a *Vorkosigan* sell himself for *money*. My career may be slagged, but so will yours, my *Lord Auditor*."

"Ah, excellent. *That's* done." M'lord kicked the door shut; it sealed with a sigh that seemed insufficiently dramatic for Vorlynkin's mood.

"*What?*" Vorlynkin's fists clenched.

"Not that every man doesn't have his price," m'lord went on amiably. "As I'm sure Wing-san would agree. I was more afraid that if he didn't come up to scratch today, I'd have that whole parade at the conference to do over again."

If the consul didn't stop inhaling, he was going to pop a lung, Roic thought. He put in peaceably, "Stop baiting the poor fellow, m'lord." *Now that you have what you want, anyway*. Roic didn't want to have to wrestle the man to the floor if he went for m'lord's throat, which he seemed on the verge of doing. Was that old phrase about being *mad enough to spit nails* supposed to apply to, like, roofing nails, or fingernails? Around m'lord, Roic had never been sure.

M'lord added a trifle impatiently, "Men like Wing don't go

around throwing their money at potential opponents at random, Vorlynkin. First they have to figure out that the target is bribable. I did my best to help him decide. Have a seat, Consul, Doctor. It's time we talked."

Vorlynkin's mouth, which had opened to emit some hot remark, sagged. "Lord Vorkosigan—is this a *sting*?"

"It is now." M'lord pulled out a station chair and plunked into it. "We weren't sure at first, which is why they sent me—I could be bait and trap at the same time, saving the Imperium on jumpship fares if nothing else."

Vorlynkin sank more slowly into a chair opposite; Roic breathed easier. The consul glanced in dismay at the secured comconsole. "M'lord—I *sent* the report."

"Don't apologize. Your next official visitor might really be on the take, after all. I don't intend to apologize to you, either, if it makes you feel any better. I've seen our diplomatic personnel bought out before. I had to make sure."

"You were... testing me?" That disturbing heat in Vorlynkin's eyes, which had started to fade, flared once more.

"Why do you suppose I hauled you along today and let you see all this?"

Vorlynkin's hands clenched on his knees, but slowly eased again. "I see. Very efficient."

"Do try to keep up." M'lord added more kindly, "It won't be easy; this case has baffled a few ImpSec analysts." He turned to Raven. "So, what did you learn of interest during the time you had with Storrs?"

Raven's mouth twisted in doubt. "I'm not sure I learned anything new. Their cryofreezing program seems perfectly legitimate—nothing wrong with their procedures from a technical standpoint. I asked to see a revival, but Storrs said there weren't any scheduled today, which by then didn't surprise me. He did show me the revival facilities. They looked quite adequate. He angled to find out if I would be interested in employment with WhiteChrys, and tried to find out my current pay rate. I said my main interests lay with cryorevival, as it's more medically challenging. He said he'd pass that along, although he didn't say who to. We came back and joined your show in progress, where you'd finished the dogs and were on to the ponies. Eh." Raven shrugged.

Vorlynkin blinked. "Lord Vorkosigan, is Dr. Durona your *agent*?"

"Civilian contract consultant," m'lord clarified, "being paid out of my case budget. Are you still collecting your Durona Group salary simultaneously, Raven?"

Raven smirked. "That's personal information."

"I'll take that as a yes. So don't hesitate to use Dr. Durona on double shifts, if needed."

Raven grinned and rose to prod the automatic beverage maker, strategically positioned near the secured comconsole and its satellite console. It coughed up something coffee-ish, judging by the smell. Raven picked up the cup and gestured politely toward his chair; Roic waved him back to it and took a position propping the wall with his arms crossed, in a pose copied from a certain former ImpSec chief.

"To bring you up to speed, Vorlynkin," m'lord went on. "WhiteChrys was vetted and cleared by ImpSec when its advance teams first scouted Komarr eighteen months ago, but ImpSec was looking for connections with military espionage and the like. Their business plan passed the local Komarran commissions, and they were in. No one would have given them a second look for years, if it hadn't been for some good old-fashioned nepotism.

"Within the last few months, as the flagship facility we saw in Wing's vid was nearing completion, WhiteChrys began collecting contracts on future customers. Not unnaturally, they targeted Solstice upper-class elderly women's clubs. At the same time, another sales team made some limited strategic stock offerings to certain wealthy and influential Komarrans, to give the local powers-that-be a stake in the future success of their operations.

I expect the two sales teams didn't compare hit lists, nor real-ize that *some* wealthy old ladies are retired Komarran traders who can read a balance sheet to a gnat's eyebrow.

"And one of those little old ladies looked at the two propos-als before her and said, 'This smells, but I don't see how,' so she took it to her beloved great-niece, who said, 'You're right, Aun-tie, this smells, but I don't see how,' who took the problem in turn to her devoted husband, better known as Emperor Gregor Vorbarra. Who handed it to his loyal Imperial Auditor, saying, and I quote, 'Here, Miles, you're better at diving into the privy and coming up with the gold ring than anyone I know. Have a go.' And I said, 'Thank you, Sire,' and took ship for Kibou-daini.'"

Vorlynkin blinked again. Deeply. Roic reflected that the Imperium's shrewd Komarran Empress served Gregor in more ways than just the joint production of their several scarily smart children.

M'lord went on blithely, "The other thing wealthy old Komar-rans tend to have is an excess of planetary voting shares—er, Raven, do I need to explain these to you?"

"Yes, please," said Raven, settling back and looking fascinated.

"The system, as usual, is a relict of Komarr's colonization history. The planet is presently unlivable—though undergoing long-term terraforming—all settlement is in sealed arcologies, the Domes."

"I knew that much..."

"Right. So to encourage the development of the domes, the early Komarran colonists set up a reward system. In addition to an inalienable one-person-one-vote that every Komarran is born and dies with, the colony awarded additional votes to those taking on the work and risk of creating more living space. These were inheritable, tradable, salable, and in gen-eral accumulate-able. The basis of the Komarran oligarchy as it now stands is clan possession of blocks of these planetary voting shares. The place is putatively a democracy, but some are measurably more equal than others. You follow?"

Raven nodded.

"So," said Vorlynkin, who had, after all, had two years to watch Kibou-daini in operation, "you think WhiteChrys plans to accumulate those votes wholesale?"

"I do now. Mind you, Komarr has a long history of attempted chicanery with its voting system. Over time it's accumulated a huge number of rules to thwart same. Among other things, voting shares can't be held outright by corporations—they have to be in the hands of individuals. There are tested systems for proxies, and so on. WhiteChrys's contracts passed muster with the Komarran regulators, and, if anybody had still been looking by that point, we'd have accepted that.

"My two working hypotheses are either that WhiteChrys has bribed some regulators—a possibility I now find quite compelling—or that they have figured out some way to game the rules system to hide their true intention till too late. Or both."

Roic couldn't help thinking that m'lord oughtn't to look *quite* so admiring, detailing this in front of the still-gently-steaming Vorlynkin. But, well, m'lord.

"The one thing that gave me pause was that there was no way this could be a get-rich-quick scheme, even if the Komarran system of voting shares gives it a turbo-boost compared to Kibou. The profit margin on what is arguably a service industry is razor-thin, yet WhiteChrys has been spending money like a drunken Vor lord. Why go to all this trouble for a payoff you'll never live to see? Until the last thing Wing said to me this afternoon, which was that he planned to have *himself* frozen on Komarr."

M'lord looked around proudly, as if expecting the room to burst into applause, and was plainly disappointed to receive three blank looks instead.

He inhaled, visibly backing up. "Unpack, Miles, right. What I now suspect is going on is a two-tiered scam. I think there is an inner cadre of WhiteChrys executives who plan to ride out the years in cryo-stasis, and all be revived in time to collect the goodies. In fact, if they're as smart as I think, they likely plan to take turns, so there's always someone on the team awake to look after their interests. While they quietly, automatically, bloodlessly *buy* Komarr. Or maybe not so bloodlessly, depending on whether you consider early freezing to be murder or suicide, or not. The slowest, subtlest, and, I have to say, creepiest planetary conquest scheme ever devised!"

Even Vorlynkin jumped at that, his lips parting in consternation. "Conquest!"

"I hardly know what else to call it. But I still have a hell of a lot of dots to connect before I can sign off on this investigation. As soon as we get your consulate deep data crawlers up and running, that's the first thing I want to look for—a list of WhiteChrys personnel who have lately shifted all their investments to WhiteChrys Solstice, and are planning to follow them in person. Because, given the numbers, I also think it possible that this could be a secret group *inside* WhiteChrys who are gutting *their own company* to feather their nests."

"Whew!" said Raven, with proper admiration. M'lord bestowed a pleased smile upon him.

Vorlynkin ran his hands through his hair. "How do you plan to nail the bastards? Bribing an Imperial Auditor may be as illegal as all hell on Barrayar, but we're on Kibou-daini. Even if you could prove it—and I'm afraid my testimony would be suspect, here—I doubt Wing would get more than a slap on the wrist."

"Actually, I would prefer not to give the slightest hint to anyone on Kibou that we've tumbled to them. The ideal revenge would be to let WhiteChrys get their hand so far into the cookie jar on Komarr that they can't get it out, then cut it off at the wrist by changing the contract rules *just* enough on 'em to make them drop the votes. Leaving them to be exactly what they feigned to be, a marginally profitable service company. *That* would hurt enough to be a warning to others. Brute nationalization is a last resort—it would piss off the rest of the

Komarran business community regardless of the rights of the case. It'll take some study—I'm afraid we're going to be up to our ears in lawyers before this is done—but with luck my part of the task will be over by then." M'lord glanced up at Vorlynkin. "So what do you think of your Lieutenant Johannes? He's young, which makes him both poorer and potentially more gullible. Is he reliable enough for this?"

"I..." Vorlynkin was given pause. "I've never had cause to doubt him."

"And your local clerk, Yuuichi what's-his-name, Matson?"

"I've never had cause to doubt him, either. But we've never had a situation like this before."

"That you knew," sighed m'lord. "Yet routine travel visas for WhiteChrys personnel have been handled through the consulate all this time."

"Yes, but all we ask is *business or tourism?* Plus a quick background check for criminal records."

M'lord's eyes crinkled in speculation. "I wonder if we should add a box to tick off—*Reason for travel: creepy planetary conquest*...no, I suppose not."

Vorlynkin said slowly, "What if I hadn't tried to turn you in just now?"

"Then you wouldn't be part of this debriefing, and I'd be on the lookout for ways to nail you to the wall, too. In passing." M'lord stretched and rolled his shoulders. Vorlynkin looked, Roic felt, properly thoughtful at last.

"Now, the other thing," m'lord began, but was interrupted when the sealed door chimed.

Lieutenant Johannes's voice issued from the intercom. "Consul? Lord Vorkosigan?"

"Yes?" responded m'lord.

"Um... Your half-sized courier's just turned up at the back door. And he's not alone."

M'lord's brows rose; Vorlynkin's drew down. Raven cocked his head in curiosity.

"Don't let him get away, Johannes," m'lord called back. "We'll be right there."

Motioning Roic to unseal the door, m'lord grabbed his cane and levered to his feet.

Chapter Nine

The kitchen of the consulate seemed homey, if spacious by Jin's standards. Maybe it was the cool dusk falling in the back garden that made it so warm and bright. Maybe it was all the dishes piled in the sink that made it look so, well, kitchen-y, as if a fellow could wander in and out to snack at will without being yelled at, even. But the noise of all the footsteps clumping up from the basement made Jin shift uneasily, and when Mina's little hand stole into his and clutched hard, he didn't shake her off.

Jin's timid knock had been answered by Lieutenant Johannes, who'd taken one look, cried *You!* and hustled them both inside, though he'd looked askance at Mina; added *Wait right there, don't move*; and thumped downstairs before Jin could get three words into his much-rehearsed explanation of how the police had taken Miles-san's money. So Jin was expecting the fierce-eyed Consul Vorlynkin, but behind him loomed the biggest Barrayaran Jin had seen yet, half a head taller than the tall consul. He wore clothes that reminded Jin of a military uniform, had short wavy brown hair and a firm square-jawed face, and looked older than Johannes but younger than the consul. Mina stared up at him with her mouth hanging open.

The big Barrayaran so filled up what had, till just before, seemed a wide doorway that it took a moment for Jin to notice the slim fellow with his hair in a neat dark braid who followed him, and another moment to spot Miles-san in their wake.

The little man shouldered past them all, coming face to face with Jin. He looked so different all cleaned up, more grownup, more . . . daunting, that it was a couple of heartbeats before Jin, recovering from his shock, inhaled and cried, "My creatures! You promised you'd look after them!"

Miles-san held up a hand. "They're all right, Jin! When you didn't come back by midnight, I copied out your instructions and gave them to Ako. When I implied I was going to look for you, she was very willing to help out."

"But how did you get *here*?"

"Walked. Took me all that night."

From behind Jin, Mina asked interestedly, "Did you get lost, too?"

"We weren't lost, exactly," Jin denied, harassed. "Just turned around a little."

"And who are you, young lady?" Miles-san addressed Mina. "I don't believe we've been introduced."

"Sister," muttered Jin. "It wasn't *my* idea to bring her."

"I *have* a name," Mina pointed out. "It's Mina. Want to see my blisters?"

Miles-san didn't even blink. "Sure! Are they good ones? Have they popped yet?"

"Oh, yes—they made my socks all bloody, too."

"Well, Miss Mina, why don't you sit down here—" Miles-san pulled out a kitchen chair with a flourish, and half-bowed Mina into it, as if she'd been a grownup lady, "—and show me." He added over his shoulder, "Johannes. Find something for these children to eat. Cookies. Milk. Gingerbread, whatever."

"Are you Jin's galactic?" Mina asked, kicking off her sport shoes and picking at her splotched socks. "He told me all about you."

"Did he?" Miles-san knelt and helped her peel off her socks; she said *ow, ow*, as they parted stickily from her scabs. "My word, those are good blisters, aren't they?" He glanced up and gave Vorlynkin-san a head-jerk that sent the consul to rummage in the other end of the kitchen.

"Aunt Lorna buys all our shoes big to grow into," Mina explained to Miles-san. "That's why they slip around like that."

Lieutenant Johannes, peering doubtfully into the depths of the refrigerator, murmured, "Beer . . . ?"

"Do you like beer, Mina?" Miles-san asked. She shook her head, making her straight black hair swing around her chin. "Thought not, somehow. You'll have to do better, Johannes. Aren't all you attaché fellows supposed to be ImpSec trained? Improvise!"

Johannes muttered something through his teeth that Jin couldn't quite make out. He then conducted a brief survey which determined that vat-octopus pizza, no onions, was universally acceptable, and trod out to order some. Vorlynkin came back with what turned out to be a first-aid kit, which he handed off to the slim man with the braid, who didn't look Barrayaran at all, but didn't talk like someone from Kibou, either.

Mina leaned toward Miles-san and whispered anxiously, "That big guy isn't a policeman, is he?"

"Used to be," Miles-san whispered back gravely, "but now he works for me. Alas, Armsman Roic had to give up all his policeman's principles when he entered my service."

The big man cast Mina a pious nod.

Mina settled back, looking relieved, and let the slim man, who Miles-san introduced as Raven and said was a doctor from Escobar, attend to her feet. Vorlynkin watched closely, frowning, till he seemed to be satisfied with the skills displayed, then straightened up and narrowed his eyes at Jin. The big fellow, Armsman Roic, filled two glasses with water and set them on the table; Mina seized hers and drank thirstily, and Jin followed suit more warily.

When he'd washed down the dry lump in his throat, which actually had little to do with thirst, Jin embarked once more on his interrupted explanation of what had happened to the consulate's money. Vorlynkin winced when Jin came to the part about the drug dealers and/or smugglers, but at Miles-san's restraining hand-gesture, the consul let Jin stumble all the way to the end before saying, "We know. We traced the packet to the police evidence rooms, and picked up your arrest report, too."

So they *did* believe him. That was something, anyway.

"Yes," said Miles-san, "and I'm sure the consul thanks you for keeping mum and preserving his reputation. Don't you, Vorlynkin?"

Vorlynkin's lips compressed in an expression anything but grateful, but he choked out a, "Certainly."

Then, through what Jin reluctantly recognized as a skillful series of questions—some put to Jin though many to Mina— Miles-san drew out the story of Jin's escape from the custody of his aunt and uncle. By the time Johannes returned, balancing a stack of pizza boxes, two liters of milk, and more beer, Jin was afraid there wasn't much Miles-san didn't understand about Aunt Lorna, Uncle Hikaru, and cousins Tetsu and Ken. It made Jin feel uncomfortably exposed.

Miles-san kicked a stepstool to the sink and made Jin and Mina wash their hands, following up himself as if to enforce the good example. Lieutenant Johannes watched him mount the stepstool, glanced at the impassive Roic, and bit his lip. Miles-san, the consul, Jin and Mina then sat four around the kitchen table, that being all the chairs there were; Roic and the others leaned against the counter. Setting out the boxes and a roll of disposable wipes, the lieutenant said, "I checked the comconsole. Both these kids were reported missing yesterday. Every police officer in town must be on the lookout for them."

Consul Vorlynkin pressed a hand to the bridge of his nose.

Jin bolted upright in alarm. "You can't turn us in!"

Miles-san waved him back down. "No one is doing anything till after we eat." He looked over the aromatic offering. "What, no vegetables? Don't you two need vegetables?"

"No, we don't!" said Mina. Jin shook his head vigorously in support.

Miles-san bit into his slice. "Ah, perhaps not. This does seem very healthy. And tasty."

Mina, at least, dove readily into the first hot food they'd had for two days. Jin, overwhelmed by the aroma, followed suit. The consulate bought *good* pizza, not the cheapest frozen kind that Aunt Lorna served. The consul barely sipped his beer, Miles-san had water, and big Roic, to Jin's surprise, after first pouring out for Jin and Mina, helped himself to a small glass of milk.

All this redirection might have worked to calm Jin, except Vorlynkin, after swallowing his first bite, said, "The consulate can't harbor runaways, Lord Vorkosigan. Their guardians must be frantic."

"We don't *want* to stay here," said Jin. "I want to get back to my creatures!"

Miles-san waved his nibbled pizza slice in the air. "Asylum?"

"That's not amusing even as a joke," said Vorlynkin. "Do you have any idea of the legal complications involved in giving political asylum to minors?"

"I'm not sure I was joking, exactly," Miles-san said mildly. "But wait for the children to eat, please."

Vorlynkin's jaw tightened, but he nodded. After Jin and Mina could eat no more, and Johannes offered more wipes and put the leftovers away in the refrigerator for breakfast, just like at home, Miles-san leaned back in his chair and said, "I suggest we repair downstairs. The seats will be more comfortable."

The other Barrayarans all gave Miles-san funny looks, but

recalling Uncle Hikaru's daily after-dinner saying, when shifting into his big chair, of *Out of the bleachers and into the box seats!*, Jin saw no objection to this. Yet when they'd all shuffled down the stairs after Miles-san, the room into which he led them only boasted four chairs, all officey-looking swivel types. Miles-san gestured Mina and Jin into a seat each, took one himself, and left the other three men to sort themselves out. Johannes parked one haunch on the long table shoved up to the wall, Raven-sensei copied him, and Vorlynkin, mouth pinched, dropped into the remaining chair.

"This is a funny vid room," Mina remarked, staring around and swinging her feet, now encased in a pair of Miles-san's socks donated to keep her bandages clean. When Roic closed the door and blandly sat cross-legged on the floor beside it, the air grew awfully hushed, and for the first time Jin wondered if this was a *safe* place to have brought her, and not just from the risk of being betrayed to the authorities. He kind of trusted Miles-san, or he would have been inclined to grab her and bolt. Though given Roic and that thick door, would that impulse have come too late...?

Miles-san laced his hands together between his knees, and said, "Suze the Secretary told me something of the story of your mother, Jin, Mina. So when I got back here I looked up what I could about her on the planetary net. It made me very curious. I really don't understand how it was she came to be frozen, when she wasn't sick or dying, or even convicted of any crime."

Jin's tasty dinner suddenly felt like lead in his stomach.

"What do you—either of you—remember about your mother?" Miles-san went on. "Not personal things, but about her work, her cause. Especially anything that might have happened about the time of the riot at her rally, or just before she was arrested?"

Jin and Mina looked at each other uneasily. Jin said, "Mom didn't talk to us much about her work. When she was doing anything, she mostly left us at Aunt Lorna's unless I was in school. Then she just left Mina."

"Aunt Lorna wasn't too happy about all the babysitting," Mina said.

"Yah, she said she hadn't volunteered for this and didn't much like being drafted."

"And she was sorry about Daddy, but maybe if Mommy really cared that much she'd do better to stay home and look after his kids herself." Mina looked away, frowning.

Jin put in hastily, "But she only said things like that when she was feeling 'specially cranky." Not that he was fond of Aunt Lorna, but these galactics were outsiders, after all, and it felt funny to be talking about his family like this in front of them. And Mom had said you should always try to be fair.

"Didn't your mother ever take you along to her meetings?"

Mina shook her head. "She said they weren't for kids, and we'd just get bored and kick up a fuss."

"Huh." Miles-san rubbed his chin. "When I was a youngster Jin's age, at home, I was often permitted to sit in on my father's meetings with his, er, professional colleagues. My grandfather had done the same with him. I learned more just by the osmosis than I realized at the time. Of course, I had to stay quiet and make myself useful, or leave, naturally."

Jin frowned. "You can't leave if you're out somewhere. Mom would have had to break off what she was doing to take us home."

"Couldn't she have just tapped—never mind. Didn't she ever have meetings at your home? In the evenings, say?"

"There wasn't much room in our apartment."

"Did no one come to visit? Ever?"

Jin shook his head, but Mina, to his surprise, spoke up. "Some people from her group did once. Late at night."

"When was this?"

Mina sucked on her lower lip. "Before she was arrested, anyway."

"Close before?"

"Yah, I think so."

"I don't remember this," said Jin.

Mina tossed her head. "You were asleep."

"What woke you?" asked Miles-san.

"They were arguing in the kitchen. Kind of loud and scary. Plus, I had to go to the bathroom."

"Can you remember what they were arguing about? Anything at all that was said?"

Mina scrunched her face in thought. "They were talking about the corps, and money. They were always talking about the corps, and money, only this time they seemed more excited. George-san's voice was really boomy, and Mommy was talking all fast and sharp, except she didn't sound mad, exactly. And the new guy yelled something about, it wasn't any temp'rary setback—this could bring the corps to their *knees,* right before he came out in the hallway on the way to the bathroom and found me. And Mommy let me have an ice cream bar and put me back to bed and told me to stay there."

"Do you know who the people were? Had you ever seen them before?"

Mina nodded. "There was George-san, he was always nice to me when he came to pick up Mommy. And old Mrs. Tennoji, she always wore a lot of perfume. They called the new one Leiber-sensei."

"Do you remember the rest of their names? Jin?"

Headshakes. Miles-san tried, "George Suwabi, by chance?"

"Might have been," said Mina, though sounding a bit doubtful.

"The timing is interesting in the extreme. And the cast. I smell a lethal secret, oh, yes." Miles-san rose and began to pace back and forth across the little room. He forgot his cane, left by his chair, a snazzier one than he'd scavenged from Suze-san's. "Suwabi and Tennoji came up in my researches. Dr. Leiber did not, I admit. Curious absence, not to be confused with an absence of curious. I wonder who the hell *he* was?"

Sounding as if he was being drawn into all this despite himself, Consul Vorlynkin said, "Could you trace these people and find out more?"

"Not Suwabi or Tennoji—they're dead. And rotted, buried for real. The other one, I don't know. Could be a long, cold trail, if he's run off-world or gone to ground well enough to escape the corps. It might be faster just to wake up Lisa Sato and ask *her*."

Mina drew a huge breath and shot to her feet, staring wildly at Miles-san. "You could *do* that? You could get my mommy back? *Really*?"

Miles-san stopped short. "Er."

Jin's heart jumped in his chest; Mina's imploring look made him feel sick. "No, of course he can't," he said angrily. "It was just a stupid joke."

Miles-san's hand went to his throat, clutching something through his shirt; some kind of pendant, Jin thought. "Damn. If I were on Barrayar, I could just *order* it done."

"But we're not *on* Barrayar," Armsman Roic muttered under his breath, almost the first Jin had heard the big man speak. Miles-san waved a hand as if to say, *Yah, yah*, though whether in agreement or protest Jin was not sure.

Mina looked crushed; her lower lip quivered. "It wasn't... wasn't a very *nice* thing to make a joke about it, if you didn't really mean it!"

"No," said Miles-san, staring, for some reason, at Raven-sensei. "It wasn't. *Could* I, ah... really mean it? Technically?"

Raven-sensei scratched his chin. "*Technically*, yes. You will forgive me if I point out that the medical aspects would seem to be the least of it?"

Miles-san waved a hand in easy pardon.

"Assuming," Raven-sensei went on, "the cryoprep was done correctly in the first place, of course. Or at all."

Miles-san's eyes narrowed, and he resumed his pacing. "Mm... no reason why it shouldn't have been. We're not on Jackson's Whole, either, I note. What all would you need to do the trick? Technically."

"A decently-equipped revival facility. This isn't something I'd choose to do out of the consulate basement's laundry tub, if that's what you're thinking. Not if there were any complications."

"We couldn't afford complications, no. Emphatically not." He glanced at Jin and Mina.

Raven-sensei nodded. "Some standard medical supplies, synthesized blood and so on."

"If I secured you a facility, could you scrounge the supplies?"

Raven-sensei got a faraway look. "Legally, or otherwise?"

A pause. "I've no intrinsic objection to legally, but it can't leave a data trail back to us. Otherwise, alternate suppliers would do. If their merchandise was of proper quality, of course."

"That goes without saying. How would you propose to gain custody of my patient?"

Miles-san's expression grew equally faraway. "Now, that's where it becomes quite interesting—"

"Lord Vorkosigan!" Vorlynkin interrupted. "What the hell are you *thinking*?" Jin wasn't sure if he really didn't know, or knew and objected. Strenuously.

Miles-san waved that airy hand again. "Any number of threads in my cat's cradle of Kibou-daini mysteries seem to run back to Lisa Sato—and stop. I'm thinking I might be able to cut the whole knot right through if I had her to interrogate. Er, talk to. Grant you, it seems a little imaginative at first glance, but the more I think about it..."

"Imaginative! It seems outright mad!"

Miles-san cast the consul a soulful look. "But Vorlynkin, it would solve all your problems with asylum for minors at a blow. Their mother being their closest possible adult next-of-kin."

"When did those become *my*...never mind."

Miles-san grinned in a glinty way that Jin did not entirely understand. "Very good, Vorlynkin."

"What are you all *talking* about?" Mina practically wailed.

Miles-san lost his glintiness at once, and dropped to one knee in front of her swivel chair. "Unpack, right. Um. You see, Mina, I was sent here by my government to check out some sneaky, nasty things that a Kibou cryocorp is trying to do back on one of my home worlds. I think your mommy might be able to answer some of my questions, or at least give me some interesting new information. Now, it just so happens that Dr. Durona over there"—Raven-sensei waved his long fingers kindly at Mina—"is a top cryorevival specialist, and he already works for me, which is what gives me this idea. See, there are three things that have to be in place before I could undertake to wake up your mommy. I have to be sure it would be medically safe for her, and I think Raven could see to that. I have to be able to secure her cry—I have to be able to get hold of her, get her away from the place where she's now held without kicking up a dust, and I think I can do that. And afterward, I have to be able to protect her from being arrested and taken away again, or it will all be for nothing, and that will be Consul Vorlynkin's job."

Vorlynkin looked startled at this news. But when Mina's anxious gaze targeted him, he returned her a flicker of a smile, the first Jin had seen lighten his face. Girls, hah. Nobody handed *Jin* smiles like that when *he* was scared...he more usually got some sort of unsympathetic and bracing advice to buck up.

"Which reminds me, Vorlynkin," Miles-san went on over his shoulder in a more clipped tone, "what are the limits of the political and legal protection this consulate can offer, once it becomes known that Madame Sato has, er, escaped custody, as it were? You're not a full-scale embassy..."

Vorlynkin said reluctantly, "By our budget, we're a branch of the embassy on Escobar. But we're legally more than a consulate, because we're the only full-time diplomatic facility Barrayar maintains here. It would be...it could be an ambiguous argument."

"And ambiguous legal arguments burn lots of time, ah. That might just be good enough." Miles-san rose to pace again.

Mina sank back into her swivel chair, her expression caught between hopeful and confused. Jin realized he'd been gripping the arms of his own chair so hard his fingernails were white, and slowly released his clutch. Mina's words whirled around and around in his head, *You could get my mommy back? Really? Really? Really...?* Who did this half-sized galactic think he was? When he'd said he was a delegate to the cryo-conference, but didn't seem to be a doctor, and the others had all called him an auditor, Jin had vaguely assumed his job had something to do with insurance. Or maybe, less boringly, insurance fraud. He seemed to know a lot about fraud, anyway.

"First things first. Johannes, what vehicles does the consulate maintain?"

Johannes jerked, as if he'd been a watcher of a play unexpectedly addressed by one of the characters. "Uh, the official groundcar, of course. And we have a lift van. I have a float bike, myself."

"Lift van, perfect. Tomorrow, then, we'll take Jin and Raven and go pick up Jin's creatures, and bring them back here to the consulate, so that'll be off his mind and my conscience."

Jin looked up, caught between thrilled and bewildered. Didn't these Barrayarans mean to let him go...? On the other hand, as long as he had his animals back, and didn't have to go back to Aunt Lorna and school, did it matter where he stayed?

"My consulate isn't exactly set up to host a menagerie," said Vorlynkin.

"No, they'll be fine here!" Jin assured him, panicked at the thought of being separated yet again from all his pets. "There's so much room. And your back garden is all walled in. They won't bother you a bit."

"What kind of—no, never mind. Go on, Lord Vorkosigan."

"At the same time, I will take Raven to meet Suze and company, and inspect the facilities. We might avoid having to retool the consulate laundry room into a cryo revival facility—" though he did not sound as if this proposed renovation gave him much pause "—if, like the installation we saw today, her old place already has one. And it's still in good shape, not stripped."

Jin said doubtfully, "If you want any favors from Suze-san, you better catch her early in the day. When she's still sober."

"Not a problem," Miles-san said. "Then, if everything proves workable, we can go on to the next step."

"What *is* the next step?" asked Consul Vorlynkin, in fascinated tones. He looked like a man staring at a groundcar wreck. In slow motion. That he was in.

"Securing Madame Sato."

"How?"

"I'm going to have to do a spot more research first, to devise the optimum ploy. According to the public records, she's being kept at the NewEgypt facility out in the Cryopolis here in Northbridge, which is actually pretty convenient." Miles-san's lips drew back on a peculiar grin. "It could be just like old times."

Armsman Roic sat up in alarm. He put in, with some urgency, "What about those commodified contracts Ron Wing was going on about? Maybe you could work out a way to just, I dunno, *buy* her. All peaceable and aboveboard." He added after a moment, "Or under the table, but peaceable, anyway."

Miles-san paused again in his pacing, as if arrested by this notion. "Shrewd idea, Roic. But she's not just any cryo-patron. I suspect that any interest in her is likely to send up a big red flag." He fell into motion again. "Still, hold that thought. It might be useful later, for the retroactive tidying up."

Roic sighed.

"The ideal," Miles-san went on, "would be to arrange things so that she wasn't missed at all."

"These commercial cryochambers are all continuously monitored," said Raven-sensei. "You'd need some way to fudge the readouts." He hesitated. "Or go low tech, and just swap in another cryo-corpse. That way, all the readings would be naturally right. They wouldn't know the difference unless they pulled it out and unwrapped it."

Miles-san tilted his head, like Gyre-the-Falcon contemplating a choice morsel of meat. "The old shell game, eh? That...

might actually be highly feasible. I wonder if I could borrow a spare from Suze? God knows, cryo-corpses are not an item in short supply around here."

Vorlynkin choked. "Do you have any idea how many different crimes you've just rattled off?"

"No, but it might not hurt to make up a list, should your lawyer need it. Could speed things up, in a pinch."

"I thought the task of an Imperial Auditor was to *uphold* the law!"

Miles-san's eyebrows flew up. "No, whatever gave you that idea? The task of an Imperial Auditor is to solve problems for Gregor. Those greasy cryocorps bastards just tried to steal a third of his empire. *That's* a problem." Despite his smiling lips, Miles-san's eyes glittered, and Jin realized with a start that underneath, he was really angry about something. "I'm still considering the solution."

Jin wondered who Gregor was. Miles-san's insurance boss?

Mina had scrunched her chair closer and closer to where Jin rocked in his. An audible sniffle escaped her, which made both Miles-san and Vorlynkin crank their heads around. Miles-san lurched and lifted a hand toward her, stopped short, and gestured at Jin instead, who, thus compelled, gave his sister a clumsy pat on the shoulder that only made her eyes fill up and overflow for real.

"Lord Vorkosigan, for pity's sake, enough for tonight," said Consul Vorlynkin. "These children have to be exhausted. Both of them."

Jin could wish he hadn't added that last. His eyes stung in contagion with Mina's. Now he was offered it, Jin wasn't so sure he wanted sympathy—it eroded his resolve as annoying bracing remarks never did.

"To be sure," said Miles-san immediately. "Baths, I think, and we can give them both Roic's room. He can bunk in with me. I expect some clean T-shirts would do for nightclothes. Toothbrushes?"

Miles-san and Vorlynkin arguing, Jin discovered, were not nearly so daunting as the pair of them united in sudden agreement. The ordinary business of bedtime blocked further tears. Jin expected Mina found the consulate house stranger than he did. He'd slept in parks, after all, and in all sorts of odd crannies at Suze-san's. Vorlynkin even donated a fancy sonic toothbrush, though Jin and Mina had then to share it, with a trip through its sterilizing holder between customers.

At last they were tucked up in clean sheets in a warm, quiet room. Jin waited for the door to softly shut, and the grownups' feet to clump away back downstairs, before wriggling up and switching on the bedside lamp. Mina threw back her covers and helped him extract Lady Murasaki's box from her backpack. She watched closely as Jin opened the lid to give their pet a breath of fresh air, and helped by tossing in one of the little powdery beige moths they'd collected earlier, while Jin's fingers blocked the prisoner from escaping. He set the plastic box back on the table between their beds.

"Is she going to eat it?" Mina asked, peering through the lid.

"I'm not sure. She might only go for live prey."

Mina frowned thoughtfully. "They have that big garden out back. I bet we could catch more bugs tomorrow."

A reassuring notion. Jin lay back down and pulled up his sheets, and Mina reached to turn out the lamp again before any betraying line of light showed under the bedroom door.

After a while, Mina's whisper came out of the dark: "Do you really think your galactic can get Mommy back? No one else ever could."

Had anyone else even tried? Jin didn't know. Miles-san, all dapper and alert and concentrated and never sitting still, was proving an alarming acquaintance. Jin wasn't sure but what he'd liked the grubby lost druggie better. Jin had a disconcerting feeling of having set a force in motion that he could not now stop, which wasn't made better by not even knowing whether he wanted to.

"I don't know, Mina," he said at last. "Be quiet and go to sleep." He rolled over and hid from it all under his covers.

Roic followed Consul Vorlynkin into the tight-room, where m'lord was already deeply involved with the comconsole, Johannes at his side, Raven leaning over and kibitzing. They all seemed to be examining some engineering schematics for the NewEgypt facility, pulled up from God knew where. Roic was relieved m'lord had finally decided to involve Johannes, if only by necessity. Backup at last! Inexperienced, but not untrained, and judging from his wide eyes it looked as if he was getting a tutorial in covert ops that would have done his ImpSec instructors proud.

M'lord wheeled in his station chair to take in the new arrivals. "Ah, Vorlynkin, good. Your clerk, Matson—he'll be back to work in the morning, right?"

"Yes?"

"I don't think we can keep those kids quiet enough to hide them from him in a house this small. He'll have to be told they are protected witnesses, in some danger. That should be enough to settle him."

"Is it true?" said Vorlynkin.

"How did someone so reluctant to tell lies become a diplomat? By the way, I can't believe, with all your training, that you failed to admire Miss Sato's blisters. What *is* it about this universal female conviction that medical conditions make one interesting? Judging from my daughter Helen, it starts younger than I would have believed possible."

"About the danger," said Vorlynkin, winning Roic's admiration by refusing to be drawn into m'lord's flight of fancy. Judging from the brightness of his eyes, m'lord was as over-stimulated right now as his own kids after one of his bedtime stories, right enough. "Is it real? Because it's unconscionable to keep those children from their guardians otherwise."

M'lord sobered. "Perhaps. This is an investigation, which

means that not all leads pan out. Or otherwise one wouldn't *need* to investigate. But I shouldn't think Lisa Sato would have been removed in that brutal and effective way for any trivial reason. Which means waking her up could actually increase their hazard..." He tapped his lips, considering this. "I suspect Jin misjudges his aunt and uncle, actually. They may not merely lack the resources to fight the good fight for their kinswoman. They may be seriously intimidated."

"Hm," said Vorlynkin.

Roic's own conviction was that as soon as that poor frozen woman had intersected m'lord's orbit, this chain of events had become inevitable. Worse than dangling a string in front of a cat, it was. He likely shouldn't explain this to Vorlynkin; an armsman was supposed to be loyal in thought, word, and deed. But not *blind*...

"But if Jin and Mina were your children, would you want some off-worlder as good as kidnapping them to use for his own purposes?" Vorlynkin persisted. "No matter how well-intentioned?"

"In my defense, I must point out, they turned up here on their own, but—if I were dead, my widow frozen, my children fallen into the hands of people either unwilling or incapable of helping them? I doubt I would *care* where the man came from who could reunite them with Ekaterin. I'd shower all my posthumous blessings upon him." M'lord wheeled around and drummed his fingers on the comconsole counter. "Poor Jin! He makes me think about my missing grandmother, actually."

"Missing grandmother?" said Raven, leaning back against the counter. "I didn't know you had any."

"Most people have two—not you, of course. My Betan grandmother is alive and well and opinionated to this day, in fact. If you ever meet her, you'll understand a whole lot more about my mother. No, it's a Barrayaran tale, the fate of Princess-and-Countess Olivia Vorbarra Vorkosigan."

"Then delightfully bloody, I daresay." Raven's sweeping hand

gesture invited m'lord to go on, not that he needed any encour-
agement. Johannes, too, was listening in apparent fascination.

"Very. If you'd learned your Barrayaran history, not that you
would be expected to, you'd know that once upon a time—all
the best stories start that way, you realize—that once upon
a time, the death squads of Mad Emperor Yuri attempted to
erase most of my family, thereby triggering the civil war that
ended, eventually, in Yuri's dismemberment. So many people
wanted a piece of him by then, they were forced to share, y'see.
The death squad shot my grandmother in front of my father,
messily. He was eleven at the time, which is part of why Jin
keeps reminding me of it.

"But you see... for all the horrors of that day, and of the
war that followed it, nobody, I'm not sure how to put this,
nobody *denied* my father his experience. Jin's mother was just
as abruptly and unjustly taken from him, but he's not been
permitted his grief. No funeral, no mourning, no protest,
even. No revenge—certainly not whatever satisfaction there
might be of knowing she was escorted down into death by a
procession of her enemies. For Jin and Mina, there's just...
silence. Frozen silence."

A rather frozen silence followed this, among the Barrayarans
in the room.

Vorlynkin cleared his throat, leaned on his hand, stared into
the comconsole. "So. Lord Auditor. And, um... just how are
we planning to give this woman her voice back...?"

Chapter Ten

"**D**on't land on the chickens," Jin said, leaning anxiously over the back of the seat between Johannes, who was flying the lift van, and Miles, occupying the passenger side.

Johannes grimaced and eased the lift van forward under the canopy of Jin's rooftop refuge, then paused again while Jin leaped out to pull the cafe table out of the way, glance underneath the van, look relieved, and motion Johannes forward. As Johannes gingerly set them down atop the roof, a woman at the back of the tent-room stood hands-on-hips, watching them in suspicion, though she smiled briefly as Jin danced up to her. The whine of the van's engines went silent.

"Ah, Ako, good, she's been faithful," said Miles, and slid open his door. "The rest of you wait here till I signal," he added over his shoulder. "We don't want to stampede the poor woman." *Or look like a clown car,* he did not add aloud. Johannes and Raven nodded silently; Roic's disapproving frown at Miles seizing point-man position might as well have been audible.

Ako was evidently attempting to feed Gyre; she wore heavy oven mitts and brandished a long fork with a fragment of raw meat fluttering from it. As she gestured to Jin, the bird stretched forward and snatched the slithery morsel, twisting its head and gulping it down. Ako jumped. "He bites, you know," she said to Jin, almost apologetically.

"Not *very* hard," said Jin.

"I needed antibiotic salve and plastic bandages the first time, thank you very much. I'll allow the bird didn't actually take off a finger." She put her hands on her hips again and stared hard at Miles. "So you're back! You gave me quite a turn, sneaking up in that van."

Miles hoped their sneaking had been successful. Though not hidden from more sophisticated scanners, at least the tent roof concealed their activities from casual observation, in this level morning light. Discreet, if not secret.

"I was beginning to think you weren't coming back, and was wondering what to do with all these animals. But you found Jin after all!" She had nearly decided, Miles read in her eyes, that he'd dodged off without any intention of finding Jin.

"We were both unavoidably delayed," Miles said. "Jin actually found me, but in any case, we're reunited. Thank you so much for looking after his creatures. They mean the world to him."

She sniffed, not displeased with some recognition of her efforts. "I know."

Jin returned from taking a rapid inventory of his menagerie, including counting his chickens. "Miles-san is going to take me and all my creatures away to, to his place. For a while," he told Ako.

Her brows tightened. "Yah?"

"Yes, and I need to speak to Madame Suze about that," Miles said. Ako looked marginally appeased at this indication of aboveboard-ness. "Tenbury told me you are something of an apprentice to the plant medtech?" Miles would be meeting her again soon, if things went as he hoped. Best to placate her.

Ako went wary. "I help her clean and things. In the infirmary."

"Just so." Miles motioned to the van; the rest of his entourage piled out.

Miles was relieved of the problem of introductions by Jin taking them over, possibly more reassuringly than Miles could have: "This is Raven-sensei, he's a friend from Escobar, this is Roic-san, he works for Miles-san, this is Lieutenant Johannes, he's all right."

Ako bent and whispered, "Jin, they're not policemen, are they? You should know better—"

"Naw, they're Barrayarans. Galactics."

Ako bit her lip, but seemed to accept this provisional guarantee. She watched as they sorted themselves out, Johannes and Roic to stay with the van till Jin got back to supervise loading it, Raven and Jin to accompany Miles.

"I should come with you," Roic muttered to Miles's ear.

"These people are justifiably nervous of outsiders. I won't get what I want if we hit them *en masse,* and you're *en masse* all by yourself." Miles tapped his wristcom. "I'll call you if I need you."

Roic returned him The Sigh, familiar shorthand for the usual argument. Miles let Jin lead him and Raven off down the exchanger tower. Ako trailed as far as the kitchen, where Miles prudently detoured to grab a carafe of coffee and some cups. She stared after them as they headed toward the stairs to Suze's suite.

As they waited for an answer to Miles's knock, he turned his head and said to Jin, "I had better pitch this to her in my own way. I'll let you know when you can chime in."

Jin, shifting from foot to foot, gulped and nodded.

A slow shuffle from within heralded the door opening a crack. Suze's bleary eye peered out. "You again!" she said. "I thought we were well rid of you." She squinted at Jin. "Of both of you." The eye traveled on to Raven. "Who the hell are you?"

"Raven Durona, from Escobar," Raven answered readily. "Pleased to meet you."

"He's a friend," Miles said. "As in, *Pass, friend.*" He brandished the carafe. "May we come in?"

"Eh..." Reluctantly, but with her one open eye on the carafe, Suze gave way. She wore the same loose black garments as before; she probably slept in them. Her inner chamber had the same close geriatric smell. She went to her window and set the polarization to admit a grudging shade more morning, and waved Miles, and his carafe, cups, and followers, to her battered seats.

"You found your wallet, I see," she said, settling across from them. At Miles's gesture, Jin hastened to distribute coffee.

"Yes, and my luggage and my friends. I'm back in business."

"And just what is your business? Thank you, Jin."

"I'm an investigator, of a sort."

Suze's cup halted on its way to her lips. Her seamed face set in stiff panic.

"Not for any authority on Kibou, however," Miles added.

"Insurance fraud," Jin put in, in hasty reassurance. "He's not a policeman. Or a doctor or a lawyer, even though he went to that conference. Raven-sensei's the doctor."

Miles's eyebrows went up at this description of himself. Clearly, at some point he was going to have to take the boy aside and explain *Imperial Auditor* to him in greater detail, but perhaps this would do for now. "Not precisely, but close enough. As it happens, the powers-that-be on Kibou are the subject of my inquiries, not its sponsors. I have no interest whatsoever in shutting down your operation. I'd actually like to make use of your facilities. I may be able to make it worth your time."

Suze's eyes narrowed over her coffee cup; she finally drank. "We get by here because we don't draw anyone's attention."

"I don't wish to draw attention, either."

Suze sat back, leathery lips pursing. "You want someone illegally frozen? Hoping you can bribe me into storing the body for you?" Her tone was remarkably neutral, neither leading nor guiding.

Her suggestion came up far too readily—ye gods, had Suze ever provided such services, perhaps for the local underworld? Did Kibou-daini *have* an underworld? Aside from the literal one he'd been lost in, that is. Could this be the source of some of her protection? Because crime lords would want to cheat death, too. Though you'd think they could afford their own private arrangements—still, they would need benefits to distribute to lesser followers. And for the discreet disposal of enemies, those ranks of anonymous drawers downstairs would certainly trump lead weights and a swim in the nearest river. It would even render murder reversible, if one had been too hasty in one's crime-lordly commands, or otherwise made a mistake. *Man, if I wanted to hide a body on Kibou*... Miles wrenched his mind from this fascinating side-path. "Have you done such favors before?" he asked cautiously.

Suze shrugged, her alarm giving way to dry amusement in the face of his consternation. "If I had, would I tell you?"

"I have no need to know," Miles assured her. *Want* to know yes, but then, he wanted to know everything. "My need is quite the reverse. We wish to do a private cryorevival. Which requires proper facilities. And discretion. You may be able to lend us both."

This took her aback. Her jaw worked, and she covered her confusion with another swallow of coffee, then grimaced. "Jin, fetch my medicine out of the cupboard," she commanded. Jin leapt up, rummaged for the square bottle, and brought it to her. At her gesture, he also uncapped and poured—scantly, both Miles and, he thought, Suze noted, but she didn't complain as the boy settled once more. "Cryorevival! How?"

"Dr. Durona, here, is a noted cryorevival specialist. If your facilities meet his specs, we'd like to, as it were, rent them."

A long pause. "How much?" Suze said at last.

"I thought I'd offer you something your money can't buy. In exchange for letting us revive our, um, patron—and for the discretion, of course—Raven will throw in a top-class revival for any other candidate of your choice."

Suze's jaw unhinged. She sank back in her chair. And after a moment breathed, "You *devil*."

Money would have worked, Miles thought. But some things worked better.

Suze jerked her head toward Raven. "Just how good is he?"

For answer, Miles unbuttoned his gray tunic and white shirt. "This"—his hand traced the spider web of pale scars—"was a needle-grenade, very well aimed, at close range. Ten years ago. Raven did my revival." *Assisted at,* strictly speaking, but Raven had acquired a decade's more experience and seniority since then. "I guarantee, as a medical challenge nothing that you have downstairs can compare."

Suze looked away as he buttoned up again. "Old age," she said, "is slower than a grenade, but a lot more thorough."

"This is unfortunately true," said Raven, "though I may have a few aids for that as well. What I would suggest is that Madame Suze, here, draw up a list of half a dozen or so candidates, and let me triage them for the maximum chance of medical success. This should produce the most satisfactory result all round."

"Mm," she said. Her hand crept up and rubbed her chest, over her heart. "Hm."

Jin, unable to contain himself any longer, burst out, "Please, Suze-san! Let them!"

The caterpillar eyebrows climbed. "What's it to you, boy?"

Jin pressed his lips together and looked imploringly at Miles.

"Are you sure you want to know?" Miles inquired.

Suze was shrewd enough to hesitate a long moment before her curiosity overcame her better judgment. "Yah."

Miles opened his hand to Jin, who cried, "Miles-san promised to get my *mother* back!"

Suze's face pinched in horror. "Oh, and you think you aren't going to draw *attention,* mister galactic investigator? Lisa Sato was all about attention!"

"We may draw some eventually, but not to you," Miles said smoothly. "As soon as her recovery permits, we'll remove her to the Barrayaran consulate and reunite her with both her children. No link to this place."

"You think so? Those that froze her will sure enough want to find out who unfroze her! Which will drop them right back in my lap, which isn't big enough to hold *them*, I promise you!"

"Yes, but the first thing they'll run into is me. I plan..." Miles hesitated. He didn't exactly have a plan, yet. More of a stab in the dark. He still wasn't sure what his blade would connect with...

"What?" demanded Suze.

"I plan to give them other worries." He glanced at Raven. "Much depends on Madame Sato, both on what she has to say and how soon she can say it. I had rather severe cryo-amnesia, myself. Which lingered uncomfortably."

"I remember that," said Raven. "Uncomfortable it may have been, but it didn't really last that long. We were just pressed for time, back then. Madame Sato—well, I can't give any guarantees at this point."

Miles nodded understanding, both of what was said and what was unsaid, and turned again to Suze. "I need one more favor. I'd like to borrow a cryo-corpse."

"*What*," Suze began in a towering tone, which weakened to, "...kind?"

"Female, about fifty kilos. As young as you have available. Anything else, Raven?"

Raven shook his head. "That should do it."

"We undertake not to damage her in any way that would compromise her future revival," Miles went on, hoping he didn't sound too airy.

"That a guarantee, galactic?"

"It won't be wholly under my control, but if things go my way, she should be all right." *I hope.* "In any covert operation, people...take their chances."

Raven winced—ah, maybe not the best parallel to draw, after the chest display.

"When?"

"Soon. Possibly tonight, no later than tomorrow night."

Suze's nostrils flared in a long, indrawn breath of doubt.

Miles held up a pair of fingers. "*Two* cryorevivals of your choice."

Suze turned her head and made a throwing-away gesture. "Go see the plant medtech. Vristi Tanaka. Jin will show you the way. *If* you can talk her into going along with all this nonsense, though I suppose you will... Talk, talk, talk. Makes me tired."

Miles rose quickly, so as not to outwear his welcome or her decision. "Thank you, Madame Suze. I promise you..." *you won't regret this* was too big a diplomacy to push past even his teeth. "...it will be interesting," he finished.

Suze's snort sent them on their way.

The infirmary turned out to be on the second floor of the facility's old patron intake building. Jin led Miles and Raven through double doors to a corridor with some two or three rooms apparently furbished up for action, judging from the fresh medical smell. They found Tenbury lingering outside of one of them, leaning against the wall with his arms crossed, a narrow float pallet grounded at his feet.

"Jin!" he said, looking pleased. "They said you'd got lost!" He looked somewhat less pleased at Miles. "You again." His brow wrinkled at Raven.

"We came to see Tanaka-san," Jin explained. "It's important."

"She's busy right now"—Tenbury jerked a thumb at the room beyond—"but they should be done soon."

Raven craned his neck to peer through a narrow glass window in the door. "Ah, cryoprep in progress? I'd like to see that."

"Raven-sensei's a doctor. From Escobar," Jin began. Tenbury looked perturbed, and began to speak. Miles cut the debate short by simply knocking.

The knock was answered by a frowning woman, brown skin like old leather, spare of build and with straight white hair where Suze was stout and frizzy, but of a like age, Miles judged, and without the alcohol fumes. Her face lightened when she saw Jin.

"Ah, you're found, Jin! And who have your creatures savaged now, and can it wait?"

"No one, Tanaka-san. But it's kind of urgent. Suze-san sent us over."

Miles let Jin run through his introductions, at which the boy was becoming nicely practiced. He picked up: "We've made arrangements with Madame Suze to use your facilities for a private cryorevival, if they meet Dr. Durona's needs. May we come in?"

"Huh!" she said, and gave way, staring at Raven. Miles wondered if he'd rumpled Raven's clothes, mussed his neat hair, and doused him with gin if he would have seemed less out of place, here, less alarming to these people. Too late.

On a table standing out from the far wall lay the naked body of a frail old man, detained, Miles thought, at the border crossing between life and death. A sheet draped across his middle lent him a scrap of dignity, as much as one could have when given over to plastic tubes and the will or whim of others. A cold-blanket wrapped around his skull sped the chilling of his brain. A tube from a tank above, divided partway down, ran a clear liquid into both carotid arteries. A wider tube, from a vein in his thigh, ran a dark pink color to a knee-height tub with a drain, with a trickle of water from a spout above to keep things flowing. Judging from the paleness of the skin and nails, and the color of the murky exit fluid, the old body was almost wholly perfused with cryo-solution.

Ako hovered, closely supervising the process; she'd evidently overheard something through the doorway, because she looked up and said excitedly, "A doctor? We're getting a real doctor?"

Miles waved down this hope, before it could grow big and bite. "Just visiting. We'll explain it all when you're finished, here."

Jin was staring; Miles wondered how disturbing this process

was to the boy, or if he'd seen it before. It was disturbing to Miles, and he'd *done* it before, or had it done to him. Maybe the more unsettling for that? For the first time, he wondered how much the news of his own encounter with the needle-grenade had felt like *history repeats* to his father, if it had triggered unwelcome old memories of the Princess-and-Countess Olivia's messy death. *I must apologize to him for that, when next we meet.*

"It almost seems too simple," Miles murmured to Raven.

Raven said, "The complexity lies in the cryo-preservation fluid, which has a whole pharmaceutical facility behind it. Or so one trusts. Where *are* you getting your cryo-fluid, Madame Tanaka?"

The medtech's old mouth set in a flat smile. "The concentrate falls off the back of a few loading docks of hospitals here in town. They discard their outdated supplies a couple of times a year. We distill our own water to reconstitute it."

Miles's brows rose. "Is that, um ... all right? Medically?"

Raven shrugged. "If the use-by dating is fairly conservative, yes."

It was not, Miles supposed, a choice between discarded fluid and fresh, but between discarded and none. He was reminded again that this place was a parasite operation, clinging to the underbelly of a more functional economy, without which it could not continue to exist. Granted, if its host economy functioned rather better, it wouldn't *need* to exist.

Medical sensors blinked timing lights. Ako withdrew the tubes and sealed the entry and exit incisions with plastic bandage, and carefully lathered the skin with ointment. She and Medtech Tanaka horsed the body into a sort of plastic body-glove, then joined forces with Tenbury to shift it all onto the float pallet, where Tenbury covered it more corpselike with a sheet. He guided the pallet out the door. "Want to help me, Jin?" Tenbury asked hopefully over his shoulder. Jin, planting his feet, doggedly shook his head. Tenbury sighed and trundled his burden away.

Ako turned to the clean-up process, Raven leaned against a counter, and Miles found a stool to perch upon. While the medtech folded her arms and listened dubiously, Miles embarked on much the same pitch as he'd presented to Madame Suze, heavy on the implication that Suze had sent them over here with her full blessing. Since Tanaka seemed susceptible to the boy, Miles also unleashed Jin for a judicious blast of heartfelt imploring.

As a result, her frown at the end seemed more technical than political. "We haven't had most of that section open for years. A lot of the equipment that wasn't stripped out when the place was decommissioned went later."

Palmed and pawned or sold, Miles presumed.

"But I do maintain . . . huh. I think we'll have to go up and take a look around."

Not a flat *no, impossible,* then. Good so far. "That's what Raven is here for," Miles assured her. "Suze said—is that her first name or her last, by the way?"

"Both," said the medtech. "Susan Suzuki."

"Have you been working with her for long?"

"Since the beginning. There were three of us put the scheme together—Suze, her sister, who was assistant to the comptroller, and me. We roped in Tenbury pretty quick, though."

"A younger man then, was he? You were critical for the cryoprep, obviously. Did you have any plans for the other end of things, the revivals?"

She blew out her lips in a short laugh. "At the time, I didn't think we'd go more than a year before we all ended up in jail. I figured it for more of a hopeless protest than anything. Then the street people started coming in, even more desperate than we were, and we found we couldn't quit. Couldn't betray them as everyone else had."

"The world is made by the people who show up for the job," Miles agreed.

Medtech Tanaka eyed Ako, who had finished cleaning up

and drifted over to listen in. "That's a true thing. Ako and her great-aunt used to run a cook-shop. The usual—the old woman grew ill, the medical bills bankrupted them, the shop failed, they were evicted . . . came in to us. Ako'd never finished school, but she knew how to clean and wasn't afraid of work, so I took her on." Earnest but timid Ako, Miles guessed, would never have gained entry to, let alone graduated from, any medtech academy. This place gave a whole new dimension to the term *unlicensed*.

"Shouldn't we take Raven-sensei upstairs now?" Jin urged.

They mounted one floor to the corridor directly above, which had apparently once been a fully-equipped cryorevival facility, with half a dozen operating theaters, a recovery room, and some intensive care booths. Most of it was dark and dusty and, indeed, sadly stripped, but Medtech Tanaka apparently maintained one operating room for procedures more demanding than what anti-biotic ointment, surgical glue, and bracing advice would cover. She and Raven fell into intense but by no means discouraged tech-speak, medical division, which ended with sending Jin downstairs to bring back Tenbury for more consultation.

"Who *is* the owner-of-record for this place?" Miles asked the medtech while they were waiting. "If it was legally abandoned, I'd have thought the city would have seized it for back taxes by now."

"There have been a couple of supposed owners, over the years. The city won't seize it for the same reason the current owner, poor slob, can't unload it. Legal liability for two or three thousand destitute cryo-corpses. He was a contractor, who bought it for what he thought was a song and only then discovered what came with it. Suze has him under control for now. We think the biggest current danger is that he'll try to solve his dilemma through a spot of arson, but we keep a watch."

"It doesn't sound like a very stable situation."

"Never has been. We just try to go from day to day. Surprising where you can end up, that way."

Raven, Miles noticed, was listening intently to all this, not in the least appalled. Well, Jacksonian-trained, after all. The Hippocratic Oath, if he'd ever heard of it, was likely only considered a guideline there.

Tenbury came back, and there followed a lot more tech-speak, then visits to other chambers with some alarming thumping and crashing. Miles sent the fretful Jin back to his roof to supervise the loading-up of his menagerie. When the noises of inventory at last died away, Raven returned.

"Well?" said Miles. "Go or no-go?"

"Go," said Raven. "There will have to be some prep, but I find these people are good at improvising. And the physical impediments are made up for by a delightful lack of paperwork."

"How soon will you be ready for me to make my snatch? I'll probably want you along on the insertion, by the way, in case we run into any snags that are medical rather than security-related. How do you feel about risking arrest, by the way?"

Raven shrugged. "I'm sure your brother will extract me if you can't. In any case, you can make your switch any time. Madame Sato can just as well wait here till we're ready."

"My time is not infinitely elastic." Besides his wanting to go home, of course, there was no telling what can of worms would be emptied onto his plate with the revival of Jin's mother. Miles was getting itchy to know.

"You can take that kid back to the consulate. I expect I'll be working late here," Raven went on. "I can get back to my hotel by public transport."

Miles pointed to Raven's consulate-issued wristcom. "Check in first. Secured channel. I'll want a report. And it may be better to send Johannes to pick you up."

"Actually..." Raven hesitated. "I think I will want to stop back at the consulate anyway. Can I use your secured tight-beam links to report in to my boss on Escobar?"

"Lily, or Mark?"

"Both. Though I'm not just sure where Lord Mark is, right now. Do you know?"

Miles shook his head. "His enterprises have become rather far-flung. I don't track him daily. Are you arranging bail in advance?"

"Well, that's a thought, but mainly because I may have found some elements of interest to the Durona group, here."

"If they impinge on my investigation, I want to be fully apprised. Or even if they don't."

"Understood."

Miles waved him back to work, then made his way back down through the basement maze and up to Jin's rooftop.

As they unloaded the van, Consul Vorlynkin came out to see what all they were dumping in his back garden. Mina danced ahead of him and pounced on Lucky with an excited cry, rubbing her face in the soft fur. "Lucky! I thought you were dead!" The old gray cat endured the hug, but wriggled free promptly. "Do you still have your ratties, Jin?"

"Yes," said Jin, lifting the cage he was lugging to show them off. "Jinnie and most of her children."

"Handsome," said Vorlynkin, inspecting Gyre, chained to his perch, from a prudent distance. "How do you keep it from eating your chickens?" Galli and Twig, released from their transport box by Lieutenant Johannes, ran past his knees, flapping their wings and squawking, then slowed to stare in apparent amazement at the grass patch before them, warm and green-smelling in the noon sun.

"Well, the big ones sort of defend themselves. I had to keep Gyre chained to his perch when the chicks were littler. I'll have to keep him chained here anyway, till he figures out this is where he belongs." Jin watched as Armsman Roic, with due care, unloaded a stack of terrariums onto the shelf they'd brought from Jin's refuge. Tucked up against the back of the house and sheltered by its eaves, concealed by the house, the tall stone garden walls, and all the trees and bushes, the shelf and its contents would be almost as safe as in his tent-shelter at Suze-san's.

"Cats and mice together as well?" Vorkynkin went on. "What next, lions and lambs?"

"Rats," Jin corrected austerely. "Though I *wish* I might have a lion...! Anyway, Lucky's too old and lazy to bother the big ones, and I keep the little ones in cages with tops." He looked around with satisfaction. "Now that I have all my creatures back, you can keep Lady Murasaki," he told Mina generously.

She made a face. "But *Lucky's* half mine. Because she wasn't yours to start with, you know, even if you did steal her away."

"I saved her from Aunt Lorna," Jin reminded her.

Lucky curled around Vorlynkin's ankles, rubbing her chin to scent-mark him as her new property and leaving a trail of hairs plastered to his formerly-tidy hakama trousers. He bent rather absently to scritch her spine, and she arched shamelessly under his hand.

Mina addressed him anxiously, "Oh sir, can we keep Lucky inside? Till she knows this is home? Cats *do* get lost, you know!"

Looking down into Mina's upturned face, Vorlynkin said reluctantly, "Is she housebroken?"

Mina nodded vigorously. "I can fix her cat pan in my room!"

"The washroom off the kitchen would likely do as well," he told her. "You and Jin...well, yes, I expect it will be good for you and your brother to look after her."

Miles-san strolled past. "All shipshape here, Jin? Then I need Johannes back." He added to Consul Vorlynkin, "We'll be in your tight-room for a time. A lot of detail-work still to do." At his gesture, Roic rose and took up what seemed his accustomed place at his shoulder.

"Is your scheme going to fly, then?" Vorlynkin asked. Miles-san nodded. Vorlynkin grimaced.

Miles-san returned a wry smile. "Flexibility, Vorlynkin. That's the key." He trod indoors, swinging his cane. Jin and Vorlynkin stared after him.

Vorlynkin voiced Jin's own half-formed thought: "Was that supposed to be reassuring?"

Chapter Eleven

Roic figured midnight would have been the right time for a body-snatching expedition, possibly in the middle of a thunderstorm. Among other things, an electrical storm might help account for any power-flicker anomalies they left in their wake. But there were no suitable cold fronts predicted any time soon, and so Roic found himself, Raven, and m'lord, with Johannes driving the lift van again, turning in at the impressive entrance of the NewEgypt facility at high noon. It was only in Roic's imagination that the dog-headed statues flanking the main gate seemed to follow them with their painted eyes.

Johannes was armed with a couple of little floral arrangements in water tubes and a script, but he wasn't called upon to deploy either; the human gate guard waved them right through.

"What t' hell," said Roic.

"It's visiting hours," said m'lord mildly. "They aren't going to harass their patrons' kin, nor their potential future customers coming in for their tour, at this time of day. This isn't a military

installation. All NewEgypt security has to worry about is theft—
which is more likely to come from an employee—vandalism,
which isn't likely to occur in broad daylight, and maybe something
like the N.H.L.L.—who would probably wait for that midnight
thunderstorm you wanted. Seems like their style, somehow."

Roic settled back with a disgruntled, "Huh."

He shifted uncomfortably in his somewhat-too-tight hospital
uniform, *XL*, scavenged by Raven and Medtech Tanaka, possibly from the same source as some of their medical supplies
now laid in and waiting back at Madame Suze's. M'lord wore
a similar set, *XS*, a bit too loose, with the sleeve and trouser
ends rolled up. Raven's set fit perfectly. Johannes was dressed
in what Roic had been assured were unexceptionable Kibou
street clothes, tidy and middle-class.

The van slipped past both the pyramid-topped building's
lobby, fronted by an inviting faux-Egyptian garden with stone
sphinxes, and the sign pointing to the loading docks for pre-
frozen patron intake, hidden on the more utilitarian backside,
then on around to a discreet side entrance meant for employees.

"All right, this is where we unload," m'lord said. "Don't look
hurried, but don't waste time."

Trying not to look hurried, not to mention harried, Roic
helped Raven open the back of the lift van and slide out the
float pallet. A stack of boxes, emptied of their medical supplies,
concealed the long shape in what Roic thought of as the freezer
bag beneath. The body bag, designed for short-term transport,
would, if left sealed, keep its contents at cryo-temperature for a
couple of days, Raven had explained to him. Roic had to grant,
it was a hell of a lot less bulky and eye-catching than a portable
cryochamber. Johannes drove off to find the visitor parking and
wait, and m'lord led the pallet and its handlers inside through
automatic doors that parted for them without protest.

M'lord checked the holomap on his wristcom and led off
through a succession of corridors. They encountered a trio of
gossiping employees and an elderly couple, clearly visitors, on

their way to the cafeteria that Roic smelled in passing, but none
spared the pallet a glance. Roic carefully did not look back.
Two more turns and a short ride down a freight lift tube, and
they were pacing along an underground corridor that stopped
at a double door, the first locked barrier they'd encountered.

M'lord opened one of the boxes, whipped out his *special*
tool kit, ImpSec standard issue with upgrades, and knelt to
the electronic lock. He muttered unreassuringly, "God, it's
been a while. Hope I haven't lost my touch..." He puttered
for a minute or two, while Roic jittered and kept glancing over
his shoulder, and Raven looked bland. The doors parted so
soundlessly, Roic was taken by surprise. M'lord looked smug.
"Ah, good. I'd hoped not to leave any evidence by damaging
the lock." He waved them through like some demented maître
d'hôtel escorting diners to the best table in the room, and closed
the doors gently again when the pallet had passed through.

The new corridor was much darker. And, Roic was surprised
to see, unfinished, which made him worry about encountering
workmen, but he supposed a construction crew would have
lights that would warn them. Beneath the pyramidal building
lay three sub-levels. Around the core stack of utilities on each
level, four concentric corridors extended outward in squares,
with radial connecting halls at the midpoint of each side. Too
regular to be called a maze, it nonetheless seemed to Roic that
it would be easy to get turned around down here. So just how
disturbing it had been to m'lord to be lost for hours in a true
maze, with *no* light?

They turned in at the next connecting spoke; m'lord's lips
moved as he counted off side branches, then set in a smile
as the core stack hove into view. Another pause, while m'lord
weaseled his way into a locked electrical access panel, did some
careful counting, and nodded. They then went out another
spoke and turned right into one of the corridors, this one
completed, dimly lit with utility lighting and lined with loaded
cryo-drawers.

"This doesn't look so fancy," Roic murmured.

"These are the cheap seats," said m'lord. "If you want to be filed away behind faux mahogany and brass fittings—or gold, I'm told—NewEgypt can supply, on the upper levels."

Even down here, a lot of the drawers had small holders set in the walls beside them for odd little personal offerings, including tiny bottles of wine, wrapped snacks, or burned-down stubs of incense sticks. Most common were flowers, mostly plastic or silk but sometimes real ones—some fresh, some brown and drooping sadly from their dried-out water tubes.

"Here," said m'lord, stopping abruptly. He craned his neck at a drawer at the top of the stack. "Read off the number, Raven."

Raven recited a long alphanumeric string, twice.

M'lord checked carefully against the data on his wristcom. "This is it."

The disguising boxes then found another use, as m'lord filched one to boost him to a convenient height to examine the drawer lock and attach his ImpSec-special door opener to it. "All right," he murmured, climbing back down. "When the lights go out, make the switch."

He unshipped his own hand light and trotted off.

Raven issued Roic a pair of insulated medical gloves, donned a pair himself, and bent to unseal the long bag. The figure revealed seemed a slender little old woman, clad in a sort of plastic caul that clung to her shape. What with the translucent protective ointment heavily slathered on her skin and the frost that instantly began to form on the exposed plastic surface, her helpless naked-ness had at least a decent veiling. Roic turned on his own hand light an instant before the corridor lights, and all the little green lights on the drawers, went black. There having proved no way to open a single drawer without setting off some indicator in the central control room, the next best thing had seemed to give the same flicker to five thousand or so drawers at once.

"Ready," said Raven.

Roic tapped the button on the unlocking device; to his relief, the drawer lock opened easily. He slid the long drawer out like opening some dreadful filing cabinet.

Inside was another female figure, also in its caul, which also frosted swiftly. Roic frowned to see that the plastic wrappings weren't quite identical—these seemed to be browner and reinforced with some sort of netting. But, bracing himself, he slid his hands under and lifted her out. Even with the gloves, she seemed to suck the warmth from him in a swift tide. He set her gently on the floor, Raven checked the name tag attached to the outside of the wrappings, and he and Raven between them lifted her replacement into the drawer. The drawer slid shut with a smooth click.

M'lord's hand light flickered at the corridor corner, and he peered around; Roic waved all's-well, and he nodded and ducked away again. By the time Roic and Raven inserted their prize into the bag and sealed it up again, the lights flashed back on. Roic reached up and carefully unsealed the unlocking device, and hid it back in m'lord's kit. He then began re-stacking concealing boxes, wondering how soon a tech crew would arrive to check out their brief power failure.

M'lord returned, and murmured, "Go, go." His eyes seemed as bright as any of the indicator lights, and Roic realized how much he was *enjoying* this caper. *I'm glad one of us is.* Raven seemed as amiable as ever, as if he indulged in this sort of chicanery every day, which Roic knew very well he did not. Roic swallowed and prepared to sprint as the hum of lift tube doors and the echo of voices drifted up the hall that radiated from the central stack, but they turned onto the outer ring before any shouts of *Hey, you there!* could find them.

A short stroll, and they were back at the underground double doors. M'lord paused to lock them again, and call Johannes on his wristcom. The lieutenant was opening the rear of the lift van as they arrived outside. The pallet-load of "supplies" disappeared soundlessly within. Roic still didn't breathe easily till the van turned out the gates and joined the flow of afternoon traffic.

M'lord checked his wristcom. "Sixteen minutes," he said, in a satisfied tone.

Raven had taken the front seat again with Johannes, which made all kinds of sense since the pair of them were by far the most normal-looking, by local standards. Johannes drove sedately but not too sedately, just as instructed. With the back seats folded down to make a cargo space, Roic crouched opposite Madame Sato's body bag from m'lord, alert to reach out and prevent it shifting should Johannes make any sudden turns. Roic had been assured that the cryo-solution and protective ointments kept cryo-corpses slightly pliable, not brittle, and that despite their temperature they wouldn't shatter like an ice cube thrown to the pavement at an accidental blow. But still.

They rode in silence for a few minutes, which Roic broke at last, low-voiced: "All this makes me think about Sergeant Taura. All these other folks got to die in some hope for their future, why *not* her? We were all right there at the Durona clinic, everything was in place for it, it wouldn't have cost much..."

Taura was one of the mercs from m'lord's old ImpSec covert ops days, before the needle-grenade and cryorevival damage had put him out of that business for good. Like Raven and the rest of the Durona cloned siblings, she was a product of Jacksonian genetic engineering; unlike them, she was a sole survivor, in her case of a failed prototype batch of supposed super-soldiers. She had escaped to m'lord's merc troop, where the super-soldier part had actually worked, m'lord testified. But her creators had built in a fail-safe mechanism for their genetic prototypes; Taura would have been dead of old age at twenty-standard without the medical intervention that the Dendarii medics and later the Duronas had supplied her. Roic had met her twice, desperately memorably, the first time when she'd attended m'lord's wedding, the second when m'lord and Roic had traveled to Escobar to attend her last days in the Durona hospice.

M'lord sighed. "I, you, Rowan, and Raven all tried to talk her into it. If her Dendarii insurance hadn't covered it, I'd have popped for it out of pocket, not that the Duronas would have let me. They still figure they owed her and all the Dendarii mercs involved for their escape from Jackson's Whole. But Taura wasn't having it at any price."

What, wake up, still a freak, in some strange place and time, with all my friends gone? Taura had said to the protesting Roic, in that terribly-wrong-for-her thready voice. *But you could make new friends!* was an argument that had failed to move her, in the exhaustion of her failing metabolism.

Roic made a helpless gesture. "You could have overridden her. After she was too far gone to tell, ordered her cryoprepped." God knew m'lord was capable of riding over any number of other people's wills.

M'lord shrugged, face sobered in the shared memory. "That would have been for our benefit, then. Not for hers. But Taura chose fire over ice. That, at least, I had no trouble understanding. High temperature cremation leaves no DNA."

She'd been indifferent to where her ashes would be scattered, except *not Jackson's Whole,* so m'lord had provided a burial plot for her urn in his own family cemetery at Vorkosigan Surleau, overlooking the long lake, a task m'lord and Roic had seen to personally.

"Nobody," muttered Roic, "should die of old age at thirty-standard." Certainly not such a blazing spirit as Taura's had been.

M'lord looked meditative. "If the Duronas' or anybody else's anti-aging research ever succeeds, I wonder if death at three hundred or five hundred will come to seem as outrageous?"

"Or two thousand," said Roic, trying to imagine it. Some few Betans and Cetagandans actually made it to almost two centuries, Roic had heard, but their healths had been genetically guaranteed before conception. For random folks alive and afoot already, not a help.

"Not two thousand, probably," said m'lord. "Some actuarially-minded wag once calculated that if all the medical causes of death were removed, the average person would still only make it to about eight hundred-standard before encountering some fatal accident. I suppose that means that some would slab themselves at eighteen and some at eighteen hundred, but it would still be the same game in the end. Just set to a new equilibrium."

"Makes you wonder about the Refusers."

"Indeed. If the God they posit waited billions of years for them to be born, a few hundred extra years till they die should hardly make a difference to Him." M'lord stared off into some sort of twisty m'lord mind-space. "All the worry people expend over not existing after they die, yet nary a one ever seems to spare a moment to worry about not having existed before they were conceived. Or at all. After all, one sperm over and we would have been our sisters, and we'd never have been missed."

Since there didn't seem an answer to this that didn't make Roic's head hurt trying to think about, he kept silent. They turned in past the sagging chain link gates of Madame Suze's facility at last.

It took many hours to bring Lisa Sato's core temperature up from deep-cryonic to just below freezing. Miles sent Johannes back to the consulate, and, as the night wore on, took turn-about with Roic napping in a makeshift bunk in a room opposite Raven's cobbled-together revival lab, set up on the third floor of the old patron intake building. Raven and Medtech Tanaka, too, took the night watch in shifts. Dawn of the new day brought the start of the critical procedures: the flushing of the old cryo-fluid, the swift replacement with what to Miles seemed vats of new synthetic blood. The skin of the supine figure on the procedure table went from clay gray to an encouraging warm ivory with the transfusion. The cryo-fluid gurgled away down the drain.

If they'd had the time and equipment, not to mention a starter-sample from the patient, whole blood identical to the original's could have been grown. The synthetic blood lacked the unique white cells the patient's own body produced, so

the revived person would have to be in isolation for an inde-
terminate time following, till her own marrow began to refill
the immunity gaps. Miles had been kept asleep through that
phase, Raven told him, but then, he'd had a lot more trauma,
surgical and otherwise, to heal from. Ako had spent all last
evening cleaning and readying the isolation booth.

Raven was maddeningly vague about how soon his patient
might be questioned, and made it clear that her children had
priority as her first visitors. Miles didn't argue with that; he
couldn't think of anything better to motivate the woman to
fight her way to her full faculties.

Miles was anxious to offer help, but as they approached the
point of no return in the procedures, Raven sat him down at
a distance on a stool with a face mask across his mouth. The
memorystick around the edges molded to his skin in a flexible
but efficient seal, and the electropores even filtered viruses.
Still, Miles wasn't entirely sure if it was only to block germs.
So he bit his tongue rather than shrieking when Raven muttered, "Damn it . . . that's not right."

"What's not right?" Miles asked, as Raven and the medtech
busied themselves about the table and didn't answer.

"There's no electrical latency in the brain," Raven said, just
before Miles started to repeat his question, louder. "It should
be coming up by now. . . . Tanaka, let's try a good old-fashioned
shot of shock, here."

Lisa Sato's head bore something resembling a swimming
cap, studded with electronics and sensors, tight to the dark
hair plastered flat with cryo-gel. Raven did something to his
control screen, and the cap made a snapping noise that made
Miles jump and almost topple off his stool. Raven scowled at
his readouts. His gloved hand went out, almost unconsciously
it seemed to Miles, to massage his patient's limp hand.

"Close that drain," Raven said, abruptly and inexplicably,
and the medtech hurried to comply. He stepped back a pace.
"This isn't working."

The bottom fell out of Miles's stomach in a sickening lurch. "Raven, you can't stop." *My God, we can't afford to botch this one. Those poor kids are waiting for us to deliver their mother back to them. I promised . . .*

"Miles, I've done over seven thousand revivals. I don't need to spend the next half hour jumping on this poor woman's corpse to know she's gone. Her brain is slush, on a micro-level." Raven sighed and turned away from the table, peeling down his mask and drawing off his gloves. "I know a bad prep when I see one, and that was a bad prep. This wasn't my fault. There was nothing I could do. There was nothing I could *ever* have done." Raven was far too controlled a man to throw his gloves across the room and swear, but he hardly needed to; Miles could read his emotions in his set face, the more fierce for the sharp contrast with his usual easy-going cheer.

"Murdered . . . do you think?"

"Things can go wrong without someone intending them, you know. In fact, that's the statistical norm. Though not around you, I suppose."

"But not, I think, in this case."

Raven's lips flattened. "Yeah. I can do an autopsy, in a bit, here." When he had recovered his tone of mind, presumably. "Find out exactly what kind of bad prep this was. There are a number of choices. I thought there was something odd about the viscosity of that return fluid . . ." He paused. "Let me rephrase that. I bloody insist on the autopsy. I want to know exactly how I was set up for this failure. Because *I don't like being set up like this.*"

"Amen," growled Miles. He slipped off his chair, jerked down his mask, and approached the table with its mute burden. The blood pump was still keeping the skin hopefully flushed, deceptive promise. Absently, Raven reached out and switched it off. The silence hurt.

How was he going to explain this to Jin and Mina? Because Miles knew that would have to be his next task. In his rush and his arrogance, he had taken away their hope...no, he'd only taken away their *false* hope. This ending was apparently inevitable, however and whenever it was arrived at, now or later, by his hand or another's. The reflection didn't console him much.

I will get you justice...no. He wasn't in a position to make any such pledges to them. And *I will try* sounded too weak, mere preamble to another adult put-off. But guilt fueled his rage against his—their—unknown enemy as nothing else could. How odd, how suspect. How futile.

A sharp rap fell on the operating room door. Roic, awake again? He wasn't going to greet the news of their fool's errand with any joy, either. Miles stretched his back, grabbed his cane, walked to the door, and glanced through the narrow glass. And was immediately glad he hadn't just yelled, *Come in, Roic!* Because standing outside was Consul Vorlynkin, looking harried, with Jin and Mina in tow, one tugging on each arm.

Miles slipped through the door and stood with his back pressed to it. "What are you doing here? You were supposed to wait at the consulate till I called." As if he couldn't tell, by the way Vorlynkin was being pulled about. He supposed it was a good thing the children seemed to have lost all fear of the man, but it would be better if he hadn't turned to putty in their hands. *Yeah, like I should talk.*

"They insisted," Vorlynkin explained, unnecessarily. "I told them she wouldn't be awake till tomorrow—*you* told them how unappetizing you looked when you came out of cryo—but they still insisted. Even if they could only see her through the glass. I don't think they slept all night. Woke me up three times... I thought maybe if they could just *see*, they'd settle down. Take naps later, something." Vorlynkin's voice slowed as he took in Miles's grim stance. So he only mouthed, and did not voice, the words *What's wrong?*

Miles wasn't ready for this now. Hell, he wasn't ready for this ever. He'd had the unenviable task before of informing next-of-kin or the friends who stood in that place, but they'd always been adults. Never children, never so wide open and unarmored.

Mina and Jin's excitement was quelled, as they looked at him. Because if things had gone well, wouldn't he be puffing it off already, taking the credit? There was no way to make this better, and only one way to make it over. He wanted to kneel, to grovel, but it seemed only right to look Jin in the eye. He took a deep breath.

"I'm sorry. I'm so sorry. Something went wrong with the cryorevi—no, with the cryoprep. There was nothing Raven-sensei could do. We tried... we think your mother died during her cryoprep eighteen months ago, or sometime soon after."

Jin and Mina stood still in shock. But not crying, not yet. They just stared at Miles. Stared and stared.

"But we wanted to see her," said Mina, in a thin little voice. "You said we would see her."

Jin's voice was throaty, husky, entirely unlike himself. "You promised..."

The trio had fallen apart from each other at the blow of this news. Quite spontaneously and uncharacteristically, Jin's hand found Mina's. Mina's other hand wavered and gripped Vorlynkin's again; he looked down at her in dismay. "Now?" he said. "Are you sure...?" His hard gaze rose as if to nail Miles to the wall.

"They have a right," said Miles in reluctance. "Though I don't know if an ugly memory is better than no memory. I just... don't know."

"Neither do I," admitted Vorlynkin.

Mina's chin jutted out. "I want to see. I want to see her."

Jin gulped and nodded.

"Wait a moment, then..." Miles slipped—fled—back through the door and said, "Raven, we have visitors. Next of kin. Can we, ah, tidy her up a bit?"

Raven the supposed Jacksonian hard-ass looked deeply shaken

at this news. "Oh gods, it's not those poor kids? What are they doing *here*? Must they come in?"

"They've a right," Miles repeated, wondering why those words seemed to resonate in his mind. He ought to know, but these days he couldn't blame every memory lapse on his own ten-year-old cryorevival.

Raven, Tanaka and Miles hurried to get the silent figure decently draped, to remove the useless tangle of technology from about her, tubes and electrodes and the strange cap. Miles smoothed the short black hair back over the ears. Its slickness rendered the middle-aged female face sophisticated yet skull-like, and Miles wondered how the children's mother had worn her hair. Weird little things like that could matter all out of proportion. A swift and useless tidying-up, this.

Over, let it be over. Miles went to the door and held it wide.

Jin and Mina and Vorlynkin filed through. The look Vorlynkin flicked at Miles in passing had very little love in it. Jin took the consul's free hand as they came up to the tableside. Because who else was there left to hang onto, in this spinning hour?

The children stared some more. Mina's lips parted in bewilderment; Jin raised his eyes to Miles with a half-voiced *Huh?*

Drawing back in something between outrage and scorn, Mina said, "But that's not our mommy!"

Chapter Twelve

Miles just barely kept himself from blurting, idiotically, *Are you sure?* Neither set young face held the least doubt. "Then who," he choked, wheeling to stare at Raven, at the draped figure on the table, "was it that we just..." *Murdered* was unfair, as well as inaccurate. And, he suspected, would also be deeply offensive to the upset cryorevival specialist. "That we just..." Fortunately, no one here seemed to expect him to fill in the blank.

"Her numbers were right," said Raven. "...Or anyway, her numbers were the ones you gave me."

So either Miles had grabbed the wrong drawer code from the cryo-storage data, which he knew very well he had not, or the numbers had been fudged somewhere upstream. By somebody. For some reason. Concealment? To protect Lisa Sato's cryo-corpse from kidnapping by her supporters, or someone like the N.H.L.L.? Or by Miles—no, Miles didn't think anyone on Kibou-daini could have imagined a nosy Barrayaran

Imperial Auditor taking this interest. Or might it have been a genuine error? In which case—Miles pictured the millions of cryo-drawers in, under, or around Northbridge alone, and his heart sank. The thought that *nobody* might actually know where Lisa Sato had been stashed was too horrible to contemplate for more than an instant.

Or—and the notion was so arresting, Miles caught his breath—someone else had been ahead of him, with the exact same idea. In which case... No. Before his inner visions could proliferate madly, he'd better fasten them down with at least a few facts. Physical ones, not all these trailing tenuous tentacled inductions.

Miles took a deep breath, to slow his hammering heart. "All right. All right. We'll start with what we *can* know. First is to ID that poor, um, patron. Make that a priority for your autopsy, Raven. I'll go back to the consulate tight-room and—" Miles broke off as Vorlynkin cleared his throat, ominously.

Vorlynkin nodded to Jin and Mina, clinging together in white-faced silence. Miles wasn't sure whether to read their postures as fear, or anger, though at least they weren't weeping. In either case, Vorlynkin was probably right—it wouldn't do to discuss the gruesome details of an autopsy in front of them just now, even if the subject wasn't their mother after all. Children, as Miles had reason to know, ranged naturally from deeply sensitive to remarkably bloody-minded; sometimes, confusingly, the same child at different times. Was dealing with women *practice* for dealing with children? It was likely just as well he didn't have time to follow up that thought. With a sweep of his arms, Miles shepherded Vorlynkin and his charges back out into the corridor.

"I'm so sorry about all this," Miles repeated inanely. "I promise you"—damn, he really needed to cull that phrase from his vocabulary—"I'm still going to look for your mommy. The problem has just suddenly become a lot more interesting. Er, difficult. It's just become a bit more difficult. I need more data, d—" *Need more data, dammit,* was an old mantra of his, almost comforting in its familiarity. Some setbacks were simply setbacks. Others were opportunities breaking down the door in disguise. He was reasoning ahead of his data—*remember, data?*—to imagine this was the second sort. Well, that was what experience could grant one—a high degree of certainty while making one's mistakes...

Mina said, "But what's going to happen to us, now?"

Jin added anxiously, "You're not going to make us go back to Aunt Lorna and Uncle Hikaru, are you?"

"No. Or at least, not yet. Consul Vorlynkin will take you back to the consulate for the moment, until we get somewhere with all this, or..."

"Or?" Vorlynkin repeated, as Miles trailed off.

"We'll get somewhere." *I just don't know where.* "I'll stay here for the clean-up, then join you all there later. When you get back, Vorlynkin, put Lieutenant Johannes on a preliminary data sweep-search for me. I want to try to find that Dr. Leiber, the one who was associated with Lisa Sato's group here in North-bridge eighteen months ago." Not much of a clue, but he had to go with what little was in hand. Miles wondered just how common that surname was on Kibou. Well, he'd find out shortly.

Vorlynkin nodded, and herded the kids off. Jin looked around as if regretting his lost refuge. Mina reached up and took the consul's hand, which made him twitch a little, possibly with guilt, but he manfully endured. This was clearly distressing for the children. *Hell, it's distressing for* me.

Roic, sleep-rumpled, stuck his head out the door of the improvised bunk room and squinted as the trio vanished around the corner. "I heard voices. What's going on?"

Miles brought him up to date. His expression, when he learned that they'd just deftly snatched the wrong body, was all that Miles had pictured. Of, course, you had to have been around Roic for a while to read all the nuances of *bland* his face and posture could convey. Was there some sort of secret school for armsmen to learn this, or was it all apprenticeship? Armsman-commander Pym was a master, but Roic was catching up.

"Y'know," said Roic, as Pym would not have, because Pym would have had an exact bland to cover it, "if you'd quit while you were winning, right after Wing, we'd be on our way home right now."

"Well, I can't quit now," said Miles tartly.

"I can see that, m'lord." With a sigh, Roic followed him back into the lab.

Raven had tidied up and was getting ready for his next task. Medtech Tanaka was laying out an array of rather disturbing instruments on a tray next to the cryorevival table. She looked up at their entry and asked, "Will we still get our free cryorevivals, then?"

"Yes, of course," said Miles automatically. "Rent, after all." He was surprised she still trusted them for the task, but was vaguely heartened that she evidently agreed with Raven's analysis. He did not add, *And we might be back*; he was growing more cautious. Belatedly.

Raven tapped his fingers on the table and looked over the instruments. "Do you want me to send any samples out to a commercial lab for analysis, or try to set up something here?"

"Which is faster, and which is better?"

"If I wanted to do a good job here in-house, I'd need to bring some of my team from Escobar. This would likely take more time than sending samples out. Either risks drawing attention. Results ought to be the same."

"Hm. My instinct is to keep this close till we know what we're dealing with. I'd say, go as far as you can on your own, and then we'll take stock. My working hypothesis is that this was a deliberate substitution, sometime in the past eighteen months. If we knew who this woman was, where she came from, it might tell us something about who could have put her in Lisa Sato's place." *Or not.* "Makes a difference if she was just swapped out, or if she was actually frozen in place of Sato from the get-go, in which case..."

Raven frowned. "You think Jin and Mina's mother might

still be alive out there? In that case, why didn't she let her poor kids know?"

"Depends entirely on how dangerous that knowledge might have been."

Raven's frown deepened.

"Well, I can tell you one thing straight off," said Medtech Tanaka, bending to retrieve a scrap of plastic caul from the waste bin and holding it up to the light. "This woman here wasn't frozen in place of the one you're looking for, not in the past eighteen months at least. This is an older style of wrapping."

Three heads turned abruptly toward her. "How old?" said Miles. "And how do you know?"

Her wrinkled eyelids narrowed. "Oh, heavens. I haven't seen this brand with the hexagonal netting inside since my student days. At least thirty years old, maybe fifty?"

Miles groaned. "So this woman could have come from any time in the last two hundred and fifty years?"

"No, because there were other styles and brands before then. And after. This type was only on the market for about three decades."

"Thank you, Medtech Tanaka," said Miles. "That's a start."

His mystery, it seemed, had just split into two. Mystery mitosis. It seemed a retrograde sort of progress.

Raven lifted his first instrument and bent to his patient-turned-subject.

It was very quiet in the lift van for the first part of the trip back to the consulate. Jin's throat was choked with disappointment. Mina, strapped in the middle of the next seat to the rear, was pale and withdrawn. Vorlynkin negotiated traffic by hand till they were well away from Suze-san's, then linked to the municipal control grid and leaned back with a sigh.

He hitched around sideways to regard Jin and Mina both. "I'm really sorry about all this mix-up."

"It wasn't *your* fault," Jin conceded.

Vorlynkin opened his mouth to say something, evidently thought better of it, and substituted simply, "Thank you." After a moment he added, "Although if you two had been my daughter, I'd have been furious to have you dragged into something like this."

Before Jin could say, *But I thought we dragged you in,* Mina piped up eagerly, "You have a daughter? How old is she? Can she play with us?"

Vorlynkin grimaced. "Annah's six, so she probably would like to play with you, but I'm afraid not. She's on Escobar. With her mother."

"Are they coming back soon?" asked Mina.

"No." Vorlynkin hesitated. "We're divorced."

Both Jin and Mina flinched a little at the scary word.

"Why are you divorced?" asked Mina. If they'd been sitting together, Jin could have kicked her in the ankle to shut her up, but unfortunately she was out of reach.

Vorlynkin shrugged. "It wasn't anyone's fault, really. She was an Escobaran. I met her when I was stationed at the embassy there as a junior secretary. When we first married, I thought it was understood that she would follow where my career took me. But by the time I was offered the promotion and the transfer to the Barrayaran embassy on Pol, Annah had come along. And my wife changed her mind. With a baby to look out for, she didn't want to leave the security of her family and her homeworld. Or she didn't trust me enough. Or something."

After a silence, which Jin endured in faint embarrassment and Mina, apparently, in deep fascination, Vorlynkin added, "My ex-wife remarried recently. Another Escobaran. She wrote me that her new husband wants to adopt Annah. I don't know. It might be better for her than a father she sees for maybe three days every three years. It's hard to decide. To let go." He had been talking to his lap but, unexpectedly, he raised his shrewd blue glance to Jin and Mina. "What do you think?"

Mina blinked, and blurted, "I'd want my real daddy."

Vorlynkin didn't look terribly cheered by this reply. Jin said more cautiously, "It depends, I guess. If he's a nice guy or not."

"I assume so. I haven't met him yet. I suppose I ought to take some time and go do that, before signing off. Maybe visiting again would just confuse Annah. Surely she can't remember much about me."

"Don't you send her messages and stuff?" asked Mina, frowning.

"Sometimes."

Jin said slowly, "Couldn't you have chosen to stay with your wife back then? Instead of going to Pol?" Wherever that was. Pretty far from Escobar, it sounded like. "Being a diplomat isn't like being a soldier, is it? Aren't you allowed to quit?"

Vorlynkin gave Jin an ironic salute, just a finger-touch to his forehead, and Jin felt even more uncomfortable. Maybe he shouldn't have pointed that out?

"Yes, I could have made that choice. Then. I couldn't go back now, of course. That chance has gone beyond recall."

Mina's frown deepened to a scowl. "It sounds like you already picked."

"My younger self did, yes. I have to wonder about him, some days..." The autopilot beeped as they approached the consulate, and somewhat to Jin's relief Vorlynkin turned away to re-take the controls.

Back in the consulate kitchen, Vorlynkin fixed them all a snack, then went off to the officelike front room to see about something his clerk wanted. Mina snitched Lucky and went upstairs. Jin went outside to check on all his creatures. By the time he arrived in the bedroom he shared with his sister, she was curled up on her bed around the cat, possessively. Lucky endured being clutched like a stuffed toy without protest beyond a lazy tail-twitch or two.

Jin was much too old to take a nap in the daytime, but his bed did look awfully inviting. He supposed if he tried to take Lucky away from Mina, she'd just set up a screech. Maybe wait till she fell asleep? Her face was stiff and blotchy, her eyes red, as if she'd been crying.

As he sat on his bed and plotted his recapture of the cat, Mina sniffed and said, "They lied."

"Grownups always lie." Jin brooded. "*Mom* lied. She always said everything was going to be all right, and it *wasn't.*"

"Huh." Mina curled tighter, face scrunching, and sniffed again. In a little while, both face and grip relaxed, and Jin bent over and fished Lucky back, careful not to wake Mina. He stroked the cat till she purred in concession to the trade, then went to curl up with her on his own bed. It was a nice bed, nicer than anything he'd had at Suze-san's, but he still wished he was back there. Maybe grouchy old Yani had been right after all to want to leave Miles-san in the street...

He was wakened by Roic calling his name, big hand gently shaking his shoulder. Mina was already sitting up and rubbing the creases from her pillow out of her face. Lucky had gone off somewhere. The light on the carpet had shifted around. Jin glanced at the clock and realized that a couple of hours had slipped away.

"Sorry to wake you," said Roic. "M'lord wants you to take a look at something on the comconsole in the tight-room."

Roic waited patiently while both children visited the bath-room, making sure they'd washed their hands before following him downstairs. Now that he was getting used to the big man, Jin kind of liked Roic. For Miles-san, it must be like owning your own private grownup, following you around and doing stuff for you. Except you got to tell him what to do, instead of the other way around. Jin wished he owned a Roic.

There was a crowd in the strange sealable basement room where, Jin had figured out by now, the consulate kept all the nifty secret spy stuff. Miles-san and Vorlynkin sat at one com-console. Raven-sensei had returned, and was bent over the long table along with Johannes, attending upon a small machine.

Jin dodged over to them. "What's that?"

"DNA scanner," said Johannes.

"Is that what you used to check Miles-sa—Lord Vorkosigan's thumbprint, that first day?"

"Yes."

"Handy," said Raven-sensei. "There should have been one at Madame Suze's, but evidently it was sold off or broken some time ago. I was afraid I was going to have to take the tissue sample to a commercial lab for even this basic data."

Jin's interest rose. "Could I make scans of my creatures' DNA on it?"

"It's not a toy," said Johannes. "We use it for making positive IDs of people wanting travel documents and so on." He looked at Jin and weakened. "You'll have to ask Counsel Vorlynkin."

Miles-san called Jin over to his comconsole, where Mina was already standing and shifting from foot to foot. Still-shots of four different men hovered in a row above the vid plate. Two had gray hair. One wore a white laboratory coat.

"Miss Mina, I'm hoping you can help us out, here," said Miles-san. "All these men are different Dr. Leibers who live around greater Northbridge. We've already eliminated the female Dr. Leibers, trusting none has made a trip to Beta Colony lately." His mouth twisted up at some joke that Jin didn't understand, although Roic did, judging from his short smile. "Do any of them look like the man you overheard talking to your mommy, that night? Or, do any of them definitely not look like him?"

Mina peered anxiously at the scans. "It was a long time ago. I don't really remember."

"Do you remember anything at all? Was your Dr. Leiber young, or old?"

"Oh, old."

"Gray hair?"

"No, black. I do remember that much. I'm not too good at telling grownups' ages. But he was real old. Thirty, maybe?"

Miles-san and Vorlynkin exchanged a look; the consul's lips twitched, but he didn't say anything.

"So, old but not gray." Miles-san tapped the vid controls, and the two gray-haired men vanished. The other two looked rather alike, with similar haircuts, except one's face was bonier and the other's more round.

"When I was a wee little kid," remarked Roic, watching over their shoulders, "there was a time I thought that any skinny old man I saw was my grandfather. It was pretty confusing."

"Nevertheless," said Miles-san. "Jin, do you remember ever seeing either of these two men in your mother's company? Even if you weren't introduced?"

Jin shook his head.

After a long hesitation, Mina pointed at bony-face. "That one. Maybe. The other one seems too fat."

"He might have gained weight," Jin offered helpfully, getting into the spirit of this.

"Show her scans of a hundred fellows," said Roic, "or even ten, and I doubt she'd be able to tell, m'lord. You're leading your witness."

"If we had to look at the entire pool of elderly gents of thirty on Kibou, that would doubtless be true," said Miles-san. "Fortunately, we have some other sorting constraints." He pointed at round-face. "This Dr. Leiber is an obstetrician at a replicator clinic in a northern suburb." His finger swung to bony-face. "*This* Dr. Leiber is a biochemist working for NewEgypt Cryonics. Given that Mina's witness does not positively eliminate him, that combination puts him at the top of my to-do list."

"What happened to your theory that the fellow must have fled?" asked Roic. "This Leiber doesn't look much like an activist. I mean—good salary, stock options, cryo-insurance. A company man, belike."

Miles-san sat back and rubbed his chin. "That is a problem, true. Maybe I was wrong, before."

Roic gave him a head-tilt, which induced a fleeting grin on Miles-san's face for no reason that Jin could see.

Johannes and Raven-sensei had finished their task at the table and taken over the satellite comconsole. Now Raven-sensei said, "Ah! Is there a face scan of her? I have fingerprints and footprints for back-up, but—no, we're not going to need them, are we."

Miles-san shoved his chair back with his feet and swung around. "What have you found over there?"

Roic bent and peered. "Aye, that does look like our woman, doesn't it? Look at her cheek bones. And her ears. And that same mole above her left eyebrow. This scan must have been taken pretty near the time she was frozen."

"Can't say as I'd noticed her ears..." Miles-san grabbed his cane and stood up to get a better view.

Jin wriggled in to look, too. Comparing the picture of the live, smiling woman with that still, alien figure they'd seen on the treatment table made him queasy all over again. Would his mother look all strange like that if she died for real?

"Good, this file has it all," said Raven-sensei. "Biographical data, medical history, date of cryoprep... well, her contract and her financial data would seem to be cross-referenced elsewhere. Alice Chen, poor unlucky woman. I suppose I'm glad to know her name."

"That was fast work," said Miles-san. "Good job."

"These patron data bases are pretty open to the public," said Johannes, though he straightened a little at the praise. "Anyone from lawyers to academics doing demographic studies to medical researchers to just genealogists scouting their family trees can get in." He sat back, staring into the screen of data the vid plate had flung up. "Looks like she was frozen about forty-five years ago. That's lucky. You get back more than about a century and the data banks tend to have holes, from one cause or another."

"Yeah, when I was, uh, working in my prior career, this planet used to be a favored source for untraceable false ID's," said Miles-san. "It was the only reason I'd ever heard of the place, before this investigation." He squinted and pointed to a line. "What the devil's that unpronounceable polysyllable?"

Raven-sensei looked. "Debilitating blood disease. Might have been why she chose to freeze a bit early."

"Cause of death, do you think?"

Raven-sensei shook his head. "No, it shouldn't have affected her revival. She would have needed treatment later, though."

"Could she have had it? Effective treatment, that is?"

"Oh, yes, that one's under control these days."

"So what," said Miles-san, "was a woman frozen nearly half a century ago doing in Lisa Sato's cryo-drawer with Lisa Sato's ID tag on her foot? It's plain she didn't get there by herself. While someone could have just cooked the drawer file numbers in the data banks, that damn tag pretty much guarantees it must have been a physical switch."

"Where are your Madame Chen's remains now, by the way?" said Consul Vorlynkin. "They really ought to be returned to her next of kin at some point. There may be an inheritance tied up, or who knows what. And her death is recent enough that someone still alive may have an emotional interest in her fate." He hesitated. "Not that I'm looking forward to the lawsuits."

"She's tucked away downstairs at Madame Suze's, for now," said Raven-sensei. "Tenbury helped out."

"Will she keep?" asked Miles-san.

"Indefinitely."

Miles-san opened his hand to Vorlynkin. "Keep she must, till I've untangled all this. But hold that thought. So, now we have two ends, our straying dead lady and Dr. Leiber. It remains to follow them up and see if they meet in the middle. Was she frozen by NewEgypt, by the way?"

Johannes scrolled down. "By one of the cryocorps that New-Egypt later took over, I think."

"On that same site?"

"I don't think it was built out there yet, forty-five years back." Johannes bent to a flurry of searches. "Ah, here we go.

The place she was originally kept seems to have been decommissioned about ten years ago. Torn down. They moved her out to the new facility at the Cryopolis then."

"That would certainly have made it easy for someone to swap her out," said Miles-san. "Especially if the swapper was already on the inside, like an employee. I'm thinking Madame Chen was chosen at random. Who they *wanted* was Lisa Sato."

"Are you saying somebody *stole* Mommy?" asked Mina, a quaver in her voice.

"It's beginning to look that way..." Miles-san narrowed his eyes at the vid screen.

Vorlynkin's grip on his shoulder and exasperated head-jerk toward Mina returned Miles-san's attention to her. She looked like she was trying not to cry.

Miles-san made quick revision. "Although you have to figure, whoever took her had to care about her. You don't steal something you don't value. Suggests they would be careful with her."

Grownup lies? On the whole, Jin liked that Miles-san didn't talk down to him and Mina, but this was all just too weird.

As Mina failed to look encouraged, Miles-san babbled on, "After all, the portable cryochamber I was in was *lost* for a time, but it all came out right in the end."

"Lost from your side's point of view," said Raven-sensei. "From our point of view, it was found."

Miles-san gave Mina a big *There, see?* sort of smile, which faltered at her blank stare. Vorlynkin and Johannes were gazing at him in horrified fascination.

Miles drew himself up. "I'm going to go talk to this Dr. Leiber. In person. Not at his work, I think," he added, his voice slowing in thought.

Roic's mouth set in a grim line. "You *will* have a proper security perimeter."

"Certainly. We'll even take Johannes, so you won't have to be the perimeter all by yourself."

"It's a start."

Miles-san studied Mina, who was still shifting fretfully. "The connection between Dr. Leiber and your mother exists nowhere in the records I've seen so far—only in your witness, Miss Mina. If anything comes of it, it will be entirely due to the valuable intelligence you supplied."

She cheered a little at this, or at least her lip stopped quivering. "Really?"

"Really. And valuable ImpSec informants get paid, you know. So do couriers, I am reminded," he added with a glance at Jin.

"But I didn't finish the job," said Jin.

"Capture by the enemy rates hazard pay, actually."

"How much?" asked Mina, brightening a lot more.

"Ah, I like the way you think, kid. There's actually an official pay schedule. In Barrayaran marks, of course. It has codes for various services. I'll have Roic check it, and do the conversions to Kibou-daini money."

"You propose to pay them *adult* rates?" asked Vorlynkin. Jin thought he sounded more startled than disapproving, and hoped he wouldn't try to talk Miles-san out of this wonderful idea.

"Damn straight." Miles-san added, "My case budget allows for a lot of discretion, you know."

"Then I wish you'd buy some," snapped Vorlynkin. He shut his mouth abruptly, as if startled at what had fallen out of it.

Miles-san merely grinned at him. His stiff consul-face back in place, Vorlynkin shepherded Jin and Mina back up to the kitchen to feed them again. Jin glanced back over his shoulder at the four men turning intently back to their comconsoles, as that heavy door swung shut. He hoped the consulate had *good* spy stuff.

Chapter Thirteen

D r. Seiichiro Leiber proved to live in a rented row-house in a residential district on the west side of Northbridge, not far from his work. Miles had Johannes, driving the lift van, circle the block to give him a feel for the neighborhood. On this pleasant weekend morning, not a few folks were out tending their tiny plots of greenery; a gang of children raced noisily across the lawns, got yelled at by a gardener, and vanished, giggling, around the corner. Jin and Mina might well have grown up in a place much like this.

Miles's more focused researches last night had mainly turned up Leiber's school records, with police records drawing a bland and virtuous blank. He wasn't listed on any of Lisa Sato's rosters of supporters or contributors, nor did his name appear among the arrestees at the rally riot, most of whom had been released without being charged. Charges had been made but later dropped against the two dead and the three, including Sato, who'd been suspiciously frozen. All tidy and quiet now.

This Dr. Leiber had acquired his Ph.D. at the unprecocious age of twenty-eight, and gone directly into employment with NewEgypt for the four years subsequently. His thesis, which Miles had read—well, skimmed—had focused on improvements in cryonics fluids, which, given that a consortium of cryocorps had funded his scholarship, seemed perfectly reasonable. Several of the larger cryocorps maintained research departments that, in addition to overseeing quality control, worked on proprietary advances in their procedures designed to lure customers from their competition. Nothing odd about that, either.

Miles had Johannes pull up at the corner. "I think our biggest problem here is going to be nosy neighbors, not electronic surveillance. You aren't going to be able to sit or stand around without people coming out to see what you're up to. So I'll run an open comlink to you, Johannes"—Miles set his to *record* while he was at it—"and you find a place to pull in and buy coffee or something. Drop Roic around back on the way." Miles eyed his bodyguard, dressed fairly neutrally but not quite locally. "I wish we could disguise you as a lamp post or something."

"I'll manage," said Roic.

Miles nodded, waved Raven to follow him, and descended to the sidewalk.

The door buzzer was answered by a dark-haired, blinking fellow with a tea mug in his hand, wearing a T-shirt and trousers, barefoot. Despite the weekend jaw shadow and lack of a lab coat, he was immediately recognizable as Miles's quarry.

Miles smiled. "Dr. Leiber?" Not giving the man time to answer, he continued, "My name is Miles Vorkosigan, and this is my associate, Dr. Raven Durona of the Durona Group."

A flash of recognition crossed Leiber's face at the latter name, followed by puzzlement. "Durona?" said Leiber. "From the Escobar clinic?"

"Oh, you've heard of us?" Raven smiled sunnily.

"I read the journals."

Miles forged on, "We were both in town for the inter-Nexus cryo-conference last week, and hoped to see you. May we come in?" Leaving implied that the *associate* was *bio-research*. Miles would save the insinuation of *interstellar cops* for after they'd made it through the front door, and only if needed.

At this reasonable-sounding explanation, Leiber gulped down his last swallow of tea and gave way. Miles hustled gratefully inside. He let his host guide them into his little living room, and took a seat promptly, the harder to be dislodged. The others naturally followed suit. "Did you attend the conference? I don't recall seeing you." In fact, Miles had checked—Leiber hadn't been there.

"No, but I was sorry to have missed it. Were you fellows caught up in that mess I saw on the news with the N.H.L.L.?"

"I wasn't, but Raven here was—" Miles gave Raven a go-ahead, and Raven supplied a few ice-breaking anecdotes about his brief adventures as a hostage, with the Barrayaran connections downplayed. Raven then went into a technical riff about the conference, drawing Leiber into questions in turn, equally divided between biochemistry and scurrilous gossip. He also touched on Leiber's thesis, which Raven had actually read all the way through last night without his eyes glazing over. By this time Leiber seemed fully at ease.

Miles decided on a direct approach. "I'm actually here this morning on behalf of the next-of-kin of Lisa Sato. I believe you had some dealings with her eighteen months ago, just before her arrest?"

Shock and dismay bloomed unconcealed on Leiber's face. Well, he was the scientist type, not a con artist, nor, probably, a very good liar. *Fine by me.*

"How do you know—what makes you think that?" Leiber fumbled, confirming Miles's judgment.

"Eyewitness testimony."

"But no one saw—there wasn't—but Suwabi *died.*"

"There was one other."

Leiber gulped and seemed to pull himself together. "I'm sorry. It was an awkward time. A frightening time."

Miles prepared to utter something soothing, but his witness leaped to his feet. "I'm sorry, you've rattled me a bit. Some tea. I'll fix some more tea. Would you like some tea?"

Miles would rather not have given him time to invent lies, which they would then have to spend more time pulling apart, but he was already headed to his tiny kitchen. Miles waved an assent that Leiber didn't even look back to see.

Raven raised an eyebrow at Miles. "Congratulations."

"Indeed, a hit, a palpable hit."

Dishes rattled, water ran. A faint squeak and quiet tick of a door opening and closing...

"Whoops." Miles grabbed his cane and lurched to his feet.

The kitchen was empty, silent but for the simmering electric kettle. Only one door led out. Onto the patio, its alley gate swinging.

Miles lifted his wristcom to his lips. "Roic? Our suspect just ran out the back."

"I'm on him, m'lord," Roic said grimly.

The thump of big footsteps, quick gasps. A yelp, not from Roic. More footsteps. "*Crap.*"

That last had been Roic. "What happened?" Miles demanded.

Roic, a little breathless, returned, "He just dodged into a neighbor's place. Gone to ground. There's a woman and two kids staring at me out the glass. Now she's arguing with Leiber. Well, she's arguing, he's wheezing." And, after a moment, "You *don't* want me to go in there. Trespassing. Assault."

Roic's very firm tone of voice discouraged Miles from descanting on diplomatic immunity. He continued, "Now she's gone off. To call the police, I'm guessing. What did you two do to the fellow?"

Nothing was plainly not the right answer. "I'm not sure," Miles said. "Well, withdraw for now and rendezvous with Johannes."

"Understood."

Miles turned to Raven. "All right, we have maybe five minutes to go over the place here. You take downstairs, I'll take up."

"What are we looking for?"

"Whatever he's hiding."

Upstairs held a bedroom, a bedroom-turned-office, and a bathroom. An endearingly tame, by galactic standards, porn collection in the bedroom was out in plain sight, suggesting Leiber did not have a girlfriend at present. The closets held clothes and shoes, and a residue of old sporting equipment. Miles was just eyeing the comconsole in the next room in frustration—he likely didn't have time for a stealth download before the locals arrived, and besides the ImpSec devices that made such tasks a snap were back at the consulate—when Raven's voice came from his wristcom.

"Miles?"

"We've got to fly, Raven—I expect the police are on their way by now."

"I don't think he'll have called them, actually." An arresting remark, for all that it was delivered in an amused drawl.

"What have you found down there?"

"Come look."

Miles made his way down the stairs with rather more care than he'd pelted up them, collecting his cane on the way.

The lowest level—it was not quite a basement—of Leiber's townhouse was much as one might expect: a laundry area, the mechanical and electrical guts of the dwelling, a larger room left half-finished for dirty projects or whatever were the owner's needs. Leiber's need seemed to be for a great deal of junk stowage. Raven stood between a dusty exercise machine and a long shape covered with an old bedspread.

"Tah-dah!" he cried, and whisked off the bedspread. Revealing a portable cryochamber. Plugged into the house power. Running, and apparently occupied.

"Do we know what we're both thinking?" asked Raven.

"*Yeah*," said Miles, with proper admiration. "Although . . .

could it be it normal to keep frozen people in your basement? Around here, I mean?"

"Don't know," said Raven, running his hands over the machine in a search for identifying marks. "You'd have to ask Johannes, or Vorlynkin. Or Jin. What *I* wonder is how he ever got it in here."

"Dark of night, at a guess."

"No, I mean how he got it down the stairs. It would never make the turn. There has to be—ah, garage door. That's better." Raven climbed over some junk, opened it, and stuck his head through. "Ooh, nice float bike."

Miles checked underneath the cryochamber. It was a less expensive model, without a built-in float pallet, but it was propped up on stacks of miscellaneous bricks, concrete blocks, and a wedge of squashed flimsies—the top one seemed to be a scientific paper—revealing where a float pallet had been slid out from underneath. No sign of the pallet in the other piles.

He raised his wristcom. "Johannes?"

"I just picked up Roic, sir," Johannes returned at once. "Should we swing around to get you now?"

"One question, first. Do you still have the float pallet on board that we used the other day?"

"Yes, sorry, I haven't had time to return it to the rental place yet."

"Excellent. Come around to the back of the row. There will be a sunken garage entry. We'll meet you there. I have some heavy lifting for you."

"On our way."

Raven raised his eyebrows. "Isn't that theft? Breaking and entering?"

"No, the homeowner let us in. Breaking and exiting, maybe. If it's theft, I'm guessing it's the second time around for this item. And while it's not true that you can't cheat an honest man, crooked men are less likely to complain to the authorities, afterward. I don't think Leiber will tell anyone." He went on, still peering underneath, "Did you spot any IDs on this thing?"

"Maker's mark. It's a common brand. Ah, here's a serial number. That may help."

"Later, yeah." First things first. *If I don't know how to recognize and seize a tactical moment by now . . .* He could be spectacularly wrong. Or spectacularly right. *In any case, it'll be spectacular.*

By the time Johannes and Roic arrived with the van, they had the garage door open. Leaving muscle to do what muscle did best, Miles repaired upstairs to the kitchen and searched for something to write with, and on. A half-composed grocery list and a stylus came to hand. He thought, turned the list over, bent, and scribbled.

Roic came up to find him. "A bit awkward, but we horsed it in. Had to lean on the rear hatch to close it. What are you doing?"

"Leaving Leiber a note." Miles affixed it to the refrigerator door.

"What t' devil . . . ?" Roic bent to read it. "What kind of burglar leaves a *note*?"

Miles was actually rather proud of the vague wording. *Call on me at my consulate at your earliest convenience.* Not even an initial in signature.

"We never finished our conversation," Miles explained. "We now have something he wants. He'll come. Saves putting a trace on him, at least. Damn. Johannes is the only one of us he hasn't seen yet, but I need him for other tasks. You'll be glad to know I now regret not having brought that ImpSec team you always want."

"Cold comfort," sighed Roic. "Why not just wait for Leiber to come back?"

"He won't, not while we're here. If I've guessed right he risked his job, maybe his life, to secure what we found in the basement. He'll be skittish, till he has time to calm down and think it through." *And then he'll be terrified.*

After considerately closing the garage door behind them,

they all piled back into the lift van. "To Madame Suze's," Miles directed Johannes. "Circuitously and sedately."

Raven leaned over the seat back. "You know, if we've just stolen that poor man's grandmother, we're going to be very embarrassed."

Miles grinned, exhilarated. "Then we'll simply return her. Leave her on the lawn after dark. Or maybe ship her back anonymously. No, it would take a lot more than that to embarrass me."

The thought was less amusing when Miles remembered yesterday morning's debacle. He wasn't sure if that noise from Roic was a sigh or a snort, but in either case, he elected to ignore it.

Back when he'd been a young municipal street guard for the town of Hassadar, Roic had undergone first-aid training. Later, after taking the solemn oath of a Count's Armsman, he'd been sent off for a much more advanced course in military field aid. It had included how to do an emergency cryoprep, with practice on a disturbingly realistic and anatomically complete model person and fake cryo-fluid. It hadn't given him nightmares. Helping shift Madame Sato's body onto the procedure table, he wasn't so sure that would remain the case.

Cutting away the protective caul and prepping the still form, Raven and Medtech Tanaka were too professional to permit much embarrassment on the helpless woman's behalf. But she didn't look like the model, she didn't—quite—look like a corpse, and she didn't look alive, either. Maybe no one had a slot in their old ape brain for this. Yet if he ever had to perform a cryoprep for real, God forbid, Roic suspected this experience would help him do a better job, knowing what all those rote steps were aimed at. He was conscious of an odd sense of privilege.

At least m'lord had made damned sure he had the right woman this time, after that unholy mess day before yesterday. Fortunately, he'd stopped short of bringing in those poor kids to ID his new prize last night, after they'd got her to Suze's and unwrapped her. This time around, Jin and Mina hadn't even been told she was found yet. When he'd asked m'lord, *But which is better?* M'lord had replied simply, *Neither.* Which just about summed it up.

Roic tried not to flinch as Raven punched the assorted tubings through thawed skin and carefully seated them in his vessels-of-choice. Roic did start at a brief rap on the door, and turned on his heel, alert.

Consul Vorlynkin stuck his head in. "Lord Vorkosigan, a message came—oh."

"You didn't bring the kids this time, did you?" demanded m'lord, alarmed.

"No, no. Johannes is baby-sitting. They still don't know."

"Whew. Though perhaps you could bring them over soon, if all goes well."

"And if it doesn't?" asked Vorlynkin grimly.

M'lord sighed. "Then maybe I can bring them."

"You can come in," said Raven over his shoulder, "but you have to put on a filtering mask. You can't hang in the doorway like a cat."

Ako hastened to hand Vorlynkin a mask, and helped him adjust it; he grimaced as the memoryseal bonded to his skin. He came cautiously up to the procedure table. "I did wonder what this was like."

"Any problems so far?" m'lord asked. He was perched on a tall stool, partly to oversee the procedure, but mostly, Roic suspected, to block him from pacing.

"Not yet," said Raven. He reached over and started the first flush of warmed, hyper-oxygenated IV fluid. His patient's skin began to turn from clay gray to an ethereal ice-pale. Someone had made an unexpected effort to preserve her long hair, treated with gel and rolled in a wrapping; it lay curled like a snail shell above her shoulder. Ms. Chen's hair had been cropped in a medically utilitarian bob.

Madame Sato was taller than Roic had expected, fully five-foot-eight. That and her dark hair gave her a slight, unsettling resemblance to m'lord's wife Lady Ekaterin, actually, which Roic elected not to point out. Sato's face was a rounder shape, if also stretched over a fine symmetrical scaffolding of jaw and cheekbone, and her body was thinner in a way that suggested stress rather than athleticism. An elf-lady strung out on bad drugs and bad company.

"She's not what..." Vorlynkin stared, mesmerized. "I thought you said she'd look terrible. Skin flaking and bleeding, hair falling out and so on."

"There wasn't a thing wrong with her when they put her in cryo-stasis," said Raven, "and this appears to have been first-class prep, and recent at that. When he arrived on our operating table, Lord Vorkosigan was in much worse shape than average. To put it mildly. I suppose someone has to be better, to keep the average balanced."

"She looks like something out of a fairy tale."

"What," said m'lord, swinging one heel to tap upon a stool leg, "Snow White with just one dwarf?"

Vorlynkin reddened, an *I-didn't-say-that* look in his eyes.

M'lord snickered at him. "Now all we need is a prince."

"So who's t' frog?" asked Roic, secretly glad not to be alone in his fanciful impressions.

"Different fairy tale," m'lord told him kindly. "I hope."

Raven switched tubing, and the clear fluid was replaced with dark red. The ice-woman look slowly changed, the skin tone shifting through faint pinkness like a chill spring to a warmer gold-ivory, as though she was receiving a transfusion of summer. At length, Raven closed the exit line draining from her leg, sealing vein and skin with plastic bandage. Raven and Tanaka fussed about with the leads and wires and the strange cap. "Clear," Raven called, looking up to be sure his amateur audience had stepped back. The snap of the electrical stimulus was quieter than Roic had expected, but still made him recoil.

For the first time, the silent woman's chest rose, and her skin seemed suddenly not just pliable but *alive*. A few moments of uneven stuttering, while Tanaka watched their monitors and Raven stared narrow-eyed at his patient. His face was calm but his gloved hands, Roic noticed, were clenched. Then her lips parted on a longer indrawn breath, then another, and Raven's fists relaxed. Roic remembered to exhale before he disgraced himself by passing out, but only just.

"Got it in one," said Raven, and shut down the external pump.

M'lord's eyes squeezed closed in gratitude. Vorlynkin, transfixed, breathed, "That's astounding."

"I just love this part," Raven confided, to the air generally as far as Roic could tell. "It makes me feel quite godlike. Or at least wizardly."

M'lord's lips twitched. "Are you saying this is an ego-trip for you?"

"The best ever," agreed Raven. "I *live* for these moments."

"Always glad to see a man happy in his work," m'lord murmured.

Raven circled his patient's body, tapping here and there with a stylus in a pattern Roic suspected was meaningful. And very old. "We have reflexes. Peripheral nerves are firing up nicely," he reported. He returned to her head, smoothing a stray strand of hair back from her forehead in a curiously tender gesture. "Madame Sato?" he called. "Lisa?"

The eyelids fluttered, opened, squeezed shut. The lids bore the epicanthic folds of her Earth ancestry, the eyes the classic almond shape. The irises were a rich, dark brown, further reducing her resemblance to Lady Vorkosigan, whose eyes were a striking blue-gray.

"Hearing's working," Raven murmured. "Grossly, at least." And, "Lisa?" he repeated. "Are you with us yet?"

It could hardly be reassuring to the woman to open her eyes on a circle of masked faces, like bandits. Especially if the last thing she remembered were the faces of her all-but-murderers.

Had they been leering? Coolly professional? Indifferent? But bandits indeed, stealing her will, her world, her life from her.

Roic leaned in. In his best reassuring guardsman's tones, he tried, "Ma'am, you're all right. Safe and alive. *Rescued.* Your children are both safe and secure as well. You'll get to see them soon."

Another fluttering of lids; a moan.

"And larynx," said Raven happily. "That should please you, my Lord Auditor."

"Indeed," said m'lord.

She sighed again, the tension passing out of her.

"She'll sleep for some hours, after this," said Raven. "The longer, the better."

"We'll clean her up and move her to the isolation booth," said Medtech Tanaka. "Ako, you can help with the skin treatment."

Tubes and needles were pulled away, lines coiled up, machines turned off. Roic helped shift the *live woman* off the procedure table onto the transfer cart. M'lord slid down from his stool, stretched his back, and leaned on his cane. "How soon till we can move her to the consulate?"

"Depends on her white blood count, and a few other things," said Raven. "But possibly as early as the day after tomorrow. You'll have to keep her quiet in one of those upstairs bedrooms for a few days."

"We can do that," said Vorlynkin.

M'lord turned his head toward the consul. "Wait, why are you here? Has Leiber shown up?"

"No, not yet. You have a sealed message from Barrayar that's arrived in the tight-room. We can't access it, so I don't know how urgent it may be." He added with reluctant honesty, "Also, I was curious how this was going. Given the need to deal with Mina and Jin." He didn't want to be blindsided again, Roic read this. Understandable.

"Ah, all right," said m'lord. "Raven, if you're on top of things here, I guess I can go back."

Raven waved assent and turned to follow the medtech and Ako, trundling his patient away. The room seemed very empty when they'd left, disconsolate and messy like the morning after a winter solstice party.

Vorlynkin blinked and rolled his shoulders, as if trying to come back into himself from somewhere far away. "That was very strange. I've never seen anyone die, but this—it was like watching time run backwards. Or something."

"I have, and yes," said m'lord.

"Were we playing god?" Vorlynkin asked uneasily.

"No more so than the people who put her down in the first place. And our cause is much more just." M'lord added in a mutter, "I hope." Frowning, he fished out his Auditor's seal on its chain for a slightly cross-eyed downward glance. "Sealed message, eh? You know, when I was Jin's age, I'd have been thrilled to own a secret decoder ring. Now I have one, it feels more like a sack of bricks. There's something sadly out of phase about that."

When m'lord limped off to exchange one last word with Raven, Roic found himself briefly alone with the consul, who gazed in bemusement up the corridor after the short, retreating form. "Lord Vorkosigan is not exactly what I expected, when I was told the consulate should prepare for a visit from an Imperial Auditor."

Roic, stoutly, didn't snicker. "The nine Imperial Auditors are actually a pretty varied lot, once you meet them. Lord Auditor Vorthys, who's also m'lady's uncle, looks like a rumpled old engineering professor because that's exactly what he is. There's this crusty admiral, a retired diplomat, an industrialist . . . m'lord's become more-or-less Gregor's galactic affairs expert. The Emperor's uncannily shrewd at matching his Auditors to their cases. Although I suppose we'll have to hit a dud one of these days, he hasn't sent us off-world on a fool's errand yet." Roic actually hoped for a dud case, someday. It could be restful.

"That's reassuring." Vorlynkin hesitated. "I think."

Roic smiled crookedly at the codicil. "Yeah."

❧   ❧   ❧

Back in the consulate's tight-room, Miles saw the address code on his message and relaxed. It looked to be the weekly report from Ekaterin, which explained why it didn't bear any of the usual *urgent* markers. Something nice, amid all this muddle. Reflecting on the difference between *urgent* and *important,* he leaned forward to let his Auditor's seal swing out on its chain, and unsealed the message.

His wife's face appeared, smiling, above the vid plate, and he paused the vid just to get a good look at her. She sailed through her days under such a constant barrage of interruptions, lately, he hardly ever saw her holding still unless she was sleeping. Clear blue-gray eyes raised in a candid gaze, sleek dark hair untouched by frost although she was his age plus a couple of months. Considering that he'd stuck her with four offspring in under six years, her lack of gray hairs seemed increasingly remarkable. They'd all been gestated in uterine replicators, but still. He'd been an only child himself, racked from birth by medical issues now not so much solved as exchanged for new ones. Perhaps—no, make that certainly—he'd underestimated how much work normal healthy children would take, even with all the help his money and position could buy. For there were some tasks you didn't *want* to delegate, because then you'd be missing the best parts.

She was actually staring at a vid pick-up, not at him, he reminded himself, but under the weight of her faintly ironic look he set her back in motion, irrationally guilty at delaying her.

"Greetings, my love," she said. "We've received your latest here with much relief and rejoicing, though fortunately I didn't tell the children about that first alarming message before the second had overtaken it. I shudder to think what your parents went through during your old career. Though I suppose your father kept his high-Vor upper lip suitably stiff, and your mother, well, I can scarcely imagine. Said tart Betan things, I suppose."

Actually, he'd dodged those issues during his covert ops days by almost never sending any messages, or updates. It wasn't as if his father couldn't have demanded a report on his missions from the head of ImpSec any time he wanted one. *Or nerved himself to it,* he imagined his mother's voice remarking tartly.

Ekaterin swung into a crisp recounting of a few Vorkosigan District matters, before the news from his household, always first things first—if ever she put matters the other way around, he'd know to be really alarmed for his family. He was reminded that he was neglecting duties down in the District, as well, although this week there did not seem to be anything that called for an urgent message to his—his father's, really—voting proxy in the Council of Counts. But both his parents were off tending to the Emperor's business on Sergyar, viceroy and vicereine respectively, and had been for some years.

A fine tradition of neglect of one's own in service to the Imperium, those Vorkosigans. At a cost. Miles recalled with a touch of wry pride what a District village speaker had once said to him of Ekaterin: *We feel as though you belong to the Imperium, but Lady Vorkosigan belongs to us.*

Indeed.

"On the home front," Ekaterin went on, "here's the latest achievement..."

The vid cut to another, less steady. "Good job, Helen," said Ekaterin's voice as a room spun dizzily—the library at Vorkosigan House, Miles recognized despite its rabbiting speed, "but pan more slowly or you'll give your papa vertigo."

"What's vertigo?" came a young voice from off-side—Sasha? no, Lizzie, good heavens—and Ekaterin responded at once, "Dizzy."

"Oh." The new word was duly accepted.

The vid steadied on Taurie, ten months old, gray eyes wide under a mop of wispy black curls, clinging grimly to the edge of a low table. Sasha, five going on six, as he and his twin, Helen, phrased it, and their sister Lizzie, three, sat on a couch in the background, Sasha watching with interest, Lizzie looking bored and kicking her feet, as if to say, *I've already done this, what's the fuss?*

"Come on, Taurie," Ekaterin's voice cooed. "Come to mama." Effective—Miles undertook not to fall through the vid plate, reaching for that seductive voice.

Taurie turned, rocking, on her stout little legs, releasing one hand, which waved for balance. Then the other. Then began a bow-legged toddle toward her mama's outstretched arms. How any child learned to walk while swaddled in a diaper, Miles didn't know, but there she went, thump-thump-thump, to fall chortling into Ekaterin's arms and be swung high in triumph.

"Let *me* try her," said Sasha, much as if his little sister were a robot car. He slid to his knees on the rug across from Ekaterin, and called encouragingly, "Come on, Taurie, you can do it!"

Fresh from her first victory, Taurie screeched and toddled toward him even faster, promptly falling on her chin and setting up a wail, clearly more of outrage than pain—Miles could discern the different timbres while still lunging up from his sleep. Sasha gathered her up, laughing. "Hey, you're supposed to learn to walk before you run!" He got her turned around and aimed back toward her mama, and the trial was repeated more successfully.

Lizzie, who had slid down off the couch during all this, gave up spinning herself in circles singing, "Vertigo, vertigo, vertigo!" and made a grab for the vid recorder, which, judging from the way the view jerked wildly, her elder sister promptly raised out of her reach. "No, *I* wanna run the vid now," came Lizzie's voice. "Let me, let me! Mama, make her let me...!"

Too soon, the domestic drama came to an end. Miles backed it up and re-ran it, wondering if these were indeed Taurie's first steps, or a reenactment for his benefit. The vid recorder suggested the latter.

Ekaterin's face returned against the cluttered background of her third-floor office, the one on the north side overlooking her Barrayaran garden through the Earth-import treetops.

"I'm so sorry Sergeant Taura never lived to see her name-sake," she said, looking reflective, "but I'm glad you were at least able to tell her about Taurie, before the end. Maybe we should have given her name to Lizzie, sooner, rather than your Betan grandmother's. Oh, speaking of names. Sasha has now announced that he is Alex, I suppose because he gave up trying to talk everyone into Xander. Lexie and A.A. appear to be permanently rejected, now, too. Same rationale—if we don't call him Aral because of Grandda Aral, we shouldn't call him Sasha because of Grandpa Sasha, either. He seems to be stick-ing to this one, however, and he has Helen on his side at last, so in your next message, be sure to call him Lord Alex. That much logic and determination should be rewarded, I think."

Indeed. Miles had been deeply alarmed, earlier in his father-hood, by what seemed Sasha's—Alex's—delay in verbal devel-opment, compared to his age-mate Helen, till Ekaterin had pointed out that the boy's sister never let him ask a question for himself or get a word in edgewise after. He wasn't delayed, merely amiable, and had caught up with complete sentences soon enough thereafter, as long as Helen wasn't in the same room translating for him.

"Come to think of it," Ekaterin went on, "didn't you once have some trouble deciding what you wanted to be called? And at a much older age. History does not so much repeat as echo, I suppose.

"But he loves you, whatever he's named. We all do. Take care out there, Miles, and hurry home when you can." The vid went dark.

If only I could crawl through that vid plate and have myself beamed back to Barrayar at the speed of light . . . Miles sighed. All his life, his home had been something he couldn't wait to escape. How had his polarity become so profoundly reversed?

Roic's remark stung: *If only you'd quit while you were winning . . .* Well, this tangle on Kibou-daini wasn't all of his own making.

He wished Leiber would show the hell up. *Now* would be

a good time. Miles was surprised he was taking so long. He might have to send someone to collect the man after all. Or if Lisa Sato woke up with temporary cryo-amnesia, or simply didn't know the answers. *No, she has to know whatever Leiber knows. Because I'd bet Betan dollars to sand he's the one who told her in the first place.*

Leiber's evident alarm niggled at Miles. *Why should he have been so afraid of us? He didn't even* know *us.* Leiber was obviously responding to some local threat, perhaps the very one that Miles wanted to know all about. But Miles was still having some trouble guessing what it might be.

Just as Sato was bait for Leiber, the pair of them would be bait for...who? Why? Miles had staked people out like goats to draw the tiger *du jour* in the past, but not, knowingly, when they had children in tow. *Or had you just never noticed their webs of relationships, before?* He couldn't remember. But if he didn't have the personnel here to chase down Leiber, he surely didn't have the personnel to put a round-the-clock guard on the consulate and the people it sheltered. Roic and Johannes between them weren't enough, even if they hadn't had other duties—handing the task to them without support would be downright abusive. Raven wasn't the only one who didn't like being set up to fail.

Despite the distance it put between him and his family, Miles felt a little shiver of gratitude to Gregor for sending him so far afield on his sporadic Auditorial labors. Because it put that same distance between his family and whoever his investigations managed to piss off. *Pissing off bad guys for the greater glory of Barrayar, that would be my job description, just about.* Speaking of being happy in one's work.

He bent to the comconsole and began composing an Auditorial requisition to the Barrayaran embassy on Escobar for a security team, to be dispatched immediately, with a heads-up to put an ImpSec forensic accountant and, perhaps, legal team on stand-by. He knew nothing of his invisible enemy but that they played for keeps. *Five days for the squad to get here, at their best speed.* Had he known enough, five days ago, to ask for this? *I suppose not.*

Miles called up the background data on NewEgypt Cryonics once more, and began to slog through it. Lisa Sato could not regain her voice soon enough.

Chapter Fourteen

B y mid-morning of the day after Madame Sato's successful
revival, when Dr. Leiber still hadn't contacted the consulate, m'lord allowed as how he might have been mistaken, and
dispatched Roic and Johannes to find the man. Roic thought
it might have made his job easier if m'lord had come to that
conclusion earlier. He began with the two obvious first ploys,
calling the man's residence—no answer—and his work, where
he learned that the researcher had called in sick the morning
before, some stomach bug, he'd told his assistant, and he'd likely
be out for a couple of days. *Right.*

Roic then had Johannes pack up some of the consulate's better surveillance equipment and drive him back out to Leiber's
townhouse. A complex under construction that had caught
his eye the previous trip did so again, as they passed. Roic
cranked his head around to study the sign. *Century Estates*, it
read, and *Were you born between 150 and 130 years ago? See
us!* "What's that all about?" he asked Johannes.

"A generational cohort enclave," said Johannes. "You see them here and there in the bigger cities. Revives, at least those who wake up with enough money and health for it, often find they don't like the new Kibou so much after all, and end up clustering together trying to recreate their youths."

"Huh," said Roic. "A sort of do-it-yourself historical reenactment? At least you'd have someone to talk to who gets all your jokes."

"I guess," said Johannes, a little doubtfully.

Roic had Johannes pull in the van at the back of the house row while he tried Dr. Leiber's front door. No answer. After a few minutes Johannes opened it from within. "He left the garage unlocked. Float bike's gone."

"Right. Let's take a look around, then visit his comconsole."

No room, closet, shower, cupboard, or dustbin large enough to hold a body did so. M'lord's thoughtful burglar's note was gone from the refrigerator, which was still stocked with an assortment of bachelor rations. The kitchen was tidied, the bed upstairs more-or-less made, or at least the quilt pulled up. Clothes and shoes might have been taken—enough to fit in a duffle strapped to the back of a float bike?—but there was still a good bit left. Toiletries were absent.

Johannes had started on Leiber's comconsole, sucking a copy of its contents through the umbilicus of the secured cable onto his ImpSec recorder, watching the progress on his holoscreen.

"Hey!" he said after a moment. "This thing is monitored. I wonder if Leiber knew that?"

Roic leaned in. *Hey, indeed!* "This process won't stir up his watchers, will it?"

"It shouldn't," said Johannes.

Not very reassuring. "Can you trace the bug?"

"Partly. I might be able to finish the job from the tight-room."

"Give us a look at his communications over the past two days, since our first visit."

There were only three. Yesterday morning, Leiber had called

in sick, purchased a jumpship passage to Escobar, and emptied most of his remaining savings account onto a couple of universal credit chits. There were no personal messages to relatives or friends. He might have left a door key or instructions with the folks next door, Roic supposed, but on the whole he thought not, and he was unwilling to go stir up trouble by asking around. People might remember their visit from day before yesterday. He wondered what tale Leiber had told his neighbor lady about them. Not the truth, he suspected.

"This jumpship doesn't leave till tomorrow evening," Johannes pointed out.

"Yeah, I see."

"Think he might have gone aboard already?"

Roic frowned at the schedule. "Ah. No. That one doesn't even make inbound orbit till this afternoon." He thought a moment. "The minute he passes inside shuttleport security, he's back on the grid, lit up for anyone who can look. And if we can spot him then, belike his enemies can, too—I don't think they're operating on a shoestring, not if they're backed by one of those cryocorps. He'll wait to the last to board. So he has to have gone to ground somewhere."

"With a friend, maybe? Could be hard to find." Johannes squinted at the comconsole. "Although this could help."

"If he's in as much fear for his life as this flight suggests, he might not want to endanger a friend," said Roic slowly. "He didn't strike m'lord as the ruthless type, he said."

"It's a big city," observed Johannes.

"So, let's start with the obvious." Roic climbed to his feet. "Pack up here and drive us out to the shuttleport."

In the lift van, Roic opened its—ImpSec secured—comconsole and ran a search on lodgings around the shuttleport. Two were inside the security perimeter, half a dozen scattered in the surrounding light-industrial area. He balanced *closest* against *cheapest*, and decided to start with *cheapest*. As they threaded their way to it, he had time to reflect on how Nexus-wide transportation tech had shaped the cities it served, giving more sameness planet to planet than he'd expected, before he'd ever left Barrayar. *This provincial boy's come a long way.* In a way, he was glad no good fairy had ever endowed him with the future he would have picked for himself when younger. It would have been so much smaller.

"Now what?" asked Johannes, as they swung into the budget hostel's lot. "Stake the place out? Ask at the front desk?"

"Not sure anyone would remember Leiber even if they saw him," said Roic, "and this is one of those self-serve places." Not as cramped as some Roic had encountered on space stations, where sleep cubicles, rented by the hour, seemed a cross between a closet and a coffin, but the building's utilitarian lines didn't invite lingering. It was a shadowed place even in the mid-morning, huddled down below a long concrete road abutment and some sort of manufacturing plant. "Circle the lot. We'll look for his float bike."

Around the building's back, an open-faced shed sheltered a float bike lock-down. Roic recognized Leiber's bike nestled among half a dozen others.

"Right the first time!" said Johannes, in a tone of admiration.

"I've had some practice, trailing m'lord around," said Roic modestly, leaving out the *dumb luck* part. Well, smart luck, perhaps. Roic would have been surprised not to have turned up something within his first three tries. They sat in the van for a few minutes while Roic tried to think it through the way m'lord would. No, scratch that idea. He'd likely do better trying to think it through like Leiber. Or better still, like Roic.

Would the enemy send cops or goons to collect their quarry? If it was a cryocorp, they could likely get all the cops they wanted—charges of employee theft would do the job—they had only to wait at the pinch-point inside the shuttleport and pick the man off as he scurried through. But that would leave a trail, names, security vid recordings, a whole lot of witnesses not under anyone's direct control. A private goon squad pick-up before Leiber hit the port, that would be the quieter way to go about it. And if Roic could figure out where to look for the fellow, presumably all those smart men in the fancy trousers could, too. Roic wasn't the part of his team born with the silver tongue in his mouth—could he persuade Leiber to come to the safety of the consulate, when m'lord had not? *Guess I'll have to try.* He glanced up. "What's that?"

A pulsing blue light was reflecting off the concrete wall, coming from the front of the building.

"Blue's the color they use around here for emergency vehicles," said Johannes uneasily.

"Pull around front."

They arrived to see a pair of emergency medtechs dressed in blue scrubs yank a float pallet from the back of an unmarked van and hurry inside the sliding glass doors to the lobby. Both big fellows—one was tall, and the other looked as though he'd had some of those traditional wrestlers in his family tree. On both sides. Didn't emergency services usually try to pair a woman in such a team? Well, not always, belike. With round the clock scheduling, as Roic knew from grappling with the guardsmen's roster for Vorkosigan House and m'lord's other two official residences, you took whatever combinations you could get.

"Wait here." Roic slid out of their own van and went to take a peek in the back of the other. The rear doors had no windows, but had been left unlocked. Careless of the techs, if it was carrying drugs and expensive equipment. Roic quietly opened a door, looked inside, and raised his wristcom to his lips. "Interesting, Johannes. The cupboard is bare. This isn't an ambulance, just a van."

"Uh-oh."

"Think I'll just take a stroll inside and intercept those fellows coming out. You watch my back from there." Roic still wasn't *sure* what was happening, here, although he was formulating some rapid guesses.

An anxious young lady desk clerk was peering up the central hallway when Roic entered the lobby.

"What's going on?" he asked.

"One of our guests reported in very sick, apparently. He should have called the front desk—we would have assisted him..."

"Was he from off-world? D'you think he might have brought in something bad?" asked Roic. "Contagious?"

"No, no. Some sort of sudden seizure, I gather. He was lucky he could use his wristcom." The clerk gathered her nerve. "I should go and lock up after them, make sure the gentleman's property is secure." She glanced back at Roic. "Were you checking in, sir? There's only me on duty right now..."

"Take your time. First things first." Roic waved her away. She trotted off up the hall to where a loaded float pallet was already being shifted out a doorway and turned. The tall man hitched an IV to a pole, bent, and checked his patient. Roic glimpsed a blanketed male form, firmly strapped down, an oxygen mask in place across his face muffling his moans. Roic stepped forward, radiating curiosity and concern, as the pallet floated out into the lobby flanked by its two escorts.

Dr. Leiber blinked up with bleared eyes and groaned behind his plastic mask.

"What happened?" Roic asked, following along out the front doors. "Is it anything dangerous? Do you need any help?"

"Thanks, no," the tall one told him. "Everything's under control."

"So was it a heart attack?"

"We don't know, yet," said the tall one. "He just collapsed."

"Drugs? Is this a bad area? I just landed, myself." For once, Roic's not-from-around-here looks and accent worked in his favor. "I was about to check in at this place and sleep off the jump-lag, but now I'm not so sure."

The broad one scowled at him in irritation. "No, it's fine. Go check in." The pair swung the van doors wide and slid the pallet aboard, both climbing inside to secure it.

Roic stuck his head in after. "You sure?"

"Yes, it's safe," said the tall one, exasperated, from the windowless cargo area.

"Good," said Roic, pulled his stunner, and shot them both.

That would save some heavy lifting. And scuffling. Roic hated scuffles. Just because he was big didn't mean he liked getting hurt.

Johannes's breathless voice sounded from his side, not his wristcom. "What the *hell* is going on?" When Roic had said *Watch my back,* he hadn't meant from this close, but he couldn't fault the lieutenant for curiosity. Johannes's eyes widened, peering into the shadows.

Roic tucked his stunner away in its shoulder holster. "We just rescued Dr. Leiber. I'm not sure if he'll see it that way, though." He climbed into the cargo area, first checking both his victims for health. Stunner fire was by no means safe; it could trigger all sort of problems in people with underlying medical issues. Happily, these two seemed extremely fit. Having assured himself of their continued cooperation by the simple means of a light repeat stun to the base of each neck, he arranged them more tidily. He then turned to Leiber.

Roic was not called upon after all to trot out his encouraging *We've saved you, be grateful, I'm taking you to a place of refuge* speech, in which he had no faith; Leiber had lost consciousness. Roic hoped to hell it had just been a hypospray of knockout drugs, and not some deadly poison. Even if some bloody and secret murder was planned, if he were Leiber's enemy he'd sure want him alive to question under fast-penta first. Actually, Roic wanted to question Leiber under fast-penta on his own behalf. That decision would be up to m'lord, though.

Leiber's breathing continued evenly, and his skin did not turn any alarming colors. All right so far.

"Follow me to Madame Suze's place," he instructed Johannes. Dr. Durona would be there, among other useful amenities. He thought a moment. "No, better—*lead* me to Suze's."

He locked the back of the van, doused its flashing lights, and followed Johannes in convoy out of the parking lot. Roic wondered if m'lord's approach to life, or at least to his Auditorial investigations, was rubbing off on him. He'd never used to be this cavalier about due process. It was hard to tell, sometimes, if m'lord's style was the result of single-minded dedication to duty, habits of overweening Vor privilege, or simple insanity. Roic only knew that he had an inexplicable desire to whistle cheerfully, right now.

Instead he raised his wristcom to his lips, called m'lord, and gave a concise précis of his morning's mission, if m'lord's laconic order of, *Roic, go nail that twit* could be so grandly styled.

And then, being alone in the driver's cab, he whistled all the way to Suze's.

His imagination afire with possibilities, Jin sat at the consulate's kitchen table and counted out, again, his share of the money Roic had solemnly distributed to him and Mina at breakfast that morning. Mina had already secreted hers in her backpack upstairs, but she watched him with interest as he reshuffled his stack of currency—five thousand nuyen, more than he'd ever had at one time in his life. Back in the good times, before his father had died, Jin had never been given more than five hundred even for his best birthday.

"What are you going to do with yours?" Mina asked.

"I'm not sure yet. I could buy food for my creatures for months with this. Or get something new. I always wanted to try keeping fish, but Aunt Lorna would never let me, and there was no way at Suze's. You can't cart fish around with you if you might have to go live on the street."

Mina's eyebrows knit. "Do you guess we're going to be here that long?"

Jin hesitated. "I don't know."

"Do you think I have enough for a pony?"

"Where would you keep a pony? You need, like, lots of

terraformed ground, I think. The back garden here's not big enough."

"Aunt Lorna's patio sure wasn't big enough," Mina agreed. "At least Consul Vorlynkin has grass."

Jin tried to picture this. The consulate's patch of back lawn was barely larger than its living room. Nice for a chicken run, but he didn't think it would work for anything much bigger. "Anyway," he said bracingly, "you still have Lady Murasaki. Pony's got four legs, spider's got eight, so she has to be twice as good, right?"

Mina cast him a look of cold scorn. "I'd like to see you try and put a saddle and bridle and stuff on her."

Jin tried to imagine spider-sized tack—knotted thread, perhaps?—and what kind of insect could you persuade to ride a wolf spider? That the spider wouldn't eat? Riding would be a much more exciting sport, he thought, if ponies ate prey like spiders did. Did the consulate have any thread they could borrow...? But before he could pursue the vision further, Consul Vorlynkin and Miles-san came through the kitchen pulling on their jackets.

"Vorlynkin is going to drive me down to Madame Suze's to see about something," Miles-san told them. He and Roic had been spending a lot of time there lately, Jin thought, and come back looking grim and thoughtful, though no one had said why. And Raven-sensei hadn't come back at all. "Yuuichi Matson's here, so you won't be alone. But if any strangers come in on consulate business, you'll need to stay out of the front rooms and hall. Upstairs should be all right, or the back garden, if you don't make too much noise."

"I'll be back directly," Vorlynkin promised.

Mina looked up. "Do you think you'll ever find Mommy?"

"We hope to have good news soon," said Miles-san.

Jin wasn't sure how to interpret that soothing tone of voice. More grownup lies? By her scrunched face, he didn't think Mina was buying it, either.

But what she said was, "Lord Vorkosigan, if you had children you'd give them ponies, wouldn't you? *Not* spiders?"

He looked a little taken aback. "I do and I have. Ponies, not spiders. Although I suppose they could have spiders if they wanted some. God knows we have butterbugs. *Monogrammed.* Didn't I ever show you my pictures?"

And then, to Jin's surprise and growing dismay, he pulled a holocube out of his pocket and proceeded to show off scans of a regular-sized, dark-haired woman—Jin could tell she was regular-sized because there were some shots of the two of them together, and the top of Miles-san's head barely reached her shoulder—and a bewildering succession of children at different ages. Jin didn't quite sort them out till they came to a group shot—a dark-haired boy and a red-haired girl a bit younger than Mina, an infant in the pretty woman's arms, and a leggy toddler in the middle of the pack. *Four* children. He hoped Mina would muster the wit to look interested and not distraught. He still wasn't altogether sure what Miles-san was, but he seemed to have a lot of clout. Even the consul did whatever he said.

"And here's Helen on her pony down at Vorkosigan Surleau—it's a place we have in the country, on a lake—and here's Sasha petting his. Xander. Alex, I mean."

Jin wondered what kind of inattentive father Miles-san was, that he couldn't seem to remember his own son's name. There was only the one boy, after all. It wasn't as if he needed to run down a list till he got to the one who was irritating him, the way Uncle Hikaru had with him and Tetsu and Ken sometimes.

But Jin had to admit, they were very fine-looking ponies, one dappled silvery-gray, the other a glossy dark brown with black socks and mane and tail and a white star on its forehead, both with dark, liquid, friendly gazes, seeming tolerant of their child-admirers. Mina goggled, her mouth dropping open in naked longing. Yah and double-yah—a big place in the *country.* With lots of animals—there had been dogs and cats and birds in the backgrounds of some of those shots, and who knew what creatures lurked in those wooded hills? And fish in a real lake, not just in some little glass tank, and maybe creeping and crawling native marvels living in the streams running down into it—better than Jin had dared to dream.

And all belonging to these *other* children. Children who had a live mother and father, too. What was that line of Uncle Hikaru's? *Them what has, gets.*

And those that didn't have, didn't get, Jin supposed was the unspoken half of that lesson. He looked at those other children, and at Miles-san, so obviously pleased and proud, and didn't doubt that Mina probably felt like crying. His own throat was tight with envy and ridiculous anger. It wasn't as if Miles-san had kept his family a secret on purpose, just to bait Jin so belatedly.

"I wouldn't have dared not teach them to ride," Miles-san went on. "My grandfather's ghost would have haunted me if I hadn't, not that the old buzzard doesn't anyway. The Vor were a military caste, back in the Time of Isolation. Knights, of a sort—or bandits, perhaps, depending on your point of view. Horse soldiers, in any case. It's a tradition." He gave that last word a peculiar emphasis, as if it tasted funny in his mouth. "A perfectly useless skill, nowadays, but we keep it up all the same."

"Perhaps we'd better go," said Vorlynkin, and "Yeah," said Miles-san. He pocketed his holocube carefully, like it was something special to him. They went off through the garden toward the big garage.

Jin and Mina stared at each other.

"Well," said Mina at last. "At least I was right about the ponies." She blinked rapidly, and rubbed her reddened eyes.

Jin glowered down at his little stack of money, which had seemed such a big pile of possibilities just minutes ago.

"It's no good, after all," said Mina. "Maybe it never was. Maybe we should just go back to Aunt Lorna and Uncle Hikaru's."

Stop struggling? "You could, maybe," Jin said bitterly. "Not me. No, wait, you couldn't either—you'd gab."

Mina looked indignant at this accusation. With a "*Huh!*" she rose to go back upstairs. At the archway into the kitchen, she flung back over her shoulder, "*Two* ponies have eight legs, so there!"

Jin couldn't think of a counter-argument to that.

As Jin was fingering his nuyen and wondering if he dared help himself to a snack, the consulate clerk wandered into the kitchen to refill his mug of green tea. He leaned against the counter and stared at Jin, who fidgeted under the cool regard.

"You're Lisa Sato's children, aren't you? The cryo-rights activist?"

"Uh ... yah?" Jin wasn't sure if that was supposed to be a secret here, but Matson-san obviously already knew.

Matson-san took a sip of tea and frowned. "Nobody's really told me anything. But, ah ... if you want me to call the police for you and your sister, before the Barrayarans all get back, I could ... ?"

Jin shot to his feet, almost knocking over his chair, and cried in horror, "No!"

Matson-san sloshed hot tea, swore, set the cup down, and wiped his scalded hand on his trousers.

"It was the police who *took* Mom!" said Jin.

"Call your relatives, then?"

"No! That's even worse!"

"Er," said Matson-san. "So you two kids are not, um, not ... prisoners, here, are you?"

"Of course not! Miles-san is helping us!" He considered events so far, and amended that to, "Trying to, anyway." And then, because that sounded weak and ungrateful, "Nobody else has ever tried like him," which was certainly true.

Matson-san scratched his head and grimaced. "Ah." He took up his tea again. "Well, if you change you mind, you can tell me, all right?" Jin glowered at him in a dismay that made him hold up a placating hand. "Just trying to help, too."

Jin wanted to cry, *If that's your idea of help, don't!* but it seemed too rude a thing to say to a grownup. He settled on, "All right. But I won't. Change my mind."

Matson-san shrugged uneasily and went back out to that front office-room. Jin gathered his money and fled upstairs to hide it away.

With three of the four people he wanted to interrogate at Suze's place still out cold, bless Roic, Miles perforce began with Madame Sato.

Inside the glass-walled, softly-lit isolation booth, she was sitting up in her narrow bed, looking pale and exhausted but on the whole very good for a new revive. She was clean in a crisp patient gown and warmly padded robe, each extra layer of cloth providing protection from exposure both to germs and prying eyes. Miles suspected—no, knew very well—from his own too-frequent hospitalizations that the latter could be more important to one's morale than the former. Ako had washed the gel from her hair; it lay undamaged in a silky fall over her shoulder.

He eased into the booth, wondering if he seemed menacing to her or merely weird. Hard to tell from her stern glare. He adjusted his filtering mask and cleared his throat.

"Good afternoon, Madame Sato. My name is Miles Vorkosigan." He smiled reassuringly, then realized she couldn't see his mouth. "Sorry about the mask. But Dr. Durona says your immune system's coming back fast. We should be able to dispense with the sterile precautions and get you out of here fairly soon."

"Are you a doctor?" Her voice was raspy but functional.

"No, your revival was done by Raven Durona, a specialist from Escobar. Who works for me," Miles realized he'd better add. Explaining himself to her was going to be an uphill slog.

"I saw him earlier." She swallowed—partly nerves, partly still getting used to being back in control of her body, he expected. "Where is here? They said I was in Northbridge." Her tone said she doubted this. Doubted everything, right now.

Miles glanced around. The view from the booth took in only the shadowed, deserted recovery room, which had no exterior windows, not even looking out on the wall of another building. "Northbridge, that's right. You're in an old, decommissioned cryonics facility on the south side, which has been taken over by some rather clever squatters."

"Someone said you have my children..." The tightening of her throat smeared that last word nearly soundless.

Miles now wished he'd brought them along, even though he was still nervy from his prior failure. "Yes, Jin and Mina are safe at the Barrayaran consulate." He added after a moment, when she still didn't seem to know whether to parse this as a comfort or a threat, "Jin has all his creatures there, even Gyre-the-Falcon and your old cat, so he's content for now. Mina is pretty much sticking with Jin." This familiar reference to the traveling zoo would convince her of his veracity, he hoped.

"The Barrayaran consulate! Why?" She swallowed again. "Who *are* you? Why are you here?" She didn't add, *Why am I here?* but Miles thought it was implied.

"What do you remember?"

Her lips clamped shut.

Miles tried again. "The last thing Jin and Mina remember of you is your arrest by the Northbridge municipal police, eighteen months back. Two days ago, my people and I found you frozen in a portable cryochamber in Dr. Seiichiro Leiber's townhouse basement. I'm now trying to close that eighteen-month memory gap. For both of us, I suppose."

That last plainly shocked her; her stare at him shifted from fear and misplaced anger to sheer bewilderment. "What?"

Miles sighed, hitching himself up on the stool at the end

of her bed. An Auditor was supposed to listen, not talk—one of Gregor's wee jokes, was that?—but this woman had earned her briefing. Besides, it was quite likely that Lisa Sato didn't know enough about Barrayar to point to it on a wormhole map. "I expect I had better begin at the beginning. I'm a galactic. My official job title is Imperial Auditor. That's a high-level government investigator for the Barrayaran Imperium. You no doubt wonder what I'm doing on Kibou-daini." Miles wondered himself, some moments. "I was originally sent to check out a smelly situation with a large WhiteChrys company franchise on Komarr—that's the second planet of our empire—" As succinctly as he could, he explained the WhiteChrys scam with the Komarran planetary voting shares, including his successful bribery sting. For the first time, she looked faintly cheered.

"Yes, hit them where they keep their hearts, in their wallets," she murmured with satisfaction. "Although WhiteChrys isn't even the worst of the corps."

"Hold that thought, we'll come back to it. Now I need to explain how I met your son Jin, and found this place..." Necessarily, he backed up to his attendance at the cryo-conference, and the attack upon it by the N.H.L.L.

"Those murderous idiots!" said Lisa Sato, her voice hearteningly enlivened with scorn for someone other than Miles.

"In their defense, they don't seem to have succeeded in killing anyone, this round. If not for lack of trying. I actually feel I owe them—they opened up my case for me in ways I'd have had trouble finding on my own, although I suppose the Komarr scam part would have run on rails regardless. Anyway, after I broke away from them I ended up lost in the Cryocombs..."

That part held her nicely spellbound. Miles had the mother-wit to save most of his embroidering for after Jin had joined his tale, which drew her in fully. She had less trouble following the explanation of Suze's schemes than Miles had, first encounter.

"But why was Jin here?" she asked, at a loss. "I'd left the

children with my sister Lorna. I only thought I'd be gone overnight, maybe a day or two, until I could get a lawyer—eighteen *months*?"

"Do you remember being taken to be frozen? Who did it?"

Her brow furrowed in an effort of recall. "I was in what was supposed to have been a temporary cell, more of a room, really, at the municipal police station. A man came in. I thought he might be from my lawyer. There was a hypospray, then...." She shook her head, then winced. Post-revival headache, no doubt. His had been a doozy.

Hypnotic or knock-out drug, it hardly mattered which she had received. Miles suspected that not even more time to overcome any lingering cryo-amnesia—of which she showed very few signs—would recover anything after that.

"After you were illegally, or in any case extra-legally, frozen, your sister and brother-in-law naturally looked after their nephew and niece. I gather that Jin ran away from your sister due to conflicts over his creatures in her crowded household. Mina stayed on. She was doing well in her second year of primary school"—that seemed a safe assumption—"until I inadvertently caused Jin to be returned to his aunt, and they both ran away together to, well, me." At her *Why you?* look, he added, "Jin can tell you all the details when you see him." Miles hoped Jin was enough of a Barrayaran partisan by now to convey the Lord Auditor's good intentions. Good performance was still to be tested, unfortunately.

"But enough about me." *Let's talk about you.* It had been a very long time, thankfully, since Miles had attempted to pick up a woman in a bar—and even that had been in the line of duty—but his sense of desperate seduction wasn't altogether misplaced. He needed to persuade Lisa Sato to trust him, and quickly. "What was your connection with Seiichiro Leiber, and how did it come about?"

For a long moment he feared she was going to clam up again, but after another cool look, she began, "Seiichiro came to us—to our political action council—with a secret he'd discovered through his work."

"How many times did he visit you?"

"Two or three."

"Who all did he tell? Did he ever meet with all of you?"

"George and Eiko and me, at first. There was one later meeting with all of us, when we planned the rally—George Suwabi and me, Seiichiro, Lee Kang, Rumi Khosla, and Eiko Tennoji."

Those last names were all too familiar to Miles from his researches. "Let me guess. You decided to make a public announcement of the secret at the rally, where things went so wrong."

Her gaze flicked up from her lap to go knife-narrow at him. "It wasn't *our* people who made the trouble. We were hit by a counter-rally—a collection of thugs from the N.H.L.L. They were supposed to have stayed at the other end of the park, that night. We couldn't afford to rent a hall, and neither could they."

"Was it really the N.H.L.L., or could it have been a gang hired to impersonate them?"

"It was really them—I recognized a couple of the fellows involved. Locals."

"Mm, they might still have been employed for the task. Set upon you."

Her head tilted in consideration and half-agreement. "The police broke up the fight. There seemed to be an awful lot of police for the size of the scuffle, and they arrived very quickly. As if they'd already been warned. I saw several people with bleeding heads, or pushed to the ground." The memory seemed distressing; to her, it was literally only yesterday, Miles was reminded. "That's not the kind of protest we *ever* were. I think the N.H.L.L. is like the other side of the coin, literally, from the cryocorps. The N.H.L.L. frets about the money they don't have, the cryocorps fret about money they do have, and neither one cares about anyone's lives but their own."

A shrewd judgment, Miles thought. "May we come back to

Dr. Leiber?" *And his secret.* "He does seem to have been the key man, in several senses."

She regarded him and seemed to come to a decision. "I suppose if you are some sort of bizarre cryocorp spy, you already know. And know that I know." *So what more is there to lose?* hung unspoken.

"For what it's worth, I already have a big pointer in the fact that Dr. Leiber researched preservation solution chemistry for NewEgypt Cryonics."

She gave a gingerly half-nod. "What Seiichiro had discovered was that a certain formulation of cryo-preservative that was on the market a generation or so ago broke down chemically after a few decades. There must be thousands, maybe millions of people who were treated with it locked up in the corps freezers who are truly dead, not revivable. Meaning their votes are void and their assets due to be returned to their heirs. There must be *billions* of nuyen at stake from that alone. And that's without even getting to the vast legal costs, plus all the procedures that will have to be devised to figure out which patrons from that period are which."

Miles blew out a soundless whistle, pieces of his puzzle slotting into place at light speed. *Commodified contracts, indeed!* Oh, he wanted an ImpSec meta-economics analyst to go with the forensic accountant from Escobar, and he wanted them *now*. With all the data-penetrating equipment they could carry, pre-keyed to the peculiarities of Kibou's planetary net.

And he'd order them the moment he was back at the consulate. But for the next few days, he was stuck with his old original organic brain. A used model, at that, sadly battered by all the wear and tear.

What he said out loud was, "Yeah, that would sure account for it all." Including, perhaps, poor Alice Chen, who'd been left by Leiber in Sato's place—as a decoy, or as a clue? Or as a time-bomb?

"We thought this was a revelation that could *truly* jolt the cryocorps' hold on Kibou," said Lisa Sato. "Even break their grip." She stared around her cubicle, down at her lately-thawed hands. "I suppose we were right." Her brow furrowed. "Wait. You mean to say they've still kept this silent for the past year and a half? It wasn't a secret the corps could keep forever— as more and more bad revives turn up from that generation, disproportionately, people are bound to notice the pattern. That's part of why George wanted to strike quickly, for the maximum public impact. Why didn't...oh." She turned suddenly bleak eyes upon Miles, who flinched in anticipation of what was coming next. "What happened to the six of us? Why didn't anyone get the word out, after I was taken away? Were we *all* taken away?"

"I am sorry to be the bearer of bad tidings, Madame Sato, but that's what it looks like. Kang, Khosla, and you were all frozen under questionable diagnoses within a few days of the rally. George Suwabi supposedly crashed his lightflyer into a lake, and Madame Tennoji fell from her apartment house balcony to her death, after excessive drinking. Needless to say, I should think it most interesting to see someone from your police homicide bureau re-open those two cases. Er...*did* she drink to excess?"

She frowned, even paler about the mouth than her revival had left her. "Well, yes. She was in a lot of pain from her joint deterioration. But she didn't fall off of things. Oh, no, poor George...."

"The odd man out in all this is Dr. Leiber. He simply went back to work for the past eighteen months."

"That makes no sense."

"Fortunately, I'm going to be able to ask him about it. When he wakes up."

"Was he frozen, too?"

"Ah, no. He had an encounter with a simple sedative this morning, according to my man Roic. Raven—Dr. Durona, that is—confirms. We've detained him here at Suze's while he sleeps it off. He was trying to leave the planet when Roic picked him up. Somebody else was trying to prevent him, I think. It's going to be an interesting interrogation." Miles hesitated. This was, after all, Jin and Mina's mother. Those two had to have inherited, or perhaps learned, some part of their admirable wits and determination from her. And you couldn't demand trust without giving some in return.

"Would you like to sit in?"

Chapter Fifteen

Miles was itching to get to Leiber, but was diverted by Roic to consider his other captives. Thanks to one of Raven's potions, both now slept peacefully on the floor of an empty office—or possibly abandoned utility closet—adjoining the underground garage of the former patient intake building. Roic had spent the time constructively going through wallets, IDs, and the lift van.

"This wasn't what you might call deep covert ops, here," Roic said, sorting out the wallets to demonstrate. "The van is registered to NewEgypt, and the scrubs they're wearing are company issue. They were carrying all their own identifications. Hans Witta and Okiya Cermak. Johannes did some back-checking. T' one is actually the senior officer for plant security, and t'other used to be a regular guard till eighteen months ago, when he got a big raise in pay and a promotion to *personal assistant* to his chief."

"Interesting," murmured Miles.

"Ayup. I'd say Dr. Leiber's kidnapping was something they put together in a hurry, out of resources they had to hand. If they'd nailed him at work, or anywhere on the NewEgypt properties, they wouldn't even have had to bother with that much. Thing is, now what do we do with 'em? We can't keep 'em sacked out on the floor forever. I mean, you got to let a man pee sometime. And their bosses have to know by now that something went wrong. Catch and release? I figured to set them back in their van not far from Leiber's hotel, and let them wake up on their own."

"Hm. Have you and Johannes rendered the van unlocatable?"

"Of course, m'lord," Roic said, his prim tone adding, *I do my job.*

"But they did see you."

"Unavoidable, I'm afraid. I don't think they saw Johannes, though."

"Is kidnapping kidnappers still kidnapping?" Miles mused.

"Yes," said Roic, unhelpfully.

"Not that NewEgypt is likely to bring charges."

"Naw, they'd do something else."

"I am reminded. I could have Suze freeze and store them for us, I suppose. Technically."

Roic gave him the Look.

"If push came to shove. As a Kibou-daini problem-solving technique, there seems to be precedent."

Roic said nothing, firmly.

"Ah, well," sighed Miles. "Lock the door and let them nap, for now. Onwards."

Working around Madame Sato's bio-isolation proved only a brief challenge. Miles set up his interrogation chamber in the empty booth next to hers, and lent her Raven's wristcom to listen in. With his booth brightly lit, hers not, and the curtain mostly drawn on her side of the glass wall, it was as good as a one-way mirror as long as she didn't move around too much. She understood, if perhaps did not entirely approve, his plan to split the interrogation into two parts, the first with Leiber unaware of her presence, to see if the same story was extracted both ways. Miles wasn't sure when to spring her on Leiber for maximum utility. It would doubtless come to him.

Leiber was still woozy when Raven and Roic guided him into the booth and sat him in a chair. Roic took a wall-propping pose against the door. With no bed, the booth wasn't exactly crowded even with the four of them, but its slightly claustrophobic air was more of a feature than a failing, in Miles's view.

"You again!" Leiber said, staring at Miles.

Raven, with a benevolent air, bent to press a hypospray against Leiber's arm.

Leiber jerked. "Fast-penta?" he growled, looking helpless and angry.

"Synergine," Raven soothed. "That headache should clear right up."

Leiber rubbed his arm and scowled, but, after pressing a suspicious hand to his forehead, blinked in surprise and, in a moment more, belief.

So, and when did you ever have fast-penta, that you can tell the difference? Miles added the question to his long list. Miles waved Raven to a chair against the wall, and took one himself at a not-too-looming distance from his subject. Although to loom properly, he supposed he'd have to stand *on* the chair, which just wouldn't have the same effect. Best to delegate that task to Roic.

"So, Dr. Leiber. We might have saved steps by having this conversation day before yesterday, but I suppose your living room might have been monitored like your comconsole. Maybe it's just as well. Here, I can assure you, we are totally private." Miles smiled toothily. *Imperial Auditor, threat or menace? You decide.*

Leiber's lips moved, *My comconsole!* "Dammit, I thought I'd taken care of that. So that's how you traced me?"

"That's how the two gentlemen dressed in the medical kit

traced you, I imagine. Armsman Roic, here"—Miles waved his hand; Roic nodded amiably—"I'm sorry I didn't get a chance to introduce you two properly earlier—Roic followed them. More or less. And took you away from them. Did you recognize them, by the way?"

"Hans and Oki? Of course. The Gang of Four's pet muscle."

"Highly paid, these coworkers of yours?"

"Oh, yah." Leiber smiled sourly. "And great job security, too."

"As good as yours?"

"Not as far as I know. Lucky for them." Leiber squinted. "Took me away how?"

"Stunner," said Roic.

"That's illegal!"

"No, actually, I have a local permit. Bodyguard, y'know."

Official government bodyguard, in point of fact. Which was as close as Vorlynkin had been able to get to *Armsman* on the Prefecture's application form. Roic had acquired even odder designations in past ventures, true.

"Who the hell *are* you people, anyway?" Leiber sat up indignantly; Roic tensed a trifle. "Did you steal Lisa from me?"

"Her cryochamber is safe," said Miles, truthfully. It was still tucked away down the hall.

"Not for long if NewEgypt's onto me!"

"You're safe too, for the moment. We're holed up in an old decommissioned cryofacility on the south side of town, if you want to know. Out of sight, out of mind."

"Not likely," muttered Leiber, subsiding.

"How about this," said Miles. "I'll tell you what I know, and you tell me what I don't know."

"Why should I?"

"We'll come to that. To start with, I really was a Barrayaran delegate to the cryo-conference."

"You're no doctor. Or academic." Leiber frowned. "Prospective patron?"

Not if I can help it. "No, I'm an Imperial Auditor. A high-level investigator for my government. Among my several tasks here is to study the social and legal problems Kibou-daini faces as a result of its deep engagement with cryonics. I shall inevitably be tapped as an advisor to upgrading Barrayar's admittedly-archaic legal codes, to avoid repeating your mistakes, if we can." Granted, that wasn't his explicit task, but Gregor was bound to think of it sooner or later. Miles shuddered to foresee another few years of arm-wrestling subcommittees from the Councils of Counts and Ministers, just like his last gig about galactic reproductive and cloning technologies. On the bright side, he could go home every night; on the less bright, work would follow him there. . . . "The punishment for a job well done, as it were. But it didn't take long to figure out that the only troubles the conference seriously addressed were the technical ones."

Raven waved agreement.

Miles went on, "The rest was pretty much cryocorps sales pitches. So I went looking on my own."

"For troubles? Well, you've found mine."

"Indeed, and instructive they are."

Leiber hunched, looking offended.

"So far, I've discovered that Kibou's scheme of proxy votes for the frozen, originally devised on the assumption that people would be revived sooner and in greater numbers, has proved a fascinating demographic trap. Still thinking about that one. Also, that a certain brand of cryo-preservative from about a generation ago turned out not to be good for more than about thirty years, and that NewEgypt and presumably all the other corps are sitting on a financial time-bomb of unreviv-able corpses, for which, sooner or later, someone is going to have to pony up. And NewEgypt has gone to great lengths to insure that the someone won't be them."

Leiber went rigid. "How—!"

He'd doubtless twig to how Miles knew in a bit; Miles had no intention of hurrying his thought processes. "I know that you figured this out, that you went to Lisa Sato's political action group for help, and that the result was a riot at their rally that ended with three of her people frozen and two murdered. Did you set them up at NewEgypt's behest?"

"No!" cried Leiber indignantly. But then, deflating, "Not on purpose."

"Betray them for money?"

"No! The bribe came later, just to make it look that way."

Miles hadn't even gone looking for evidence of bribes, yet. *Ah, yes, deliver yourself into my hands, Doctor. You know you want to.* "Then what did happen? In your own words."

Leiber clasped his hands and stared at his feet for so long that Miles began to fancy fast-penta, with or without his subject's permission, but at last began, "It all started about two years ago. I was assigned the problem of figuring out the unusual number of bad revivals we were getting from that era. When I'd narrowed it down to the decomposing cryo-fluid, I went to my boss, who went to his bosses to report. I thought they'd do something about it, I mean, right away, but weeks went by and nothing happened."

"Who were these bosses? Which men were told about this?"

"The Gang of Four? There was my R & D supervisor, Roger Napak. And Ran Choi, the chief operating officer, and Anish Akabane, he's chief of finance, and Shirou Kim, the NewEgypt president. They clamped down and kept the information tight right away.

"They promised me something was going to be done about the problem. I began to figure out they didn't mean the same problem I did when Akabane unveiled his commodified contracts scheme. They weren't trying to do anything about the bad preps, just about NewEgypt's financial liabilities! When I complained to Rog, he told me to pipe down or I'd be fired, and I pointed out that if I were fired, I'd have no reason to pipe down, and he went real quiet, and then he promised me he'd do something. By that time, I didn't trust their ideas about problem-solving one bit.

"I'd been following Lisa Sato on the news for a year or two by then. She seemed to me one of the few people on Kibou who wasn't just arguing about the money. I mean, *moral* arguments, you know?"

Her detractors had certainly been arguing about the money, though, from the bits Miles had seen. The corps claimed her schemes would just set up a rival corp run by the government for the poor, for which everyone would pay. Illogically, they also claimed her scheme would damage their business, but if they weren't taking in those poor patrons anyway, Miles didn't see how they were losing anything. The N.H.L.L. just wanted to set fire to all the metabolically disadvantaged regardless of net worth. Though they certainly wanted to start with the rich, which suggested a certain shrewd efficiency in liberating their hypothesized legacy.

"So I went to see Lisa Sato in person. I didn't even make an appointment over the comconsole, just went and knocked on her door one night. And she was everything I'd hoped she would be! I went again, and gave copies of all the data I had to her and George Suwabi, poor guy, and that's when they came up with the rally speech idea, to release it all at once in a way the corps couldn't quash. I thought it was all fixed.

"A few days later, when I went into work, Rog called me in to his office, and suddenly I was being given a shot of fast-penta. They squeezed everything out of me." He hesitated. "Almost everything. Everything about the rally plan, and then they ran off in a hurry to do something about it. That's where Hans and Oki first got into it, I think—they did the legwork setting up the riot. I think Oki had a relative in the N.H.L.L., actually, which gave them their in."

"Who all was present at this interrogation?"

"All of them. The big four, I mean."

"Was that legal or illegal here? The use of fast-penta on an employee, I mean?"

"Kind of legal. I guess. I mean, they're allowed to use it in suspected cases of employee theft and crimes on the premises and so on. You have to sign a release when you're first employed."

"I see."

"There are rules about how it has to be conducted to make it admissible in court, later. But I don't think they were paying much attention to those in my case. Because the last thing they'd want is for any of this to get to a court. Because *then* they locked me up in Security's holding area."

"Was that also kind-of-legal?"

"They're allowed to hold suspects till the real police arrive. Except, of course, the police never did. By the time they let me out, two days later, it was all over for Lisa and her people." He bit his lip, clenched his hands. "I was helpless. Although not as helpless as the Gang of Four had figured, thanks to Lisa."

"How was that?"

"When I brought her and George the data, she told me to place a copy somewhere secret—lawyer, bank vault, wherever— with instructions to simultaneously release it to a bunch of places—the courts, all the Prefecture departments of justice, the news, the net—in the event of my death, freezing, or disappearance. Which I did."

"And that bought you protection from your bosses?"

"No, they had the location out of me in no time. Thing is, Lisa and George *also* hid copies, and by the time NewEgypt figured this out, they were both . . . well, Lisa was frozen and George was dead. The Gang searched, but they never found the other two copies."

"How do you know?"

Leiber smiled grimly. "I'm still above room temperature and walking around."

"Ah. Reasonable inference." Miles rubbed his lips. "Were Suwabi and Tennoji murdered on purpose, then? By Hans and Oki, perhaps?"

"By Hans and Oki, but I don't think they were told to kill anyone. I think those were attempted snatches that went wrong.

They managed to get Kang and Khosla and Lisa, though." Leiber's lips twisted. "Speaking of job security. Both were given bonuses and raises, after, despite the big screw-ups. I wasn't privy to the under-the-table agreements. They can't turn in their bosses without incriminating themselves, and vice versa. And I think the Four kind of liked the idea of owning their own dirty-work squad. In case they needed someone to handle people like me again.

"Anyway, the impasse bought everyone time to calm down and think, even me. I felt so badly about it all. Especially Lisa. I mean, I'd destroyed everything she'd worked for, even though I was just trying to help. So when I was offered the bribe, I took it, even though I didn't believe it for a minute, because I thought it would pacify *them*." He brooded. "They'd bribed Rog a lot earlier, I think."

"What form did this bribe take?"

"Nothing immediately useful, they knew better than that. It's all unvested stock options that cut in after a certain number of years. I always figured they'd fire me just before they had to pay anything out, but I don't know. They did let me do some real work—I developed a noninvasive scanner test for the bad preps, which wasn't a task they could have assigned to anyone else, after all. The first payment option was due to cut in soon, though, and that's what I set my plan on."

"What plan?"

"To rescue Lisa." Leiber's eyes brightened, and he met Miles's gaze for almost the first time. "It's what's kept me going for the past year and a half." His voice lowered, beseeching. "I *had* to keep my job with NewEgypt in order to have access to her cryochamber, do you see? I realized it practically right away. Originally, I figured to save enough money to rescue them all, Kang and Khosla and Lisa, ship all three cryochambers secretly to Escobar for revival there. But it cost a lot more than I thought it would. Time was drawing on, I thought the Four were finally dropping their guard on me a bit, so I revised the plan to take just Lisa, alone. Take her to Escobar, make the charges against NewEgypt and the whole corrupt system from there, where we'd be safe."

"You've thought about this a lot, I see," said Miles neutrally, and pressed his hand to his lips to prevent the escape of any premature editorials.

Leiber's expression grew almost exalted. "It would have worked! We could have been safe, together. We wouldn't even have had to come back to Kibou, if we didn't want. With my credentials, I could have found a job, supported us both."

A slight, indignant disturbance of the curtain, Miles saw out of the corner of his eye. He carefully didn't turn his head that way.

Leiber cast a speculative look at Raven. "Maybe even a place like the Durona Group." His gaze grew more urgent. "Maybe, if you people could help me, it still could still work out—"

Leiber's heroic visions were abruptly interrupted by the curtain being yanked back, and Madame Sato pounding on the glass and yelling something, alas made unintelligible by the barrier. Miles pointed helpfully to his wristcom.

Leiber nearly fell off his chair. "Lisa!" he cried, whether gladly or in terror Miles wasn't sure.

Madame Sato apparently didn't get the message about the wristcom, because she clenched her fists and whirled to dodge out her booth door, instead. Raven lurched up to intercept her, although only to hastily make her don a filtering mask before their own booth door slammed open—Roic had prudently moved out of the way.

"Seiichiro Leiber, you moron!" cried Madame Sato, which was approximately what Miles had guessed she'd been trying to say, since he'd been hard-pressed not to say it himself. "What were you *thinking*? You were going to *kidnap* me, take me *off-planet*, and *abandon my children*? And trap me there, with no money to get home?"

"No, no!" said Leiber, rising hastily and turning his hands out in pleading. "It wasn't like that! Wasn't going to be like that!"

It had been going to be exactly like that, in Leiber's mind, Miles guessed. A princely rescue, with Leiber in the starring role, and the happily-ever-after, if not planned, at least much wished upon. Had Snow White in her glass coffin ever had a vote? Or a voice?

"Lisa, I know this was all my fault! I was going to make it right, I swear!"

Behind her mask, Miles thought Madame Sato was sputtering, almost beyond words. He could see her point. She snarled, "Make it right? Make it worse!"

Raven put in, "You know, upsetting and stressing a new revive is not good for their immune system. Or any other system."

Some milder exercise than towering rage was indicated, certainly. Strokes were another real possibility in the more fragile revives, Miles dimly recalled. Interested as he was in what more might be squeezed out of Leiber, it was time to intervene.

"Well, his plan is certainly thwarted now," Miles soothed her. "We'll have to see if we can't come up with something rather better." He jumped up and dragged Raven's chair around. "Please, Madame Sato, do sit down. I should be extremely glad of your input, at this point."

Out of breath, Madame Sato sank into the seat, her brown eyes still glaring at Leiber over the top of her filtering mask. Leiber, too, sank down, or maybe his knees gave way.

Madame Sato rubbed her furrowed forehead, a gesture that made Raven frown medically. Her voice drooped in exhaustion along with her body. "If the corps have grown so corrupt and above the law that they can get away not just with theft, but with *murder,* what hope is there left for Kibou?"

"Escape?" Leiber offered.

Her eyes shot sparks of scorn, over her mask. "Leaving my children to be chewed up in this maw?" She drew breath. "Everyone's children?"

Miles said mildly, "NewEgypt hasn't got away with murder yet. In fact, their very secrecy suggests they're still vulnerable on that point. A big enough stink bomb, suitably aimed, might still land on the target."

Madame Sato shook her head. Miles wasn't sure if her spasm of despair was the result of post-revival exhaustion, perfectly understandable under the circumstances, or of an acquaintance with Kibou-daini's troubles much deeper than his own. Raven's glower at him suggested the former, though.

"Roic," he said over his shoulder, "I want you to run a fast-penta interrogation on both those goons we have downstairs. Focus on the murders, but get as much else as you can, especially about their bosses. Shoot the recordings over to the consulate, secured link."

"Will such confessions be admissible to the local courts?"

"Mm, I need to think about that. The fact that we're *not* the local authorities may put a wrinkle in it. Vorlynkin can ask the consulate lawyer." Miles wondered what that as-yet-unmet woman was making of the recent stream of bizarre legal questions from her client. Well, it was doubtless time she earned her retainer. "In any case, I want to secure the evidence for my own purposes. Birds in the hand and all that."

"Do we still want to release them, after? If they're murderers?"

"It sounds as if they were amateurs, not contract killers. And bungling amateurs at that. Eh. Depends on what turns up in the interrogations. Raven can assist, but don't let them see him. No point in letting them know any more than they do already."

"And if either or both of them are allergic?"

An induced, and fatal, allergy to fast-penta was not uncommon among galactic covert operatives; Miles wasn't sure about these civilians. "Have Raven check first. The test patches are in my kit along with the fast-penta. If so, call me."

Roic nodded. Miles was confident in Roic's interrogation skills on criminal matters; this was one task he might safely delegate.

"The larger issues..." Miles's voice slowed. "I don't have a handle on yet. It's hard to see how this technology, widely adopted and combined with human nature, wouldn't run into the same traps everywhere, in due course. In a broader sense, this is Barrayar's problem, too, or will be." Good, he had an all-purpose defense for his expense reports for this case. That had been a minor but growing concern.

Roic scratched his head. "Thing is—everyone here's headed for the same end. If the higher-ups allow the whole system to get too corrupt, how do they expect to assure their own future revivals?"

"Never underestimate the human capacity for wishful thinking and willful blindness," said Miles. Such as a whole society of people who became so wrapped up in avoiding death, they forgot to be alive?

Roic tapped his fingers on his trouser seam. "Yeah, belike."

A motion caught Miles's eye—the outer door of the recovery room opening. Vorlynkin appeared, being anxiously towed by Jin and Mina.

Miles pointed. "Madame Sato, I believe you have some visitors."

Her head turned. She gasped, under her mask, and her eyes widened. She scrambled from her chair, Raven springing to the alert in case the sudden motion made her dangerously dizzy, but she was already banging out of the booth.

"Jin! Mina!"

"Mommy!"

The pair raced forward, but, since they did not let go of Vorlynkin, the man was pulled into a few long, unbalanced strides that brought him face to face with Madame Sato. She fell to one knee to clutch her children to her, first one, then the other, then both together, as hard as she could hug. Miles thought she might be crying. He made his way to the booth door and leaned on the jamb, watching. Even Jin, with all the austerity of his almost-twelve, didn't reject the huggy-kissy stuff now.

"Mina!" Madame Sato held her daughter a little away from herself, and stared over her mask. Her voice shook. "You've *grown*!"

For the first time, Miles thought, those eighteen missing months and what they'd stolen from her was brought home. Proof she could touch, not just words and more words.

She looked up at last, in some bewilderment, at Vorlynkin. "And who's this?"

Mina answered eagerly, "It's Vorlynkin-san, Mommy. He took care of us at his house. It has a great garden! All Jin's creatures like it, too." She grabbed Vorlynkin's hand and swung on it, without the least dismay on his part.

Vorlynkin smiled and offered Madame Sato his other hand up, which, after her first wobbling attempt to rise, she realized she needed, and took. He was tall enough that she actually had to look up—she'd been eye-to-eye with Leiber.

"Stefin Vorlynkin, Madame Sato. I'm the Barrayaran Consul to Kibou-daini. I'm very pleased to meet you at last."

She made an abortive motion for her daughter to stop using the consul as a swing-set, but Mina had already abandoned the hand and was running around the pair in excited circles. Jin hopped up and down in a burst of explanations, most of which seemed to turn on the continued health and well-being of his creatures, with special reference to Lucky.

"You've been looking after my children?" she said uncertainly.

"Only for the past few days, ma'am. You have a couple of really good kids, there. Very bright."

Miles thought a flicker of a smile might have turned her mouth, under the mask. It was certainly the first time he'd seen her dark eyes crinkle with pleasure.

Raven intervened at this point to run his still-new revive back to her bed, but he indulgently allowed the family reunion to go along. Miles watched through the glass, the children waving their arms and explaining their lives for the last eighteen months, Madame Sato looking dismayed as she struggled to keep up.

Vorlynkin came to watch over his shoulder. "So glad to see her awake and cognizant. It solves several legal conundrums for me. Now I can actually protect those kids."

"Just so." Miles smiled.

Roic collected Raven and padded off about their next task. Leiber, looking confused, waved inarticulately through the glass at the Sato family and said, "But now what do I do?"

Miles turned to him, folding his arms and leaning against the wall. "Well, you're certainly not a prisoner. The only people on this planet I have the legal authority to actually arrest are other Barrayarans."

"Uh, but what about Hans and Oki?"

"I didn't arrest them, I kidnapped them. According to Roic. I see I shall have to explain to you the difference between permission and forgiveness, sometime."

"And what is the difference?" inquired Vorlynkin, brows rising.

"Success, usually. In any case, Dr. Leiber, you are free to leave at any time. I just don't *recommend* it, not unless you have a better plan for hiding out than your last one. Presuming Hans and Oki are not your bosses' only resource for legwork."

"No, they're not," sighed Leiber.

"You are also free to stay. Camping here overnight would make a better hiding place than any commercial venue, to be sure. We could all use a little time to digest all this, I suspect. Although I'd also suggest you re-think any attempt to make your orbital shuttle tomorrow afternoon. You'd certainly not make it past the shuttleport."

"No," Leiber agreed unhappily. "Not now."

"And what are you going to do next, my Lord Auditor?" asked Vorlynkin.

Miles rubbed his jaw and scowled in thought. "What any commander does when he's outnumbered, I suppose. Look for allies."

Chapter Sixteen

Roic's interrogations of their inadvertent prisoners ran as smoothly as Miles expected, though Hans and Oki's anxious self-justifications leaked through even their slap-happy fast-penta hazes. As Leiber had guessed, the two deaths had been more the result of clumsiness than malice, although the verbal picture of the pair of goons chasing the frightened old lady Tennoji around her apartment and over her balcony was sickening enough. Their attempt to force down George Suwabi's lightflyer might actually have worked, if he'd crash landed on dry ground instead of deep water. They could have pulled him out of the safety cage and whisked him off to the freezer openly feigning a quick-thinking rescue of an otherwise fatally injured man. As it was, his drowned corpse had been fished from the waters far too late for even Kibou-daini's medics to help.

Whether the strict legal definition of their acts was murder or just manslaughter, Miles was still left with the dilemma of how, now, to be rid of his unwanted guests. Catch and release

254 Lois McMaster Bujold

was off the table. They, and their confessions, needed to be turned over to a local police authority, but not one that could be bought by their NewEgypt bosses. Not that it would play out that way, Miles guessed. Roped together by their shared guilt, Hans and Oki would be instant sacrifices, and their bosses would purchase their own freedom through a screen of expensive lawyers. Yet Miles wanted to bring down the whole NewEgypt crew, if he could.

The meticulous Roic did get to escort his captives, individually, to the loo, and give them water. For the moment, Miles had Raven put them back into a light medicated doze, although that wasn't going to be a long-term answer either. Freezing was looking better all the time. Miles damn well wasn't packing that pair home with him. *Barrayar isn't suffering a goon shortage, and anyway,* ours *are more competent.* On the bright side, the Gang of Four must be thoroughly alarmed by now at the disappearance of their minions and Leiber, hours after they should have reported in. Yeah, it might be time to start rattling a few chains.

The recordings dispatched to the consulate, Miles was at last clear to tackle WhiteChrys, where all this had started what was beginning to seem a rather long time ago. Happily, he had no trouble bulling through to an immediate appointment with Ron Wing. Miles spent the drive out to the west end mentally rehearsing his role, so as not to crack his cover while still accomplishing his aim.

They were met in Wing's outer office by a smiling executive secretary, who rose to greet them. Also rising from a comfortable-looking chair in the corner, though with a yawn not a smile, was a startling catlike creature, with the tawny body of a miniature lion and wings not unlike Gyre's, but a disturbingly human-looking face. A colorful little striped head-cloth in the style of Egyptian statuary was tied under its feminine chin. It trotted to Roic, who froze, appalled, as it wound around his legs. It butted his knees—it must have weighed ten kilos—looked up, and opened its mouth not to say, *What goes on four legs in the morning, two legs at noon, and three legs at night?* but a mere breathy half-meow.

"Stop that, Nefertiti," scolded the secretary, and hoisted the beast to deposit it on her desk. The creature switched its tufted tail and looked offended.

Miles held out a hand for it to sniff as the secretary went on, "It's all right, she doesn't bite or scratch. She does shed, though." She added in cheerful explanation to the still stunned-looking Roic, "They were this year's promotional give-away by our competitor and neighbor, NewEgypt."

"I didn't see them at the conference," said Miles.

"Oh, they all went the first day. Very popular. They come fitted with a vocabulary of over a dozen words, and are supposed to be great with children. And good for home security." That last was delivered in a less confident tone.

"Where, um, did they have them made?" Miles inquired.

"Some bioengineering company on Jackson's Whole, I understood," she said.

Of course.

"They were shipped frozen, and NewEgypt was able to save money by reviving them in their own labs. But they prove rather tricky to maintain. Very finicky eaters."

"Cat genes...mostly?" said Miles.

She looked rather doubtfully at the mini-sphinx, who stared back sphinxlike. "I would think so. Wouldn't you? I'll tell Mr. Wing you are here, Lord Vorkosigan."

Wing bustled out promptly to greet his self-invited guests. Leaving Roic in the outer office to chat up the secretary, and perhaps exchange riddles with the sphinx, Miles allowed himself to be ushered into Wing's inner sanctum by the man himself and settled in a comfy and elegant gel-padded visitor's chair. Nice corner suite, windows on two sides overlooking the buildings and serene gardens of the complex; Miles was weirdly reminded of Suze's lair.

Wing took a seat behind his big black glass comconsole

desk, folding his hands and looking up in wary inquiry. "You say you have an emergency, Lord Vorkosigan?"

Miles picked a sphinx hair off the sleeve of his gray jacket and tried to remember what he was about. "No, I'd say you do." He sat back and scowled, wishing his feet touched the floor.

Wing seemed alert, but not alarmed. "How so?"

"I've spent a few days poking around Northbridge after the conference, and after *our* conference. Figuring out just what I'm getting into with my new investment. There turns out to be a hitch. Did you know?" Miles let his scowl go suspicious, in hopes of putting Wing on the defensive.

Wing merely said, "Hm?"

Miles reminded himself to keep in character while he delivered the bad news; smart enough to be believed, not so smart as to be a threat. "The structure of my compensation for services to be rendered depends on the value of my WhiteChrys Solstice shares rising, not falling. If they fall, I will be left holding not a profit, but a debt!"

"They won't fall," said Wing confidently.

"I beg to differ. Your parent company, here, is about to suffer a major financial blow."

Wing did not immediately go on soothing him, but said, "How so?"

"You know all those commodified contracts you've bought from NewEgypt? You've been sold a lot of dud dead. It turns out that a particular brand of cryo-fluid on the market between fifty and thirty years ago breaks down after a couple of decades, rendering patrons nonrevivable. Brains turned to slush, as my technical consultant so vividly phrased it. Increasingly, any revivals from that period which used that product are likely to fail. Your patrons' kin are owed back millions in nuyen and all those votes."

Wing's lips parted in genuine surprise. "Is this true?"

"You can check it yourselves, as soon as you point your labs in the right direction."

Wing sank back in his chair. "I certainly shall."

"NewEgypt is your culprit. The commodified contracts scam originated from there, as I understand it—generated by a fellow named Anish Akabane, their chief financial officer."

Wing nodded slowly. "I know him. Clever bastard!" He sounded more admiring than outraged.

"It seems to me you have a clear case against NewEgypt, you and every other cryocorp in Northbridge who's been suckered. You might even combine forces in a joint suit."

Wing squinted in no-doubt-rapid thought. "Only if it could be proved they knew."

"It could be proved they knew at least eighteen months ago. You can certainly bring the bandits down."

Wing held up a hand. "Slow down, Lord Vorkosigan! I share your outrage, but I don't think the course you suggest will work to protect your investment."

Leaving aside the airy nature of Miles's *investment*. "Sir?"

"This is confidential? You've told no one else?"

"I started with you. I'd planned to go on down the row of every corp in the Cryopolis, after."

"I'm so glad you came to me first. You did the right thing."

"So I hope, but what do you mean?"

"We have to think first of protecting the value of WhiteChrys and the interests of its shareholders, including yourself. First—after checking the facts, of course—we have this clear, if obviously limited, opportunity to unload our own liabilities. It would be the height of irresponsibility not to seize it. It would be far better for WhiteChrys to let this problem come out slowly and naturally from other sources, rather than springing it on the public all at once and creating an avoidable crisis."

"I'm not sure I follow you." *I'm afraid I do. Damn. This dog won't fight.*

Wing shook his head. "Every other responsible cryocorp operating team would agree with me. This isn't something to publicize. It could be very damaging not only to WhiteChrys, but to the whole industry, even to the economy at large."

"So you're talking not a joint suit, but a, but a, a joint cover-up?" *Don't sputter,* Miles told himself.

"Cover-up is too strong a term." Wing sighed as if in regret. "Though it would certainly be preferable all around. But if this problem has come so close to the surface that even an off-worlder's casual inspection can uncover it, it's clearly far too late for concealment to be effective. The news must be about to break."

Not so casual as all that, but Miles wasn't about to tell Wing the details.

Wing tapped his fingertips on the black glass of his desktop. "A small head-start for us, I think. And then—yes—I think it would be best for me to go to our competitor colleagues myself. Considering the aspects of this that threaten us all. Perhaps in a few weeks. Ah, yes! Lord Vorkosigan, your investment will be safe with us. Just leave it to me!" He sat back, smiling again, although gears plainly turned behind his eyes.

"But where, in all this, do those NewEgypt bastards get nailed to the wall?" Miles tried to keep his tone plaintive and not outraged.

"Have you ever heard the phrase, *Living well is the best revenge?*"

"Where I come from, someone's head in a bag is generally considered the best revenge."

"Well, ah, hm. Different cultures and all that. Well. You have delivered me a great deal to do this afternoon, none of which was on my previous schedule." A broad hint, that, for Miles to decamp and let Wing go grapple with his damage control.

Miles could just picture it; the corps drawing together not in collision but in collusion. "You've given me a lot to think about, Wing-san."

"And the reverse, I'm sure. Some tea, before you go?" Wing was clearly torn between social etiquette and getting on with this new crisis.

Cruelly, Miles said, "Why, yes!" Thus combining living well and revenge, he supposed, if a petty one. They repaired to the outer office, where the secretary was already engaged in filling Roic with green tea and almond cookies, and giving him admiring and grateful glances. The sphinx made plaintive noises from behind the bars of a large...sphinx-carrier.

"I'm so glad you're taking her," said the secretary, with a nod at the cage while pouring for Miles and her boss from a delicate porcelain pot. "She's a very loving creature, and quite tame, but she just doesn't fit our décor."

"Ah!" said Wing, brightening. "Have you finally found her a home, Yuko? Good work! I'll be so glad to get that litter box out of the executive washroom."

Miles stared reproachfully at Roic. "We're getting a sphinx?" *Why?* Or possibly, *Why me, God?*

Roic looked uncomfortable. "I said I knew someone who'd love t' have her."

"Ah." Miles trusted Roic had received some value in return. Information, hopefully. The secretary seemed a little too old for him, but whether her interest in his Barrayaran manliness was romantic or maternal hardly mattered, as long as it was friendly. And forthcoming.

Miles limited his revenge to one cup, then let himself be gently ushered out. Two underlings were produced to cart away the sphinx's food, dishes, toys, extra hats, and sanitary arrangements. Roic lugged the carrier, and oversaw it all stuffed into the back of the consulate's lift van. The sphinx's voice rose in unholy protest as they drove under the red torii gate once more. "Aowt! Aowt!"

"Which way now, m'lord? Any other stops?"

"Not...yet, I think. My brilliant plan for fixing this mess and getting us all on our way back home just tanked. Tell you all about it on the way back to town."

"Yes, m'lord."

ↀ⃝   ↀ⃝   ↀ⃝

Jin let himself quietly out of the isolation booth, where both his mother and Mina were napping, Mina curled on the foot of the bed like a cat. His mother looked washed-out and pale, a little scary but nothing like that other woman Miles-san and Raven-sensei had failed to revive. Jin's joy at finding her alive had crashed through him like a great wave, but now that the first flush of relief was receding, he felt all tumbled and strange. Everything was uncertain again, with the grownups back in charge. Where would they go to live now? What would happen to his creatures? Would they make him go back to school? How soon? Would he have to be stuck in with kids a year younger than him?

Could it all be taken away again...?

Ako, keeping watch in the recovery room, gave him a friendly nod from her chair. Jin heard voices out in the corridor, and went to see who it was.

He shut the door behind him to find Vorlynkin-san, looking startled, confronting Raven-sensei and two new people. Jin's mouth, too, fell open as he stared at the couple.

The man was almost another Miles-san—same height, same looks—except twice as wide, and with no gray in his hair. He wore a sharply-cut suit in black on black with more black that somehow made his girth look trim. The woman was even taller than Jin's mother, with bright blond hair swept back in a cool knot, and eyes almost as blue as Consul Vorlynkin's. Her suit was more flowing, in soft gray, with a silky white top and a glint of gold at her throat and ears. Her outfit reminded Jin of Miles-san's shirt, simple yet somehow extra... *extra*-looking. Her smile down at him made him feel warm all over.

"Jin," said Consul Vorlynkin. "I was just coming to find you. I was about to run back to the consulate for a bit, but..." He stared at the new not-Miles.

"Mom and Mina fell asleep," said Jin.

"Ah, good," said Raven-sensei. "I'll just go check on them, and have a word with Ako, and be right with you all." He slipped into the recovery room.

The blond lady's eyes glinted merrily at Jin, like sunlight off a lake in summer. "And who's this, Consul?"

Vorlynkin seemed to pull himself together, though why the arrival of this pair should have scattered his wits Jin was not quite sure, well, except for the short man's surprising looks. "This is Jin Sato. He's the son of the woman the Lord Auditor and Dr. Durona have just revived here. Lord Vorkosigan met him, well, I'll let him tell it when he gets back. Jin, this is Lord Mark Vorkosigan and his partner, Miss Kareen Koudelka. From Barrayar."

Miss Koudelka held out a slim hand for Jin to shake, just as if he were a grownup, and the man, after a beat, followed suit. Jin wondered if *partner* meant girlfriend or, like, coworker. The pretty woman seemed like she ought to be a corp executive, the expensive-looking bag slung over her shoulder sized for business gear, not cosmetics.

"Are you Miles-san's brother?" Jin asked. *Like Tetsu and Ken?* Jin stood, he realized, eye-to-eye with the man just as he did with Miles-san, but somehow the extra bulk made Lord Mark seem taller. And his smile didn't lurk in his eyes the way Miles-san's did.

"Twins, born six years apart," the man said, sounding bored and rehearsed. "It's a long story." Clearly, not one he was about to tell Jin.

"You don't look, um . . . exactly alike," said Jin. Lord Mark also lacked Miles-san's cane, and he seemed to move more fluidly. Maybe he was the younger brother.

"A distinction I go to some trouble to maintain," said Lord Mark.

Raven-sensei let himself back out of the recovery room. "I think you should meet Madame Suzuki first, Lord Mark."

"Must we deal with her? This Ted Fuwa fellow is the sole owner-of-record."

"Only of the physical plant. For our purposes, the physical plant is—well, not nothing, but interchangeable. It's the human liabilities—and opportunities—it contains that made it worth dragging you here for a closer look. And Madame Suze is unquestionably the mistress of that particular court of chaos."

Lord Mark gave a short nod—listening, not arguing.

"Did your brother know you were arriving, Lord Mark?" asked Vorlynkin. "He hadn't mentioned it to me. Nor had Dr. Durona." His glance under his lashes at Raven-sensei was not very friendly.

"We caught an earlier ship than expected," said Miss Koudelka.

"I actually haven't any interest in impinging on whatever hornet's nest Miles is presently poking," said Lord Mark. "We don't normally comment on each other's enterprises. Think of it as the parallel-play stage of siblinghood."

His partner-lady put in smoothly, "Actually, I understand one of the functions of the consulate is to assist Barrayaran business people on Kibou."

Vorlynkin nodded warily. "Although the Auditorial investigation naturally takes precedence, just now." He added under his breath, "Whatever the hell he thinks he's doing..."

"Of course." Miss Koudelka's smile grew blinding; Vorlynkin blinked. "Perhaps, Mark, Raven, the consul should come along? Then we'll only need to explain things once."

Vorlynkin looked nonplussed. "Jin, do you mind?"

"Oh, Jin is welcome, too," said Raven-sensei airily. He added aside to Miss Koudelka, "Native guide and all that."

She nodded agreeably, and favored Jin with another sunny look.

Raven-sensei led off, Jin tagging along in silent wonder, down and under and through and up to Suze-san's door. Lord Mark and Miss Koudelka looked all around as they walked, very keenly, the blond lady taking vid scans on the way with a tiny hand-held.

At the corner suite, Raven-sensei knocked briskly. The door was opened surprisingly soon not by Suze-san, but by Tenbury-san. "What's all this?" He peered suspiciously through his hedge of hair. "You've gone and brought new people in without asking!"

"Asking is just what we came for," said Raven-sensei. "I'm glad you're here. May we come in and talk to Madame Suze?"

"I suppose." Tenbury squinted down at Lord Mark. "God, it's another one. How many of these sawed-off galactics do you have up your sleeve, Raven?"

Lord Mark's eyebrows twitched, but Raven-sensei replied soothingly, "Just the two," and Tenbury gave way.

Suze-san was sitting by her window playing mah-jong and drinking something that probably wasn't tea with Medtech Tanaka; Tenbury had apparently just risen from the third seat. Their eyes opened wide at Lord Mark's party.

"Now what, Raven?" said Suze-san. "I thought I'd settled with you. When do I get my two revivals, eh?"

"We're considering changing the Deal," said Raven-sensei.

Suze-san's scowl deepened.

"Instead of two, how would you like two thousand?"

Her brows went up, though her frown still bent down; but she waved a wrinkled hand, and the whole mob filed in and pulled up seats around her. Raven-sensei first introduced Consul Vorlynkin, who, indeed, had been running in and out of her facility for the past several days, as she likely knew perfectly well. Jin cast her a nod, trying to say, *This one's all right.* Tenbury half-sat on the wide windowsill, frowning and pulling on his beard.

Raven-sensei repeated his introductions: "Madame Suzuki, may I present my employer, Lord Mark Vorkosigan—he's also Lord Auditor Miles Vorkosigan's younger brother—and his partner, Miss Kareen Koudelka. Lord Mark is a co-owner of the Durona Group, my clinic on Escobar."

"Who's the other co-owner?" Suze-san asked, staring hard at Lord Mark.

Lord Mark bowed slightly and said, "Dr. Lily Durona. Who is also founder and clone-progenitor of the original Durona Group of Jackson's Whole. I acquired my interest a decade ago when I helped expedite the group's removal from the ownership of Baron Fell, there, and emigration to Escobar."

"You a doctor, too? Researcher?"

Lord Mark shook his head. "Entrepreneur. My primary interest in the Durona research is to support development of an alternative to the clone-brain transplant method of life extension that will knock it out of business."

"That technique's illegal!" said Medtech Tanaka.

"Not on Jackson's Whole. Unfortunately."

Jin tugged Vorlynkin's sleeve and whispered, "What are they talking about?"

He whispered back, "Some bad rich people try to get young again by having their brains transplanted into the bodies of clones, purpose-grown to match them. Very dangerous operation, and the clone's brain always dies."

"Eew!"

"I agree." His brows drew down as he frowned anew at Lord Mark. He made a hand-down motion to Jin, *Be quiet and listen,* and set the example.

Lord Mark tapped his spread fingers together in a gesture very like one of his brother's, and said, "The Durona Group is considering expanding its cryorevival services to Kibou-daini."

Suze-san's lip curled. "That would be a waste of—oh, wait. Cryorevival, you say? Not cryo-storage?"

"Cryo-storage seems to be a fully mature industry here, with no room for start-ups. I think there could be far more opportunity in an arena the current cryocorps are neglecting. Raven tells me you have over two thousand unlicensed, illegal cryo-patrons stored in your lower levels. A liability that has rendered this facility unsalable by its present owner-of-record, one Theodore Fuwa."

"Yah, when the idiot bought the place for development he didn't know we were here. He tried to get rid of his dilemma by arson, once," said Suze-san. "Anyway, it's closer to three thousand, by now."

"Even better."

"And what would you do to get rid of 'em?"

"Why, revive them, and let them walk out on their own."

Suze-san snorted. "Only if you've found a cure for old age."

A weird little smile turned Lord Mark's lips, showing his teeth. "Just so."

Medtech Tanaka's head came up. In a voice of slow wonder, she said, "What have you people *got*?"

He nodded to her. "Not, alas, a fountain of youth. It may prove to be a fountain of middle-age, however. We don't think it'll do much for anyone under sixty, but from there up it seems to knock off about twenty years. So far. Not a single-pronged treatment—sort of a cocktail, really, as it presently stands—but our R & D group has finished virtual and live mammal trials, and we're almost ready to move up to clinical trials on humans."

"Has it been tried on any humans?" asked Tanaka-san.

"Just one, so far," put in Raven-sensei.

"One trial?"

"One human. Lily Durona, as it happens," said Raven-sensei. "You can imagine how riveted the whole Group is by the outcome."

"Can you guarantee the results of this treatment?"

"Of course not," said Lord Mark. "That's why it's called a *trial*. But by the time we work through two or three thousand varied test cases, all the bugs should be ironed out."

"You'll never get permissions," said Suze-san.

"On the contrary. Escobar has reciprocal medical licensing arrangements with Kibou-daini. Any facility I might buy here would move under the Durona Group's regulatory umbrella from the instant the purchase was registered. No need to stir things up by reapplying for, ah, anything." Lord Mark rubbed his double chin. "If the trials worked out, the enterprise might become self-supporting in as little as two years."

"And after twenty years," said Tenbury, "what happens to people? Can they go around again?"

Lord Mark shrugged. "Ask me in two decades."

"Damn," said Suze-san. "This sounds like a license to print money, you know that, young man?"

Lord Mark made an impatient throw-away gesture. "A side-venture, from my point of view. It will be safer than the clone-brain transplant, to be sure, but the sort of octogenarian customer who would buy a body of an eighteen-year-old is hardly going to prefer a body of sixty. We have to do better, somehow. But this could be another small step in the right direction."

"Will it only work on revives? Frozen folk?" asked Tenbury.

"Oh, no. I expect it will work even better on the never-frozen."

Suze-san's wrinkled lips drew back in a fierce smile. "Who wouldn't choose it over a risky illegal brain transplant, hell. Who wouldn't choose it over *freezing*?"

"People are strange," said Lord Mark. "I make no predictions."

Medtech Tanaka said, "But what about the poor?"

Lord Mark gave her a blank look. "What about 'em?"

Their stares of mutual incomprehension lengthened. Miss Koudelka put in, "If I may offer an interpretation, Mark, I believe Madame Suzuki and her friends feel just as strongly about Kibou's poor being shut out of their chance at the future as you feel about the Jacksonian clones being shut out of their chance at a future. Or they wouldn't have been running this place as a protest for more years than you've been running the Durona group." She turned to Suze-san. "Mark, and Dr. Durona for that matter, were both raised on Jackson's Whole, where one must hustle constantly to survive, and there is seldom margin to think of others. They're both getting over it, slowly. I suggest we all take the chance to consider the wider aspects of this while we look around. Mark and I hoped to inspect the place before our first meeting with Mr. Fuwa."

Suze-san sat back, looking strange and stern. "And if not...?"

Lord Mark shrugged. "Then we'll just have to meet with Fuwa without your input."

Suze-san's eyes narrowed. "Think you hold all the cards, do you?"

Miss Koudelka said, "It's hardly such a zero-sum game. A cooperative venture might yield major advantages to all, according to their varied needs."

"Yes," said Suze-san slowly, "I need to think." She sat forward and jammed the cork into the top of her square bottle with a hand that shook slightly. "Tenbury, take 'em around. Let them see whatever they like."

Tenbury nodded and pushed off the wall. "Follow me, then, folks..."

They all shuffled out after Tenbury, except for Suze-san and the old medtech, who bent their heads together before the door even shut. Out in the corridor, Jin edged close to Consul Vorlynkin, and whispered up to him, "What did they mean? I didn't understand any of that. Why was Suze-san mad?"

They trailed the group not quite out of earshot. Vorlynkin rubbed his knuckles across his lips, looked down at Jin, and lowered his voice. "If Lord Mark has the money, and I gather he does, he could buy this facility outright and there would be nothing Madame Suzuki could do about it. He could do—well, not anything, because he'd pick up liability for all those cryo-corpses downstairs, but in theory he could clear out all the live people here as trespassers and dump them back on the street."

"That's not right!" said Jin indignantly.

Miss Koudelka cast him a glance over her shoulder, and a funny smile. Jin blushed furiously.

"I'm not sure that's quite what he has in mind," murmured Vorlynkin, "but I guess we'll have to see."

Jin frowned, trying to sort it all out. "How come Miles-san is Lord Vorkosigan, and his brother is Lord Mark, if their last names are both Vorkosigan?"

"Both are the sons of Count Aral Vorkosigan. Your, er, friend Miles-san is Lord Vorkosigan because he is his father's heir.

Lord Mark, as the younger brother, has a courtesy title with no direct political duties."

"Oh."

The consul had a very thoughtful look on his face as he followed Tenbury and the new Barrayarans. Jacksonians. Whatever. So if Lord Vorkosigan and Lord Mark were brothers, how come they'd been raised on different planets? Did all that creepy clone history have anything to do with them? And was that five-year-old boy, the one with all the confusing names his own parent couldn't remember, lord anything?

Jin thought of Miles-san's story about being allowed to sit in on his father's conferences, if he was quiet and useful, so shut his mouth and hurried to keep up.

Two hours later, Jin was yawning. He wondered if Miles-san had ever fallen asleep at any of those old meetings. Maybe his dad's business, whatever it was, had been more interesting than this. They'd trailed Tenbury-san all over: up and down and through parts of the facility even Jin had never seen. The talk was all boring grownup stuff about finances and drains and regulations. It never did get back to more strange stories about cloning and medical murders. Tenbury showed off his shop and tools and tricks, Lord Mark taking it all in expressionlessly, Miss Koudelka outright encouraging the custodian to drone on forever with way too many questions. Jin thought of abandoning them and going back to the recovery room to see if his mom and Mina were awake yet. He was getting hungry.

They were crossing the parking garage under the old patient intake building, when everyone's heads turned at the sound of pounding and muffled yells coming from a door marked *No Admittance.*

"Hadn't someone better let that person in? Or out?" asked Miss Koudelka.

"Out, and no," said Raven-sensei. "They're Lord Vorkosigan's prisoners. They must have woken up. I hadn't wanted to give them too much sedative, atop the fast-penta and the stunner hangovers."

Lord Mark held up his hands, palm out. "No affair of mine, then." He didn't sound surprised that his brother went around drugging and detaining people, but merely asked, "When is he thinking of removing them? I expect my deal to be moving rather quickly."

"Don't know." Raven-sensei shrugged. "They're his puzzle-pieces." As the pounding continued, he added, "All the same, I'll wait till Roic comes back to go in and settle them. They're a nasty pair."

Jin tilted his head and ventured nearer to the door. "Hey! That's old Yani's voice!"

"Who?" said Raven-sensei, and "Are you sure?" said Tenbury.

"Hey, Yani! Is that you in there?"

The pounding stopped. A quavery voice cried, "Jin? Is that you? Unlock the door and let me out!"

"Where are the two guys?" Jin yelled back.

"I heard someone thumping and carrying on and went to go look," Yani returned, muffled. "What call they got to go locking people up around here?"

Raven-sensei threw up his hands and clenched his teeth. "Oh, my Lord Auditor will not love this." He bent to the lock.

Lord Mark stood back, drawing a businesslike stunner from his black jacket. Miss Koudelka didn't get behind him, but rather, circled to cover another angle, hitching her shoulders and flexing her hands and suddenly looking very athletic.

A tense pause, and the door fell open.

Yani stumbled out, swearing. He looked rumpled and wild, with a big bruise on his forehead and dried blood around his nose.

Raven-sensei peered within. "Crap. Gone!"

Chapter Seventeen

As Roic drove them into the underground garage, Miles flinched at the sight of the mob clustered around the open door of the office where they'd left their prisoners. His eye skipped to the empty space across the concrete where the captured NewEgypt van had been parked—and widened, when he spotted the sleek blond head bobbing above the dark ones. He didn't even need to look down to know who he'd see standing level with her shoulder.

"What t' hell?" said Roic, pulling to a halt. "What's Miss Kareen doing here?"

"Trailing my brother, no doubt. What I want to know is what the hell *Mark* is doing here."

They disembarked, and Miles shouldered swiftly through the gawkers to stare into the barren office. But even his best Auditorial glare couldn't make Hans and Oki magically reappear. Not that he wanted them, exactly... He turned to sort out Tenbury and Raven, Mark and Kareen, Consul Vorlynkin,

Jin jittering at his elbow pouring out the escape tale in a rapid high voice, and battered old Yani, looking something between irate and contrite. But no worse, thank God, and by his complaints still oblivious to his close encounter with one of Kibou-daini's shadier death angels.

"How long ago did this happen?" Miles tried to cut to the essentials.

"Very soon after you left, at a guess," said Raven ruefully. "I'm afraid I under-medicated. Sorry..."

Miles waved a hand, in understanding if not absolution. "So they've been gone at least two hours, maybe almost three. Plenty of time to get home. Or somewhere."

A tactical tree began to sketch itself in his mind. If the pair had bugged out intending only to save themselves, they might be anywhere, but were unlikely to come back, and certainly not with reinforcements, the police and their own bosses being equally dangerous to them in such a flight. If they'd dutifully returned to NewEgypt...the possibilities grew more complex. *I wonder if we passed them on the road? Too late...* The two goons had gained a good look at Roic, might have glimpsed Raven, had not yet seen the memorable Miles, but Roic was pretty remarkable all on his own; and once he'd been identified, the trace back to Miles could be swift, if rather baffling from NewEgypt's point of view.

And NewEgypt now knew the location of Suze's facility, and they had to be pretty sure Leiber, their original target, had come here, though they couldn't be sure if he was still here. Had NewEgypt figured out yet that their employee—former employee, by now, no doubt—had absconded with Sato's cryo-corpse? And if so, would they imagine she'd been revived already, or would they still picture Leiber carting her about in a cryochamber like some especially awkward souvenir? Could they track back to whatever security vids they maintained from the day Miles and his strike force had liberated her unfortunate substitute Chen? And what would they make of it if they did? And...

"Damn," Miles muttered. "I have to talk to that idiot Leiber again." If he was to second-guess their thinking, he wanted more details on those key NewEgypt execs. He sighed and raised his voice. "And hello, Mark. Why are you here? And so unexpectedly, too."

Mark tilted his head in un-apology, smirking a bit.

Miles eyed Raven. "I thought we'd had an understanding about such surprises."

Looking faintly guilty, Raven shrugged and mumbled, "Earlier ship."

Miles abandoned the unfruitful point. "Hi, Kareen."

She glinted back at him, reassuring in a way. Sort of. "Hi, Miles. How's it going?"

"Not as well as I thought, evidently." He peered one last time into the drab little office—still empty—and turned away. Tenbury, bless him, was soothing Yani and ushering him off to visit Medtech Tanaka.

A penetrating yowl rose from the back of the consulate van. "Aowt! Aowt!"

Vorlynkin's brows rose. "Have you kidnapped someone else?" His tone seemed more resigned than disapproving. Miles thought of those tales about water wearing away stone; the consul's edges were growing more rounded, at least.

"Not this time. Jin, Armsman Roic has a present for you. Live cargo."

"Really?" Jin was instantly diverted; Miles jerked his head at Roic, who led the boy out of earshot to meet his new pet. *Good with kids*, Wing's secretary had promised.

And you trust those people, why?

Kareen, curious, followed Roic. Miles lowered his voice to Vorlynkin and Raven. "Raven, how soon could Madame Sato be moved out of medical isolation?"

"To the consulate?" said Vorlynkin.

Miles nodded. "If secrecy, which was our first defense, has failed, then the consulate would be a better location for fending off legal attacks. Granted it hasn't much advantage for illegal, physical attacks. I have some help on the way for that, but they're not here yet."

Raven's lips pressed together in medical reluctance. "Tomorrow? Not that her bio-isolation isn't compromised already, with those kids in and out. Little vectors that they are."

"Well, load her up with every immune system booster in your arsenal—"

"I already have."

Miles made a thumbs-up gesture. "Then plan to decamp as early as possible tomorrow. In fact, Vorlynkin, if you could stay here tonight, and be ready to move her and her kids out at a moment's notice, that might be, um, prudent." He added reluctantly, "Leiber, too."

"Do you think NewEgypt will react that quickly?" asked Vorlynkin.

"I truly do not know. My impression of all these cryocorp chiefs so far is that they'd rather hunker down behind a wall of lawyers than, say, hire mercs, but this crew has already shown it can move fast at need. And, despite the lethal screw-ups, their actions eighteen months ago must have seemed successful at the time. I wish them a distraught and sleepless night figuring it all out, anyway."

Vorlynkin frowned, taking this in.

Miles turned to his clone-brother. "And you?"

"Kareen and I jumped over from Escobar to look into a real estate deal Raven spotted," said Mark, unperturbed by the foregoing. "The short version is, Madame Suze's set-up could be the perfect venue for large-scale human trials of the Durona Group's latest life-extension treatment. If so, I mean to buy the place from the unhappy current owner-of-record, this fellow Fuwa—lock, stock, and liabilities." Mark jerked a thumb downward to indicate the frozen sleepers stacked in the hidden corridors below. "I'd take it as a personal favor, Lord Auditor Brother, if you don't mess up my Deal."

Miles's lips twitched. "Happily, Vor views on nepotism remain culturally generous, even in what our late grandfather would have called this degenerate age. But don't mess up my case."

"Haven't the least interest in your case, thanks. Which is what, by the way?"

"Raven didn't apprise you?"

"No, he's been virtuously closed-mouthed."

Well, no one could say that a Durona didn't earn his or her pay. "It all started with an attempt by a Kibou cryonics company called WhiteChrys to expand onto Komarr."

"*That* smells."

"Oh, you've heard of it?"

"Not before now. But at a glance, there's a physical, financial, and cultural distance that doesn't explain itself." Mark's lips curved slightly. "And then there's you, popping up in the middle of it. Always a tip-off."

"Mm," said Miles. "Well, the WhiteChrys part is a train that has left its station, and can run on rails to its appointed end. So far. This NewEgypt involvement is a side-issue that grew complicated." His jaw set. "I'm trying not to leave undue collateral damage upon a local kid who befriended me, at some cost to himself. Good intentions, Mark. My path is paved with them."

"So glad I don't have any of those." Mark's glance grew uncomfortably shrewd. "It's not your planet, you know. You can't fix it."

"No, but...well, no. But."

"Well, try not to leave too much rubble in your wake. I can use this place."

"So you said." Miles hesitated. "Life extension, you say. Does this one look better that the last two Durona developments you were so excited about? That, excuse the expression, died on the lab benches?"

"Maybe. The one human trial looks hopeful so far. Lily Durona, if you were wondering."

It was Miles's turn to raise his brows. "All right, I'm officially impressed, if Lily was willing to try it on herself."

Mark's smile went a little flat. "Lily," he said, "ran out of time to wait."

Miles drummed his fingers on his trouser seam. "Has it been tried on an older male, yet? Speaking of running out of time."

Miles and his clone-brother exchanged very similar looks.

Mark said, "Do you think he could even be persuaded to try it?"

"Mm, not by me, perhaps. Our mother might give it a go. Betan, you know, anything for science."

"That's one more reason I'm anxious to move these human trials along."

"You might actually be more successful at persuading him if it were still billed as dodgy. Hit those old Vor service-to-the-Imperium reflexes, and all."

"That's so strange."

Miles shrugged. "That's the Count-our-father." He added, "So, if your deal goes through, would you and Kareen be spending much time on Kibou?"

Mark shook his head. "Once it's set up and running, I figure to turn it over to Raven to develop. Past time he was promoted. So far, this is not the knock-out competition to the clone-brain transplant business I was hoping for, but it's early days yet." Mark smiled slowly. "On the other hand, if it proved sufficiently profitable, maybe I could hire my own space mercs and attack the Jacksonian cloning lords directly."

Miles grimaced. "Do you remember the last time you tried that?"

"Vividly. Don't you?"

"Patchily," said Miles dryly.

Mark winced.

"In the event, though I've no doubt Admiral Quinn could do the job, I would beg you to hire a different outfit." Just in case this wasn't quite a joke. With Mark, on this subject, it could be hard to tell. "What are you two doing next? Do you have a hotel?"

"No, we came straight from the shuttleport. Next, we've made arrangements to meet Fuwa here."

"Isn't that after local business hours?"

Mark shrugged. "I'm on system ship-time."

"Can I sit in?"

"Sit in, yes. Mix in, no."

"Mm," said Miles, but Jin, Roic and Kareen returned before he could take exception to this. Jin was bouncing with pleasure, but he paused to stare in the usual amazement at Miles and his clone-brother standing toe-to-toe. Miles still wished Mark hadn't picked weight gain as a way to differentiate himself, but Mark's grim glee at his progenitor-brother's discomfort with the choice was probably just a bonus, from his own point of view. Complicated man, Mark.

"I want to show my sphinx to Mom and Mina!" said Jin.

"You mustn't take it into her booth," said Raven, coming alert.

"*I* know that," said Jin. "But I can hold it up to the glass. Can Roic-san help me cart everything?"

Roic glanced at the empty office and cast Miles a tiny head-shake, bodyguard-conscious again. Vorlynkin caught it, and said smoothly, "I'll give you a hand, Jin."

Raven added prudently, "I'll come along."

"Actually," said Miles, "I think Leiber's still up there; we'll both come."

Tenbury returned then, to continue the interrupted tour; with no more than an eyebrow-twitch from Mark and a farewell smile from Kareen, the three went off toward another exit. Miles followed Vorlynkin, who carried the sphinx-carrier in Jin's train. Plaintive cries of "Aowt! Hum!" drifted back through the stale shadows of the underground garage.

Out. Home. You and me both, Sphinx.

His mother's reaction to the sphinx was disappointing, Jin thought, but not surprising. Familiar, in fact, and comforting thereby.

"Jin, no!" she said, holding her hand to her lips. "Where would you keep it?"

Nefertiti squirmed in a disgruntled fashion under Jin's arm as he hoisted her up on his hip for his mother to see, and attempted to flap her wings, but practice handling the fiercer Gyre left Jin undismayed. "I'll take good care of her! Don't I always? She came with a file of instructions, too, so nothing can go wrong."

In her bed beyond the glass wall, his mother rubbed her forehead. "That's not the point, this time, Jin love."

Mina, who had been lurking on the foot of the bed all day, sat up, interested. "She's huge! Bigger than Lucky and Gyre put together. She sort of looks like Lucky and Gyre put together, really. Oh, say yes, Mommy!" She wriggled down and exited the booth on a slight puff of positive air pressure.

"Did Tenbury get the intercom working?" Jin asked, realizing a bit belatedly that something new had been added. "When did he come by?"

"No, it was Consul Vorlynkin," said Mina, bending to stare into the sphinx's slow blink. "She has a funny face..."

"Oh, how?"

"I found the on-switch," said Vorlynkin, leaning one shoulder against the glass wall and watching all this in some bemusement.

Raven-sensei bent to capture Mina's mask and pop it into the sterilizer box for re-use.

Nefertiti flexed her claws and growled, and Jin set her down on her four paws, where she flapped her wings with a burring noise for all the world like one of the chickens.

"Does she fly?" asked Mina, holding out a hand for the sphinx to sniff.

"I don't think so," said Jin. "Her wings are almost the same size as Gyre's, but she's way heavier."

"These custom genetic constructs are usually made to be decorative, not functional," advised Raven-sensei. "Depending on what the buyer orders, of course."

Mina frowned. "That seems mean, to give her wings she can't fly with."

Jin crouched on his heels and scratched the creature's shoulder blades, between the wings, which folded tamely again as she stretched into the caress. She could not lick her fur like a cat, nor preen her feathers like a bird, so Jin would have a lot of interesting grooming to do, according to the care instructions in the file. "I wonder, do they lay eggs, or have live babies? One at a time, or a litter like kittens? I wonder if there are any male ones, left over?" And if he could find one, somehow...

"There may not have been any males made," mused Raven-sensei. "I believe sphinxes were traditionally female. But these proprietary constructs normally aren't given the ability to reproduce. You'd likely have to clone her, and hand-raise the babies."

Jin's imagination took fire. Home cloning of small animals wasn't that hard, if you could get the right equipment, from a pet supply place or hobbyist who was upgrading or quitting. Hardly something to be found in an alley scavenge, but there ought to be used stuff for cheap somewhere...

"Hum!" said the sphinx, plaintively.

"She talks!" cried Mina, her face breaking into a delighted smile.

"They come with about a twenty-word vocabulary, according to the file," said Jin. "I don't know if you can teach them more, like a parrot."

"We can *try*..."

Beyond the glass, their mother made a noise of hopeless maternal protest, much like the halfway point of other such negotiations, so Jin took heart. But this time, she said, "Jin, we don't even have a home to take her to, right now. Oh, no, I just thought of that! What's happened to our apartment, and all my things? Nobody could have been paying rent for a year and a half, with no one living there. Oh—and my bank account—what happened to my money, after I was frozen? If I have no job, no money, no place for us to live—"

"Aunt Lorna has some of your clothes in boxes in the attic, I know," Mina piped up. "And she took my stuff and Jin's. She had to sell the big couch, and the kitchen table, and a couple of the other big things, because she didn't have room, though."

Consul Vorlynkin turned and spoke through the glass, earnestly. "These are all solvable problems, Madame Sato, but none of them need be solved today, or all at once. As part of the Lord Auditor's case—a protected witness, more or less—your immediate needs will be covered by our consulate."

"My committee, my friends—what's happened to them all, beyond the ones you say NewEgypt murdered or took away? What if they—" Her voice shrank to silence.

"Your first task must be your own physical recovery," Raven-sensei put in, with a look of concern at her sudden distress. "Your normal mental resilience will follow. In two to four weeks, not two to four days—you have to give yourself time."

"I've never had enough time." She pressed her hands to her temples. "And that appalling creature—!"

Vorlynkin cleared his throat. "I'm not sure the Lord Auditor was thinking it through, when he accepted the animal. Nevertheless, it may be kept in the consulate's back garden with the rest of Jin's creatures, for now. They're doing no harm at all, there. Livens the place up, really. The space was underutilized."

She sighed, folded her arms, half-laughed, quelling Jin's growing alarm. "I suppose it just looms so absurdly large because it's closest." But her eyes sought Jin and Mina, not the sphinx.

Since they weren't going back to the consulate tonight after all, Vorlynkin let Jin speak on his wristcom with Lieutenant Johannes, and talk him through how to care for his creatures till Jin returned tomorrow. Johannes didn't even sound sarcastic at the added chores. So that was all right, for now.

Miles-san and Roic had taken Leiber-sensei off to another room to talk, right after they'd come in. They returned at length, toting, unexpectedly, a big stack of dinner boxes from Ayako's Cafe. Miles-san let it be known this bounty was courtesy of

Miss Kareen, who had somehow found out where to get it, how to have it delivered to the facility, and had paid for it all, too.

They all ended up having a sort of picnic in the recovery room; Raven-sensei even took in a box to Jin's mother, so that when he pulled back the curtains after his medical check, it was almost as if they were all eating a family meal together again. Jin thought she looked a bit better after she ate, sitting up less wearily, and with more color in her face. But then, Ayako's curry was always very good.

It was funny to watch big Roic sitting cross-legged on the floor, being instructed on how to use chopsticks by Mina. Miles-san handled his pretty well, for a galactic; he claimed he'd practiced on the ship coming here, and at other times in the past. When he let slip he'd been to Old Earth itself, twice, Mina made him tell stories of his visits, though he mainly told her about his second trip, his wife, and gardens, lots of different gardens. All he said of his first trip was that it was purely business, he'd never got out of one city, and that it was the first time he'd met his brother, which last remark seemed very weird to Jin's ear. Consul Vorlynkin pulled his lip and looked thoughtful at this, but he didn't ask any helpful questions, and Miles-san didn't expand.

With frequent references to the instruction file, Jin fed tidbits to Nefertiti, who apparently could eat some kinds of people food but not others, at least not without messy digestive consequences. Unfortunately, Ako came in just as the sphinx was having an accident in the darkest corner, which was Jin's fault really because he hadn't paid enough attention to her little mutters of *Poo! Pee!* during her restless explorations of the recovery room. Ako was very upset, and made Jin clean it up, which was fair, but then insisted the creature couldn't spend the night in here. Raven-sensei, at least, seemed undisturbed by biological messes, and stayed out of the debate. Jin finally promised to take Nefertiti back to his rooftop hideout for overnight, which satisfied Ako, but then Mina wanted to tag along and see the place.

Miles-san and Roic had gone off by then to meet with Lord Mark and Suze-san, so Consul Vorlynkin, after a glance through the glass at Jin's worried-looking mother, volunteered to go along and help lug the sphinx carrier, and make sure that all was well. Jin's mother smiled gratefully at him, so Jin supposed that was all right, too.

They were filing down the end stairs when they met Bhavya, one of Ako's friends, panting up.

"Jin! Have you seen Ako? Tanaka-san wants her on the second floor—an emergency cryoprep. Some poor old lady collapsed in the cafeteria, all in a heap, they say."

"She's up in the recovery room with my mom." Jin pointed back up the stairs. "Raven-sensei's there, too."

Bhavya nodded and ran on, waving thanks without looking back.

Vorlynkin wheeled to stare after her. "Should we go try to help?"

Jin shook his head. "Naw, this happens all the time. Well, not all the time, but every week or so. Tanaka-san knows what to do."

Vorlynkin looked doubtful, but followed Jin down to the tunnels.

"The layout down here is very confusing," he remarked.

"Yah, the tunnels below are all offset from the buildings above, and run underneath the streets, too. And some go down four levels, and some five or six. You kind of have to memorize them."

Jin had no trouble finding his own familiar route, even when they passed out of range of the lit section, and Vorlynkin drew a small hand light from his jacket to illuminate the steps. Mina, who had walked on her own thus far, took a prudent grip on his wide coat sleeve in the deepening shadows. They trudged upward five flights to come out at last from the exchanger tower door onto Jin's roof. Vorlynkin wasn't wheezing too badly, for a grownup, despite carting the carrier.

Jin had lost track of time in the windowless recovery room, but it seemed to have grown very late. The air was damp and chill, lit by diffuse reflections from the street lights in the area that gave everything a funny brown tinge. The city noises had quieted down the way they usually only did after midnight. But around the side of the tower, Jin found his tarps were all still up and taut, not blown loose by the weather yet. His little refuge was littered with a dreary residue of things not taken away the other day—not needed for his creatures, or too big and awkward to fit in the lift van, or too junky to salvage. He'd taken his own hand light down off its wire and packed it along, so it was now less-than-usefully back at the consulate, but Vorlynkin amiably shone his around while Jin explained his old life up here to Mina, and Mina made admiring and envious noises.

When they let her out of her carrier, Nefertiti did not at once take to her new environment. She stared around warily, crouching, then at last went off in a stiff-legged reconnoiter. Jin followed along, explaining to Vorlynkin about the gruesome fate of the baby chicks who couldn't fly yet. "I can't tell, if she went over the edge, if she'd just plummet, or flutter down like the big chickens, or even fly away." The dense muscles Jin had felt beneath the golden fur didn't help him decide. "Maybe I'd better tie a line around her leg like Miles-san."

"Hm?" said Vorlynkin, so Jin explained his first night's safety procedures, which just made Vorlynkin go "Hm!" and set his teeth to his lower lip. But from the way his eyes crinkled, Jin didn't think he was mad or anything.

Jin's old bedding of shredded flimsies was still piled against the wall; if he slept out here, he could keep an eye on his new pet. Would Mom miss him? She'd have Mina—or would Mina try to stay out here with him?

Jin rose on his toes to make a grab when Nefertiti stretched her considerable length, put her front paws on the parapet, and peered over, but she drew back without any effort to launch herself fatally over the side. She visited Jin's latrine corner, and used it properly—Jin explained about the bucket-flushing to Vorlynkin—and Jin made sure to praise her, after the confusions about the corner of the recovery room. The sphinx did not quite look as if she believed him. She stretched and flapped her wings, but folded them again when she went to look over the parapet on the opposite side, toward the narrow parking lot behind the old complex.

And stiffened, growling, staring down with a predatory intensity like Lucky regarding the rats, back when Lucky had been much younger. The fur went up in a ridge along her back, and her wings spread and quivered, making a sinister rustling-rattling noise. Her tufted tail lashed.

"Foes!" she whined. "Foes!"

"What?" said Vorlynkin, sounding startled. He stepped up to peer along with her; Jin joined him.

Mina, who was not so fond of heights, hung back a few paces and asked, "What does she see?"

Jin wasn't sure what kind of night vision the sphinx had, but what he saw was a van parked in the shadowiest part of the lot, and some dark-dressed men moving about below. One swung some sort of long hammer or bat, three or four dull thumps, and Jin heard a ground-floor window pop out and fall from its frame, inward, perhaps onto a carpet, he guessed from the muffled clatter.

"Somebody's breaking into the building," he whispered back over his shoulder to Mina, who at this news overcame her nerves and joined him to stare.

"Maybe it's robbers," she whispered back.

"What would anybody want to steal out of *here*?" The building had been stripped of usable furniture and equipment long ago; anything left inside was valueless or non-portable.

Two of the men lugged a big barrel-like thing from the van; they did something to it, then hoisted it through the window and let it fall and roll. A strange pungent aroma seeped up through the night mist, which made Vorlynkin jerk back and swear.

"Not robbers," he said through his teeth. "Arsonists!" He grabbed Mina's hand and looked frantically around.

Below, one of the men threw something through the window, and they all ran for their vehicle. They'd evidently left a driver waiting, because they shot out of the lot, past where the chain-link gate had been broken open, in a spray of gravel before the van doors were even all the way shut.

A flash of orange light; below Jin's feet, the building quaked as a boom echoed out across the lot and broke into mumbling thunder against the buildings across the street. A greasy boil of flame belched from the window, a licking tongue two meters long.

"Fire!" screamed the sphinx, all her fur on end, and her eyes like gilded saucers. "Fire! Foes! Fire!"

"We have to get out of this building, right now!" said Vorlynkin; Mina yelped as his hand tightened on hers. Vorlynkin lurched toward the towers. "Which stairs are farther from the fire?"

"Not that way!" said Jin. "There's an outside ladder drops down to the alley on the other side."

Vorlynkin nodded and ran, jerking Mina along with him; Jin grabbed up Nefertiti and ran after him. The sphinx struggled and hissed in his arms. Was there time to stuff her back into her carrier? Maybe not. Vorlynkin reached the opposite edge of the roof and found the steel staples.

"I have to go first, to let down the extension!" Jin yelled to Vorlynkin.

"Mina next," said Vorlynkin.

"I can't reach that far!" Mina sounded like she wanted to cry.

"I'll lower you over, and hold you till you get your grip," said Vorlynkin. "Go, Jin!"

"Who'll carry Nefertiti?"

Vorlynkin choked back something short, and said, "I will."

Jin dropped Nefertiti, hoping she wouldn't bolt away, vaulted over the parapet, and slapped down the rungs faster than he'd ever gone in his life. Unlatched the ladder, thumped at it, prayed it wouldn't stick or hang up. It rattled, then reached its full extension with a clang. "All right!" he called up.

Mina's kicking legs dangled over his head, then she found her footing and started down with no more than one scared meep. The rungs really were too far apart for her to reach comfortably. Above, Jin heard Vorlynkin swearing, and the scrunch of his footsteps, and the sphinx screaming, "Fire! Foes! Fire!" and, apparently confused in her vocabulary by the commotion, "Food!"

Vorlynkin yelped in pain, seemingly from some greater distance, and swore some more. Jin reached the ground and stretched up to catch Mina, whose sport shoes wavered in the air when she ran out of rungs before she ran out of space. "You're all right! Just let go!" She fell into him, knocking him to the ground; they both rolled, then scrambled to their feet and stared upward. At that point, Jin found out how well sphinxes could fly when Nefertiti sailed over the parapet, wings flapping madly, and descended. She neither plummeted nor soared, but she did land right-side-up on all four paws like a cat, hard enough to grunt when her belly hit the ground, but not hard enough to break anything.

Vorlynkin's big dark shape finally swung out over the edge; he dropped the last two meters, hit with knees bending like the sphinx's, staggered, but didn't fall. Blood was running down his face from a deep triple scratch below his left eye.

"Jin!" Vorlynkin's voice was sharp and hard, brooking no debate. "Take Mina straight to your mother, and do what Dr. Durona tells you to. If this fire spreads, they may have to evacuate all the buildings in the complex." He raised his wristcom to his lips and began snapping connect-codes into it.

Jin dove for Nefertiti, who flapped away screeching.

"Leave the bloody animal!" Vorlynkin snarled over his shoulder, already starting away down the alley. "Both of you, run!"

Chapter Eighteen

Ted Fuwa, the old cryofacility's putative owner, turned out to be more or less what Miles had expected—a big, harried man in his late forties who looked as if he'd be more at home on a construction site than in a conference chamber, even one so strange as Madame Suze's quarters at midnight.

A less-expected presence was the consulate's local lawyer, an alert, composed, compact woman, with wiry salt-and-pepper hair, who stood barely taller than Miles himself. Kareen, Miles was unsurprised to learn, had persuaded her to come here after hours. Madame Xia stared back at him with at least as much covert interest, as the source of the increasingly bizarre stream of legal questions she'd been fielding for the past week or so from her formerly staid and routine client. Miles trusted she was having her accumulated curiosity satisfied tonight.

Miles missed Vorlynkin, told off to stay with Sato and her children, and Suze wasn't happy that Tanaka had been called away to deal with some medical crisis, so he supposed the shifting sides, however you counted them, were still evenly matched. Suze and Tenbury versus Mark and Kareen, Miles as unruly witness with Roic his silent partner, the attorney throwing in comments and questions now and then that gave everyone pause, and Fuwa versus everyone, although Miles wasted little sympathy on him.

Madame Suze folded her arms and stared hard at Mark. "You still have given me no guarantees whatsoever about future provisions for the poor."

"I'm not running a charity, you know," Mark returned, irritably.

"*I* am," snapped Suze.

"Yes, but for how much longer?" asked Mark. "Sooner or later, and more sooner than later, I think, it would be your turn to go downstairs. And you would lose control of this place in any case. Tenbury and Tanaka might hold things together for a while, but after that—what?"

"It's what *I* was waiting for," put in Fuwa, a bit mournfully. Suze shot him a scornful look and sat up straighter in her big chair, as if to imply he'd be waiting for a while yet. Miles was less sure. Suze's skin bore more than a little of that pallid slackness that was the harbinger of decline. One couldn't say she glowed with health, not even in her irate stress.

"If the Durona Group doesn't step in," said Mark, "the inevitable end game is that this place will go to the city or the Prefecture, or to Fuwa. And in either case, patron intake stops. The life of one person isn't *long* enough to see this venture out."

"Although that might change in the future," Kareen observed.

"Or cryofreezing will become obsolete technology, and this whole demographic mess Kibou has created for itself will be naturally swept away," said Mark.

"I'm not so sure of that," said Miles thoughtfully. "If people start getting frozen at eight hundred instead of eighty, the game will still go on, just set to a new equilibrium. Although at eight hundred, it's hard to guess how people will think. At twenty, I could not have imagined myself at almost-forty. I can't imagine eighty even now."

Suze snorted.

Mark shrugged. "That will be for them to decide, however many decades or centuries from now. I expect death will still be cheap and always available, doesn't take high tech."

"During the initial transition period," Kareen said, wrenching things back from this flight of speculation to the practical present, "treatment actually will be free, if the subject is willing to sign up for the experimental protocols and give the legal releases. And anyone coming in can give their own permissions." Not needing, this implied, any cooperation from Madame Suze and company. "I expect the Group will prefer to have a few more healthy live subjects to start on, before tackling the more difficult complications from death trauma and cryorevival. Although they'll certainly want data on those as well."

Suze growled. Tenbury scratched his beard.

Kareen regarded her fingernails, looked up, smiled. Miles wasn't sure if anyone else caught Mark's small gesture, two fingers held out and then curled once more atop his stomach. The pair had the good-cop-bad-cop routine down to an art, Miles thought with admiration, and it would be a naïve observer who concluded that all the bad-cop ideas came from Mark—or the good-cop ones from his partner, for that matter. Kareen continued serenely, "The Durona Group will be doing a lot of local hiring, if this goes through. For example, if you, Madame Suzuki, were to sign up for the first round of protocols, and they proved to work as well as we hope, the position of Director of Community Relations could be made open for you. Which would put you in place to work on these problems on an on-going basis, right from here. This is all too complex to be solved in a night, but that doesn't mean it's too complex to be solved ever."

"Buy me off with an empty title? Oh, as if I haven't seen how that works before!"

"What you make of it could be largely up to you," said Mark, sounding as if he didn't care one way or another. "But in three years, when all those chambers below stairs are emptied out, it may be a whole new situation, here. Employment would keep you in the center of things, with real input."

It wasn't the future Suze had set her mind to; Miles fancied he could hear her imagination creaking with the strain of change, like a gate almost rusted shut. Almost. She said querulously, "What about the rest of us?"

"Tenbury, I'd hire tonight," said Mark readily. "We'll be wanting a Director of Physical Plant first thing—the place certainly needs significant upgrades and repairs, starting from the laboratory core outward. We'll likely"—he flicked a glance at Fuwa—"need a local contractor. Medtech Tanaka as well, Raven vouches for her. The rest on a case-by-case basis. I do require competence. Certification can be arranged."

Suze glowered in suspicion. Tenbury raised his hairy eyebrows.

The lawyer, Madame Xia, put in smoothly, "By the tacit contracts argument, Ms. Suzuki is the tacit proxy holder for all who have been frozen here, and can give blanket protocol permissions for all who entered here under her care. I believe I can make this argument work for the city adjudicator, since the city doesn't want the liability for several thousand destitute cryo-corpses."

"Not even if the city could register their votes?" asked Miles. "Seems to me that would be enough to swing a city election, if not one on the Prefecture or planetary level."

"I think I could guarantee—or at least plausibly suggest— expensive legal challenges about that, which the adjudicator would not relish." The lawyer smiled quietly. "Unless disunity among the petitioners forces the matter to go before a judge, in which case I cannot guarantee the outcome, because at that point the issues will become public and political. I actually spend most of my working time keeping my clients *out* of court."

"Public and political sounds like a job for Madame Sato's group, or something like it," Miles said. "I regret that we didn't snatch the other two members of her committee while we were at it. We'd have them now." Although an attempt to carry off three cryo-corpses from NewEgypt's coffers would certainly have taken more time, and might have gone less luckily.

"Client confidentiality has certain limits, Lord Vorkosigan," Xia warned him. Kindly, he thought.

"Diplomatic immunity?"

"Works for you. Not for me. But in this event, with criminal charges certainly coming down on NewEgypt, there may be legal ways to wrench Mr. Kang and Ms. Khosla away from their captors. Subpoena them as witnesses, for starters."

Miles tilted his head in appreciation. "If one could keep them from being destroyed by NewEgypt *en route*."

"That would be an important consideration in designing the approach, yes."

Mark pointed. "Kareen, put her on retainer."

Xia smiled warily. "My plate at work is actually rather full. I was only able to come here tonight because it's after hours."

"Partner or employee?"

"Me? I'm one of three associates in the galactic business law department of my firm. We work under a partner."

"The Durona Group will certainly be needing full-time local legal advice," murmured Kareen. "Perhaps we should talk instead about salary . . . later."

Xia waved this away, provisionally. "In any case, Ms. Suzuki, I'd invite you to think about what is the better long-term practical result for your patrons. You serve one community; this technology has the potential to serve the planet. If the—"

An echoing boom from outside rattled the windows. Roic shot to his feet and peered into the night. "What t' hell . . . ?"

"That sounded awfully close," said Xia uneasily.

"Was that *us*?" said Madame Suze. "Tenbury . . ."

"Could be the plastics fabricator next door," said Fuwa, joining Roic. "Though I can't think what they'd be doing over there at this hour. Or something from the street . . . collision?"

But with the municipal traffic control net here, collisions were vanishingly rare, Miles had thought.

"It's hard to tell the direction," said Tenbury, craning his neck as well.

"Go up on the roof and look," directed Madame Suze.

Tenbury was halfway out the door when Miles's wristcom chimed, emergency secured channel. *Vorlynkin. Not good.* Miles found himself on his feet without remembering standing up. "Vorkosigan here."

"Lord Auditor." Vorlynkin sounded winded. "An arson team—I counted four men—just put a fire bomb through a ground-floor window of the heat exchanger building. Asterzine, I think—it was a two-part liquid fire-starter, anyway."

"Call the local fire guards!"

"Already did, sir." The cadence of Vorlynkin's language was reverting to old military training, Miles noted in passing. "Police, too. They should be here in moments."

"Good man."

"I'm looking now to see if there are more intruders. Haven't spotted any so far. I'm fairly sure there's no one left in the exchanger building—can't speak to under it."

"Keep this channel open."

"Right, sir."

Miles wheeled to find everyone staring at Fuwa, who stared back in horror.

"It wasn't me!" the contractor practically wailed. "Not this time! Why would it be me, *now*? I'm about to get *rid* of this mess!"

"My exchanger towers!" cried Tenbury, starting for the door again. "If they go down, everyone'll start to thaw!" Suze grabbed his sleeve.

"*My* exchanger towers!" cried Fuwa. "My *facility*!"

"Tenbury." Madame Suze shook the custodian's arm, for emphasis. "Tell everyone you see, get out of the buildings and assemble on that patch of open ground in front of the intake building. I'll wake up and warn everyone on this floor."

The front of the patron intake building was on the opposite

side of the four-building complex from the fire-so-far, a map of the layout burning, so to speak, in Miles's mind's eye. So the arson had occurred as far as possible from the intake building, and the people now in it. This stank of diversion.

"Should we go to Vorlynkin?" asked Roic, jittering like a horse at the start of a race.

"No. To Leiber. Anything interesting will turn up at Leiber."

Roic's eyes widened as he took in the implications; Miles didn't have to spell them out. "Ah."

"Suze, we'll go warn them in the intake building," Miles added.

Madame Suze, already short of breath and with her hand pressed to her heart, nodded and said, "I know Vristi Tanaka is on the second floor. I think she just started a cryoprep."

"We'll get the word to her, as well as to our people."

She waved thanks and tottered out, Xia going with her in support and asking shrewd questions about where else all the sleeping residents were to be found at this hour. Tenbury sprinted ahead of them. Miles and Roic followed, turning in the opposite direction for the nearest stairs.

Through the office doors, Miles glimpsed Mark and Kareen braking Fuwa, one at each elbow providing a combined resistance that plainly surprised the big man, as he was yanked backward almost off his feet.

"Fuwa-san," Mark began in his most urbane voice, "let's talk fire sale."

Jin staggered up the last flight of stairs, puffing, lugging Nefertiti. For no discernable reason, she'd shied and bolted back past him in the alley below the exchanger building as Vorlynkin had disappeared around the corner, and Jin had caught her on a lucky tackle. Well, it had seemed lucky at the time. The sphinx seemed to have at least doubled in weight since then. She growled continuously, and shed fur and feathers on his shirt, but didn't try to scratch him.

"Get the door," Jin wheezed, and Mina nodded and swung

it wide. It was labeled, on this side, *Fire Door: Do Not Block.* So did that mean it would stop a fire? Jin hoped they weren't about to find out.

Nefertiti wriggled some more, and finally lunged from Jin's sweaty, failing grip just as they made it down the corridor to the recovery room, so Jin was at least able to spill her into this more confined area. Leiber-sensei, who was slumped in a battered folding chair staring anxiously into space, jerked upright at their entry.

"I thought you went to get rid of that thing!" he said, eyeing the sphinx with disfavor.

His mother sat up in her bed. "Jin? Mina? What's going on?"

"It was ninjas, mommy!" Mina declared breathlessly. "We saw them! They set fire to Jin's hideout!"

"*What?*"

"It was not either ninjas," said Jin impatiently. "It was just some stupid guys dressed in black stuff."

"Was that anything to do with the strange thump we heard through the walls a few minutes ago?" asked his mother.

Jin nodded. "It was even louder close up. Consul Vorlynkin said it was some kind of liquid fire-starter."

His mother gasped. "How close were you?"

"We were on top of the roof, looking right down at them!" said Mina. "The fireball was all orange and black!"

Leiber-sensei stood up and gripped the back of his chair, looking very uneasy.

"Where's Raven-sensei?" said Jin. "Vorlynkin said we were supposed to tell him about the fire, and then do what he said."

"He went down to the second floor to help Medtech Tanaka with a cryoprep," said Leiber-sensei.

Jin's mother slid out of bed and came to the wall of her booth, standing with her hands pressed against the glass. "Jin, maybe you'd better run downstairs and tell them what's going on. Was the fire spreading very fast?"

"We couldn't tell yet."

"Maybe I'd better find a room with a window and look," said Leiber-sensei.

"Where's Stefin gone?" asked their mother. "He was supposed to look after you two!"

"I think he went to look for more ninjas," said Mina.

She touched her hand to her lips. "Isn't that the sort of thing that Armsman Roic fellow is supposed to do?"

"He's probably with Miles-san," Jin called over his shoulder, heading toward the door again. "Mina, don't let Nefertiti get out!"

Leiber-sensei followed close on Jin's heels. And then cringed backward as the door was kicked open from the corridor side. Mina shrieked.

So did Nefertiti. "Foes, foes!" she screamed, flapping madly around the room and up onto a table.

Oh, Nefertiti, you're so right, thought Jin, backing up as Chief Hans and Sergeant Oki shouldered into the recovery room.

The pair seemed out of breath, and angry, and much, much bigger when looming vertically than when they'd been laid out on the floor of the garage office, drooling as they snored. They'd changed their clothes from the rumpled blue medical smocks they'd worn earlier, and were now dressed in uniformlike gray trousers and heavy cloth jackets, with equipment belts and big clumping boots, but without any insignia or name tags or identifying markers.

"There you are, you stupid turd! Finally!" growled tall Hans to Leiber-sensei, who'd backed up against a table and turned pale.

"What the hell . . . ?" said broad Oki, staring around at their audience. "What are these kids doing here? That jerk Akabane didn't say anything about kids."

"Never mind, just grab him."

Oki strode forward and did so, yanking Leiber-sensei around, doing something with the policeman's baton he carried in his hand, and hauling the scientist's arm up behind his back. Leiber-sensei yelped.

"Let him go!" cried their mother through the glass.

Hans's head turned, and his eyes narrowed. "I'll say *what the hell*! It's that bitch Sato! They must have woken her up. Isn't this the jackpot! Grab her too, Oki!"

"You'll have to. My hands are full," snapped his companion. Leiber-sensei tried to resist by going limp, and almost succeeded in slithering out of his captor's grip, but Oki jerked him upright once more, freed the hand with the baton, and slapped it with a loud electric pop against Leiber-sensei's thigh. Leiber-sensei yelled really loud. With a surprised gasp, Oki flinched and almost let him go, as the electric jolt evidently traveled through his victim's body and bit his gripping hand. But he renewed his clutch before the shuddering scientist could escape it.

Hans strode toward the booth and hit the lock control; the door slid back, and air puffed out.

"No!" said Jin, panicking so much that his vision blurred. "She's not supposed to come out yet! She'll get sick!"

"She's going to be a lot sicker when Akabane gets done with her," Hans snarled. He lunged for their mother, who hopped up and across the bed, and almost made it around the end to the door and freedom before he lunged again, caught her by the arm, and swung her against the glass wall with a sickening thud. He manhandled her out of the booth, stumbling, her long hair tumbling down all over.

"No, you can't have my mommy!" screamed Mina. "We just got her back!" She grabbed the folding chair, flopped it shut, and swung it as hard as she could. She might have been trying to hit the security chief in the stomach, but Mina was pretty short, and her aim was rather blind, as she whirled around. Instead, the chair legs took him square in the crotch—but not quite hard enough.

He bent over, saying really *horrible* words, but didn't let go of their mother's arm. With his other fist, he backhanded Mina, who fell on her butt, crying. Their mother tried to kick him, more accurately than Mina had, but she was barefooted and frighteningly breathless. "How dare . . . you *touch* . . . my children, you . . . horrible murderer!"

Remembering the blood running down Vorlynkin's face, Jin dodged around the table where Nefertiti stood stiff-legged, wings flapping, fur on end in a dark ridge running down her back, tail lashing, and shrieking incoherently. He grabbed her up and flung her at Oki, who was closest. The wide man yelled, waving his snapping and popping stick but only connecting with wing feathers, which scorched with a dreadful stink. Nefertiti leaped off him, shredding his jacket but only getting in one shallow bleeding scratch on his thick neck. Leiber-sensei broke from his grip, though. The scientist lurched and limped, dodging out of the way of the swinging baton.

"Oh, for God's sake!" said Hans. "Akabane didn't say we'd have to capture a damned *tribe*!" As Jin made a head-down rush with some wild idea of head-butting him in the stomach, Hans shoved their mother away hard, so she fell and skidded on the floor next to Mina, who scrambled to reach her. The tall man grabbed for Jin instead, catching him by the hair and swinging him around. Jin yelled, tears of pain starting in his eyes. He heard a strange snick by his ear, and looked down cross-eyed to glimpse a steel blade at least fifteen centimeters long glint past his face and lodge below his upraised chin.

"Everybody, freeze!" bellowed Chief Hans.

Everybody did. Hans added impatiently, "Not you, Oki!"

"Hans, no, he's just a kid!"

"After the day we've had, *don't push me*."

The belief and terror in Oki's face convinced the others that this was no bluff as nothing else could have, Jin thought. He could feel the edge pressing into his skin, and strands of hair popping from his stretched scalp.

"All right," said Hans. The big chest against which Jin was now pressed heaved for air, and maybe for balance. Could the tall man actually be frightened, too? That was a weird thought, and not reassuring. "Behave, all of you, or I'll cut the damn kid's throat, got it? You, quit wriggling!" He shook Jin's head back and forth by the hair.

Jin's mother, still on the floor, glared up cold and furious, but said in a voice sharp with dread, "Jin, hold still!"

Jin could see Leiber-sensei swallow. The limping sphinx had taken refuge in the shadows under a table, where she crouched and mumbled piteously, "Foes, foes, hurts, aowt, hum, hurts!" That, and people breathing, were the only sounds in the windowless room.

Hans straightened. "That's better. Now, you, kid, stuff your hands in your pockets." Jin, after a glance at his mother, complied. "You, Sato, stand up. You too, Doctor, and put your hands on top your head. Sato, take the mini-bitch by the hand with your right hand. Now, you're all going to march out in file, and Oki with his stick will keep you all in line. Set it on *high*, Oki!"

The broad man gulped, nodded, fiddled with the control in the base of the handle.

"Now, you all follow Oki out the door and turn right. Sato first, Leiber next, then me."

Their mother, her face utterly still and intent, grasped Mina's hand convulsively; they both stood up together. Her bare feet moved soundlessly on the floor, her padded robe flapping around her calves. Mina, sniffling and scared, trotted alongside. Leiber-sensei would have looked silly with his arms up like that, as if he were playing some toddler's rhyming game about touching your nose and ears and head, if he weren't so grim and pale and shivering. Jin waited for the grip on his hair to slacken, the knife edge to press less deeply, so that he could twist away and run, but the big fists holding him didn't ease.

They followed the others out into the corridor, Jin's feet barely touching the floor as he was yanked along, and turned right. They took maybe three steps toward the end stairs.

A bellow from behind them, Armsman Roic's deep voice: "Halt!"

Chief Hans whirled, still holding Jin in front of him. Up the corridor from the other end-stairs strode Roic-san, with Miles-san running at his elbow and Raven-sensei sort of dodging behind him. Roic raised his right arm, something in his fist too blurred for Jin's pain-teared eyes to make out. His expression was very strange, cool and remote, like no expression at all.

Jin felt his captor flinch. The knife edge bit harder. Hans yelled back, "You again! Drop that damned stuh—"

A white light flared from Roic-san's hand, and a strange buzzing noise. The world, or maybe it was Jin's head, seemed to explode in a jagged shower of colored rain. The rain turned black, and drowned him deep.

Chapter Nineteen

To Roic's surprise, he was actually aided in his capture of the remaining NewEgypt security fellow by Dr. Leiber. Oki had grabbed the scientist when Roic had shouted, presumably to keep him from bolting, but then found him harder to get rid of; Leiber hung on to the thick left arm that was trying to shake him off, turning and twisting and evading what looked to be a heavy-duty shock stick, just long enough for Roic to close the distance and aim his stunner between Oki's eyes at point-blank range.

"Give it up, Oki," Roic advised genially. "It's been over ever since I sent your confessions off in a bottle. I'd have thought you people would have realized that."

Caught and nailed by Roic's steady and implacable gaze as much as by the weapon aimed at his head, Oki reluctantly held his right arm wide and released his shock stick, which fell with a clatter. As he slumped, Leiber stood away from him, wheezing but with his spine actually straight for a change.

Unasked, Oki folded his hands atop his head and stood look-ing downright miserable.

Madame Sato, distraught, slid to the floor to gather up her son's limp body. The unconscious boy was pale, but Roic saw with satisfaction that the cut on his neck was a mere shallow scratch, barely bleeding.

"I'm sorry Jin was caught in my stunner nimbus, ma'am," Roic said to her. "But I've found it's usually better to resolve these hostage situations as directly as I can. Bad to let them spin out."

"This is a nightmare," she groaned.

Roic granted this with a nod, but said, "Cut short now, ma'am. Raven will get Jin some synergine *right away*"—Roic rolled his eye compellingly at Raven—"and he won't even wake up with a headache."

Raven took the hint and scurried back to the recovery room for suitable supplies.

M'lord strolled up, possessed himself of the shock stick, and regarded their captive with a curious and thoughtful air, like a biologist planning out the dissection of a promising new specimen.

Oki regarded him back, bewildered. "Who the hell *are* you people, anyway?"

"From your point of view," said m'lord, "I suppose we're your karma delivery service. Why the devil didn't you and your buddy Hans run and keep on running when you had the chance, earlier today? Yesterday, by now, I guess. Why ever did you go back to your bosses?"

"We got *families*, you know."

M'lord's brows rose. Had this not occurred to him before now, Roic wondered? "If you didn't want to be a disgrace to them, you're about eighteen months too late, I think."

Oki rocked a bit. "That, and the money."

M'lord brows went up a bit further. Oki said defensively, "For the first time in my life, the money was good. We bought a *house*."

Oki's was not exactly a world of riotous living, Roic suspected. If NewEgypt's plant security hiring practices were any good, he'd probably been an honest man, before he'd been sucked down into this bog by his bosses. Roic glanced at m'lord, prepared to give a hint and a nudge, but m'lord was on it already.

"It's not too late even now to limit your damages. What's the local equivalent of turning Emperor's Witness around here, does anyone know? They must have one."

"Prefecture's Evidence, I believe, m'lord," said Roic.

"I happen to have a good lawyer on retainer who can advise you, if you cooperate with me in a timely fashion," m'lord told their captive. "That means, instantly."

Roic took the cue and a tighter grip on his stunner, staring along its length into Oki's eyes for emphasis.

"Where were you taking Leiber and Sato just now?" asked m'lord. "Not for a walk, presumably."

"Akabane's waiting for us out front in the street with the van," mumbled Oki.

"The NewEgypt finance chief? Alone?"

Oki wet his lips. "It was just supposed to be Leiber, see."

M'lord's eyes lit. "*That* one we want, Roic—*in flagrante delicto* and arrested on the premises, if possible. An enemy's mistake is a tactical gift that must never be wasted."

Oki added, unasked, "It was going to be wall-to-wall lawyers for *them*—President Kim, and Choi who runs Operations, and Napak, that research head. Akabane caught us after the big meeting—said it was plain that him and us were going to be the goats, that the other three would hand us over without a blink in the morning if nothing was done. But he knew from the last time that my brother-in-law was with the Legacy Liberators, and..."

"Division and panic, ah," said m'lord, sounding quite satisfied. "That explains much. Hurry, Roic. Akabane's bound to bolt as soon as the police show up in force."

Raven was returning with a medkit. Roic passed his stunner

briefly to m'lord, circled Oki and fastened his wrists behind his back with his own tanglecuffs, was blandly handed back his weapon, grabbed Leiber's arm, and jogged for the end stairs.

"What do you want me for?" asked Leiber, sounding a touch alarmed, as they scuffed rapidly down the steps.

"You can ID Akabane for me. I wouldn't want to stun the wrong fellow, after all."

"You're pretty free with that thing."

"It's all right. I have a license to stun."

"I thought that was supposed to be a license to kill."

Roic grimaced. "That, too. But you would not *believe* all the forms that have to be filled out, afterward."

Leiber looked as if he weren't sure if that was a joke or not, which was all right, since Roic wasn't sure either. The procedures hadn't been all that amusing at the time. Or in retrospect.

They pushed through the heavy metal doors at the intake building's far end, turned left, and rounded the corner onto its long front side. A short, U-shaped driveway in the center led to a covered entry space, where patients and visitors had once been dropped off, no doubt. The drive embraced what had likely been a sweep of tidy lawn and landscaping, but now was a sad stretch of weeds. There was no security lighting, but a lot of flickering hand lights revealed a herd of elderly people in all sorts of dress and undress, milling about on the drive and the ex-lawn. To Roic's relief, no orange fire-glow reflected in the night mist from the other side of the complex, but various colors of flashing emergency lights did, which helped illuminate the scene in a dance-party sort of fashion.

A double row of parking spaces ran the length of the facility's front—Roic could see the end of the administration building, beyond the intake building, and mentally located Madame Suze's corner office on its top floor. Beyond the parking row, the facility was bounded by the dilapidated chain link fence.

In the street beyond, only one or two dark and distant vehicles were parked, but just past the gate with its tumbled-down old security kiosk, a familiar van lurked in the shadows. The gate, interestingly, had been forced open and left standing wide.

"All right," said Roic. "Wait'll I take cover behind that gate kiosk, then go out to the end of the lawn and mill around like the others. Make sure you can be seen from the street, but don't get within arm's length of the drive."

"Wait, what, you want to use me as bait?" said Lieber, indignant. "I thought you wanted me to identify Akabane!"

"This'll do that," said Roic reasonably. "Nobody else here is going to go grabbing for you. Plus it will lure him out of his vehicle and onto the grounds." *I hope.*

"Why bother?"

"First, I can't stun him through the side of the van, and second, if nothing else, Lord Mark can charge him with trespassing. Which will hold him for the night, and by morning it'll be too late."

"I thought that fellow Fuwa owned the place."

"If Lord Mark doesn't own it by now, I don't know him." Not that anyone did really know him, not even m'lord. Well, maybe Miss Kareen. "Go on." Roic gave Lieber a little encouraging shove, then drifted away unobtrusively through the intermittent shadows to take cover on the facility side of the gate kiosk, out of sight of the street.

Leiber stumbled around quite convincingly among the weeds, albeit at a few meters farther range than Roic would have preferred, looking up and around as if in bewilderment, showing profile and full-face. For a minute, Roic wasn't sure if Akabane would rise to his bait, and was just trying to think of a next ploy, when the van eased past the kiosk. Roic crouched down in the shadows.

For a horrible instant, he wondered if he'd misjudged the situation—if Akabane just lifted the van to head-height and brought it down hard enough atop his victim, Leiber would be in no shape to confess anything to anyone again. Someone had tried to do that to m'lord once, as he'd told the story to

Roic, with several passes like a big stomping boot coming within centimeters of reducing him to a smear on the pavement. Roic tensed like a runner at the start of a race, getting ready to sprint to his bait's rescue.

But maybe these local vehicles had safety sensors to prevent those sorts of accidents, or maybe Akabane was inhibited by the hundred or so witnesses. In any case, as its side door slid open the van merely lurched up onto the lawn, cutting Leiber off from the sight of the old folks, who were mostly turned away craning their necks toward the source of the flashing lights.

A dark shape leaped from the van toward Leiber, who recoiled. Roic took a sweeping knee shot and brought the figure down in a muffled cry of astonishment and rage. A few swift paces, and Roic was in position to put his favorite low-stun immobilization into the back of the fellow's neck, at can't-miss range.

"Quick, help me toss him back into his van," Roic told Leiber, who, puffing, nodded and complied.

Chief Financial Officer Akabane proved a local-looking sort—he might have been Raven's middle-aged wicked uncle, if the Durona clone had owned any uncles of any description. Although Akabane did not look especially wicked at this point, just pale and limp. And, Roic hoped, defeated.

For all the days m'lord had been playing against the New-Egypt cabal, this was the first direct view Roic had gained of the enemy's face, except for a few vid scans. It had all been action at a distance, like a space war. Or perhaps some bizarre mutant form of chess where the rules changed every two moves. M'lord's formidable father, who'd once been a space admiral, might have felt at home, and m'lord had scarcely been given pause, but to Roic it felt strange and bloodless and removed, though he was very grateful for the bloodless part.

And then Roic wondered how m'lord's sudden trail of chaos through their affairs, erupting out of seeming-nowhere, must have felt to the confused cryocorp men, who'd thought they'd had it all locked down. That was a vision to make a fellow smile, though it was a smile that made Leiber draw back in unease.

From the corner of his eye, Roic saw the lights of emergency vehicles turning into the street; they'd be through the gate in seconds. "Melt into the crowd and meet me back at the end door," he told Leiber, and swiftly followed his own advice. Melting into this crowd proved a bit of a trick, as he was a head taller, as well as about a century younger, than anyone else around him. But there was plenty enough else going on right now that no one spared him much attention.

Leiber arrived a few paces behind him. "That's it?" he asked.

Roic nodded. "M'lord will arrange the rest. Stunner tag's over." Roic took a moment's modest satisfaction in his job performance. "It's all words from here on. Which are not my department." He added after a reflective pause: "Thankfully."

Jin blinked open his eyes to discover himself staring at a ceiling—of the recovery room, he realized after turning his head. He touched his face, which was tingling, and scrunched his eyelids open and shut a few times, but he didn't feel especially sick or dizzy. He didn't feel especially good, either. Sort of blah, really. He seemed to be lying on one of the room's several raised, narrow bed-tables, though it didn't have any sheets, and its brittle old plastic felt nasty on his skin.

"Jin, are you all right?"

He sat up on one elbow to find his mother leaning over the side of the bed-table. She was wearing her filtering mask again, her robe all belted up tight, and her eyes searched him anxiously.

"I guess so." He rubbed his face some more, then scrubbed his scalp where it still hurt from the hair-pulling.

Mina skipped to their mother's side and looked up at him with great interest. "Armsman Roic shot you. I'd never seen anyone get shot for real before."

Neither had Jin. It felt very strange to have been shot. For the first time, he wondered what it had really been like for Miles-san when he'd been shot with that needle-grenade. Of course, that was nothing like being merely stunned, Jin supposed, but that weird moment of looking into Armsman Roic's unyielding face, and feeling so helpless and *too late* and that his world was being taken away from him by people he didn't, couldn't, control... He scowled, not liking that feeling much.

"It's not broken," came Raven-sensei's voice, and, "You couldn't prove it by me," Vorlynkin's voice returned.

Jin twisted around to find the pair of them at the next table over. Vorlynkin was sitting up with his legs dangling. His wide-sleeved coat was off, tossed aside, along with his undercoat, and his shirtsleeves were rolled up. Raven-sensei stood in front of him, poking at his left arm, which Vorlynkin was holding rather defensively.

Vorlynkin's face was all washed, and Nefertiti's claw marks were now three thin red lines beneath a shiny layer of transparent plastic bandage. There was a lot of drying blood soaked on his shirt collar, though, and spattered elsewhere on his clothes, and Jin cringed in guilt for his new pet.

"You will have some magnificent bruises," Raven-sensei continued.

"A crowbar will do that. I'm lucky I didn't get my face bashed in."

"Vorlynkin-san found more ninjas," Mina confided to Jin. "They had a fight. Vorlynkin-san won."

Vorlynkin looked over and smiled rather ruefully at her. "Fortunately for me, not ninjas. They were just a couple of borrowed thugs from the local chapter of the N.H.L.L. Finally trying to carry out their slogan, I suppose."

"I thought they were all arrested after the conference kidnappings," said Raven-sensei.

"That was an especially radical splinter group, apparently. Their organization is not very unified at the best of times, I gather." Vorlynkin added to Jin, "I found the pair of them around the far end of the next building over from your hideout, trying to pry the door open and get down into the tunnels with more fire-starter. If they'd succeeded it would have been a major mess."

Raven-sensei's eyebrows lifted. "Would the arsonists even have gotten themselves out alive?"

"Hard to say. It seems awfully easy to get turned around down there. But the department was able to get the fire in the exchanger building under control quickly, once I'd told them it was asterzine. Ugly product, asterzine. You *don't* want to put water on it, and it would have been a horrible surprise for the firefighters if they had. You can believe *they'll* be going after the N.H.L.L. in the morning."

Jin's brow wrinkled. "Why a crowbar? The door around the next side after that is always left unlocked."

Vorlynkin blinked, then laughed, then winced, touching his scratched face. "Just as well that none of us knew that, I suppose. After I confiscated the crowbar, I was able to hold them till the police arrived. Some of the firemen were more than eager to help. The pair fingered the NewEgypt security guards as having engaged them, evidently just to create a diversion for Dr. Leiber's re-kidnapping, though I gather that some of the Liberators grew over-eager and exceeded their instructions. But it should lead back nicely to the senior men Lord Auditor Vorkosigan wished to target."

Their mother rubbed her forehead, frown-lines deepening around her eyes. "If they don't manage to suppress it all, again."

"Not this time, I suspect," said Vorlynkin, smiling at her in reassurance.

"Where's Nefertiti?" asked Jin in sudden alarm.

Mina pointed at the desk built into the far wall, along with a lot of cupboards. From the shadows beneath came a mumbling sort of growl. "She's hiding. Maybe you can get her to come out after she calms down. I tried some food, but I don't think she's hungry right now."

Raven-sensei stepped around the tables to smile at Jin, peer into his eyes, thumb back his eyelids, and feel his pulse. "Headache? Nausea?"

"Not really." Jin felt down his tingling face to find a strip of plastic bandage across his neck.

"Just a nick," Raven-sensei assured him.

"My face is a little numb."

"That's normal. It'll pass in another hour. If it doesn't, let me know." Raven-sensei paused and cleared his throat. "Lord Vorkosigan said to tell you when you woke up, those few minutes of delay you and Mina caused with those NewEgypt thugs made all the difference to us. The rescue party, as it turned out."

"Oh," said Mina, sounding pleased.

Raven-sensei nodded. "If they'd hustled you out of the building before we arrived, he said, it would have been a long stern chase—one of his military turns of phrase, that—meaning, we'd have had a hell of a time catching up with you. Although I imagine he would have, somehow. He, ah . . . tends to be persistent."

For the first time, Jin sat all the way up. In the glass booth next to his mother's, the two big NewEgypt guys were penned, and Jin flinched in fear, till he saw that Hans was still out cold on the floor, and Oki was sitting with his hands fastened behind his back and his shoulders slumped, not paying attention to anything.

Jin pictured it—all of them dragged away in some windowless van to who-knew-where, and Mom *taken away again* . . . He gulped, which made the bandage tug on his skin. His desperate struggle with those big men hadn't seemed to do much good at the time, had seemed utterly futile in fact, but maybe . . .

Miles-san himself blew in then, his step brisk, with Armsman Roic in tow. Oki still didn't look up, and Jin was reminded that you couldn't hear anything in those booths.

"Ah," said Roic, smiling at Jin and giving him a friendly wave. "You're awake. Good."

Jin scowled back, not quite able to get that new picture out of his mind's eye of Roic looking through him like he wasn't there while he aimed the stunner. Roic's face fell, a little, though he then tried his smile on Mina to better effect. Was it all a fake, that smile? Which was the real Roic, the big smiling man or that cold, intent, scary one?

"You're all here, excellent," said Miles-san to the room at large. He hopped up on a chair like a teacher about to give a lecture, commanding everyone's attention, and making himself quite as tall as Roic. It should have looked silly, and Jin wasn't sure why it didn't.

"The Northbridge police will be here in minutes to start recording statements, and to take delivery of our NewEgypt guests," Miles-san went on, with a wave at the jail-booth. "We should be getting a couple of sleepy lawyers by then, too. Madame Xia has categorically insisted she has no expertise in criminal law, but we've woken up a couple of associates from her firm's criminal department. We'll have the senior partner in later today, when we're all back at the consulate and have rested up a bit."

Jin's mother stiffened. "We never had good luck with lawyers before."

"This time, they'll be on your side," Miles-san promised. "Meanwhile, Raven, Dr. Leiber, Consul Vorlynkin, we have just time to get our stories straight."

Raven-sensei looked interested, Leiber-sensei alarmed, and Consul Vorlynkin resigned.

Miles-san went on, "This whole chain of events is too complex and interlocking to adjust much, but on the whole I'd prefer to be less prominent in it, for reasons having to do with the other half of my investigations on Kibou. Which do not concern and should not impinge on your affairs, Madame Sato, so don't be alarmed. Fortunately, Raven and Dr. Leiber, here, are well positioned to be the local heroes."

Raven-sensei's brows rose. Leiber's stare at Miles-san grew glumly suspicious.

"Short version is, when Raven and I visited you that first

day, Dr. Leiber, it was because Raven was head-hunting a top cryo-preservatives chemist for the Durona Group's proposed new expansion to this Northbridge facility. Which is a position you will in fact be offered, by the way, assuming we can keep you out of jail."

"Oh!" said Leiber-sensei, sitting up, his sudden smile surprised but gratified.

"At that time, Dr. Leiber explained his renewed plans to blow the whistle on NewEgypt for the decomposed cryo-solution and commodified contracts scandal, and that he had abstracted Madame Sato's cryo-corpse to assure her safety as a future witness. Seizing his opportunity, he engaged Dr. Durona to revive her, as part of his price for employment, and Dr. Durona, anxious to secure his services, agreed."

"And carried her stolen cryochamber off to my secret laboratory on the spot?" inquired Raven-sensei, a bit dryly.

"Precisely." Miles-san smiled cheerfully at him. "Though let's not use the term *stolen* in your statements, should the issue arise. *Rescued* would be all right, or *secured*."

Raven-sensei waved assent. "And then what?"

"Dr. Leiber's attempt to leave Kibou for Escobar was a feint, to draw NewEgypt off, and out, till Madame Sato was revived and ready to testify. Unfortunately, it worked a little too well. But his rescue by Roic, at Raven's request, was allowed by me as a nepotistic favor to my brother's company.

"I was along for the ride tonight merely to keep an eye on Mark, whose movements are of on-going interest to Barrayaran Imperial Security for purely Barrayaran political reasons. Which also happens to be true, by the way. Having concluded that there is no current threat to the Imperium from Mark's new enterprise, I shall be withdrawing from Kibou-daini shortly to tend to my own urgent affairs."

Jin blinked at this news. Yah, well... of course it had to be that way. People always left. Nothing was ever really secure, or safe. He bit his lip.

"I suggest we not volunteer any information on the late Alice Chen tonight, and I think her existence is unlikely to come up as yet, but if it does, Raven abstracted her at Dr. Leiber's request as well, as independent physical evidence for the effects of the bad cryo-solution. Raven being enough of both a scientist and a businessman not to put his company at risk on mere hearsay."

Raven tilted his head and grinned at this. "That works for me."

Miles-san rolled his shoulders and stretched. He did look a little gray-faced, a very four-o'clock-in-the-morning look, if no more tired than anyone else here. His eyes were bright, though. He turned to Jin's mother. "I have an experienced forensic economics analyst already en route from the Barrayaran embassy on Escobar. As it happens, my need for him has been largely short-circuited the events of the last day, but to justify the expenses of his journey I will make you a loan of him for a few days. I expect he could be of considerable help in strategizing your next moves, should you decide to try to revive your political action committee. Or even if you don't."

Jin's mother rubbed her forehead. In a rather thick voice, she said, "But what if the police try to take Jin and Mina?"

It was a horrible thought, one that Jin had been trying not to think ever since Miles-san had announced the imminent arrival of the authorities.

"I think they are unlikely to question minors when abundant adult witnesses are ready-to-hand. You are next-of-kin; they'll have to request your permission to interrogate your children, which I suggest you deny for now on the grounds that the pair are too traumatized by the recent fright of their thwarted kidnapping."

Mina made a faint indignant noise at this. Jin wasn't so sure.

"The lawyer will support you," Miles-san went on. "If it becomes an issue, which I doubt it will in this immediate aftermath, tell the police to come see them later at the consulate if needed—which, by then, I suspect it won't be, and in any case we'll be on home ground there."

Vorlynkin nodded reassurance at her. She shook her head in doubt, but Jin thought some of the strain eased around her eyes.

Jin glanced up to find Armsman Roic eyeing him closely. Jin shrugged uncomfortably and turned his head away.

"Madame Sato," came Roic's slow, deep voice, "can Jin and Mina come out in the corridor with me for a moment? I'd like to show them something."

Jin looked back, about to decline, but Mina was already hopping up and down in agreement, readily prevailing over their mother who seemed to want to say something to the consul anyway, so Jin ended up letting himself be shepherded out with his sister. Roic closed the door firmly behind them.

To Jin's surprise, Roic went down on one knee, which made him, well, not much shorter than Jin and still taller than Mina.

"I thought," said Roic, "that you might like to try firing my stunner." He drew the weapon that had hurt so shockingly out of the holster under his jacket, and Jin flinched.

"Ooh, ooh!" said Mina. "Wow, can we?"

Which made it impossible for Jin to say *No*. He nodded warily.

"You must never point a weapon at a person unless you intend to fire," Roic began a short tutorial. "No matter if you think it's uncharged, or the safety lock is on, or what. Make it an absolute habit, and it will never be a question." He pointed out the various features of the device, including a sensor in the grip that was keyed to his own palm, and which he turned off with a code. Then he let Jin take it, making sure it was pointed up the empty corridor.

The grip was still warm from Roic's hand, like a chair you'd sat down in too soon after someone else got out of it. The stunner was lighter than Jin expected, but solid enough. The power pack in the grip gave it the most of its heft. It didn't feel like a toy.

Jin stared down the sight the way Roic told him too, and squeezed the trigger. The buzz in his hand startled him, but there was no recoil, and he managed not to drop it.

Encouraged, Jin let Roic show him how the automatic laser sight worked, and fired again. This time, he didn't jump. And again. The charge hit the wall pretty nearly just where he'd intended, this time. Jin didn't exactly smile, but he felt his jaw ease.

Mina was by this time eager to try, *Let me! Let me!* so Jin reluctantly gave the device up to her. Roic went through his instructions once more, prudently kneeling behind Mina and keeping a hand hovering to help steady her—she had to hold the thing up in both fists—and the drill was repeated.

Roic stood up, reset the code, and holstered the weapon. "Better?" he asked Jin.

"Yah," said Jin, in some wonder. "It's like a tool. It's just a tool."

"That's right."

This time, when Roic smiled down at him, Jin smiled up. He let the armsman lead them back into the recovery room.

Miles leaned forward and spoke earnestly into the secure holovid recorder. "I just want you to know, Gregor, that if the planet melts down over all this, it wasn't my fault. The trip-wire was laid long before I stumbled across it."

He considered the opening remark of his report cover for a moment, then reached out and deleted it. The one good thing about the very asynchronous vid communication entailed by Nexus info-squirts, moving at light speed between jump points and ship-carried through them, was that if you didn't think before you spoke, you could at least think before you hit *send*. Not that he hadn't generated some of his best ideas as his brain raced to catch up with his moving mouth. *Also, some of my worst.* He wondered which kind his recent examples would ultimately prove to be.

He glanced around the consulate's tight-room, which he had all to himself, having run out the exhausted Johannes before embarking on this private and personal recording. Since Johannes

was the closest thing to an ImpSec analyst the out-of-the-way
consulate boasted, Miles had spent much of the past two days
in training him in just what information, out of the uproar
of the local planetary feeds, to screen and forward to Galactic
Affairs on Komarr. Multitasking, always a good thing. Johannes
proved a diligent enough student. If the attaché had been one
of the Imperial Service's brighter stars, he'd have been sent
to some hotter posting, but if he'd been less responsible, he
wouldn't have been sent to such an autonomous one.

Miles added a note commending the lieutenant's conscien-
tiousness, while he was thinking of it, which reminded him in
turn of his early suspicions of the clerk, Yuuichi Matson. He'd
caught the tail end of a short conversation between Matson and
his boss Vorlynkin in the kitchen, day-before-yesterday, when
the media siege of the consulate was just beginning.

"People told me I'd be able to pocket a tidy amount of
baksheesh in this job," the clerk complained, "but in five years
nobody offered me *anything*. And when they finally do, it's
because they want dirt on Sato-san. *Sato-san*. As if I would!
Agh!"

Vorlynkin's blue eyes crinkled. "You were doing it wrong,
Yuuichi. You're not supposed to wait for offers, you're supposed
to ask. Or at least hint. You should ask the Lord Auditor for
pointers."

Matson just shook his head and stalked off, nursing his
green tea and his umbrage. Miles grinned and bent to add a
kind word for the overworked clerk, as well.

Trying to bring his mind back into focus, Miles scanned
down the long index of attachments, both raw data and his
synopses, that he'd generated for HQ, a tedious but necessary
chore. This should suffice to keep some unfortunate team of
ImpSec Galactic Affairs analysts busy and happy for a week
or three, till he caught up with them in person. Well, busy,
anyway. The Imperial Councilor, as the Barrayaran viceroy on
Komarr was dubbed, would be invited into the loop as well

when this arrived by coded tight-beam. A full analysis of the planetary voting shares scam should be awaiting the Lord Auditor by the time he made Komarr orbit, and a plan for suitable countermeasures for the vote-theft, as well.

Miles indulged himself with a brief fantasy of Ron Wing and friends waking up from cryo-stasis, expecting to have stolen a planet, as destitute and distraught as old Yani. Alas, the affair would doubtless be wound up before matters progressed that far. Cosmic justice was very appealing, but the regular kind would also do.

Putting together his Auditorial report had also sufficed to keep Miles out of the way of the consulate upstairs, and out of sight of its visitors, as the consequences had spun out from that very useful night at Madame Suze's. The NewEgypt execs were under arrest for conspiracy, and possibly murder, and as the degenerated-cryopreservatives-and-commodified-contracts scandal hit the newsfeeds in force, it was likely that enough other charges would be thrown in atop to keep them from wriggling out. The attempted kidnapping involving real kids looked to prove especially damaging to their cause, score another point for Jin and Mina, which Miles must remember to tell them. Lawsuits on behalf of Madame Sato and her group were in preparation, and she'd given her first interview, under the watchful protection of Vorlynkin and with the shrewd advice of her new attorney, who was working, very enthusiastically, on contingency.

WhiteChrys and a number of other cryocorps, shoved into premature responses by these breaking events, were making noises like outraged victims after all, and Miles, smirking, wished Ron Wing all the luck he deserved in his damage control. Asterzine was all very well for setting a building on fire, but if one wanted to set a world alight...well.

Miles hardly needed, he reminded himself for the *nth* time, to mix in further, above-stairs. Consul Vorlynkin was doing a fine job of looking out for Barrayar's interests, not to mention

those of the Sato family, and Mark was atop affairs from the
Durona Clinic end. Miles had danced uncomfortably close to
jeopardizing his primary mission with WhiteChrys on these
fascinating side-issues with NewEgypt, but given Mark's new
enterprise, they might not prove so sidewise after all. Miles was
not above taking credit for accidental foresight; really, none of
this would have come to pass if he hadn't gone on poking just
a little farther than he'd needed to. He must be sure to point
that out to Gregor.

Ah. Gregor. The cover message would go to the Emperor's
eyes and ears only. For inspiration, Miles called up a still vid
of Gregor in full uniform and his sternest glower, the official
pose that Gregor had dubbed *the rod up my Imperial butt look*.
Alas, it only inspired Miles to want to clown till he made that
grave face crack a smile. No, Gregor had clowns enough in his
life. Starting with about half of the Council of Counts, though
they seldom made him smile.

Miles hit *record* once more, and began with crisp efficiency.

"Good day, Gregor. As my follow-up note to Vorlynkin's little
misguided emergency message last week indicated, suspicions
of WhiteChrys chicanery on Komarr have proven correct. The
raw data and my summations are in the main body of my
report. I'm not sure what to do with the bribe. I'm not going
to give it back, but it's not going to be worth what Ron Wing
promised, either, which makes dumping it directly onto the
Imperial Service Veterans' Hospice a questionable proposi-
tion. But we can deal with that later. I'll stop at Solstice on
my return trip if ImpSec Komarr and the Imperial Councilor
want to ask further questions, though really, this should be
enough to get them started.

"Oh, and with respect to Vorlynkin, I want a suitable Auditorial commendation to go on his diplomatic department record
for exemplary assistance during my visit, or, ah, visitation. And
after, as I'm running away tomorrow and dumping all of the
cleanup on the poor fellow." *Better him than me.*

"Meanwhile, I suppose I'd better give you a quick synopsis of the erupting NewEgypt scandal, as it has impinged on my investigation. It all started when the local loony party broke into the cryo-conference and failed to carry me off, which I described in brief in my last report, but after that..."

As succinctly as he could, Miles summarized the events of the past days, from Jin's arrival at the consulate's back door through the successful arrest of the NewEgypt crew. He was a little out of breath by the time he finished. Miles tried not to wince as he imagined the look on Gregor's face as he heard all this out. Nonplussed? Pained? Bland? Gregor could out-bland Pym.

"So far, no criminal charges have been leveled against me, and I trust I'll be long gone from Kibou-daini before anyone on the other side thinks of it," he concluded in cheerful reas-surance.

He sought for an upbeat note on which to end. "In the department of *only on Kibou,* we actually got to summon the dead to testify against the bad guys, which is a moment of cosmic justice if ever there was one."

What was that creepy old quote...? Something read in his Academy days, or more likely on one of his Academy leaves, an ancient tale from Old Earth. Before cryonics was invented or even imagined, so seeming strangely prescient. The words were branded in his brain, though their literary source was long forgotten, buried under the chaos of his intervening decades and possibly a touch of lingering cryo-amnesia. *I will break the door of hell and smash the bolts; I will summon the dead to take food with the living, and the living shall be outnumbered by the host of them...*

Ah, not something he cared to share with Gregor, that. Gregor, as Miles had reason to know, already had enough creepy crap stuffed into his Imperial head that it was a wonder his skull hadn't exploded. But it did bring Miles to his finale.

"I shouldn't wonder if Mark's rejuvenation research here

doesn't turn out to be more important, in the long run, than my mission. Too early to judge, but the Durona Group will be something to keep an eye on, and not just ImpSec's spy-eyes, either. A private word in the ear of Laisa's great-aunt, if she's looking for a better investment than WhiteChrys Solstice, might be a suitable reward for her first bringing the affair to our attention, come to think.

"I missed today's commercial jumpship to Escobar, but I've snagged berths on tomorrow's. I'm eager to get home.

"And oh, tell Laisa from me—*Good catch.*"

Miles closed the recording, security-sealed it, attached it to his coded report, and sent it on its way.

Chapter Twenty

The afternoon sun warmed the consulate's back garden, murmurous with creatures. Gyre preened and muttered on his perch. The chickens scratched in the grass or dozed in their nest boxes. The sphinx nosed and mumbled among the flower beds, occasionally sneezing just like Jin's mom. Gracing the tabletop, the turtle slowly crunched a piece of lettuce, donated from Mina's lunch salad. Lucky sat in Jin's mother's lap and purred, unsheathing her claws whenever the stroking hand stopped, apparently demanding to be petted bald. Granted that the rats, let out for a run earlier and then fed special tidbits, just curled up and slept in their cages, but then they never made much noise in the first place. It was all very *alive* out here, Jin thought with satisfaction.

They had brought out a table to eat lunch under a tree, Mom and Jin and Mina and Consul Vorlynkin, and Aunt Lorna, invited for the first time to visit her revived sister. Jin had been horrified when he'd learned she was coming, but

since she wanted him back in her household quite as little as
he wanted to go there, they'd actually ended up on the same
side, in a weird sort of way. She still seized the chance to chide
him for running off. Both times.

"She's right, Jin," his mother endorsed this. "They were all
very upset when they didn't know what had happened to you.
You might have been killed, for all she and your uncle knew."

"But if I hadn't run away," Jin said, "I'd never have met
Miles-san. And Mom would still be frozen."

Vorlynkin-san grinned at Aunt Lorna's flummoxed expression.
"Unassailable logic, I'm afraid." He'd taken off his business coat
in the warmth, and leaned back in his chair in his shirtsleeves,
looking more relaxed than Jin had ever seen him. But then,
most of the time he'd been following Miles-san around, and
Miles-san had a way of un-relaxing people.

Miles-san and Armsman Roic had left yesterday, to board an
orbital shuttle and catch a jumpship to Escobar, from where,
Consul Vorlynkin had explained to Jin and Mina with the aid
of a wormhole map, the Lord Auditor would transfer to a ship
bound for the planets Sergyar and Komarr, and finally to Barrayar, where his real home was. The one with all those children
and ponies, Jin supposed. Despite the steady procession of lawyers, police, and journalists into and out of the consulate, not
to mention Jin and Mina and their mother and now relatives,
Jin had to admit it had grown a lot quieter around here since
the little man had left. It had all been very exciting for a time,
but Jin wasn't sorry for the slow-down. In any case, the parade
of people had been closely supervised by the consul, at his most
formal and intimidating, not to mention Barrayaran and tall, and
nobody had tried to take Jin's mother away again.

Mina had gone inside to go to the bathroom, but now the
back door slammed open and she rushed out in excitement,
a familiar box in her hands. Lieutenant Johannes followed
warily, saying, "She'll be much happier returned to her natural
habitat, I'm sure."

"Jin! Mommy!" said Mina. "Look! Lady Murasaki's babies all hatched!"

Their mother valiantly replied, "That's nice, dear," although Aunt Lorna winced. Mom stared down through the transparent lid, and added faintly, "My goodness, she has a lot of children, doesn't she? Perhaps it's time to move them to a larger home."

Like us? thought Jin. *Let it be like us.* He eyed Consul Vorlynkin in fresh speculation.

"Lieutenant Johannes says I have to put them all out in the garden." Mina frowned, evidently trying to decide if this was a good idea or not. Behind her, Johannes made motions that seemed to indicate he didn't want to share the consulate with a hundred active spiderlings, which Jin thought quite narrow-minded of him.

"Excellent notion," said Vorlynkin, tactfully. "I understand their webs look quite attractive in the morning light, after a heavy dew."

Jin embarked on a hasty tutorial about what kinds of spiders did and didn't spin webs, and the web designs of various species in relation to their prey, while Mina went off to find some especially pretty flowers on which to release the new family.

Johannes muttered to Vorlynkin, "When she shoved that box under my nose, I thought I was going to throw up."

Vorlynkin's eyes crinkled. "I didn't know you were arachnophobic, Trev."

"You realize, the garden is going to be *swarming* with those gigantic spiders?"

"Actually," said Jin, "the chickens will probably eat some of them."

Johannes eyed the chickens with approval for perhaps the first time ever.

"Don't tell Mina," Jin added.

"Wouldn't dream of it," said Johannes, and, after a polite nod at Jin's mother and aunt, went back inside.

Not five minutes later, the back door opened more sedately,

and Raven-sensei strolled through. Jin had never been more glad for an interruption, as the grownups had started talking about Jin's missed school, and what was to be done about it, and how soon. Raven-sensei gave a general wave to everyone—Mina waved back enthusiastically—and came to a stop at the table, with a lift of his eyebrows at Aunt Lorna. "Ah. Sister-san?"

Jin didn't think Aunt Lorna looked that much like her older sister, being both shorter and rounder, with bobbed hair, and more peevish, although any peeve evaporated as she stared up, wide-eyed, at the Escobaran surgeon. Vorlynkin hastened to introduce them, and Aunt Lorna actually smiled and shook hands, and, when Raven-sensei turned away to greet Mina, whispered to her sister, "You didn't tell me your doctor looked like *that.*"

"Decorative *and* functional," Mom murmured back. "His clinic has quite the reputation on Escobar, I'm told."

For a moment, Consul Vorlynkin frowned, as if worrying whether to try to look decorative or functional, but settled on diplomatic, which suited him better anyway.

Raven-sensei returned from admiring the spider family, and Jin, at a nod from his mother, gave up his chair to the new guest. This wasn't so bad, as Jin then went to lean on her shoulder, and she slipped her arm around his waist. Lucky, with a grumpy noise at the loss of the petting hand, jumped down.

"I thought you would like the word at once, Madame Sato," said Raven-sensei. "We retrieved Mr. Kang and Ms. Khosla last night, and I did both revivals this morning. Entirely uneventfully, I'm pleased to report. Both spoke briefly, and about as lucidly as could be expected, before I put them back to sleep. As soon as your head cold passes off, you may come down to the facility and see them."

Jin felt his mother's body tremble; her eyes squeezed shut in brief thanksgiving. "Thank you for your excellent work, Doctor."

"Truly," said Consul Vorlynkin. He tilted his head in concern at Jin's mother, but eased back in his chair again when she dabbed her eyes and relaxed. "How soon will they be able to speak to the lawyers and the police detectives?"

"They will, of course, have to stay in biological isolation for a few days, but I'd expect their recoveries to be almost as swift as Madame Sato's. They may be coherent enough to give depositions through the booth intercoms as early as tomorrow evening, but I told the authorities to come the following morning, to be sure."

"And their physical security, meantime?"

"Miss Koudelka has arranged that, as part of setting up security for the new clinic. She turns out to have a knack for that sort of thing. Did you know her mother used to be a bodyguard to the Emperor of Barrayar, when he was a child? ImpSec trained, I gather, and she passed it along in the family."

"Yes, I believe Lord Vorkosigan did say something about that, before he left. He does seem to know the most extraordinary range of people. Only to be expected, given his background."

"What *is* this Lord Unpronounceable you keep talking about, anyway?" asked Aunt Lorna.

"What, or who?" said Raven-sensei. "Although I gather that for him, the two are nearly inextricable."

"Either. Both."

"He investigates insurance fraud for somebody," Jin supplied. "His boss is named Gregor. He talks about him a lot."

Vorlynkin blinked; Raven-sensei laughed, and Jin twisted his toes in unease. "Isn't that right?" he asked.

"Well, yes," said Vorlynkin, smiling again. "Emperor Gregor Vorbarra, that is. But a Lord Auditor investigates all kinds of fraud and, er, other difficult situations that may arise that affect the Imperium, on the Emperor's direct orders. At the highest levels, generally, and with very little oversight."

"He once called himself the Emperor's stirrup-man," Raven-sensei confided. "I wasn't sure if that meant a guardsman who rides at his leader's side, or a man who holds the stirrup while he mounts. Very Barrayaran turn of phrase, though, I thought."

"*Rides at his side* is more correct," said Vorlynkin. "Although the other isn't out of line."

Jin's mother tilted her chin in interest. Aunt Lorna's eyes widened a bit.

"I didn't know he was *that* important," said Jin, thinking back to his first view of the tattered lost druggie. And a great deal of really strange behavior and babble subsequently. Miles-san had never acted at all high-nosed or stuffy. On the other hand, he'd never acted like the rules applied to him, either.

"His father, Count Aral Vorkosigan, is Viceroy of Sergyar," Vorlynkin explained to Jin's interested female relations, "and his mother, the famous Countess, is Vicereine in her own right—her title's a co-appointment, not a courtesy just because she's his wife. His viceroyalty caps a long career in service to the Imperium."

"Very hard act for Miles to follow, I gather," Raven-sensei put in.

Jin thought of his own father, frozen in time by his death more permanently than by any cryonic procedure. Jin would never be more than seven, in those fading memories. Never seventeen, or twenty-seven, or almost thirty-eight from the other side. What would it be like to have a father when you were both grownups at the same time? It seemed a strange, uncomfortable, tantalizing thought.

"Royalty?" asked Mina, who had drifted back to her mother's other elbow in time to hear this. "Is Miles-san's daddy some kind of prince?"

"A viceroy is a—hm," Vorlynkin paused as if to choose words especially for her. "Emperor Gregor can't be on all three worlds at once. So he stays on Barrayar, mostly, and sends people to represent him on the other two planets. The Imperial Counselor on Komarr, the Viceroy and Vicereine as a team on Sergyar. Same jobs, really, just under two different titles because the planets are rather different." He glanced at Jin's mother, as if to check how she liked this explanation about his home.

"So, they're like... deputy emperors?" asked Jin.

Vorlynkin's brows rose in approval. "Yes, actually. Except they are appointed, serve terms, and then stop. *Emperor* is a life sentence. So to speak." A wry smile crossed his lips.

"So Miles-san has an important job *and* an important family," said Mina, testing out these ideas. Jin wondered if she was thinking about those ponies.

Aunt Lorna grimaced. "Is his important relative why he was given the important job?"

"No," said Raven-sensei judiciously, "I expect Miles was given his job because he's a damned weasel. There's a reason *ferret out* means what it does. You have to have noticed that the man is a hyperactive lunatic, surely." With a fair-minded air, he added, "To the benefit of me and mine, to be sure."

"Well..." Vorlynkin trailed off vaguely. And diplomatically, Jin supposed.

Jin heaved a sigh. "I wish I might have a ferret!"

Jin's mother choked; Vorlynkin glanced at her, and at Nefertiti who was now nosing among the violets, and put in, "You just got a—er—almost a lion, at least. Possibly enough wildlife wishes granted for the moment."

Mina twined her arms around her mother and rested her head on the maternal shoulder. Mom hugged her back. *There's a wish*, thought Jin. *There's a real big wish, to have granted.* Bigger than a ferret any day. Bigger than a lion, even.

Although—Jin had seen pictures—ferrets were really cute. Cute-and-furry was always an easier sell than carapaced-and-multilegged, for some obscure reason. Grownups, so unreasonable...

The grownups started talking about lawyers and lawsuits and NewEgypt's evil executives, all under arrest, and Mom's old political action committee and what would happen to it next, which they'd been doing nonstop for *days,* practically the whole week since Suze-san's place had almost been burned down, so Jin drifted away to watch Nefertiti. Mina, equally bored, followed him.

The sphinx was crouched down in the patch of purple and white violets.

"Oh, no!" cried Mina. "She's eating them!"

Jin, worried that the consul might be attached to his violets—thin green stems, at this point, mostly—grabbed the sphinx and dragged her away, scolding.

"Fud," mumbled Nefertiti, squashed lavender petals dribbling from her mouth.

"Vorlynkin-san!" Mina called in anxiety. "Will eating violets make Nefertiti sick?"

Jin's mother gulped in dismay, except that she was also laughing, but Vorlynkin seemed barely taken aback. "I shouldn't think so. Edible flowers are sometimes put on salads, and violets, I believe, are among them. They're also served candied. It would doubtless be prudent not to let her eat too many at a time, however."

Jin and Mina both slumped in relief, for slightly different reasons, perhaps. Vorlynkin-san knew all *kinds* of nifty things. And he smiled at Jin's mom. And Jin's mom smiled back, which wasn't something she'd done much, lately. He was actually an all-right-all-round sort of fellow, though he needed to be brought up to speed on zoolology, if he was... going to stick around.

So that's all right, thought Jin.

Miles selected a table at the edge of the balcony overlooking the Escobar transfer station's main concourse. From here, one had a doubly dizzying view, of the people passing two floors below, and of a broad slice of star-specked space and Escobar's rim, glowing with light and color, through the transparent wall above. He set out three coffee bulbs, took a seat, and gestured Roic to another.

The armsman accepted a coffee bulb but shook his head at the seat, preferring to lean against the balcony rail and gaze around, appearing, alas, exactly like a bodyguard trying to look like a tourist. Roic was not fond of these exposed positions.

Miles always enjoyed this cafe, when passing through here—this addition to the station was about ten years old, he recollected.

Mark appeared, spotted him—well, Roic—waved, and trod over. Miles's commercial ship was not leaving for some hours, so Mark had delayed catching the hourly downside shuttle in favor of a few more minutes with his brother. Sharing the same ship from Kibou-daini had thrown them together for a longer stretch of time than they'd had in years, even if they'd both spent much of the time *en route* in their separate cabins devising detailed directives to send ahead to their respective associates. Busy and absorbed was, on the whole, good. Beat the hell out of *insane and dead,* for example.

Mark sat down, swept up the last bulb, popped the cap with his thumb, took a swig, and grimaced. When he had time, Mark was a bit of a gourmet, finicky in his tastes for food and drink. Miles didn't think the flavor was so bad, for transfer station bulb coffee. As a practical matter, you had to allow the modifiers.

"Sorry I'm late," said Mark. "At the last moment before disembarking, I got a message from Kareen, and I wanted to play it right away."

In the privacy of his cabin. Miles nodded understanding. Mark had left Kareen and Raven behind to start the set-up for the new Durona clinic, and incidentally keep an eye on the progress of Jin's affairs, while Mark went ahead to deal with the details on the Escobar end. The separation from his partner, temporary though it was, left him notably cranky. Miles thought of Ekaterin and sighed.

"News good or news bad?" Miles asked. Though if there were anything very bad, he should have received a tight-beam from Vorlynkin.

"Not bad. Kareen reports Raven successfully revived those two missing friends of Madame Sato's, and they've given some useful testimony to their authorities. Legal actions against NewEgypt proceed apace, by legal standards, which means glacially by human standards, but they are apparently moving in the right directions, so far. With the murder charges laid, the NewEgypt execs remain in custody. The locals accepted a plea bargain of some sort from your friend Oki, whatever you call it when you rat out your comrades in exchange for a lighter sentence." Mark didn't sound especially disapproving.

Roic, listening, raised his coffee bulb in salute and drank. Oki hadn't been the worst of the bunch, to be sure.

"I trust my name hasn't turned up in the proceedings," said Miles.

"They don't know you from a hole in the ground," Mark assured him, and grinned like a fat shark at his pained expression. "Did Kareen really have to sit on you to keep you from giving interviews?"

"That was a joke, and she knew it," Miles said austerely.

"Yeah, right."

"What's next for you?"

"I descend on the Durona Group with a long list of chores not in their prior schedule, much as you will when you hit home, no doubt. I hope to have the set-up team for our first off-Escobar satellite clinic assembled and on their way in a week. Fuwa's repairs are in hand, which is a relief; most contractors in my experience are only just barely faster than lawyers. Kareen says his work looks good so far, so we'll be able to employ his company some more. Seems the least I can do for the man."

"How little *did* you get him down to, that night?"

Mark gave a smug duck of his chin. "That's proprietary information. But to thwart seller's remorse, I plan to swing him a lot of construction business."

"Bet he'll try to pad his estimates."

"Oh, of course." Mark waved this away as a given.

Miles wondered if sending Mark to batten on Kibou-daini would prove adequate revenge for WhiteChrys's ploy on Komarr. On the whole, he thought it might.

"And you?" asked Mark. "Are you going straight back to Barrayar, or will you stop at Sergyar to see our parents?"

Miles rubbed his knuckles across his mouth, frowning. "There was no chance to go downside on my outbound trip, of course. Though I did snatch twenty minutes to talk in real time with Mother, from the orbital transfer station."

"How was she?"

"No more harried than usual. I'd promised to stop on the way back, but my case ran a couple of weeks over what I'd initially planned—did that one to myself, true—and I might need to spend a few days on Komarr, setting up the trap for WhiteChrys with some folks, which also wasn't in my initial plan. So I may have to wait till they come home for Winterfair, if they do, this year. Will you and Kareen be coming home then?"

"Not sure yet."

"I was thinking you could pitch your new procedure to the Count-our-father in person."

"We'll see how good it's looking at that point. We might actually have some preliminary results. Or not."

A few passers-by turned their heads to stare at the two not-quite-twins, slouching, for the moment, in identical poses in their bolted-down chairs opposite each other. Miles studied his clone in a little frisson of wonder he'd never quite lost.

"What?" said Mark, tilting his head in an invitation to be amused by his progenitor-brother's infamous babble.

"Thinking about the uncle we neither of us ever knew. Our father's older brother, who was killed in that same attack that took out our Barrayaran grandmother, in the opening salvo of Mad Yuri's war. He was in his mid-teens, I believe. I was thinking how strange it was that I had a brother I never knew till I was an adult, and our father had a brother everyone had forgotten by the time he was an adult. Were you ever told anything about him at all, when you were being trained about Barrayar?"

Mark shrugged. "Just a name. No time was spent on him, when there was so much else to learn."

"That's about all I've ever gotten from Da, either. A painful period of his life, I gather. Maybe if you and Kareen do Winterfair, we can tag-team him and get him to disgorge more. Because I'm thinking...there's hardly anyone else alive who knows anything about the fellow, by now."

Mark nodded. "It's a deal. If we come. Could be interesting. Or hair-raising."

"Or both. I sometimes wonder how different things would be if he'd lived. Our father would never have become the count, for one. Maybe not even Lord Vorkosigan, if his brother had managed to pop an heir before our grandfather died. He'd have spent his life as Lord Aral."

"I'll bet he'd still have had a military career, though," said Mark judiciously.

"Perhaps. Or perhaps, with the responsibility for our House taken up by someone else, he'd have felt freer to rebel. Do something else, be someone else."

"Huh," said Mark.

Miles fingered the holocube in his pocket. There was no point in pulling it out and showing it to Mark again, as he'd already done so. Twice. "You and Kareen planning kids yet? Not to mention marriage," Miles added in an afterthought. The couple's informal partnership, which would have been unremarkable on Beta Colony, had been a difficult pill for Kareen's very Barrayaran parents to swallow, but after several years the senior Koudelkas seemed pretty reconciled. And Kareen had three older married sisters, all of whom had sprung at least one sprog, so there wasn't the family pressure on her that there had been on, say, Miles.

"Children frighten me," Mark confessed. "You had your Da as a role model, but all I ever had growing up was an insane Komarran terrorist who spent all his time trying to train me to be you."

"Da spent a good bit of time trying to train me to be me, too," said Miles, "but it wasn't at all the same thing."

Mark snorted. "Indeed."

We can laugh about this now, sort of, Miles thought, pleased and bemused. *What a journey that's been.* "You'd have Kareen for a co-parent," Miles offered. "She's one of the sanest people I know."

"There is that," Mark admitted. "So what's your greatest terror, now you're a Da yourself?"

"What if..." Miles pulled at his hair, looking up cross-eyed to see if he could spot any of the sneaky gray ones, but this cut was still too short. "What if my children find out I'm not really a grownup? How dreadfully disappointed would they be?"

This time, Mark laughed out loud. It was a very good sound, Miles thought, and he grinned back ruefully at his brother.

"I think your wife already knows," said Mark.

"I'm afraid so." Miles rubbed his lips. "Heh. D'you think Vorlynkin and Madame Sato will make a match of it?"

"Good God, how would I know?"

"I thought he had that look in his eye. Not as sure about her..." Which gave Miles a rather comradely feeling toward Vorlynkin, now he considered it. He wished the man luck.

Roic stiffened, peering down into the concourse.

"What?" said Miles.

"There's Colonel Vorventa," Roic answered. "Wonder what he wants?"

Miles leaned toward the railing and craned to see. The Barrayaran officer was, among other duties, senior ImpSec liaison from the local Barrayaran embassy on this main transfer station; Miles had dealt with him before, though more often with his predecessors. The colonel looked up, saw Roic, then Miles, waved in a wait-right-there sort of fashion, and made for the lift tubes at the end of the concourse. "Us, I'll bet. Or me." ImpSec would have known when their ship was coming in, of course.

"You, I hope," said Mark. "I've had a few conversations with him. I don't think he trusts me."

"He's actually pretty cosmopolitan, for a Barrayaran," said Miles. "One of Da's New Men. Blast, I hope he's not bringing me more work."

It was a compelling and unwelcome notion. If some fresh forest fire involving Barrayar's interests had sprung up somewhere on this end of the Nexus, well, here was one of Gregor's most notable firemen already halfway there. Miles's lips twisted. *No, I've just been! I want to go home now!*

"That's funny," said Roic, in slow speculation. "I don't think I've ever seen him wearing his dress greens before."

Miles hadn't either. "That's true. He always wears local civvies, trying to blend in."

Not today. Vorventa wore a high-necked military tunic in forest green, all his rank tags and decorations squarely in place, the green trousers with the red side-piping tucked neatly into mirror-polished riding boots, and a more inappropriate garb for a space station Miles could scarcely imagine. "Damn, but he looks shiny. Wonder what's up?"

"We'll find out in a minute," said Mark, turning in his chair to watch the officer make his way among the tables toward them.

Vorventa's steps slowed as he approached, and his eyes searched his quarry, though his face remained stiff. He halted at the table's side, cast Mark and Roic a grave nod, came to attention, and offered Miles a very formal salute, though Miles was in no kind of uniform at all except his gray trousers and jacket.

The messenger moistened his lips, and said, "Count Vorkosigan, sir?"

Aftermaths

A drabble is a story in exactly 100 words.

Aftermaths: Five Views

1 MARK.

Mark had once shot a man with a nerve disruptor; seen the surprised eyes go blank as the charge burned out the brain behind them. He didn't know why watching Miles take in the news of their father's death made that black memory surface. No buzz or crackle from a weapon here; just three quiet words.

It wasn't for hours, after the scramble to rearrange travel, that he realized he'd witnessed the truth. As if harnessed in tandem to the Count-his-father, Lord Vorkosigan had died in that moment, too, old life draining away along with the color from his face.

2 MILES.

Count Vorkosigan stared at his face in the mirror. "Fuck."

Fuck. Fuck. Fuck...

"Are you all right, m'lord?" called Roic from the fast courier's cabin.

"Of course I'm not all right, you idiot!" Miles snarled, and then, in a smaller voice, "Sorry. Sorry. I feel like my brain's been pulled out, and there's nothing in my skull but loose wires waving from my spinal cord. God. Why are we in a hurry *now*? Days too late?"

"The Countess, er, the Dowager Coun... your mother is waiting for you on Sergyar."

"Ah," said the Count. "Yes." And, "Sorry."

"We'll manage, m'lord."

3 CORDELIA.

It wasn't Cordelia who'd found him, but it was she who'd decided. A brain aneurysm, a warm afternoon, two hours gone while the servants assumed the white-haired man had fallen asleep in his armchair, as he did after lunch these days.

Miles's voice was ragged. "Couldn't you have had him cryo-prepped anyway? The technology might progress..."

"To wake without mind or memory, soul in tatters? He told me himself once; no man would want to live on like that."

Or else wake with the burden of his memories intact, hardly less a horror. Could Miles understand?

Ensign Dubauer, I'm sorry.

4 IVAN.

The state funeral ran for a grueling week. Ivan watched Miles mount the podium to present the eulogy. Gregor'd lent his best speechwriters; Miles had edited. Still, Ivan held his breath when Miles clutched the flimsies in a shaking fist and almost, almost cast them away to deliver his wounded words *ex tempore.*

Till his eye fell on his children, squirming and confused in the front row between their mother and grandmother. He hesitated, smoothed out the flimsies, began reading. The new Count's speech was everything it should be; many wept.

Ivan wondered what the old Miles would have said.

5 GREGOR.

The interment at Vorkosigan Surleau was private, meaning a hundred or so people milling around. The grave was double but only one side dug; the earth waited like a bridal bed. The pallbearers were six: Ivan, Illyan, and Koudelka, of course; Duv Galeni for Komarr; Admiral Jole for Sergyar. And one other.

Lady Alys, to whom everyone owed their sanity, pointed out that Gregor's place was with the chief mourners.

"The man has carried me since I was five years old," answered the Emperor of Barrayar. "It's my turn."

Alys gave way as Gregor went to help shoulder the bier.

Miles Vorkosigan/Naismith:
His Universe and Times

CHRONOLOGY	EVENTS	CHRONICLE
Approx. 200 years before Miles's birth	Quaddies are created by genetic engineering.	*Falling Free*
During Beta-Barrayaran War	Cordelia Naismith meets Lord Aral Vorkosigan while on opposite sides of a war. Despite difficulties, they fall in love and are married.	*Shards of Honor*
The Vordarian Pretendership	While Cordelia is pregnant, an attempt to assassinate Aral by poison gas fails, but Cordelia is affected; Miles Vorkosigan is born with bones that will always be brittle and other medical problems. His growth will be stunted.	*Barrayar*

CHRONOLOGY	EVENTS	CHRONICLE
Miles is 17	Miles fails to pass a physical test to get into the Service Academy. On a trip, necessities force him to improvise the Free Dendarii Mercenaries into existence; he has unintended but unavoidable adventures for four months. Leaves the Dendarii in Ky Tung's competent hands and takes Elli Quinn to Beta for rebuilding of her damaged face; returns to Barrayar to thwart plot against his father. Emperor pulls strings to get Miles into the Academy.	*The Warrior's Apprentice*
Miles is 20	Ensign Miles graduates and immediately has to take on one of the duties of the Barrayaran nobility and act as detective and judge in a murder case. Shortly afterward, his first military assignment ends with his arrest. Miles has to rejoin the Dendarii to rescue the young Barrayaran emperor. Emperor accepts Dendarii as his personal secret service force.	"The Mountains of Mourning" in *Borders of Infinity* *The Vor Game*

CHRONOLOGY	EVENTS	CHRONICLE
Miles is 22	Miles and his cousin Ivan attend a Cetagandan state funeral and are caught up in Cetagandan internal politics.	*Cetaganda*
	Miles sends Commander Elli Quinn, who's been given a new face on Beta, on a solo mission to Kline Station.	*Ethan of Athos*
Miles is 23	Now a Barrayaran Lieutenant, Miles goes with the Dendarii to smuggle a scientist out of Jackson's Whole. Miles's fragile leg bones have been replaced by synthetics.	"Labyrinth" in *Borders of Infinity*
Miles is 24	Miles plots from within a Cetagandan prison camp on Dagoola IV to free the prisoners. The Dendarii fleet is pursued by the Cetagandans and finally reaches Earth for repairs. Miles has to juggle both his identities at once, raise money for repairs, and defeat a plot to replace him with a double. Ky Tung stays on Earth. Commander Elli Quinn is now Miles's right-hand officer. Miles and the Dendarii depart for Sector IV on a rescue mission.	"The Borders of Infinity" in *Borders of Infinity* *Brothers in Arms*

CHRONOLOGY	EVENTS	CHRONICLE
Miles is 25	Hospitalized after previous mission, Miles's broken arms are replaced by synthetic bones. With Simon Illyan, Miles undoes yet another plot against his father while flat on his back.	*Borders of Infinity* interstitial material
Miles is 28	Miles meets his clone brother Mark again, this time on Jackson's Whole.	*Mirror Dance*
Miles is 29	Miles hits thirty; thirty hits back.	*Memory*
Miles is 30	Emperor Gregor dispatches Miles to Komarr to investigate a space accident, where he finds old politics and new technology make a deadly mix.	*Komarr*
	The Emperor's wedding sparks romance and intrigue on Barrayar, and Miles plunges up to his neck in both.	*A Civil Campaign*
Miles is 31	Armsman Roic and Sergeant Taura defeat a plot to unhinge Miles and Ekaterin's midwinter wedding.	"Winterfair Gifts" in *Irresistible Forces*

CHRONOLOGY	EVENTS	CHRONICLE
Miles is 32	Miles and Ekaterin's honeymoon journey is interrupted by an Auditorial mission to Quaddiespace, where they encounter old friends, new enemies, and a double handful of intrigue.	*Diplomatic Immunity*
Miles is 39	Miles and Roic go to Kibou-daini to investigate cryo-corporation chicanery.	*Cryoburn*